RACING CAN BE MURDER

Speed City Indiana Chapter of Sisters in Crime

Edited by:
Brenda R. Stewart and Tony Perona

Compiled by: Mark Zacharias

Blue River Press
Indianapolis, Indiana

Cover designed by Phil Velikan

Printed in the United States of America
10 9 8 7 6 5 4 3 2 1

Published by Blue River Press

Distributed by Cardinal Publishers Group
2222 Hillside Avenue, Suite 100
Indianapolis, Indiana 46218
www.cardinalpub.com

*This book is dedicated to the members
of Sisters in Crime everywhere.*

Sisters in Crime is an international group of women and men who are professional mystery writers or mystery enthusiasts formed to "combat discrimination against women in the mystery field, educate publishers and the general public as to the inequalities in the treatment of female authors, and raise the level of awareness of their contribution to the field."

Racing Can Be Murder is an anthology of short stories revolving around the Indianapolis 500 Mile Race and its festivities. Nineteen members of the Speed City Indiana Chapter of Sisters of Crime have contributed stories to this work.

Introduction

Early in 2006, I was asked to address a group of writers known as the Speed City Indiana Chapter of Sisters in Crime. The organization is composed of budding mystery writers from all over the country, and, appropriately, the meeting place was a bookstore in Carmel that specialized in mysteries and crime novels.

My reason for being invited was to give them a brief lecture on the history of the Indianapolis Motor Speedway and the Indianapolis 500 and help them determine if there was sufficient material on which to base a future mystery, using the race and the track as a backdrop. It was a most reasonable request. After all, in the scheme of things, the Indianapolis 500 is *THE* most important event in the history of this community. For nearly 100 years, it has been the site of some of the most incredible drama ever witnessed in the world of sports. Each May, the eyes of the world focus on the Indianapolis 500, and the sport of auto racing is in itself a struggle of life over death.

So what better location on which to base a "Who-dunit" story? If the Speedway and its famed 500-mile race do not present an exciting background for a mystery novel, what other topic would? With that in mind, I tackled my assignment.

I spoke for nearly an hour, sharing stories and anecdotes I believed might be helpful in tying their interest to my area of expertise. Afterward, there was a question-and-answer session, although I might be more accurate in using the term "interrogated." I was, after all, being queried by a group of mystery writers! Seriously, though, the questions were both serious and thoughtful. Each member of this group had a genuine interest in producing the perfect mystery involving the race to give it a genuine Hoosier flavor.

A year later, a second request was made for my services. This time, my expertise as a writer was sought in putting together an introduction for what has since become an anthology of mystery stories involving the Indianapolis 500 and the Speedway.

The end result is an enjoyable grouping of 19 different works, collectively entitled *Racing Can Be Murder*. With each writer taking her (or his) own approach, *Racing Can Be Murder* offers 19 short mysteries involving the Indianapolis 500 and the Speedway. The stories range from a variety of 500-related topics, including the drivers, the track, the 500 Festival Parade, the selection of the 500 Festival princesses, the caterers, the race parties that are prevalent during the month of May and even the land that surrounds the complex. One writer uses the historic Tuckaway House as a setting, while another writer has a story based on an early air show that was staged at the Speedway.

I won't give away any of the plots or endings. You'll simply have to read each story for yourself. But while you are reading this book, I hope you will find it an enjoyable experience prepared by a most enjoyable group of people.

Rick Shaffer
Greenwood, Indiana
February 27, 2007

Rick Shaffer is the author of *Autocourse Official History of CART and* co-author of *Autocourse Official History of the Indianapolis 500.*

Acknowledgements

We would like to thank the Speed City Indiana Chapter of Sisters in Crime for not only their support and invaluable assistance in making this anthology a reality, but their faith in the validity of the project itself. In particular, we would like to thank the editors, Tony Perona and Brenda Robertson Stewart; Kit Ehrman for her invaluable assistance; Mark Zacharias for the huge job of compiling the book; Jim Huang for his never-ending support; Wanda Lou Willis for the endless hours she spent researching and writing a large number of the transition pages of true facts about the race track, the drivers, the traditions and the men and women behind the scenes; Phil Dunlap, Andrea Smith, Sheila Boneham, Lucy Coyle Schilling, Tony Perona, and Ann Collins for contributing true facts' transition pages; Adriane and Tom Doherty from Cardinal Publishers for their trust in the value in this anthology; and Rick Shaffer for his endless supply of stories about racing. Most of all, we would like to thank all the authors who submitted such wonderful stories of malice and justice.

Table of Contents

INDIANAPOLIS 500 WINNERS

By Wanda Lou Willis

YEAR/WINNER/AVG. MPH

2007 - Dario Franchitti, 151.774
2006 - Sam Hornish, Jr., 157.085
2005 - Dan Wheldon, 157.603
2004 - Buddy Rice, 138.518
2003 - Gil de Ferran, 156.291
2002 - Helio Castroneves, 166.499
2001 - Helio Castroneves, 153.601
2000 - Juan Pablo Montoya, 167.496
1999 - Kenny Brack, 153.176
1998 - Eddie Cheever, Jr., 145.155
1997 - Arie Luyendyk, 145.827
1996 - Buddy Lazier, 147.956
1995 - Jacques Villenueve, 153.616
1994 - Al Unser, Jr., 160.872
1993 - Emerson Fittipaldi, 157.207
1992 - Al Unser, Jr., 134.477
1991 - Rick Mears, 176.457
1990 - Arie Luyendyk, 185.981
1989 - Emerson Fittipaldi, 167.581
1988 - Rick Mears, 144.809
1987 - Al Unser, Sr., 162.175
1986 - Bobby Rahal, 170.722
1985 - Danny Sullivan, 152.982
1984 - Rick Mears, 163.612
1983 - Tom Sneva, 162.117
1982 - Gordon Johncock, 162.029
1981 - Bobby Unser, 139.084
1980 - Johnny Rutherford, 142.682
1979 - Rick Mears, 158.899
1978 - Al Unser, Sr., 161.363
1977 - A. J. Foyt, Jr., 161.331
1976 - Johnny Rutherford, 148.725
1975 - Bobby Unser, 148.725
1974 - Johnny Rutherford, 158.589

1973 - Gordon Johncock, 159.036
1972 - Mark Donohue, 162.962
1971 - Al Unser, Sr., 157.735
1970 - Al Unser, Sr., 155.749
1969 - Mario Andretti, 156.867
1968 - Bobby Unser, 152.882
1967 - A. J. Foyt, Jr., 151.207
1966 - Graham Hill, 144.317
1965 - Jim Clark, 150.686
1964 - A. J. Foyt, Jr., 147.350
1963 - Parnelli Jones, 143.137
1962 - Rodger Ward, 140.293
1961 - A. J. Foyt, Jr., 139.130
1960 - Jim Rathmann, 138.767
1959 - Rodger Ward, 135.857
1958 - Jimmy Bryan, 133.791
1957 - Sam Hanks, 135.601
1956 - Pat Flaherty, 128.490
1955 - Bob Sweikert, 128.213
1954 - Bill Vukovich, 130.840
1953 - Bill Vukovich, 128.740
1952 - Troy Ruttman, 128.922
1951 - Lee Wallard, 126.244
1950 - Johnnie Parsons, 124.002
1949 - Bill Holland, 121.327
1948 - Mauri Rose, 119.814
1947 - Marui Rose, 116.338
1946 - George Robson, 114.820
1941 - Floyd Davis, 115.117; Mauri Rose, 115.117
1940 - Wilbur Shaw, 114.277
1939 - Wilbur Shaw, 115.035
1938 - Floyd Roberts, 117.200
1937 - Wilbur Shaw, 113.580
1936 - Louis Meyer, 109.069
1935 - Kelly Petillo, 106.240
1934 - Bill Cummings, 104.863
1933 - Louis Meyer, 104.162
1932 - Fred Frame, 104.144
1931 - Louis Schneider, 96.629
1930 - Bill Arnold, 100.448

1929 - Ray Keech, 97.585
1928 - Louis Meyer, 99.482
1927 - George Souders, 97.545
1926 - Frank Lockhart, 95.904
1925 - Peter DePaolo, 101.127
1924 - L. L. Corum, 98.234; Joe Boyer, 98.234
1923 - Tommy Milton, 90.954
1922 - Jimmy Murphy, 94.484
1921 - Tommy Milton, 89.621
1920 - Gaston Chevrolet, 88.618
1919 - Howdy Wilcox, 88.050
1917 - 1918 – No race held due to World War I
1916 - Dario Resta, 84.001
1915 - Ralph DePalma, 89.840
1914 - Rene Thomas, 82.474
1913 - Jules Goux, 75.933
1912 - Joe Dawson, 78.719
1911 - Ray Harroun, 74.602

A Sure Bet

by Judith Skillings

Judith Skillings is a mystery novelist, playwright and a graduate of the Bertil Roos race-driving school. She and her husband own a Rolls-Royce and Bentley motorcar restoration shop which inspired the setting for her Rebecca Moore mystery series: Dead End, Dangerous Curves *and* Driven to Murder. *A contributing author to* Mystery Muses: 100 Classics That Inspire Today's Mystery Writers, *she has just finished a suspense thriller set in the Yucatan,* My Brother's Killer.

Overdressed? I don't think so. Rebecca Moore slid the strap off her heel and let the shoe plop onto the grass. A hiccough escaped, releasing a whiff of Curacao. *Too tipsy, maybe.* Had that been Nate's problem? One minute he'd been toying with the hem of her sweater, the next he'd set his drink behind a carving of a pregnant woman and announced he needed fresh air. He'd lurched past her and banged his hip on the slider opening onto the deck. "You could come along, you know. But you're way overdressed for a tryst on the dock."

"Did you say tryst?"

"Is good word," Nate said. "Reporter should know it."

He'd oozed around the corner so quickly he missed her saying, "I'll tell my uncle and join you down there." Or maybe he'd heard and chose to ignore her. Hard to tell. She'd just met Nate that afternoon. And now it was what, ten, eleven?

She felt her wrist. No watch. She'd worn the bracelet Uncle Walt had given her years ago—silver links with fourteen charms having to do with open-wheel racing. He'd introduced her to the sport, and she'd embraced it with a passion most adolescent girls directed toward horses. Summers, she'd learned about car mechanics with her elbows pressed onto his work bench. Learned to love auto racing sitting beside him glued to ESPN. Now, for the first time, she would see the Indianapolis 500 live.

"The weekend's on me," Walt had said when she'd phoned with news of her job offer. "I'm so proud of you, even if I'm not a fan of the *Washington Post*'s politics. You'll be within spitting distance of the shop, Reb. Any day you get bored, you come on out."

"You're dreaming. My first year in DC I won't have time to read a newspaper."

"But you'll make time for the race weekend." It wasn't even a question.

Rebecca flopped forward to remove the other shoe. A strand of hair, smelling of shampoo, swung across her eyes. She twisted her lips and blew at it, set it fluttering as she padded across the lawn to the opening in the hedge. There she rested her sandals on a boxwood that had been given a flattop. They balanced for a second before the thin heels scratched through the twigs and sank down out of sight, like the path leading to the dock. Edged with lumber and spacious enough for a couple to stroll between the shrubs, it descended like a slalom course. Solar bulbs had been embedded in each riser. From a boat the lights would have looked magical, like oversized fireflies winking in the mist, but they did nothing to illuminate the dock. Nor did the handful of stars just becoming visible overhead.

It couldn't be far. By blocking out the chatter from the party, Rebecca could hear frogs croaking, crickets, the rhythmic creak of an articulated walkway as waves slapped the breakwater. And the air was laced with a hint of boat exhaust. *Just follow the red brick path*, someone had said. *Piece of cake*. Of course, whoever said it was inside, placing bets on Sunday's race and munching hors d'oeuvres at tables spread with black-and-white checkered cloths.

She fingered the charms at her wrist, found the race car and spun its wheels. How long ago had Nate left the party? Twenty minutes at least, maybe forty. What were the chances he was still dangling his feet in the water? Or doing it alone?

Did she care? *Maybe*.

She'd first seen Nate that afternoon at the track, one leg up on the low wall that separated the pits from the foot traffic. A rangy blond with a twice-broken nose, he was heckling a crew member bent over the back end of a car. Craving an audience, he'd snagged Rebecca's elbow. "And here I thought that the pressure on the pop-off valve was pre-set, didn't you?"

"It is, by race control." Since he grinned at her, she went on. "But if you figure a way to increase the pressure without getting caught, you increase the boost, which translates into more horsepower on the straightaway."

"Aha. Hear that, Lauer. She's more than a pretty face." He held out a hand. "Nathaniel Spenser. Nate. Delighted to meet you." Keeping hold of her hand, he pulled her to the wall, yelled in her ear as a racer roared by, spitting dust. "It looks as if my friend and a crew chief wannabe, Jack Lauer, is attempting to do just that. If he doesn't watch it, he'll get the car disqualified."

The comment was too pointed for Lauer to ignore. He unfolded, rubbing the back of his hand across eyes better suited to an eighteenth-century poet. "Get lost, Spenser. You know jack-shit about race cars."

"Nonsense. Daily I fool three-quarters of a million readers with my race acumen. Including this well-educated example." He breathed into Rebecca's ear. "Tell me you subscribe to the *Indianapolis Star.*"

She nodded. "Each year, for the month of May. My uncle has it mailed to me."

"An out-of-state female race fan with the credentials to access the pits. I may have to interview you. Hell, I may have to marry you. What are you doing tonight?"

"Not eloping."

"No? Well then, how about a party?"

And here I am. Rebecca smiled as her feet slapped the damp bricks, raising liquid footprints in her wake. Each step down, the noise from the party became more muted as if the volume was being lowered notch after notch, fading like the drone of the power boat heading toward the dam at the far end. She winced when she stubbed her toe on something at the side of the path, softer than a rock but not by much. She wiggled her toes to stop the throbbing, shrugged out of the sweater Walt had made her wear over the strapless dress and tossed it at the branch of a flowering tree. It caught, scattering petals onto the lawn beneath.

The night air raised goose bumps on her sunburned arms. Tomorrow would call for a hat and sun block if the weather held. She wondered if Nate would be covering the pit area during the final practice sessions. She'd like to tag along, unless Susan Hazleton had the same idea. Something other than racing had been on Susan's mind that afternoon. Blond hair sparkling, she'd trapped Nate on his way out of the track and rewarded him with a lemonade and a kiss on the cheek. "Hey, it's my favorite reporter. What insights have you lined up for Sunday's paper?"

"Usual stuff, Susan. Rules, modifications and what the teams are doing to eke out as much horsepower as possible."

"Such as? You know I don't read your rag."

Nate had rattled the ice in the cup, slurped the drink instead of answering.

She patted his arm. "So secretive. Give me a hint."

"Ask your fiancé. He's right behind you."

Susan let out a whimper as Jack Lauer, the man from the pits, slid his arm around her. Oblivious to the chill between the men, she'd clung to Jack while continuing to engage Nate in race chat. Midtwenties, she'd mastered the politician's knack of registering appropriate emotions without engaging the muscles of her face. Even in jeans and motorcycle boots she looked like a rich kid slumming.

Inside her parent's home on Geist Reservoir, Susan looked like a rich kid rebelling. For the party, she'd changed into a thigh-hugging black dress with an uneven hem and a lace shawl that drooped off her shoulders as limp as a cobweb brought down by a storm. She'd cornered Rebecca just inside the door and waved a fan of colored tickets in her face. "For every hundred dollars, you get four tickets to bet on the winner, second place, first out of the race—you know, a crash or engine failure, or something—and the most improved. Just drop the ticket in the goblet with the driver's name. It's simple. If you need help, Jack knows everything about racing."

With only a second's hesitation, Rebecca had handed over a big chunk of her first paycheck as a reporter. "Do the proceeds go to charity?"

"Charity?" Susan ran her tongue along a tooth to clean off a fleck of lipstick. "No. The winners divide the pot. What's the point of gambling if you don't win something major?"

"Fun?" said Rebecca.

Susan had blinked as if the word were an obscenity. Rebecca was saved from elaborating by Nate, who'd snuck up behind her. He'd moved her toward the betting table. His breath was warm on her neck as he whispered, "Never make Susan think. Leaves her looking perplexed. That causes wrinkles."

Rebecca couldn't stifle a grin. "Is she really marrying a mechanic? She must be doing it to annoy her parents. Judging from her outfit, shocking them is her goal in life."

Nate glanced over his shoulder and whistled. "I hadn't noticed her dress. She looks ready for Halloween. Unlike you, who looks— "

"Don't." Rebecca held up a hand. "It was the only dress I brought with me. I'd planned to treat Walt to dinner at St. Elmo."

"—stunning." He drew a lazy finger along her collar bone. "But now that you mention Elmo's, I'll amend that to as delicious as one of their steaks. Looking at you makes me hungry."

Smiling at the corny compliment, Rebecca turned her back on him and placed the WIN ticket in Jacques Villeneuve's goblet. He'd come in second in 1994, close enough to smell victory. He'd go all out this year.

Nate reached around her to deposit his ticket with hers. "I see Jack's returned from a run to the liquor store. Not Villeneuve, Lauer. And to answer your question: I can't imagine Susan's father approving of a mechanic for a son-in-law. Yet there are rumors that Hazleton plans to start his own team with Jack as the crew chief."

"Humoring his daughter in hopes she'll get bored and dump Jack?" Rebecca hesitated over choosing Paul Tracy for the DNF. He was crazy enough to crash out on the first lap, but strong enough to make it to the end, if he stayed patient. "Would that please you as well? Susan was very friendly this afternoon."

He laughed. "We dated a few years ago, part of a group. Nothing serious. And when she's friendly, watch out. The smile is to distract you from the sound of her rattle."

Nate went off to get them drinks.

Rebecca watched Susan slither through the crowd, mentally sheathing her in the skin of a diamond-back until a voice at her shoulder made her jump. "I hear you're a reporter for the *Washington Post*." Broad knuckles pressed manicured nails into the flesh of her arm. They belonged to a silver-haired stranger with wide nostrils and Susan's eyebrows. "Ed Hazleton. How about you come out in September for my daughter's wedding? Write it up for your paper. Thanks to my wife, it'll top any East Coast affair. Four hundred guests. My company has international connections. You'll have heard of it."

He named it; she hadn't. "Sorry," Rebecca said. "I do investigative assignments: political scandals, insider trading. Tedious stuff. No weddings." She tried to keep the smile on her lips, but the assumption she wrote for the society page rankled.

"Then how about you send out the sports writer, a real one?" He gripped her elbow tighter. "Have him call me. I'll treat him right. Suze is planning to marry into the race world. Jackson Lauer is the best crewman in the business, according to her." He leaned in, dropping his nose close enough to sniff her cleavage. "If you haven't bet yet, put your money on the Walker Team's rookie to win." He winked. "You could say I have insider information. But if you say it in print, I'll sue." His laugh released a wave of garlic from the marinated calamari.

Rebecca stepped out of range. "Team Green has it sewn up. The car has the speed on the straightaway. Villeneuve can handle the corners."

"You're entitled to your opinion. But Jack won't let me down. He has too much riding on the outcome."

The conversation left Rebecca feeling uncomfortable, as if Hazleton had fed her innuendos, hoping she'd pass them along. To whom? Did he expect her to run to Nate and confirm his suspicions that Lauer was up to something worth reporting? Hand him another nail for the coffin lid?

She wormed her way into the kitchen, where she bumped into Lauer replacing a liquor bottle in the refrigerator and coming out with tonic water. He seemed more relaxed away from the crowd. Working at the counter his hands moved swiftly, shoulders tensed only when he spoke to her. "Do you really know anything about pop-off valves?" He asked the question without turning. "You don't look like a race groupie."

She considered showing off, but Nate was waiting. "Just what I pick up from the TV announcers while passing around the nachos."

He'd squeezed a wedge of lime into the glass and nodded as if that was what he expected.

At the edge of the wharf the night seemed too quiet. The crickets or whatever she'd heard on her way down had gone still. No breeze ruffling the leaves. Not even the hum of a mosquito. The only noise came from a loon, or some other sea bird, announcing her presence with a muffled lowing that was almost a moan.

She stepped onto the walkway. The creaking boards silenced the loon and left her feeling alone. Exposed. She whispered, "Nate?"

No answer.

Had he given up on her and returned to the party through the front while she was coming out the back? He could be on the shore, hugging the shadow of a tree to surprise her. Or he could have gone in for a midnight swim. He claimed the reservoir was manmade, that it had been a farm town, flooded in the name of progress. She pictured clapboard houses rotting in the watery dark, bones being cleansed of their flesh, while pleasure boats skimmed the waves. The fine hairs rose up on her neck; her palms turned as clammy as her bare feet.

She hugged her arms and took another step. Boards scraped together, ripples oscillated away from the dock. *No.* She shook her head. If Nate was waiting he'd be in the motorboat, invisible under the awning that hung low on the sides to keep the sun from fading the paint. It was a perfect place for a tryst.

Horseshoe shaped, the dock flanked the front and both sides of the power boat. She started down the right walkway, humming snippets from *Margaritaville* to fill the silence. Not looking for a lost shaker of salt, she was searching for a good-looking man. "Some people claim that there's a woman to blame, but I know it could be my fault."

She gripped an aluminum upright to keep her balance as she stooped over, intending to peek under the canvas into the boat. She was fully expecting to see Nate's grin, hear him ask what took so long. Maybe feel his arm encircle her waist, pull her under the awning and onto his lap.

What she didn't expect were fireworks. Real ones. But without warning the sky exploded. Red-and-blue sparks streaked through the darkness. Trailing booms echoed over the water. They came from the house on a spit of land not far away. Another party of race fans celebrating the Indy 500 in advance.

"Nate." She was already moving to the end of the dock. "Nate. Come on. You don't want to miss this." She dropped down, setting the wharf rocking. It had been years since she'd seen fireworks over a lake or the ocean. The reflection, the contrast of fire and liquid, was an irresistible lure. That and dangling her feet in the cool water like a kid. It brought back a Fourth of July when she was a teenager; the first time she'd been kissed in earnest. "Come on, Nate. If this is how you impress all your dates, don't change it. It's working."

She was grinning when her toes tickled the water and sank below. She frowned when they hit something soft. Something bobbing just below the surface.

Her legs jerked out of the water.

She flipped them under her and shot up on her knees, shuddering for breath. Gripping the edge, she peered over. A bundle of clothes, paler than the inky water, swayed with each wave— expanding and contracting, banging gently against the end of the dock.

"Nate? Nate!" She was screaming.

The fireworks answered. Green and gold lit the sky.

Fingers stretching, she reached for the bundle. It sank beneath her touch. She tried again. Her knee slid away, propelled by something slick on the deck. Her chest banged against the edge. She pulled her leg in, collected herself, balanced and leaned farther. Her hand made contact, gripped the fabric, closed around it. With her left arm flapping in the air, she rose up on her haunches, lifting the sodden cloth. A fingernail snapped. Water ran down her arm onto the shirt, still buttoned around a body. She gasped as its weight pulled her forward, heard the material start to tear, felt the cloth slip through her fingers. Watched it sink. Relieved of its weight, she toppled backward onto the dock. As she scrambled to regain her feet, her hand smacked against fabric. The awning covering the boat.

The boat.

There should be an oar, a pole, rope, something. She squirmed on the deck to get upright. She was almost erect when she felt hands on her back. Cool fingers pressing into her skin.

"Nate?" Was he all right? Had she panicked over nothing? "Is—" She had time to utter the one word before she was airborne, heading for the water.

Two hours later, she was shivering from more than a dunk in the lake.

"Someone pushed you?" Hands on his belt, the county sheriff scuffed the toe of his shoe along a smear of vomit. "Looks as if you upchucked at the sight of your boyfriend floating like a log. Then you slipped on the stuff and fell in."

"The vomit was already there. I knelt in it. Nate must have been sick and lost his balance. Did he hit his head?"

No response.

Flares marked the steps. A floodlight had been set on a tripod. It lit the dock area from the shore, making it an over-exposed negative, all shadows and highlights. Rebecca dropped her eyes away from the glare. She picked at the stains on her dress rather than watch the medics strap Nate's body to the stretcher. They'd examined him, pronounced him dead and were ready to lug him up the steps past the fairy lights to the lawn, where a few guests lingered, too enthralled to go home. "I felt a hand on my back. Hands, on my shoulders."

"But you didn't see anyone?"

"It happened too fast. I hit the water and went under. When I surfaced, I heard footsteps running away. I cried for help, but the person kept going." Her voice was wavering, rising in pitch.

Walt tucked the blanket tighter around her. He looked as bewildered as she felt. "Whoever pushed Reb must have been hiding in the boat. Probably ducked there when he heard her coming."

She shook her head, sending shivers down her spine. "But why not help Nate out of the water? Unless—"

"Unless," the sheriff cut in, "this unknown had something to do with the vic's being in the water and didn't want you making the connection. Is that what you think?"

Rebecca plucked at the charms. *She wasn't sure what she thought. She was certain she hadn't pushed Nate into the water. Wouldn't have. She felt for the wheels on the race car, but it wasn't there. She'd lost her favorite charm as well as Nate.* Her head popped up. Tears threatened.

"Okay, okay." The sheriff backed off. "How long after you found him did you go for help?"

"I don't know. I dragged him along the dock until I could stand and wrestle him onto the breakwater. Then went to the house."

"We found the pole."

"Good for you. I didn't."

"That's peculiar. It was wet, like it was used recently to fish something out. Or hold someone under."

Rebecca was shivering so hard her teeth threatened to break. She couldn't prove she hadn't held Nate under. She was an outsider, some woman he'd picked up at the track. She'd followed him to the dock and now he was dead. Who needed a motive when the circumstantial evidence was so compelling?

Walt tightened his grip on her shoulders. "Sheriff, how about we go inside where it's warm?"

"No need." Susan Hazleton clattered down the steps. "I brought hot coffee." Once in the light, she raised Styrofoam cups and a thermos to demonstrate her thoughtfulness. She beamed like Hostess of the Year, although she looked like one who'd been through the wringer. Her skirt was damp, leaf debris was caught between the straps of her shoe. The shawl, tied at her waist, bunched over her arms. Its black fabric and her pallor made a ghostly combination, relieved only by a glint of metal in the weave. From the distance, it looked like a tiny spider. Perhaps the designer had intended to create a cobweb effect after all.

Susan handed her a cup then moved on to a technician, offering to exchange coffee for the sample jar he was holding. He shook his head. "Got to test this for toxins." Backed by the light, the contents glowed green.

Rebecca recognized the vomit from the dock. She shrugged off the blanket and stood. "Excuse me, what toxins will you test for?"

The kid sought permission from the sheriff before answering. "The usual ones. Unless you know something specific worth looking at?"

"I might." Rebecca reached for her uncle's arm. "Nate and I were drinking Tequila Sunrises: sweet, deceptively strong. Mine were golden, as was his first one. The next was a vile green. He said they ran out of clear Curacao and switched to blue. He said it tasted nearly the same. It should have tasted *exactly* the same. The only difference is the color."

Walt's eyes grew worried. "You're thinking it was spiked with something that would change the color, but not do much to the taste? Something common like antifreeze? It's mostly green, depending on the brand, and one heck of a poison."

"And sweet. That's why you're careful disposing of it at the shop, so animals won't lick it up and die. The taste would have been masked by the liqueur."

"Wait a minute," the sheriff said. "You think the vic's drink had antifreeze in it? Was he complaining of a headache; unsteady on his feet? Three, four ounces of ethylene glycol will take a man down within twenty-four hours."

"It would act that quickly?" Susan jumped in before Rebecca could describe Nate's lurching and sudden departure from the house. "Who'd do such a thing at a party?"

Her exclamation was punctuated by footsteps marching down from the lawn. "Who indeed?" The voice was Edwin Hazleton's. He stopped one step away, with Lauer inches behind him.

"Who?" Rebecca turned to the men. "Someone clever enough to know that with forty or fifty people milling about, blame would be hard to pin down. Sheriff, I can show you where Nate set his glass on the mantle. And I'll bet there's a bottle of clear Curacao in the refrigerator, isn't there, Jack? That's what I saw you exchanging for the tonic water."

"I shoved it aside. So what? Anyone could have put it there. Lots of people were mixing drinks."

"Lots of people weren't angry at Nate, but you were. He'd caught you fiddling with the pop-off valve and let you know it. Were you afraid of losing your job if he went public with his suspicions? Or of losing Hazleton's support for a new team? What was the plan—to make Nate sick enough that he'd miss Saturday's practice and not be able to write his Sunday column? Give you breathing room to correct the adjustment and get away with it? No harm, no foul." She ran out of steam. "He wasn't supposed to die, was he?"

The question hung in the air. No one moved.

Then Lauer pushed past Hazleton to face her. In the half-light his eyes were sunken, rimmed with charcoal, but the tension had left his body. "It was just a splash, not even an ounce. It shouldn't have acted like that. I figured he'd get sick at home, maybe spend the night in the emergency room. I didn't know he'd hit his head and accidentally drown."

"Your friend drowned all right." The sheriff got between them. "But I never said he hit his head. Only bruise was on his shoulder. Matches the tip of that pole used to hold him under. He was too weak from the poison to struggle much. He was murdered."

Someone sucked in a breath. Rebecca sighed, expelling one. "But not by Jack. He was in the kitchen when I started down."

"So?" The sheriff slapped his thigh in frustration. "The vic left a half-hour ahead of you. Lauer just confessed to doctoring his drink. He had time to hold him under before returning to the party."

"Then who pushed me in? It had to be Nate's killer—the person who'd followed him to the dock and got trapped there when I came stumbling and singing my way down. Not Jack, but someone who has as much to lose as he does."

The sheriff shifted his weight, uncomfortable with his options.

Rebecca moved level with him. "What if Nate had ingested two doses of antifreeze, hours apart? Would that explain its effecting him so quickly?"

"Where'd he get the first dose?"

Shielding her eyes against the lights, Rebecca said, "In a lemonade handed him by Susan Hazleton around three o'clock as he exited the track."

"Susan?" Jack whispered.

"What?" Edwin Hazleton swung an arm toward Rebecca. "You're crazy."

She shied out of reach. "Just a little slow. If you check her shawl, sheriff, you'll find a silver charm caught in it: an open-wheel race car missing from my bracelet. It must have snagged when I struggled to stay on the dock. I felt cloth behind me and assumed I'd hit the awning."

Susan looked at the shawl and frowned. "You were crowding me at the party." She ripped at the glint of silver with red nails. "The stupid thing could have caught then."

"But it didn't. I was playing with it when I tripped over shoes left by the side of the path. Your shoes. Flower petals that I shook loose are still caught in the straps." Everyone except Susan stared at her feet. Rebecca leaned closer. "Did you go barefoot so Nate wouldn't hear you coming? Was he standing, back to you, enjoying the stars over the water? Or bent over being sick? Did you even speak to him? No, I'll bet you just pushed him in, and got your dress wet kneeling on the dock while you held him under. Were you afraid that Jack wouldn't go through with it?"

Susan's eyes narrowed before her father squeezed her arm to silence her. "She's being absurd, Sheriff," he said. "Susan had no motive. It didn't matter if Lauer was cheating to win. It had nothing to do with her. She wasn't really going to marry him."

"Wasn't I?" Susan spit it out and jerked away from her father. "Is that what you thought? That if you'd play along for a while, I'd get bored and give him up for one of the country club preppies you throw at me? Don't you get it? I have no talents, nothing but ambition I inherited from you. But Jack has real genius. We make a good team. He needs me."

"And to secure Jack's future with a team of his own you killed Nate?" Rebecca felt the night chill burrow into her bones. "You held him under, didn't you?"

"No." Susan reached out to Lauer. "I tried to talk to him, to make him understand how important this race win is to us. Nate stumbled trying to get away and fell in. He just floated there face down. I didn't know what to do."

Lauer stared at her. "You could have run for help." His voice broke. "For Nate."

"And you should have been more realistic, son." Walt's voice was tinged with sorrow. "You live in the pits, you know racing is unpredictable. Upping the boost might give you an edge, but it wouldn't guarantee victory. Your driver could crash, or the engine blow. Get caught and you're labeled for life. Even with Nate dead, you could have been found out. Rebecca knew what you were up to."

The truth of Walt's statement registered on Lauer's face. He stood, arms rigid, hands balled into fists. Unlike Susan, he felt the enormity of what his ambition had set in motion. It ended his friend's life and changed his forever.

Rebecca sagged against her uncle and spoke softly to Lauer. "You shouldn't have been so desperate. Nate had faith you'd succeed without Hazleton's backing. It might have taken longer and not been as easy, but you'd make it. He wouldn't have turned you in. He was just letting you know that someone was watching, for your own good.

"When we were placing our bets he said, 'Susan is making Jack crazy right now, dangling her father's influence in front of him like the proverbial carrot. He'll be fine in the long run; he has the talent. Unlike Villeneuve, Jack Lauer is a sure bet.'"

(Note: In 1995 Jacques Villeneuve was a very good bet. He led only fifteen laps, his engine stalled twice, and a fuel hose jammed, delaying his exit from the pits, but he won the Indy 500. Jack Lauer was not as lucky. Lawyers for Susan Hazleton argued that Lauer was a bad influence on her, forcing her to poison his friend so he could later administer the fatal dose. She assured them that she was trying to fish Nate out of the water, not hold him under.)

The Feminine Influence

by Wanda Lou Willis

"The Greatest Spectacle in Racing." Since 1955 the world has known this famous phrase. It was made famous by Sid Collins, chief announcer for the Speedway Radio Network. However, it was actually created by a young lady.

From the mid-1920s, radio broadcasts of the 500 consisted of only a few minutes covering the start and the finish of the race, and in between, brief updates aired every 15 or 30 minutes. In 1952 the track created its own network using the same coverage format until 1953, and history was made when the race was covered in its entirety with only commercial breaks.

Subscribing stations requested that their engineers be alerted to an impending commercial break by some kind of a standard out cue. This request was handled by the sales staff of Indianapolis' WIBC, the 500 network's flagship station. It was Alice Greene, a young female copywriter, who suggested the lasting classic: "Stay tuned to 'The Greatest Spectacle in Racing.'"

Other females have also left their mark on this sport's classic. It was Speedway owner Tony Hulman's wife, Mary Fendrich Hulman, who suggested the release of multicolored balloons on race morning. By 1950, the release coincided with the final notes of "Back Home Again in Indiana."

Louis Meyer was a good son and evidently always listened to his mother even when he entered Victory Lane after earning his third 500 win in 1936. His mother told him drinking buttermilk would refresh him. And today, every winner has his drink of milk, though it's no longer buttermilk.

Murder at the Snakepit Ball

by Chris Wright

Chris Wright has been a television and radio meteorologist since 1987 and currently serves as Chief Meteorologist at WTHR, Channel 13, in Indianapolis. For his work as a meteorologist, he has been honored with numerous awards, including six Emmys from the National Television Academy. His writing career has flourished as well, and he is the author of nine mysteries and three children's books.

The clouds were dark gray, the air thick and heavy, but the isolated thunderstorms the weatherman predicted never appeared. Not that anyone cared about the weather on this evening. As many as thirty limousines lumbered through downtown Indianapolis, and the normally congested Saturday night traffic was clogged from Washington Street through Monument Circle back to Meridian Street.

Designed to resemble the courtyard of a Spanish coastal village, the Indiana Roof Ballroom was built in 1927. A forty-foot domed ceiling creating the illusion of a star-laden night sky towered above the 8,700 square-foot dance floor. The ballroom was refurbished in 1986, and now, thirty-four years later, the facility would host the social event of the season.

Klieg lights waved back and forth across the facades of buildings and danced upward to illuminate the cloud-laden sky. Plush red carpet was rolled out, and the entranceway was well-lit for the live television broadcast of the 2020 Snakepit Ball Red Carpet Show.

Lights flickered and flashbulbs flashed as patrons strolled by the bank of television, newspaper and magazine photographers into the sold-out event. A long white car stopped and the driver quickly circled the vehicle to open the door. Three political power brokers who were virtually inseparable on the campaign trail arrived together as planned.

Two-term Indianapolis Mayor Steve Campbell and retiring Governor Bart Peterson climbed out, followed by gubernatorial candidate John Stehr. The sixty year old, a former television newsman, had served as the first mayor of Zionsville after the city was incorporated and was making a strong bid for the state's highest office.

Two of the wealthiest men in America would also be in attendance tonight. Arthur Alexander Cantwell, of Cantwell Motors and Edward Holcomb, of Holcomb Ethanol and Lubricant Processing, climbed out of their respective limousines and gave brief media interviews before entering the party. The parade of locals, celebrities, politicians and athletes continued and the evening's festivities began.

A lavish selection of items was available with proceeds from the silent auction benefiting St. Vincent Children's Hospital. Mary Stirsman and the Dayside Trio entertained during the cocktail hour. The popular ensemble dominated the local jazz music scene and had just signed a record deal with Mercurial Records. Cat Palermo was wonderful on the piano and J. D. Carroll and Paul Williams accompanied on the bass and drums.

Stirsman's soulful crooning and spicy ballads were perfect for the evening, but later that night the music would take on a more up-tempo flavor. Dinner was served at seven o'clock, and the sumptuous meal was followed by a short program at eight p.m. Native son and comedian-turned-national-television-talk-show-host Martin Summers was emcee.

"Welcome to the fifteenth Indianapolis 500 Festival Snakepit Ball," Summers began. "The one hundred fourteenth running of the Indianapolis 500 takes place tomorrow afternoon, and we'll get the party started tonight. Bon Jovi is in the house and they are ready to rock! We'll have a couple of special presentations before the music begins."

After remarks by the governor and mayor and two check presentations, the concert everyone eagerly anticipated started. At eight-thirty the New Jersey rocker and his band took the stage and began playing the hits that had made them stars worldwide. Lead guitarist Richie Sambora was in top form, and the band showed why they were still chart toppers even after more than three decades of making music. The rock-and-roll party continued, and stylishly dressed party-goers danced into the night.

While the band played, Patrice Ellingham Holcomb perused the silent auction items. As wife of the state's wealthiest man, she wanted for nothing but always enjoyed the thrill of the bidding process. Bred in a family of old money, she had attended charitable events far too numerous to mention, but she always took time to participate in the silent auctions. She always bid generously. Many times she would purchase items at one event and donate them to be used to benefit another cause.

As Patrice casually examined each item, her husband Edward swilled scotch and talked business with Arthur Cantwell. When Cantwell Motors began building cars that ran solely on ethanol, Holcomb became one of the most powerful men in America and was rapidly becoming one of the richest. His company processed corn into ethanol and had processing plants in sixteen states and employed over eleven thousand people.

In 2010, when Cantwell first announced that the company his great-grandfather founded would no longer produce petroleum-powered vehicles, Edward Holcomb began constructing factories to produce fuel for Cantwell's cars. Holcomb grit and Ellingham money merged to manufacture fuel for Cantwell's vision of freeing America from its dependence on foreign oil.

The first cars were met with skepticism but within ten years ethanol-powered vehicles outsold gas-powered cars three to one. Japanese automakers and the Big Three in Detroit eventually followed suit, eliminating America's trade deficit with the Middle East and dropping gas prices to fifty cents a gallon. Arthur Cantwell was named *Time Magazine's Man of the Decade* and was hailed as an American hero.

While the two industry tycoons talked, Patrice Holcomb was approached by a familiar but unfriendly face and was soon in the middle of a heated argument.

"What are you doing here?" Patrice asked.

"Same as you. I bought a ticket," was the reply.

"Well, I guess they will let anyone into this event."

"Patrice, my money is just as good as yours."

"Don't forget exactly where *your money* comes from."

"My money comes from honest hard work. You, of all people, know that."

"If you say so," Patrice said as she brushed past her tormentor.

"He's going to leave you, you know."

"How absurd," Patrice said with a wave as she continued to walk toward the ladies' room. "I won't entertain such a ridiculous notion."

As the excitement grew on the dance floor, tension exploded in the alcove. As Bon Jovi belted out "You Give Love A Bad Name" on stage, Patrice Ellingham Holcomb was dragged into a dark corner. Before she could scream for help a thin cord was wrapped around her neck. As Patrice began to choke, she reached for the cord but grabbed her pearls instead. The pressure around her throat intensified and she fought to keep consciousness. The bind around her neck tightened more and she began to strangle. The last image she saw before death was the face of her attacker.

Patrice's limp body dropped to the floor before the killer walked away. The necklace that had once belonged to Louise Ellingham, Patrice's mother, was broken, and beads were strewn across the floor. The band played for more than an hour before the lifeless body was discovered.

As a gesture of appreciation, Lyle Corday had purchased four tables and invited thirty of his employees to the ball. Lyle and his wife Marge had taken out a second mortgage on their Washington Township home to open their first store. Now they were the proud owners of nine successful outlets. After a couple of spins on the dance floor, she was winded and excused herself.

Marge was accompanied by two other women who stopped at the bar while she continued to the ladies' room. She turned to push the door open, when she eyed several loose pearls lying on the floor. She leaned over to pick up one of the shiny beads and saw what she thought was a human shape.

Gripped by a sudden wave of intense fear, she curiously crept closer. Her breath was ragged, and although she had taken her high blood-pressure medication earlier that day her heart rate spiked. She opened her purse and, with one hand, slid on the eyeglasses she needed, but hated to wear. With her vision boosted she clearly saw a body crumpled over in the corner.

"Oh, my God!" she screamed. "Oh, my God!"

A crowd gathered quickly and all eyes focused on the same grisly sight. The elegant black-and-white gown that had been tailor-made for Patrice Holcomb was still wrapped around the woman. Her head was twisted at an unnatural angle and a thin purple bruise formed a ring around her neck. Her eyes bulged wide-open and her lipstick was smeared around her lips. Her mouth still wore the snarl she used to draw in her last breath before speaking her final words.

Word of the fallen woman raced around the room like fire through a dry woodpile. Minutes after she was found, Mayor Campbell interrupted her husband to let him know. He was still talking business with Arthur Cantwell and Governor Peterson.

"Mr. Holcomb," the mayor started. "Sir, I have some terrible news."

"Steve, you look like the world's about to end. What the hell is going on?" Holcomb replied.

"Sir, it's regarding your wife."

"No, Patrice is fine. She's around here somewhere," Holcomb said as he glanced over his shoulder.

"Yes, sir, I know exactly where she is," Campbell said as he shot a glance toward the governor. "Please come with me."

The two men had known each other for almost twenty years. Campbell's weary look told Peterson that this was a grave situation. There was a moment of awkward silence among the four men, and Arthur Cantwell was first to speak.

"Come on, Ed, I'll go with you."

The group followed Mayor Campbell around the alcove to where a group of dazed patrons stood. Nervous murmurs instantly went to silence as the four men approached. Many of the men and women struggled with their emotions and a few lost the battle. The crowd spread apart as Campbell led Holcomb toward the body.

The dress she had modeled for him, but he had barely noticed, lay before him. Vain to her last dying breath, her freshly colored hair was radiant red, and it framed her face perfectly. The scowl she still wore showed that she died in a painful struggle.

Holcomb dropped to his knees and reached out to her, but his hand was brushed aside. An off-duty IMPD traffic cop attending the ball with his fiancée had taken control of the scene until homicide detectives could be dispatched.

"Sir, I can't allow you to touch the victim. This is an active crime scene," the officer said.

"She's my wife. Why aren't you helping her?"

"I'm sorry to be the one to tell you this, Mr. Holcomb, but she's dead. I think she's been strangled."

"How did this happen?"

"Sir, I have no idea, but we'll find out who did this."

IMPD's Chief Homicide Detective was not happy when his cell phone rang. This was his poker weekend. A group of cops, some active, some retired, met once a month to smoke cigars, down some beers, and swap stories. The card game was just a backdrop for the monthly male-bonding session.

When he arrived at the ball and saw the body crumpled in the corner, he knew this was a case of murder. He received a detailed update from the forensic tech on the scene before interviewing the first officer on the scene. After talking to the young officer, the nineteen-year lawman walked across the dance floor to the stage. The band was in the middle of a song when he demanded the microphone.

"Good evening, ladies and gentleman, I'm Detective Fritz Weber. There has been a heinous crime committed in the building tonight. The perpetrator is most likely still in this room, and for your own safety, no one will be allowed to enter or leave this building until this case is solved. Law enforcement officers are posted inside and outside the facility, and I would like everyone to take a seat in the ballroom. We will make a thorough investigation. My partner Yancey Goldman and I will need to speak to each one of you. I apologize in advance for the inconvenience."

News of the body found at the Indiana Roof Ballroom was huge. The murder was the lead story on all four late-night newscasts. Although there were no cameras inside to record images on this night, the Holcomb's were Indiana's first family and there was ample file footage to help tell the story.

While the shocking tale was being told to viewers, inside the ballroom Detectives Goldman and Weber delivered on their guarantee to personally question everyone. Veterans of large-scale investigations, they were able to gather information quickly. They interviewed the first one hundred patrons in less than an hour. As Goldman questioned the party-goers, Weber kept his eye on Edward Holcomb.

The corporate baron who was always seen standing confidently in his company's ads, delivering the tagline, "Helping America stand independent, one gallon at a time," slumped in his chair. This time there was no red, white and blue flag behind him waving in the breeze; no supportive spouse off-camera smiling at him. This time there was just a broken shell of a man, wondering who killed his wife.

Sitting at the table with Holcomb was his brother Bradley, along with Arthur Cantwell and their wives. Louise Stansberry, Edward's secretary, was also at his side. She had worked for Edward long before he became the czar of ethanol production. Stansberry's husband Phil sat nervously next to the empty chair that had been set aside for Patrice.

Twelve hundred people had attended the event and as the clock approached one a.m., many grew impatient, as the investigation continued. Detective Weber concluded that since there was no robbery and the body showed no defense wounds, Patrice was killed by someone she knew. A review of surveillance cameras in the ballroom's lobby showed that no one had exited the building since the event began. Police were confident the killer was still there.

Normally in murder cases the spouse is the primary suspect, but in this case, surveillance cameras showed Holcomb in plain view standing near the bar the entire night. The only time he stepped out of sight was when he was led by the mayor to the crime scene. Still, Weber decided to talk to him first.

"First of all, I'm sorry for your loss. I want you to know that we are doing everything we can to find the person or persons responsible for this," the detective started.

"I can't believe this," Holcomb said quietly. "I don't know why anyone would want to hurt Patrice."

"Sir, you're a very powerful man. Do you know of anyone who would want to get to you by hurting your wife?"

"No, not to my knowledge."

"Is there anyone internationally who would want to harm you?" Weber asked, exploring the terrorist angle.

"My company is responsible for a two-dollar drop in the price of a gallon of gasoline. Of course I'm Public Enemy Number One in the Middle-East, but killing my wife has no bearing on ethanol prices versus gasoline."

34

"Had she received any threats?"

"No threats that I know of."

"Okay, well, we'll talk to everyone tonight, and I'll get back with you when I know something."

The murder took place in an area not covered by cameras, but physical evidence from the crime scene enabled investigators to narrow the suspects down to three. That was verified when the homicide specialist interviewed Gideon Lake.

Two years before Patrice Ellingham became Patrice Holcomb, she was engaged to Lake. The two were inseparable after meeting during freshman orientation on the campus of Valparaiso University. Three years of dating ended abruptly when Patrice met Edward Holcomb.

The eloquent poems Gideon penned for Patrice paled in comparison to Holcomb's lofty dreams of conquering the industrial world. Lake went on to become a best-selling author and lecturer, eventually becoming a professor at the university, but in spite of his personal success, his resentment of Patrice and Edward was deep.

"Mr. Lake, I know that you attended college during the same years as the victim. Do you know of anyone who would want to harm her?" Weber asked.

"I didn't just go to college with her. I was her boyfriend, at least until Holcomb came along."

The detective knew of their history from other patrons he'd interviewed earlier. He also knew the professor had an axe to grind; now it was time to see if he was the perpetrator.

"What happened between you two?" Weber asked.

"Not much. She was in love with me and we were going to get married after graduation. I was going to be a writer and she was going to teach. Holcomb came along with his mind focused solely on money and took her from me," Lake replied.

"Wasn't she from a wealthy family?"

"Yes, but the money her parents inherited was almost gone. They were down to their last million or so, and the way they spent money, they were as good as broke."

"So how often did you see the victim?"

"Actually, quite a bit. Holcomb donated ten million dollars to endow a chair in literature at the university. I always knew it was her idea since they used the money to hire me as a fellow. Patrice was also very active in fundraising for the school so she was on campus all the time."

"So, you think she wanted to have you around?"

"Yes, I do."

"Why?"

"Because, she never got over me."

"What was your relationship like?"

"Strictly professional, I was over her years ago. I felt that she had made her choice, so she had to live with it."

"I'll go back to my original question. Do you know of anyone who would want to harm her?"

"Everybody knows their marriage is shaky. I've heard the secretary is in line to become wife number two."

"Really, where did you hear that?"

"I overheard a couple of faculty members talking at our last fundraiser."

"Mr. Lake, did you kill Mrs. Holcomb?"

"No, I did not."

After talking with Gideon Lake, Weber questioned Louise Stansberry. She had served as Holcomb's assistant for more than twenty years. Next to his wife, no one knew him better. The detective knew that if the marriage was in trouble the secretary would know.

"Mrs. Stansberry, do you know of anyone who would want to hurt Mrs. Holcomb?" Weber began.

"Gideon Lake," she answered.

"Why?"

"He's still in love with her. The Holcombs would have divorced years ago but they wanted to wait until their youngest boy finished college."

"Mrs. Stansberry, are you in love with Mr. Holcomb?"

"Yes, I am."

"Mrs. Stansberry, did you kill Mrs. Holcomb?"

"No, I did not."

The blunt honesty from Louise Stansberry told Fritz Weber that he needed to talk to Edward Holcomb again.

He walked over to the man who had just stared into the eyes of his dead wife. More than two decades of listening to her voice, smelling her perfume and feeling her touch, and now she was gone. A long-term illness can be understood over time, wounds from a car accident can heal, but an untimely death in such a benign setting as tonight would never be forgotten.

"Mr. Holcomb, I know this is a difficult time for you, but I have to ask you some more questions," Weber said. "Would you please walk with me?"

The CEO of one of the nation's most powerful companies rose and complied with the request.

"I understand detective; you can ask me anything you want," Holcomb said quietly as the two men walked toward the parking garage.

"Sir, was your marriage in jeopardy?"

"Jeopardy, no, but over, yes. We were waiting for Jeremy to finish college. After his graduation we were going to get divorced."

"Why?"

"My wife was never in love with me. I was a way to restore the Ellingham wealth. I had served my purpose and she was done with me."

"Was she in love with someone else?"

"Gideon Lake was the love of her life. She should have married him instead of me."

"Why do you say that?"

"Because she never stopped loving him, I always knew that."

"Did you kill your wife, Mr. Holcomb?"

"No, I did not."

"Do you think Gideon Lake killed her?"

"Yes, I do."

"Why?"

"I think he killed her because he couldn't have her."

"But if you and your wife were planning to get divorced, why couldn't he have her?"

"He couldn't have her because I believe she was seeing someone else."

"Your wife was having an affair?"

"I think so."

"Do you know who the man is?"

"No, and I don't care."

"Why don't you care?"

"Our relationship was more like a merger than a marriage. I couldn't care less what she did or who she did it with."

"One more question, sir, are you in love with Louise Stansberry?"

"Yes, I am."

Fritz Weber knew he was working the most interesting and dynamic case of his career. A dead body found at a public event, not just public, but corporate royalty. With adultery, a pending divorce, a husband and secretary in love, and a once-jilted lover standing by unrequited and still bitter, this was a tantalizing case. At monthly poker games for years to come, this would be the gem everyone would talk about.

"When did you know? What tipped you off? And how did you figure it out?" Eager cops, young and old, would ask.

At this point Weber didn't have all the answers, but he had a hunch. His intuition had solved many a case before, and as the clock struck two a.m. he knew the time had come to unravel this murderous riddle. A brief chat with Phil Stansberry yielded nothing new. His wife was Holcomb's loyal secretary, and he appeared to know nothing about the romantic stirrings between her and her boss.

Bradley Holcomb was the last person at the table. The detective called him over to answer a few questions. The two men walked away from the ballroom, taking a seat on the steps leading to the parking garage. To the left of the stairs was an original stage door. Encased in protective glass, the door bore the markings made by two employees. The rating system gave up to four stars for each of the performances of the 1934-35 season. In this simple setting, the final interview of the night began.

"Did you and your wife come in the same car with Edward and Patrice?"

"No, my wife and I came together and have been together all evening."

"Mr. Holcomb, did you see your brother's wife this evening?"

"Of course I saw her. We had dinner at the same table."

"Were you alone with her at any time this evening?"

"No."

"Mr. Holcomb, do you know of anyone who would want to kill your brother's wife?"

"No."

"Are you sure?"

"Well," Bradley Holcomb said before a long pause. He reached in his shirt pocket for his cigarettes and grabbed a small black box instead. He absentmindedly flipped the small device over and over in his left hand.

"Go on," Detective Weber encouraged.

"Look, my brother is under a lot of pressure. He runs one of the most powerful corporations in the country, and his marriage is going bad. I don't think he would do anything this crazy, but you never know."

"So, you think your brother killed his wife?"

"They were about to get a divorce that was going to cost him tens of millions of dollars. Losing that much money might push a guy over the edge, that's all I'm saying."

"Does he have a history of violence?"

"I wouldn't say that, but he does have a temper."

"Really?"

"Yeah."

"So, let's just say he did this. What would happen to the company?"

"We wouldn't miss a beat. As the Chief Operating Officer, I handle daily operations. I'd step in and take charge."

"That would make you one rich and powerful guy, huh?"

"Yeah, but I could handle it."

"So, if your brother was convicted and jailed, the business would fall into your lap?"

"Yeah, and just between you and me, I'm more of a risk-taker, so I could take the company to the next level."

"What do you mean by that?"

"If we made a few changes to our refinement process, we could increase our profits by millions."

"Why doesn't your brother make those changes now?"

"There are some minor environmental concerns he's worried about."

"Hey, what is that thing in your hand?"

"It's an iPod. My kids got it for me for Father's Day. This little thing holds hundreds of songs."

"How do you listen to it?"

"It comes with earphones that plug in."

"Could you show me how it works?"

Bradley reached inside his coat pocket and then checked his pants, but the earphones weren't there.

"Are you looking for this?" Detective Weber asked as he held up a plastic evidence bag.

Inside the bag was a thin black cord.

"We found this near Patrice Holcomb's body. A thin bruise was also around her neck. We think this cord caused the bruise when it was used to strangle her. We know she was killed by someone she knew, and we have surveillance video of the two of you speaking in a less-than-friendly way," Weber said. "Now is there anything you want to tell me?"

"I want to speak to my lawyer."

Fast Track Ladies

by Wanda Lou Willis

There are several examples of women being admitted to the Indianapolis 500 track and pit/garage area long before credentials were issued to females on a regular basis in 1971. Amelia Earhart and Jackie Cochran (first woman to break the sound barrier) both served as honorary referee. Earhart in 1935, and Cochran in 1938, attended the drivers' meeting the day before the race and were escorted through the pits on race morning by Eddie Rickenbaker. The earliest female to ride in a race car at the track was an *Indianapolis Star* reporter, Betty Blythe. Driver Bob Burman took her for several fast laps around the track in August 1909. The following day her account appeared on the front page.

Women are a part of the racing sport as drivers and pit crew members. Though Richard Petty has not changed his mind that women should not be drivers, his team was one of the first to employ female engineers and mechanics.

Janet Guthrie in 1977 became the first female to qualify. Louis Meyer's daughter, Kay Bignotti, was the mechanic who started Guthrie's engine. Guthrie finished twenty-ninth. She competed in two more races, finishing ninth in 1978 and thirty-fourth in 1979. Her place in history is secure. She was one of the first women elected to the International Women's Sports Hall of Fame, inducted into the International Motorsports Hall of Fame, and her helmet and racing suit are at the Smithsonian Institution.

In 1992 Lyn St. James raced for the first time at Indy, placing eleventh, and was voted Rookie of the Year. She qualified six more times but never bested her 1992 record. Dedicated to advancing opportunities for female athletes, she served as president of the Women's Sports Foundation from 1990 to 1993. The following year she established a nonprofit organization dedicated to professional race car driver development, especially for aspiring young women.

In 2000 Sara Fisher became the third woman to compete at Indy. She started nineteeth and ended thirty-first. She qualified the next four years, placing thirty-first, twenty-fourth, thirty-first, and twenty-first respectively. At the 2007 Indianapolis 500 she placed eighteenth.

Danica Patrick in 2005 became the fourth female to qualify at Indy and was named Rookie of the Year. Her fourth-place starting position and fourth-place finish were the highest ever for a female. She was the first female to lead the race. Coming back in 2006, she finished eighth, a feat she duplicated in 2007.

Another milestone was reached in 2007 when three female drivers started at the Indianapolis 500: Danica Patrick, Sarah Fisher, and first-timer Milka Duno. Duno finished thirty-first.

A Little Dab Will Do Ya

by Brenda Robertson Stewart

Brenda Robertson Stewart is a figurative artist, forensic artist, horsewoman, and mystery author. Her first published short stories were included in the anthologies: Derby Rotten Scoundrels *and* Low Down and Derby. *Her mystery novel,* Power in the Blood, *featuring forensic artist Lettie Sue Wolfe, was published in 2005. She is currently working on book two in the series. She lives in central Indiana.*

Laura Chapman sat alone in her luxurious townhouse, clinging to one of her teddy bears while she sobbed and muttered, "He wasn't supposed to die." Her tears soaked the golden mohair fur of the Steiff bear.

Charlie Martinez wasn't supposed to be dead two days before he was predicted to win the pole for the Indianapolis 500. The paramedics had tried to resuscitate him, but instead of racing on Memorial Day, he was being trucked to University Hospital for an autopsy.

Laura was a hometown girl who had grown up in the Sunshine Trailer Park on the southwest side of town. Her mother had worked three jobs to support her two children, while keeping their modest home spotlessly clean. The kids at school called them trailer trash, but Mrs. Chapman said to pay them no mind. "They're just ignorant," she'd say. Both Laura and her brother Todd were determined to make their mother proud when they grew up. Todd, two years younger than his sister, became a lawyer, which was a good thing since Laura often needed the services of his law firm.

The Sunshine Escort Service was Laura's pride and joy. When she announced to a client, "We take all major credit cards and checks with proper identification," her chest swelled with pride. Her stable of girls numbered an even dozen now. They raked in enough money in the month of May to subsidize the business for the rest of the year. Men always needed a date for the race festivities or a girl to show off on their arm when they went to dinner. Over the years, Laura had made friends with many in the racing community, and she was often called upon to provide escorts for their guests.

The luxurious condominium Laura afforded on the north side of the city was the center of her business. Her computer and phone bank occupied one of the guest rooms. Her records were meticulous and up-to-date, which made the IRS happy but made some of her clients a bit nervous. *After all, an escort service was a perfectly legitimate business,* Laura thought. *The police sometimes harassed her and her girls, just didn't seem to understand that men needed dates to feel secure among their colleagues.*

The doorbell rang while Laura sat alternating between tears and muffled muttering. She checked the closed-circuit TV mounted on the wall. It looked so much like the newer flat-screen plasma televisions, no one would have guessed it was connected to the security cameras monitoring her front door. Seeing one of her girls at the door, she let her in. "Whatever is the matter, Laura?" Brooke Binghamton asked.

"Charlie Martinez died tonight. Right here in my dining room," she exclaimed, while pointing to a room off the living room. "I had put out some snacks and drinks on the table. Charlie had only taken a few bites when he grabbed his chest and fell right over the table, knocking bottles of champagne and wine everywhere. I'll probably never get those wine stains out of that white linen tablecloth, let alone the carpet."

Brooke shook her head while tendrils of auburn hair fell out of her topknot. "No, no that can't be true," she said. "I've bet a lot of money on him to win the race this year. Of course, I'm sorry he's dead, too. I didn't mean to sound callous. What do you think he died from?"

"I don't know, but he had been sweating profusely and complaining of a toothache. Said he was going to the dentist early in the morning to get his tooth fixed because he couldn't concentrate on racing with all that pain."

"He was popping some pain pills the doctor gave him when I saw him at the track yesterday. Sounds like a heart attack," Brooke said.

"That's what I think, too. You know, you hear about those athletes who just up and die from heart defects and stuff nobody knew they had. I do wish he'd died someplace else. My home is my castle, and look at the mess I'm left with."

After Brooke left, Laura went into her Collecting Room, as she called it. Glass cases, from floor to ceiling, surrounded the guest room walls, while a heart-shaped bed draped in plush pink velveteen occupied the center. Hundreds of teddy bears stared like little soldiers from the shelves. "I'm probably going to get the electric chair, little guys. I promise to find you homes before the police come to arrest me for murder." She stretched her long slim body out on the bed, letting her platinum blonde hair cascade over the side like a silver waterfall while she clutched her golden Steiff bear.

"Listen up, and I'll tell you the whole sad tale. I don't know how I could have been so stupid. You're right, though, I need to start at the beginning," she said as she drummed her long red fingernails on her favorite bear.

"It all started with that creep, Red Jenkins. He's a mechanic on Jorge Mendez's racing team. Charlie told him he was going to see me tonight. Red was the one who was here night before last. Anyway, Red said that Charlie didn't deserve to win the Indy 500, that his father had bought his ride. I pointed out that any driver in that class had to have talent, not just money. He agreed, but he wanted to at least see to it that Charlie wouldn't sit on the pole. He said if Charlie had so much talent, he could win from back in the pack. That's when Red told me Charlie was allergic to shellfish, and if I could get him to eat some, it would make him too sick to race for the pole. Ten thousand dollars is a bunch of money. I thought I could put some more with it and get my mother to move from that trailer into a real house. I agreed to do it, but Red didn't give me any down payment or anything. I bought some shrimp and made a chip dip out of it. After putting it into the food processor with horseradish, which I knew Charlie loved, and adding some jalapenos and other stuff, it didn't taste like shrimp. Well, he ate almost all of it. He was sweating when he got here, though. I should have looked up shellfish allergy on the Internet, but I didn't have time. Red said it would make him sick, but it made him dead."

Laura decided she couldn't go away with her house in such a mess, so she swept up the glass from the bottles and glasses, washed the dirty dishes, sprayed the tablecloth with something that said it would remove wine stains, put it into the washer, and started to clean the carpet. No one said anything about preserving the crime scene. *Of course, they wouldn't know it was a crime scene until they received the autopsy report,* she thought. As she was cursing Red Jenkins, the doorbell rang.

There stood Red Jenkins. She jerked him inside. Before she could say anything, Red said, "You weren't supposed to kill him, Laura. What on earth were you thinking? You keep me out of it, you hear. Nobody's going to believe I'm involved unless you open your big mouth. I told you to make him sick. You're not getting a dime out of me."

Laura started crying again. "You never told me he could die from eating shellfish. He was supposed to get sick."

"You were supposed to give him a little bit. How much did he eat?"

"Well, he ate almost all of it—about a cup, I guess."

"Haven't you ever heard of anaphylactic shock, you moron?" Red shouted.

"No. My brother's allergic to strawberries, and he breaks out in hives."

Red got up and walked to the door. "Count me out, Laura. You're on your own."

Laura got back to cleaning the carpet. If tears could remove wine stains, she'd be done in a flash, but she had to resort to chemicals. Satisfied the rug was clean, she double-checked all the locks in the house and set the alarm. Shivering as she removed her clothes, she turned on the shower and tried to warm her cold body. *She thought about how upset her mother and brother would be when they found out what she'd done. They'd never forgive her.*

After drying off and dressing in pink satin pajamas, Laura climbed into bed and turned on the electric blanket. She had never felt so cold. All she could think of was that this might be the last night she'd get to spend in her beautiful home. Still reeling from shock, she finally fell into a deep sleep.

Early the next morning, she awakened soaked in perspiration from the heat of the electric blanket. Laura jumped out of bed and took a quick shower. She dressed in a pair of pink shorts with a matching tee. There was much work to be done. After putting the bed linens in the washing machine, she ironed her linen tablecloth, noting the wine stains were gone. Slipping into her office, she decided to follow her preconceived plan of protecting her clients. She put all her computer files on CD's, which took most of the morning. Using a program she had purchased some time ago in the event she needed it, she swept the hard drive of any file remnants. She knew a forensic computer tech could still access the files, but she hoped it wouldn't come to that. Her computer skills weren't good enough to replace the hard drive and destroy the old one.

As she got into her red Mercedes convertible for the drive to the post office, Laura noticed how hot the day had become. *I'd better enjoy the sunshine for as long as I can.* She began to shiver again, but she dropped off the package of CD's addressed to her mother at the Sunshine Trailer Park.

While driving home, Laura considered her options. *It's said that confession is good for the soul. Maybe I should come clean and get it over with,* she thought. *But that psychic I went to last week said good fortune was coming my way. Obviously it wasn't coming from Red Jenkins.*

It was 4:00 p.m. when Laura pulled her car into the garage. She had made a decision not to confess. *Why should I say I did it when I didn't mean to kill him? Maybe they won't find out about the shrimp.*

The death of Charlie Martinez was the main story on all the newscasts around the city, overshadowing the Indy 500 itself. Cause of death hadn't been determined, but toxicology reports were pending. *Oh my God. I think I'm going to have a heart attack if this mess isn't settled soon,* Laura thought. It was a good thing she had a business to run to take her mind off the unpleasantness.

A few days later, Laura was parking her car in the garage after a shopping trip to buy the latest collectible teddy bear. A car with two men in it pulled up in her driveway. She assumed her number was up.

"We're with the IMPD homicide unit, Ms. Chapman, and we wanted to put your mind at ease. Charlie Martinez was killed by an overdose of acetaminophen. His liver looked like cottage cheese, and nothing you could have done would have saved him. We've arrested a woman by the name of Brooke Binghamton. Said Charlie reneged on his promise to marry her, and she decided to get even. She kept feeding him acetaminophen in large quantities for his toothache, telling him it was just over-the-counter stuff. He was also taking a narcotic with high doses of the drug in it. Binghamton used to be a nurse's aid and admitted she was so mad, she wanted to hurt him when she found out he was seeing other women. Said she didn't mean to kill him."

"Thank you so much for telling me, officers," Laura said as she clutched her new bear to her bosom. "I've been blaming myself. At least now I know I couldn't have done anything to save the poor man."

After the detectives drove away, Laura hurried into her house. *Of all the nerve,* she thought. *That Brooke was seeing Charlie off the books. Never gave me a cent. And now I'm short one girl, and here it is May, our busiest month of the year.*

HANS Saves Drivers' Necks— Wins Schwitzer Award

by Ann Collins

Chasing the checkered flag at break-neck speeds, Indy Car drivers pursue an extreme sport with maximum risk of casualties. A leading cause of racing fatalities is basilar skull fracture. In a collision, the driver's body experiences tremendous forward momentum and becomes a projectile within the cockpit. The traditional shoulder harness and seatbelt restrain the torso, but allow the driver's head to fly forward like a bowling ball on a spring. At race speeds, the sudden deceleration of a crash can subject the Indy Car driver to forces exceeding one hundred G's. This gives the head and helmet an effective weight of twelve hundred pounds, and places the neck and base of the skull in peril. Space shuttle astronauts pull only three G's at launch from Cape Canaveral.

Dr. Robert Hubbard, a professor of biomechanical engineering at Michigan State University, developed a solution to keep the driver's head on his (or her) shoulders. In collaboration with his brother-in-law, Jim Downing, a seasoned IMSA driver, Hubbard developed the HANS device (Head And Neck restraint System). This collar-and-yoke system is worn on the shoulders and connected to the helmet by flexible tethers. HANS can reduce the dangerous neck loads experienced in a crash by eighty percent. In 2001 Hubbard and Downing received the prestigious Louis Schwitzer Award in recognition of engineering innovations benefiting Indy 500 racing. Today, Indy Car drivers won't start their engines without first strapping on the HANS.

Race to the Rescue

by Andrea Smith

Andrea Smith's Chicago police detective, Ariel Lawrence, has been featured in three published short stories including A Lesson in Murder, *which was published by Delacorte. Smith writes mystery and romantic suspense. Born in Chicago, she's lived in Indianapolis eleven years.*

Friday, May 25, 2007 – 8:00 p.m.

The ornate wooden door stood open. Not something you could do in Ariel Lawrence's Chicago neighborhood even though it boasted a few corporate VPs and a judge or two. Funny how people who lived in smaller cities were lulled into believing they were immune to crime.

Ariel stepped into the foyer and set her overnight bag on the white ceramic tile floor. The aroma of her aunt's southern-style cooking made her stomach growl. "Dora? Uncle Ross?"

A still petite Dora, thick salt-and-pepper hair cut into a stylish bob, popped through a doorway on the left and hurried toward Ariel.

"You made it!" Dora pulled Ariel into a welcoming embrace. Then she stared at her hard. "I swear you look more like your mother every year. You could be her twin with that pretty chocolate skin of yours."

Ariel gave a half smile. "I guess that's appropriate since she bullied me into being her stand-in this weekend."

Ariel's mother had laid on the guilt. "Do you know what it means for your cousin Jenna to be chosen Indy 500 Festival Queen? It's a dream. If I didn't have to give English finals on Monday, I'd be waving from the front bleacher at the parade. Your aunt and uncle haven't seen you in years, so you have to go represent the family. Show your cousin how proud we are."

Actually, it wasn't guilt that made Ariel succumb to the badgering. Ariel adored Jenna. It was hard to believe the little girl she had babysat and taught to ride a bike was a college freshman and hobnobbing with Indy's elite. Ariel hadn't seen her cousin since Dora and Ross relocated. She was just coming out of her braces. Ariel couldn't wait to see the sophisticated young lady she'd grown into.

Dora laughed. "Trust me; you're going to have so much fun you'll want to come back every year. The Indy 500 gets in your blood. I hope you brought a formal for the Snakepit Ball."

Ariel made a face. "I'm thrilled; I feel like Cinderella."

"Just leave your bag there; Ross will get it later." Dora grabbed Ariel's hand and led her toward the family room. "He'll be just giddy that you're finally here."

At that moment, her mother's youngest brother came out of the kitchen, drying his hands on a towel. Ross was reed thin and basketball-player tall. He wrapped Ariel in a tight hug. "You're looking good, niece. Everybody okay in Chicago?"

"Just peachy. Where's the 'queen'?"

"At a meeting, getting final instructions for this weekend's events. She should be home soon." Dora pressed her slender hands to her mocha cheeks. "This is so exciting, I can hardly stand it. Jenna's had so much fun this month making appearances and volunteering. She met the mayor and Tony Dungy, the Colts' coach. This weekend is just going to top it off."

The doorbell trilled.

"Now who could that be?" Dora asked and floated off to the front door.

"Bet you're hungry," Ross said. "As you can see," he pointed to the buffet table that was filled with delectable-looking dishes. "Dora cooked for an army platoon."

Ariel picked up a quiche hors d'oeuvre. "She always does."

Dora returned carrying a huge basket arrangement of black roses.

Ariel chuckled. "You Indy folks really take this 500 race thing to extremes. Don't ever think I've seen black roses before."

Dora carried the arrangement to the coffee table, untied the black ribbon that was around the clear floral wrap so she could get to the card. "Aren't they lovely? There's no name on the envelope, but I'm sure they're for Jenna."

She took the card from the envelope and read it. Then she let out a blood-curdling scream and dropped the card on the floor as if it had burned her hands.

Ariel and Ross were at her side in an instant.

"What is it, honey?" Ross asked.

Dora's mouth was moving, but no sound came out.

"Don't touch it, Uncle," Ariel said. She grabbed a napkin from the table and used it to pick up the card. The message constructed from words cut out of a newspaper read: *One hundred thousand dollars in cash to see your precious festival queen again. More instructions to come.*

Ariel's heart skipped. She took a deep breath so she could speak. "It's a ransom note. Jenna's been kidnapped."

Ross's eyes widened with terror. "What?" He put his arm around his wife. Dora clutched him tightly and started to sob.

The dream had quickly turned into a nightmare.

Ariel held Dora's hand while Ross dialed 911. Since kidnapping was a federal crime, the Indianapolis Police Department immediately handed the call off to the FBI. The Bureau sent an agent named Henry Snyder. He was a scrawny man whose blond hair was going thin on top. His dark suit screamed government agent.

"Where's the note?" Snyder asked Ross. His tone was brusque, and Ariel hoped his approach wouldn't upset Dora and Ross even more.

Ariel had placed the note in a ziplock bag. She handed it to him. "I used a napkin to pick it up after my aunt touched it. Her prints should be the only ones on it—besides whoever left the note. Of course, there's no hint of what florist made the arrangement."

Snyder squinted at her. "You practicing to be a cop or something?"

"Actually, she's a Chicago police detective," Ross said. "A darn good one."

"Ariel Lawrence. I work violent crimes," she said, extending her hand.

Snyder shook it. "Chicago, eh," Snyder said.

Ariel knew what he was thinking, so she decided to reassure him she wasn't planning to tread on his territory. That she was going to follow protocol. She had no jurisdiction here, and as difficult as it might be to cool her jets, she had to let Snyder and his team do their jobs. "I'm on a few days' vacation. I came down to enjoy the 500 Festival activities and the race with my family. Sure didn't expect this."

Snyder read the note through the plastic bag. Then he handed it to a member of his team. "For processing. When did you folks last talk to your daughter?"

"Jenna called around seven-thirty to let us know the meeting was going to run over," Ross said. "It was downtown at the Girls Inc. building. She said to expect her some time after eight."

"Was she driving or did she get a ride?" Snyder asked, taking a small pad and pen from his inside suit pocket.

"She was driving a green 2003 Ford Focus. License plate is Jenna MD," Ross said. "She wants to go to medical school."

"Who was at this dinner?" Snyder probed.

"Festival organizers and other girls in the program this year. There're more than thirty princesses, and two of them are part of her court. They ride in the float with her."

Snyder looked Ross up and down. "What do you do for a living?"

Ross straightened. "I own a few dry cleaners."

"How many is a few?"

"Three locations."

Snyder raised a blond eyebrow. "So whoever grabbed your daughter knows you have a few dollars in the bank."

Ross shrugged. "I do all right, but I'm no millionaire."

"All right," Snyder said. He took his cell phone from his belt and punched in a number. "Yeah. I need a team to do some canvassing here on Lockerbie Street. And have IMPD put out an alert for a green 2003 Ford Focus. Plate is J-e-n-n-a M-D. That's the vic's car. Those techs on the way for the telephone surveillance?"

He listened. "Hurry it up."

He snapped the phone shut. "You folks are gonna need to tell me everything you can about who your daughter may have been around. And I need a good photo."

"They'll be calling with more instructions. Should we be trying to get the money together?" Ross asked.

Snyder's expression was tolerant. "We'll get to that."

"But we're wasting time." Ross turned a pleading gaze on Ariel. "Ari, what should we do?"

Then the phone rang.

9:00 p.m.

Snyder puffed up with anger. "Told them to get that tech team here. Where's an extension?"

"In the kitchen." Ross pointed to the door.

"Answer it and try to stay calm," he told Ross before disappearing into the kitchen.

"B-Burke residence." Ross listened. "Yes, this is Jenna's father." He listened some more, his face contorting in fear. "We...we...understand."

"Tell them you want to speak to your daughter," Ariel mouthed.

"How do we know she's all right? I want to talk to her." He waited. "Jen? Honey, are...Wait! Put her back on the phone!"

Ross sighed and punched off the call.

Snyder reappeared. "Voice was muffled. Couldn't tell if it was a man or woman."

Ross went over and put his arm around Dora. "They only let her say 'Daddy' but it was Jenna. They said get the money or we'll never see her again. We have until 1:00 a.m. They'll call again to let us know where to take it. How are we going to get that much money so fast?"

"My people will be here shortly and we'll be ready to trace the next call," Snyder said. He made more notes on his pad.

"I don't mean to butt in, Agent Snyder, but..." Ariel said.

He looked up at her; his expression said 'you already have.'

"Don't you think this ransom demand is kind of odd?" Ariel asked. "How do they expect my aunt and uncle to get a hundred thousand dollars in the middle of the night?"

"After twenty-five years with the Bureau, there isn't a whole lot that I find odd. Kooks will do and demand anything. Probably figure with all those stores he owns he can come up with it."

"Hey, Henry, you might want to take a look at this," a member of Snyder's team called from the other side of the family room. He'd turned on the flat screen TV that was on a black wooden stand. They all went to see. The headline blazing in front of a talking head was: BREAKING NEWS: 500 FESTIVAL QUEEN KIDNAPPED! A photo of a beautiful, smiling Jenna flashed.

Dora gasped, "Oh, God! How did they get her picture?"

"Great," Snyder hissed. "Hope this doesn't spook the creeps that snatched her."

Ariel shuddered at the thought of Jenna being held in God-knows-where by some maniacs. "Snyder, I know I don't have any jurisdiction here, but I want to help."

Snyder gave her a thin-lipped smile. "Thanks. But we've got everything under control."

At Snyder's dismissal, Ariel, Ross and Dora retreated to the long white sofa. She tried to convince Dora to go rest in her bedroom, but her aunt, dabbing at the tears she couldn't keep from welling in her eyes, stated she wasn't budging until her baby walked through the front door.

Ariel had never felt so helpless, waiting for the kidnappers' next call, waiting for Snyder to report some progress from the canvassing. From what she could tell, his teams were coming up empty. It made her wonder if Snyder's agents were talking to the right people, asking the right questions. Ariel decided Snyder owed them an update. She got up and crossed the room to where he was huddled with one of his techs.

"Can you tell me where things stand?" she asked.

Snyder twisted his mouth from side to side as if he were considering whether or not to answer her question. Finally he said, "We're making our way through the florists. So far, we've ruled out half of them. The agents assigned to interview the other girls are working as fast as they can."

That's it? Ariel thought, but said, "What about the program director?"

"We're going to get to her," Snyder said.

Ariel stared at him.

"I didn't get the extra people I requested from my office. And IMPD can't provide any more officers because they're stretched thin with extra details for the race," Snyder admitted.

It was time to kick protocol and territory to the curb. "So my cousin is just going to sit in the hands of some lunatic because you don't have enough people to handle it?"

Snyder held up a hand. "We're doing everything we can — "

"And making such stellar progress. Snyder, you need to authorize me to work this before we run out of time."

Snyder pointed at her. "We're talking about a kidnapping."

"We're talking about my cousin."

Snyder shoved his hands in his pockets. "You know I checked with the Chicago Police Department about you."

Ariel eyed him warily. "You spoke to my sergeant?"

"Oh, yeah. So I know you're notorious for not following your superior's orders."

Ariel smiled slightly. "So you also know I'm not going to just sit here keeping the furniture warm while my cousin's life is in danger."

They played the staring game for a few seconds.

"Fine," Ariel said. "Don't authorize me."

She turned to walk away.

"Hold it," Snyder said.

Ariel turned back around and waited. Snyder stepped toward her. "I'm in charge. I ask the questions. I take the notes. We do this my way."

Ariel smiled again. "What other way is there?"

10:00 p.m.

Snyder had arranged to meet Marta Witherton, the director of the Indy Festival Princess program. They met in front of the Girls Inc. building. Witherton looked like she'd dressed for a *Vogue* magazine photo shoot. Her slender frame was draped in a white Chanel slack suit. She had on black-and-white spectator pumps, and a yard of cultured pearls gleamed around her neck. Her jet black hair was swept up in a perfect updo and her make-up was flawless.

But Witherton was clearly flustered. When she spoke, her manicured hands flew as if she were using sign language. "We can't have a parade without the Queen. We have the fundraiser for the Children's Hospital. The Snakepit Ball. We have to find Jenna before it's all over the news. We need to call a press conference..."

"Whoa," Snyder held up his hands. "Take it easy. These kidnappers have given us just a narrow time frame to meet their demands. We do our jobs—and we intend to—you won't need to talk to the media until it's all over. Now if you get any press calls, I want you to pass 'em on to me and I'll have my office respond." Out came the notepad. "Tell us about this meeting you had this evening. When did it wrap up?"

Witherton twisted her pearls. She looked as if she were counting to ten. "We...we ran a little over. I think we finished around eight. Yes, just a few minutes after eight."

Ariel said, "Anything unusual happen? Did Jenna walk out with anyone? Where would they have parked? Did anyone escort them to the lot? Tell me about security here." She hadn't meant to jump in and fire the questions like that. She kept thinking about how afraid Jenna must be. She stole a glance at Snyder. Fortunately, he wasn't bristling too much.

"Security? We don't have guards. Never thought we needed them." Witherton's pearls were now in a knot. "What are we going to do?"

"We're going to find Jenna," Ariel said. "You can count on that. Can you take us to the parking lot?"

Witherton led them to more parking in the back. There were quite a few cars still in the lot. Witherton explained that after hours, people who lived in the area felt free to leave their cars in the Girls Inc. lot.

Using flashlights Snyder had retrieved from his car, they checked out each car until they found a green 2003 Ford Focus. Ariel looked at the plate and swallowed hard to get rid of the lump in her throat.

"It's Jenna's car," Ariel said.

Witherton gasped and covered her mouth.

Snyder's cell phone chimed. He unclipped it and said, "Yeah." He listened a few minutes and hung up. "We need to get back. Kidnappers made another contact."

11:00 p.m.

The call had been placed using a pre-paid cell phone, impossible for the tech team to trace.

"This is absurd," Ross said. "All this fancy equipment and they can't even pinpoint the area the call came from?"

Ariel tried to calm him. "Unfortunately this isn't like the stuff they use on the television series *24*. There's a limit to what real-life technology can do."

Ariel breathed deeply to stir up her nerve. She'd been holding back from asking her aunt and uncle the question she would have asked any other victim's relatives. "Uncle Ross, I know Jenna is a good girl."

Ross and Dora both looked at her with big fearful eyes. God, this was hard.

"Can you think of anything Jenna was involved in that might have brought her in contact with, say, less than optimal characters?"

"Why would you ask that? Of course not!" Ross said. "She studies all the time. Tutors middle school kids. She's never, ever given us any problems."

"She's a pretty girl. Were there any issues with boyfriends?"

Ross shook his head, then dropped his head in his hands.

"I'm sorry, Uncle Ross. But we have to consider all the possibilities if we're going to find Jenna. Parents don't always know everything that's going on," Ariel said. She stole a glance at Snyder who stood, hands in pockets, looking impatient.

"Well, there was that one boy," Dora said in a quiet voice. "Remember the one who wouldn't stop calling?"

Ross lifted his head. "What boy?"

Dora spoke to Ariel. "Jenna dated this young man just a few weeks. She broke up with him and he called her every five minutes after that. We had to change her cell phone number to stop the calls."

"Oh, yes. That tall skinny kid," Ross remembered. "Earring in his nose."

"He threaten her?" Snyder demanded to know.

Dora shook her head. "Jenna never said anything like that. But the way he acted bothered her enough to make her change the number."

"How come you didn't mention him before?" Snyder asked.

Dora folded her arms across her chest. It was her don't-mess-with-me gesture. "You didn't ask the question, and I've been so afraid for my daughter that I just didn't think about him."

Ariel rubbed Dora's shoulder. "That's okay. Why'd she break up with him?"

"She said he was creepy. That's the only explanation she would give us. You know young people. Never think their parents will understand anything."

Snyder said. "Sounds like we need to talk to this young man. Do you know where he lives?"

Dora went to find the address.

"There's another news report, Henry," the agent called from his post.

This time a local reporter was in front of the Girls Inc. building interviewing Marta Witherton. Her manicured hands fluttered dramatically around her face when she said, "We're all praying Jenna Burke will be found safe and…"

"Didn't I tell her not to talk to the press?" Snyder snarled.

Ross said, "What about the money? We only have an hour."

12:00 Midnight

Brock Edmunds' family lived in Broad Ripple. Filled with trendy restaurants that were open late and art galleries housed in quaint buildings, the area reminded Ariel of Chicago's north side.

It took a woman they assumed was Brock Edmunds' mother five minutes to answer the doorbell. She cracked the door and eyed Ariel and Snyder with a mixture of confusion and annoyance. She was a tall woman with pale skin and bright red hair.

"Who are you and why are you ringing my doorbell at midnight?" she said with a scowl, clutching her pink bathrobe at the neck.

Snyder held up his shield. "FBI. Are you Mrs. Edmunds?"

She stared at it. "Yes?"

"Is your son Brock home?" Snyder asked.

Mrs. Edmunds blinked at him. "No, he's not. What do you want with my son?"

"Need to ask him a few questions about an acquaintance of his. Jenna Burke, this year's 500 Festival Queen."

Ariel saw the cords tighten in Mrs. Edmunds' slender neck.

"Mind if we come in?" Snyder said.

Mrs. Edmunds hesitated before she opened the door to allow them into the front room of the small brick house.

Snyder said, "Your son had a relationship with Jenna. We've been told he didn't take their breakup too well."

Mrs. Edmunds flipped her red hair behind her ear. "He dated her. So what?"

"Where is he, ma'am?" Snyder pressed.

"Why? And why are you asking about that phony girl?"

Ariel felt herself bristle. "You don't sound like you were too fond of Jenna."

Mrs. Edmunds flipped her hair again. "A little snooty for my taste. Especially after they named her queen. But then they all are. The girls who participate in this junk—pageants, beauty competitions—think they're everything. Do anything to be 'chosen.'" She made the quote marks with her forefingers.

Ariel gnawed her lower lip, fighting the urge she had to go off on the woman. Jenna was anything but snooty. Maybe this woman's attitude had spilled over to her son after Jenna stopped going out with him. Maybe it had made Brock angry enough to do something crazy, like kidnapping her.

"We're told your son made harassing calls to her." Snyder said.

"He would have no reason to do that. He's a good kid. He had a job at the track. He even volunteered to work on some festival events. Besides, my son is handsome and charming. Girls chase *him*. Why would he want to keep running behind some wannabee beauty queen?"

Snyder gave a snort. "You don't have to admit it. We can get cell phone records. We need to talk to him, so you need to tell us where we can find him."

Mrs. Edmunds batted her eyes nervously. "I-I-I don't know where he is. We had a disagreement this morning and he left."

"About what?"

"College. He doesn't want to go, and I'm insisting that he do so."

"We're going to need a photo of your little angel," Snyder said.

Back in the car, Snyder called in a description of Brock Edmunds and the kid's car to put IMPD on the alert for him as a 'person of interest.' They headed back to Dora and Ross's house for an update from Snyder's team.

"We've talked to about a third of the girls who were at the dinner meeting. None of them remember anything unusual, and they don't remember Jenna leaving with anyone. Any luck with the Edmunds kid?"

Snyder told them where they were.

"I never did like that boy," Ross said after learning what Edmunds' mother had said about his daughter.

The phone rang and everybody seemed to stop breathing.

Snyder put on his earpiece and nodded to Ross.

Ross picked up the phone. Ariel could see his hand shaking.

"We're doing our best to meet your deadline. You have to understand, we can't get to any banks at this time of night. We need more time. We just can't get our hands on that much cash. I promise you, we're trying. We—"

Ross sighed and hung up.

"Well?" Snyder asked the techs.

"Sorry, sir. Same thing. Prepaid cell phone. Call came from a wide calling area."

Ross raked his hand over his face. "This is the last hour we have to come up with the money."

"No other instructions about where to bring it?" Ariel asked.

Snyder shook his head, turned to his lead agents. "Contact the office and tell them we need the phony money for the drop. That may be our only chance to get them."

Ariel pulled Snyder out of her aunt and uncle's earshot. "This ransom demand still feels wrong. What kidnapper would demand a large sum of money in the middle of the night? They know Jenna's parents can't get to a bank. Can't have any money wired. It's almost as if the kidnappers don't want them to make the deadline." A shudder went through her. "As if they plan to hurt her no matter what."

"Look," Snyder started, but was interrupted by his cell phone ringing. He held up a finger to signal Ariel to put their conversation on pause, and stepped away to take the call.

Ariel decided to make a call, too, and went into the kitchen.

Marta Witherton answered after the first ring.

"Sorry to wake you," Ariel said.

"Who can sleep? You have news?"

"No, we haven't found Jenna yet, and none of the leads are getting us anywhere. I'm calling for Agent Snyder. I need you to think about the 500 Festival activities the princesses participated in these last few weeks. Tell me about any problems with their behavior or the events. Doesn't matter how insignificant they might seem."

Ariel heard Witherton take a deep breath.

"There were a few glitches with vendors and coordination. The usual missteps that can make executing the program a little stressful. One printer had the wrong time on an invitation. The florist shorted us on centerpieces. And, oh yes, the caterer didn't deliver the food until the eleventh hour for one of the luncheons. But this is my tenth year directing the program. It was nothing I couldn't handle."

"You personally took care of all those details?"

"For the most part. I had a little help from a handful of volunteers."

"What about the girls? Did they get along? Any disagreements?"

"There are always issues when you're dealing with young people. There were a few, shall we say, rivalries, but for the most part, this group seemed pretty level-headed."

"Would you elaborate on the rivalries? Who didn't like each other?"

Witherton sighed. "Well, the competition for queen was extremely stiff this year. The girls went all out with their references and presentations. Especially Amber Lee. She was upset when she didn't get the spot, but she got over it. She's been a terrific asset to the program. Her appearances have been splendid."

"I see. Did you know Brock Edmunds? His mother said he volunteered to work on some of the festival activities."

"Edmunds?"

"Tall skinny kid. Lot of long shaggy hair."

"No, I'm afraid I don't know him."

"Okay, guess that's it then. I'll keep you posted," Ariel said.

"Detective?"

"Yes?"

"When do you think you'll let me know when I can move on this?"

"Move on what?"

Witherton sighed heavily. "Believe me, I'm optimistic that Jenna will be found. But if she isn't located in time for the parade, I'll need to announce Amber Lee as the new queen."

After she hung up, Ariel filled Snyder in on her conversation with Witherton. "We might have a case of 'mean girls' here. It's possible this Amber Lee was upset enough about coming in second to orchestrate Jenna's abduction. She gets crowned festival queen if Jenna's not found. A lot more publicity during the year. Scholarship. I assume your people talked to her."

Snyder crooked a finger at the agent who'd been leading the interviews. Amber Lee's story had jived with the other accounts.

"I'd like to know how Ms. Lee spent the rest of her evening," Ariel said.

Snyder agreed and they drove to Avon on the west side of the city. A plaid bathrobe-clad Joseph Lee opened the door of his brick ranch home with a scowl, but he quickly agreed to wake his daughter when Snyder and Ariel identified themselves. "Have a seat while I get her. I'd be terrified if something like this happened to Amber."

He came back with Amber and her mother. Mom and Dad sat on either side of Amber, a pretty girl with a riot of light brown curls.

"We need you to tell us what happened at the meeting this evening, and when you last saw Jenna Burke," Snyder said.

Amber turned to look at her father. The curls bounced. "Gosh, I already told the officer about it. I don't feel like going over that again," she whined.

Brat. Ariel leaned toward Amber. "A girl's life is at stake. We need you to go over it again."

Amber scrunched her face.

"Go ahead, honey," Joseph Lee urged.

Amber let out a huge affected sigh. Then she told Ariel and Snyder what she'd told the officer about the meeting. "It was so boring. Withered Up was more of a basket case than usual. Tomorrow should be the bomb, though."

Ariel noted Jenna's disappearance hadn't dampened Amber's enthusiasm for the parade. "Withered Up?"

Amber giggled. "That's what some of us call Mrs. Witherton. It's all in fun."

With Amber's attitude, Ariel didn't have a hard time believing the girl could be behind Jenna's abduction. But who was helping her? Who was holding Jenna? And where?

"Do you know Brock Edmunds?" Ariel asked.

"Sure. He used to hang out with Jenna. He's such a loser."

"Why do you think that?" Snyder asked.

Amber bobbed her head and rolled her eyes as if to say, "Duh." "He's always creeping around trying to get her back. He just couldn't accept that she dumped him. How stupid is that?"

"Did you see him tonight?" Ariel asked.

"Oh, yeah. He was there. Drooling as usual."

"He was invited to the meeting?"

Amber shook her curls. "You kidding. That weirdo? He was working. Cleaning up and stuff."

Ariel's mind flashed back to her telephone conversation with Witherton. "How interesting. I talked to Witherton on the phone. She told me she didn't know Edmunds," she said to Snyder. "Why would she lie?"

They thanked the Lees, and fifteen minutes later, were downtown ringing the doorbell of Marta Witherton's three-story townhouse. Witherton answered the door still dressed for a fashion spread. "Has something happened? Do you need more information?"

"As a matter of fact we do," Snyder said.

They stood on the landing at the door.

"What can I tell you?" Witherton asked with a smile.

"You can tell us where Jenna is," Ariel said, tired of playing cat and mouse with the woman who may have hurt her cousin.

Witherton slid her fingers through the yard of pearls. "I really don't know what you mean."

"Of course you do," Ariel pressed. "Just like you know Edmunds."

Witherton's chin jutted out. "I *do not* know the boy." She said to Snyder, "Why are you here questioning me instead of trying to find our queen? The parade is in a few hours and my superiors won't be happy that you haven't done your job."

"Nice try," Ariel said. "We know Edmunds was on the clean-up detail at your meeting this evening. He was one of your volunteers. What else did Edmunds do for you?" Ariel stepped closer to the woman. "Did he help you kidnap Jenna?"

Witherton did the jut thing with her chin again. Defiant. "Don't be absurd. Why would I do a thing like that? If this boy kidnapped Jenna, he acted alone. I mean, he's been everywhere. At the track. At all events. He even—"

"What did you just say?"

At that moment, a TV news van pulled in front of Witherton's townhouse. Witherton's eyes darted at the van. Then she glared at Ariel as if she wanted to make her melt into the ground.

"You mentioned the track. Edmunds' mother told us he had a job there. But if you don't know him, how would you know that?" Ariel said.

Two men got out of the van, one balancing a camera on his shoulder. They started for Witherton's townhouse.

"Here're your choices," Ariel said. "We can let your supervisors and everybody else in this city see you on the news doing a perp walk in those designer duds, or you can show us where you're holding Jenna."

The TV crew was almost at the townhouse steps. Witherton gave Ariel one last angry glare before she put her hand up signaling them to stop. "I'm so sorry gentlemen, but I have an engagement and we will need to cancel the interview."

"Smart choice," Ariel said.

Ariel's heart was pounding when they pulled in front of the Hall of Fame Museum at Speedway. IMPD officers met them and took Witherton into custody. Speedway security led them to the Gasoline Alley exhibit and the storeroom where Witherton said Edmunds was holding Jenna.

Guns drawn, Snyder's agents bracketed the door. Then one kicked it in. Edmunds was sitting in a chair facing Jenna, who was on the floor tied up. He stood up and one of the agents tackled him to the ground. Ariel ran to Jenna, who burst into tears.

"I wasn't going to hurt her!" Edmunds cried, trying to twist away from the agents. "I just wanted to be with you, Jenna! Jenna, I just wanted to be with you!"

Saturday, May 26, 2007, 10:00 a.m.

The spring air was crisp and the sky clear, a perfect day for a parade.

"I'm still in shock. I can't believe that Witherton woman. After all her years of working with the 500 Princess Festival," Dora said. They were sitting in the parade bleachers enjoying the high school bands and waiting for the big moment.

"That's what drove her to it. In her view, she'd given so many years for so little recognition; she felt it was her time for the spotlight," Ariel said. "She got a rush from the media attention, doing the interviews, and giving them Jenna's picture."

"But to kidnap our daughter? How could she be so cruel?"

"The poor woman had a breakdown, Aunt Dora. She was convinced a crisis would make the festival organizers realize how valuable she was. Edmunds was unstable and so crazy about Jenna, he made the perfect accomplice. He was also an easy one to pin the blame on. Witherton figured no one would believe him when she claimed it was all his doing."

Edmunds' confession that Witherton had paid him to kidnap Jenna was enough evidence to bring charges. But they also had the testimony of the florist who'd provided the centerpieces for the events. Witherton had demanded the company throw in the black roses to make up for their flubs. Edmunds had picked up the flowers and managed to leave them on the doorstep without being noticed.

Cheers turned to whistles as the float carrying the 500 Festival Queen and her court came into view.

"There's our baby!" Ross yelled. His chest swelled with pride. They stood and chanted Jenna's name.

Jenna waved and blew them kisses. Ariel thought her cousin sparkled as much as the tiara she was wearing, in spite of the horror she'd suffered. In fact, all the girls shined. Even the spoiled Amber Lee.

Ariel put her fingers in her mouth and let out a loud whistle. She *was* proud of Jenna. And she had to admit she was looking forward to the race. Heck, even wearing that formal gown and dancing at the Snakepit Ball.

Imagine that.

Winning Lip Service

by Wanda Lou Willis

Many actors and actresses from Hollywood and television have participated in numerous Indianapolis 500 activities. Borg-Warner in 1947 would have an actress presenting the Victory Lane trophy and a kiss to the winner.

The first actress to kiss the 1947 winner, Mauri Rose, was Carol Landis. Rose won again in 1948 and received his trophy and kiss from Barbara Britton.

The lady in waiting for the 1949 winner, Bill Holland, was Linda Darnell. Holland and Johnny Parsons dueled for the 1950 win. Parsons won. The winner's kiss was presented by Barbara Stanwyck, star of the recently released racing film, *To Please a Lady.*

Lee Wallard refused to give up. With a broken rear shock mount and exhaust pipe and no brakes, he won the 1951 race. Waiting to present him with his much-deserved awards was the glamorous Loretta Young. Shortly after this spectacular win he was severely burned in a sprint car race ending his career.

Arlene Dahl in 1952 planted the winning smooch on Troy Ruttman. The next two years Bill "Vucky" Vukovich was kissed by Jane Greer and Marie Wilson, respectively. In 1955 he was killed in a chain-reaction crash involving Rodger Ward, Al Keller and Johnny Boyd, who also died. Bob Sweikert won the race and was kissed by Dinah Shore.

Noted actresses Virginia Mayo, Cyd Charisse and Shirley MacLaine greeted Pat Flaherty, Sam Hanks and Jimmy Bryan in 1956-58, respectively. The tradition ended in 1959 with Erin O'Brien kissing Rodger Ward.

One Cold Dish

by S.M. Harding

As a former academic, S.M. Harding has published academic papers, essays and magazine articles. She turned to fiction a few years ago, seeing several short stories to print, including Kate's first appearance in Detective Mystery Stories. *She currently lives in Indianapolis, Indiana and works as a chef.*

If cooking is heaven, then catering is hell. And catering for race fans at the Indianapolis 500, I was sure, could be found at the lowest level of Dante's Inferno. At 3:00 a.m., two days before the race, I stood jiggling the key in a lock that wouldn't work.

Oh, Kate, what have you gotten yourself into? I muttered. On the other side of the door was a kitchen I had never seen and where I would supervise meals at 6:00, 10:30 and 1:00 from an order sheet I'd also never seen. Damn Drew, anyway! Drew Frobisher had been the sous chef when I started at L'Aigle Noir as sauté chef. We'd both come a long way. I'd worked my way up and now wore the hat of executive chef. Drew had joined Chef Express, one of the largest catering companies in the area, and was currently their most visible VP.

Minor disasters in both our professional lives had brought me here. The chef who was supposed to be running this gig had managed to upset a pot of boiling water in a fit of temper yesterday afternoon. The splash he'd received was serious enough to keep him home through the rest of the festivities. L'Aigle Noir had suffered smoke damage from a fire started in a trendy boutique next door that wallowed in ambience of the candle variety. Kismet. Last night, in a moment of insanity, I'd said yes to Drew when he'd called to see if I'd fill in. He'd given a small whoop and said he'd be by shortly to drop off my pass and the keys of the catering kingdom.

Drew had assured me everything would be just peachy. "Ronnie Sellers will be your sous chef and knows the routine pretty well," he'd said, holding out the keys.

"Then why don't you give him the job and let me putter in peace with some new recipes for the restaurant?"

"She. Rumor has it Ronnie's a woman."

"It's only a rumor?"

"Ah, Kate, you know you love a challenge. Just take the keys and let me get to bed." He waggled his eyebrows in a bad imitation of Groucho Marx.

"Ronnie doesn't like a challenge?"

"She's fine with someone at the helm. Just tends to fray around the edges when she's in charge."

He threw the keys to me and in pure reflex, I caught them. He tossed a quick, "I'll be in around 9:00. Easy gig, Kate. Cake walk," over his shoulder as he walked to a Ford Excursion parked on the street.

In the pre-dawn darkness, I jiggled the key once more, pulled it out and grabbed the knob, thinking force of personality would open the door. It did. Or the door hadn't been locked all along. I stepped into the dark space and felt along the wall for the light switches. Banks of florescent lights flickered on and hummed in the silence.

The low cement ceiling was characteristic of the cement block box by the infield grandstand called the cold kitchen. Eight battered stainless steel prep tables filled the room. In an hour, this space would be buzzing with personnel assembling the cold orders. All the hot stuff, fried chicken to mashed potatoes, was taken care of in the fleet of oversized catering trucks parked across the underpass outside. Two hot trucks, one chicken truck with huge fryers, two cold trucks for storage and prep, three for dry goods, and a bunch of smaller mobile trucks that would take the orders to their various destinations. An armada of culinary vessels—and I was the commander.

I walked to the far side of the room where a small walk-in cooler and the executive chef's office were. I flipped on the lights in the office, booted up the computer, and took a look at what the day would hold. Hell. I quickly added up the orders and found we were going to send out over twenty-five hundred meals. The day was packed with activities, beginning with Carb Day practice and running through the Freedom 100 and the Pit Stop Challenge to finish with the Carb Day concert.

The very lowest level of catering hell.

I printed out the orders and each menu and arranged them on a bulletin board according to delivery time. I searched for gaps, times we could take a breath or two, and found none. I returned to the computer and made a time schedule for myself. I'd just finished it when I heard the entry door open and slam shut. I stepped outside the office and found myself facing a short round woman with numerous tattoos on her well-muscled arms. She was carrying a chef's white jacket and ball cap with the Chef Express logo. She had the shortest hair I'd ever seen outside the armed forces.

"You must be Ronnie," I said.

"And who the hell are you?"

"Kate St. John. Drew asked me to fill in for your executive chef for a few days."

"The hell he did."

I shrugged. "Call him, check it out." This gig's level of hell had just dropped another tier. All I needed was a second-in-command who was set on mutiny. Damn Drew for not letting her know. "I'll be more than glad to stroll out the door, go home, and go back to bed. Leave you in charge. Your call."

I could read the pros and cons scroll through her mind. I hoped she didn't play much poker.

I turned around, picked up my jacket and ball cap from the office chair, and stepped back into the doorway. "Well?"

She nodded. "I don't have much choice, do I?"

"Look, Ronnie, I know what I'm doing in the kitchen; I work hard and I really like working with a team I can trust. We can do this together or I go home now."

"He should have let me know," she said, shifting her jacket to the other arm.

"I agree. It's inexcusable and I'll tell him so when I see him."

She put on the ball cap and shrugged into the jacket. "We'd better get moving."

I wasn't sure she was really onboard, but the only thing I could do was keep my eyes open. "Come on in and tell me if I've got the orders straight."

We spent about ten minutes going over the schedule, another fifteen checking the trucks. Some people were already at their stations, warming up grills, fryers and ovens; the rest were due soon. The sky was still dark, but the track was beginning to come to life. I heard gruff voices, the clank of metal, the whoosh of what I assumed were hydraulics. Everyone was gearing up for a busy day.

I walked back to the cold kitchen to actually begin the day while Ronnie headed over to the cold trucks to round up the fruit trays for breakfast. She pounded in a few minutes later, scowling. "Damn bastard had the breakfast fruit trays put in the walk-in. Nobody tells me a goddamn thing." She marched to the cooler and slammed the door open.

She stopped and backed out, looking green around the gills. "There's a dead body on the floor."

Hell. "Mouse or rat?"

"Human."

I felt my stomach drop. "Dead?"

"As a damn filet of salmon."

"Anybody you know?"

"The guy's naked except for a pillowcase over his head."

The head chef's mantra started playing in my head: *I'll think about it after the dinner rush.* It fought against the image of a naked man sprawled on the cold concrete slab, life force ebbed. I didn't have to see him to feel the sorrow.

I glanced at my watch. We wouldn't have enough time to remake the trays. And nowhere to get replacements. "Can you be very careful not to disturb anything, but get our trays out? Put them on a rack-and-roll by the door?"

"You mean like before the cops get here?"

I nodded, knowing both the cops and the Board of Health would have conniptions if they found out. I'd cross those bridges when they came, after the rush.

"If you get the rack, I'll hand them out to you."

"Good idea." We'd do the least amount of damage to the scene and still save an important part of the breakfast order. I grabbed one of the racks and propped it against the door. The first thing I saw when I stepped to the door was the dead man's body on the floor. He was in a fetal position, the pillowcase covering his head in a grey and black geometric design. I glanced at Ronnie and noticed she was being careful about where she stepped. She didn't look at the body either. In a few minutes we had the rack filled. I pushed it to the middle of the room, walked into the office and dialed 911.

Ten minutes later, two uniformed cops walked in. They checked the cooler and got busy on their radios. The tall one asked me when we'd found him. I skirted the issue by saying "Check the 911 log. I wasn't exactly looking at my watch. Will we be able to use the rest of this space?"

"Don't know, you'll have to wait for the detectives," he said, jotting something in a small battered notebook. He took my name, address and phone, then beckoned to Ronnie. She gave him her information. "We were going to assemble the orders here," I said when she'd finished.

"We can find another space. OK if we set up elsewhere?"

"You'll need to wait for the detectives." He didn't look up.

"Can we at least call some of our people to pick up these trays and get going on the rest of it?"

"We need to leave the scene as is until the detectives get here."

"But we rolled the rack in here right before we found him. It's not evidence and we really need it for breakfast." As much as I hated lying, I hated more the thought that this whole day was going to be wave after wave of disaster for Chef Express. And me.

He glanced at the rack, got back on the radio as he walked away from me. I could hear the squawk of the radio but nothing of what was being said. He turned around, nodded. "I'll go with you."

I thanked him and turned to Ronnie. "We're going to have to use your area. Or maybe we can get another tent set up."

"There aren't any other tents," she said. "This time of year, we're stretched thinner than a chicken breast for a roll-up. So are our vendors." She looked at me. "You need a cap."

"I've got one on, Ronnie."

"Not regulation. Bottom right-hand drawer of the desk. And don't forget your radio."

"OK?" I asked the cop. He nodded and I returned to the office. I found the cap with the Chef Express logo and Executive Chef embroidered on the bill. Cool. I slipped the walkie-talkie on my waistband and then thought about the timetable and orders I'd pinned to the bulletin board. I took the whole thing off the wall and joined Ronnie. The cop's eyebrows lifted, but he didn't say I couldn't take it.

I had Ronnie roll the rack to the cold truck since we still had an hour before delivery and told her not to tell anyone what had happened. I put the bulletin board on one of her tables and wondered how the day could get any worse. I started attaching the orders to the racks with duct tape. Kiwi. Damn.

"We usually use the carts," Ronnie said from behind me.

"Any reason we can't use the racks?"

Her eyebrows inched up. "No."

"We'll use whatever you're used to the rest of the day. I just wanted to get started. Do we have the kiwi trays for the Herman order?"

She groaned. "We were going to do them first thing because they don't hold."

"Let's get somebody on it."

"We can't. The kiwi are in the cooler in the cold kitchen."

Of course the day could get worse. We were slowly sinking through the levels beneath hell. "Let's go see if we can liberate them. Were they close to the body?"

"Right by it."

I wondered where the up button was.

We trotted back to the cold kitchen which was now swarming with law enforcement personnel. As I stepped into the room, I saw a familiar figure. A homicide captain who was a regular at L'Aigle Noir, John Zimmerman.

"Sorry, ma'am, you can't come in here," said a young cop with a brush mustache.

"Would you please ask Captain Zimmerman if I may speak with him for a moment?"

The cop looked surprised, ducked his head as he turned to look into the room. "You can't come in," he said as he backed toward the captain.

I nodded and leaned against the doorjamb. The cop tapped Zimmerman on the back, pointed to where I was standing. I waved. Zimmerman did a double take, straightened his jacket and walked over briskly.

"What are you doing here?" he asked. He looked at my cap.

"Doing a favor for a friend," I replied and told him the story. I introduced Ronnie and told him our dilemma. "If your techs could check the cases out for prints and whatever else, could you pass them out to us?"

"I don't know, Kate. Do you really want to use fruit that's been in the proximity of a corpse?"

"No, I don't. But I don't think we have any choice. There's no place to get replacements at this hour. Besides, the kiwi's individually wrapped. I'm up the creek and this is the only paddle I can find."

"Let me see what I can do." He walked to the door of the cooler, then returned. "They're about to bring the body out. Once that's accomplished, they'll process the kiwi. Two cases, correct?"

I saw a gurney emerge from the cooler with a body bag on it.

"Since he had no identification on him, would you both take a look and see if you recognize him?"

I nodded and saw Ronnie do the same. The coroner's men stopped and unzipped the bag. Zimmerman lifted a corner of the pillowcase enough that when we leaned over, we saw his face.

"Drew." I said. I felt something in my stomach knot, tighter and tighter. "I thought he was a homeless man who'd wandered in. But Drew."

"Oh, shit," Ronnie said.

"Drew?" Zimmerman asked.

"The friend who asked me to fill in this weekend," I said. "Drew Frobisher, VP for Chef Express."

Zimmerman took out a small leather-bound notebook and a Mont Blanc pen and began asking questions.

I went over the call, the visit when Drew had given me the pass and the keys. "It was late, considering when I needed to get up for this. Oh, speaking of the keys. I had a really hard time unlocking the cool kitchen door, maybe because it was already open. I was still half asleep."

He made more notes. "Do you know his home address?"

I looked at Ronnie. She shook her head. "Somewhere in Carmel."

"Married?"

"I've never met his wife, but he talked about her occasionally when we worked together. A Swedish name. Ingrid, Inga, something like that. She must be hot, he was anxious to get home to her." I stopped, remembered. "That's not what he said. He said 'get to bed.' He didn't mention home."

"So you have no idea where he was going after you saw him?"

"None. I haven't heard from him since, though he said he'd be in around 9:00 this morning."

"Hmm," Zimmerman said. He turned to Ronnie. "Do you know Mrs. Frobisher's name? Are you familiar with her?"

"She sure hasn't been around here," she said, pulling the bill of her cap down and looking at the ground.

Zimmerman shot me a glance. I raised my shoulders and eyebrows. Ronnie knew more than she was saying, but what was a mystery.

He nodded to me. "Thank you. I'll have the men bring the fruit over when they're finished. Where?"

I pointed to the trucks. "The one labeled 'Cold 2.' We can go on with, uh, everything? And can I let corporate know?"

"Proceed with your work, but I'll contact the corporate offices."

Fine with me. Before we reached the cold truck, I pulled Ronnie aside. "What's the story on Drew's wife?"

She crossed her arms, looked at the truck. "You knew him."

"As a co-worker six or seven years ago. Tell me the story, Ronnie. Now."

She shifted her weight, put her hands in her pockets. "She's a real bitch. Showed up at a wedding reception Drew was catering, started yelling and throwing things." She looked at me, anger in her eyes.

I could understand. Bringing personal business into catering, especially when it caused a disruption in service, was a capital crime. "What happened?"

"Guests could hear. Not to mention what she did to the mousse. So he hustled her outside."

"Physically?"

She nodded. "Haven't seen her since, and I don't think she'd dare show up again at one of his gigs. He was really pissed off."

I could also understand her reluctance to air dirty laundry in front of the cops, but this was a homicide investigation. I'd tell Zimmerman when I saw him.

He proved true to his word and the cases arrived fifteen minutes later. I rolled up my sleeves and picked up one of the kiwi cases.

"What are you doing?" Ronnie asked with a tone that sounded vinegary.

"Helping?"

She stepped closer and lowered her voice. "You're the executive chef."

"Yeah, and right now I'm helping execute an order. Go ahead and do what you need to do. I'll be along shortly."

I started with the open case, unwrapping the kiwi, filling a bowl that I would pass down the line. I'd only done a couple when I felt something sharp. I pulled out my hand and saw blood pooling on my thumb. I rinsed it off, put antiseptic on, wrapped a bandage around it, and pulled on a fresh glove. I walked back to the box and peered in, hoping I wouldn't see anything moving. I spotted a flash of gold and carefully pulled out an earring that looked like a gold-and-lapis scimitar. What the hell was an earring doing in a case of fruit? I set it on a shelf above the box and checked the rest of the kiwi. Nothing.

It was an expensive piece of antique jewelry, heavy in my hand when I'd held it. Food service workers didn't wear fancy jewelry at work, especially large earrings that could get caught in machinery or drop in food. And I didn't think it had belonged to the worker who'd packed the case of kiwi. I called a young woman over and asked her to bring Captain Zimmerman here. "He's in the cold kitchen. Tell him it's important."

She took off like the hare at the start line and came back with Zimmerman in tow. I pointed to the earring on the shelf and told him what happened. "I thought it could be evidence."

"It may very well be, but the chain's been broken," he said with a frown. He glanced at me. "The chain of evidence."

"The links are all there," I said. "You should have photos of the cases in the walk-in by the body, and each case has the invoice number on it. Your men carried the cases over, put them where they are now, and I found it. My fingerprints and blood should prove that."

His frown lightened slightly and he nodded. He had a tech photograph the scene then bagged the earring. "Again, Kate, thank you. We'll need to take both cases of kiwi."

"Can we use what have been cut already?"

He pursed his lips for a brief second. "If you must."

"Just for garnish, we'll keep them away from anything edible." I stepped outside with him. "How was Drew killed? Can you tell me?"

"A single bullet from a small-caliber gun to the head."

At least it was quick for Drew. I thought of the pillowcase. "You think he was asleep? Never knew what happened?"

"Possible."

"The body was dumped here?"

"Probable."

That's all I was going to get from him. I told him what Ronnie had said and went back to work.

We got all the breakfast orders out, the Herman order with kiwi garnish going out at 6:01. I thanked everybody for a great effort and walked back to our temporary headquarters at the sous chef station.

"Everything under control?" I asked Ronnie.

"Oh yeah, sure. Everything."

Fraying around the edges.

I asked her to bring me up to speed, and we settled into the routine of detail that makes or breaks catering. An hour later, I looked up to see a tall woman striding toward us. She was a striking woman, long blond hair rippling in the slight breeze, her figure in a summer dress like a pinup from the 1940s.

"May I help you?" I asked, wondering if she was an irate customer whose order had gone wrong or a crazy one who wanted to make last-minute changes.

"I'm looking for Drew," she said, barely glancing at me. "We were supposed to meet here to trade cars. I've got to pick up a load of antiques, and I can't very well do it in his BMW Z3."

"Drew Frobisher?"

"Yes," she said, looking at my cap. "Your boss."

"Uh, I haven't seen him walking around this morning." We were on the down elevator again. "Let me see if we can find him for you." I turned to Ronnie, who looked suddenly comatose. "Would you track down our head of security, what's his name, ah, Zimmerman and bring him over ASAP?"

Her eyes grew large. She nodded and took off for the cold kitchen at a trot.

"You must be his wife," I said, mostly to fill the uncomfortable silence.

She nodded, tapped her foot. A little gust of wind blew her hair away from her face.

I glimpsed a flash of gold and lapis, not much, but enough to make me think it was a match for the one that had attacked me in the kiwi case. I could see Ronnie and Zimmerman coming from the cold kitchen. I pushed the send button on my walkie-talkie and kept my thumb on it as I set it behind a box where she couldn't see it. An earring, a pillowcase and a naked body. Cool Mrs. F. as a jealous wife?

I looked at her. "Why did you kill Drew? And then do something dumb like dump his body in the cold kitchen?"

She gave me a long stare. "I have no idea what you're talking about."

Not the reaction I'd expect from a woman who'd just found out her husband was dead. "You should have gotten rid of the other earring."

Her hands flew to her ears. "Damn. So I've lost an earring. So what?"

"It was found next to his body."

She moved very quickly and pulled a gun from her purse. "You're going to walk me out of here."

I didn't know diddly about guns, but the one pointed at me wasn't large. "And now you're going to shoot me? In front of all these people?" My thumb was sweaty, and I was afraid I'd lose the connection.

"I would hate to do something so crass, but if I have to, I won't hesitate. Now move."

In my peripheral vision, I saw Zimmerman approaching. I hoped he could hear everything.

"Before you finish me off, just tell me why you shot Drew. Wouldn't divorce do?"

Her eyebrows shot down and she leveled the gun. "No, you nosey bitch, divorce wouldn't do. He gave me HIV, and last night he was with his favorite lay. The delicious Tommy Harmon."

"The grill chef? Drew was gay?"

"Bi, the bastard. Now move."

I did. I dove under the prep table because I'd seen Zimmerman reach out for the gun. There was a scuffle, a shot, a muffled curse. Silence.

"You can come out, Kate."

I peeked above the table and saw her cuffed on the ground. "Did you hear it all?"

He nodded. "Ronnie, would you be so kind as to get a couple of patrolmen?" He nodded toward the cold kitchen. "Inga Frobisher, you have the right to remain silent."

When L'Aigle Noir reopened, Captain Zimmerman came in for a late dinner and sent a note to the kitchen requesting my company when I had time.

He was just finishing his Bacheofe when I sat opposite him at a small corner table. He looked up with a smile on his face. "Delicious as always, Kate. A delight."

I signaled Juan to bring coffee. "I'm glad you enjoyed it."

"The prosecutor thinks the chain of evidence will hold. Thank you for coming in for fingerprints and the DNA swab. But I also taped the conversation you broadcasted. These digital, voice-activated recorders are a delight to use. So much smaller, I carry it with me."

"She's going to trial?"

He nodded. "You were very brave to face her."

"I wasn't brave. I caught you out of the corner of my eye and thought I'd be safer if I kept her talking until you could nab her." I waited while Juan served the coffee. "I read in the paper that they found Tommy Harmon's body."

"She shouldn't have dumped him in the White River, but it was handy. Harmon had a place on the river with a deck. There was a blood trail from the bed to the deck. She looks frail, but remember, she has an antique business."

"She caught them asleep." Drew never knew. That was consolation. "Did she think she'd get away with it? Two bodies?"

He shrugged. "I think she thought finding his body at work would throw us off the trail of a domestic altercation. Plus, the temperature would confuse the time of death. I don't think she really thought it through. She should have remembered that old adage: 'Revenge is a dish best served cold.'" He took a sip of coffee and smiled. "Let's just hope you don't find any more killers in your kitchen. I'd hate to lose my favorite chef."

"That wasn't my kitchen." I stood. "That was the level of hell called 'catering,' and from now on, Dante is welcome to it."

The Speedway Aviation Meet of 1910

by Lucy Coyle Schilling

In 1910, six years after their historic flight at Kitty Hawk and at the height of their international fame, Orville and Wilbur Wright came to Speedway, Indiana, for a week-long aviation meet. Although they had drawn millions of people to their demonstrations of the Wright biplane, they had consistently refused to enter any competitive meets with rivals who were challenging their patents to the plane.

Carl Fisher persuaded them to race at an airplane course he had created within the Speedway Oval. To relieve the Wright's concern about patent infringement, Fisher paid a $95,000 premium insuring their patent rights throughout the meet. The race would be open to all pilots, and every plane could be stored in the huge aerodrome Fisher had constructed on the southeast corner of the track.

The Wrights began shipping biplanes by train, and six graduates of their Ohio school made up the Wright Brother's Biplane Team. Five amateur pilots from Indianapolis, flying their own planes, would compete against them.

On Monday, June 13, Orville Wright opened the meet with a demonstration flight around the course. The spectators cheered as the plane rose in the air. At the end of the day, he climbed into his plane again to fly Carl Fisher around the Speedway track. They stayed aloft about ten minutes, dipping and turning toward the grandstand. Later in the week, heavy rain and high winds brought out the May Fly Later flags and the meet was delayed. Despite the weather, aviation records were set or surpassed before Orville Wright closed the Speedway Aviation Meet of 1910.

He and Wilbur continued their meteoric success, flying the Wright biplane before President Taft and assorted European royalty. Wilbur drew a million spectators when he flew around New York Harbor and the Statue of Liberty.

While the Wrights were in Speedway, Carl Fisher agreed to his request and drove Wilbur Wright around the brick track in a race car. The first Indy 500 was a year away.

The Early Bird

by Lucy Coyle Schilling

After graduating from college, Lucy Coyle Schilling was a magazine editorial assistant and an advertising copy writer in New York, an entertainment director for the U.S. Army in Hawaii, and a high school teacher in Georgia before coming to Indiana. She won a graduate fellowship in journalism at Ball State University and blazed geriatric trails by earning her master's degree thirty years after her bachelor's. She is currently at work on a book-length version of her graduate thesis.

Hazel and I were on the grassy Speedway infield, craning our necks with everyone else when it happened. There was a collective gasp from the small group of spectators still at the field. Hitchcock's aeroplane just disappeared. He'd reversed its course and was heading back to Speedway, when suddenly the little speck in the sky we'd all been watching was gone.

Hazel turned to me. "What happened to his plane, Eston? Did it crash?"

I could feel a muscle jumping in my cheek. Did she notice? Would my voice give me away?

"I don't know," I managed to say calmly.

Ah, but I did. I wanted to leap into the air. I'd done it! I'd brought that strutting little gamecock down.

A week ago, I didn't know who Billy Hitchcock was. Neither did Hazel. Certainly he wasn't among the members of the Aero Club or one of the gentlemen pilots who, like me, were embracing the new, daring concept of flight. But I had learned his name. I'd heard it every day that week. "Billy Hitchcock breaks the record for altitude...Billy Hitchcock breaks the record for time in the air..." His name was on everyone's lips now, especially Hazel's. The situation at the Speedway had grown more and more intolerable.

In the beginning, everyone was wildly enthusiastic when the plan was announced. Maybe it was the spectacle of Halley's Comet streaking across the sky just before the start of the May auto races, or maybe it was the balloon races a year earlier. But in 1910, everyone in Indianapolis was looking to the skies. The talk at the Speedway was about Carl Fisher's announcement of the Speedway Aviation Meet from June 13 to 19, open to all aviators—amateurs and professionals.

There weren't many of us amateurs. Owning your own aeroplane was beyond the pockets of most guys. Even owning your own race car was pretty much reserved for millionaires or their sons. The five-mile race in May for amateurs driving their own cars was dubbed the "Millionaire's Race" by the *Indianapolis Star*. I'd won that and a bunch of others with my red Fiat, even beating the famous Barney Oldfield in a couple of races. Hazel was there to greet me at the finish line then, drawing almost as much admiration as the trophy.

Hazel Stanley was my kind of girl, cool and classy, a real looker. The Stanleys had as much money as my family and they lived near us on Riverside Drive. Hazel wanted her own touring car and she'd probably get it from her doting daddy. But right now, she was as fascinated by flying as I was.

I remember the first time I took her up in my Farman biplane. Hazel climbed into one seat, her hat tied down with a scarf. From the other seat, I gripped the control lever and heard her gasp as the biplane began to ascend. We flew over the three streets in Speedway.

"That's Tenth Street with the covered bridge over Big Eagle Creek," I pointed out, "and Crawfordsville Pike is that street north of the Baltimore and Ohio Railroad."

"There's only one cross street in town," she said.

I nodded. "Winton Avenue, the only road going north and south."

From the air, it looked like a model train layout beneath us. An Interurban train pulled into the Ben Hur station just to complete the illusion.

I had no trouble slowly lowering the plane and gliding to a stop. Hazel jumped down from her seat before I could reach her. Her face was glowing.

"Eston, what a thrill! I've...I've never experienced anything like that. You were magnificent."

I'm over six feet and she only comes to my shoulder. I knew all I had to do was bend my head. But the mechanics were still there, lounging around in front of the aerodrome, and there was a week's worth of flying ahead. Plenty of time. At least that's what I thought.

On June 13, the Speedway aerodrome at the southeast corner of the brick track was filled with the eleven entries for the meet. Six of the Wright biplanes had been shipped by rail from their Ohio flight school to be piloted by a rag-tag bunch of their students. They were all in their twenties and inexperienced. One, a fellow named Hitchcock, had spent the last two years hanging around the Wright's bicycle shop in Ohio. But of the six, he seemed the most assured, even cocky.

The five other entries, like me, were from Indianapolis. All of us were race car drivers, mad about this new machine that had been around just a little over six years. We were all anxious to see the famous Orville and Wilbur Wright. They had become almost obsessive about the patent rights to their invention and refused to appear in air competitions with their rivals. But they were eager to promote the idea of flight and drew millions of spectators to their barnstorming shows. The Speedway Aviation Meet was the first exhibition of the Wright Biplane Team.

I had a good look at the brothers as they arrived. Nattily dressed in dark suits, ties and fresh celluloid collars, they looked more like businessmen than daring aviators. Orville Wright sported a black handlebar moustache and was a little stockier than his brother. He was wearing his ever-present dark bowler hat when he climbed into his waiting aeroplane to open the show. He made two laps over the course to the cheers of nearly 2,000 people.

Wilbur was a little taller, with grey eyes and a lean, strongly sculpted face. He seemed more solemn, but a little smile played around his mouth as he studied the crowd. Like most aviators, he wore a soft tweed cap. Both brothers reminded me of teachers I'd known. Their class of young aviators was obviously mindful of their instructions, except, I noticed, Hitchcock didn't seem quite as deferential as the others.

I almost felt sorry for them. They had to be intimidated by the powerful machines they were paid to fly. And not paid much, I had learned—$20 a week and $50 for every day a man went up. There was no drinking, gambling or flying on Sundays. How pathetic!

Then the meet director signaled. I was next.

Hazel, as beautiful as ever in some kind of lacy white dress and long white gloves, blew me a kiss from her seat in the Aero Club as I strode out to my aeroplane. The plane was ready for me, and I worked the controls as it gained momentum and slowly ascended. Flying east and then south over the aerodrome, I began my descent and slid along the ground before coming to a smooth stop. I heard the announcement: "Eston Carter has a total flight time of six minutes and twenty seconds." It was a record time in the air that day, and I ordered champagne when I got back to the clubhouse. Hazel raised her glass in a silent toast when it was poured.

Later in the afternoon, a pal of mine, George Friedrich, took off in his Fisher-Indianapolis biplane. His plane suddenly went out of control. We could see him struggling to keep it aloft, when it crashed and broke apart on the grassy field just in front of the grandstand. An ominous silence hung over the field as the ambulance crew rushed over to the wreckage. Then there was a ragged cheer when George was placed on a stretcher and managed a feeble wave to the crowd.

"That could have been nasty," I said. "That hard a landing the gas tanks could rupture. And boom!"

Hazel paled, but my attention was drawn back to the course. It was announced the last event of the day would be a Wright pilot attempting to increase the altitude level. The biplane had a recording device onboard to measure altitude, while the Wright brothers and a Mr. Lambert of the St. Louis Aero Club took measurements from the ground. That was when I heard his name, William "Billy" Hitchcock. He grinned at the Wright team as he tossed his cigarette aside and turned his cap backward. *He looks more like a newspaper boy than an aviator*, I remember thinking.

He circled the aeroplane course, then flew far to the south, continuing to go higher and higher. When he passed over the grandstand again, Mr. Lambert announced an altitude of 4,187 feet.

"Paulhans beaten!" one of my friends shouted.

Louis Paulhans had set the previous record at 4,165 feet in January at the Los Angeles aviation meet. But the biplane, just a speck in the sky now, flew back around the course for one more measurement. The excited crowd was chanting "man-bird" as the megaphones echoed the final reading of 4,384.5 feet! Hazel was standing, her hands folded almost in prayer over her lips. She watched like everyone else when Hitchcock dipped the front of his plane toward the earth to begin his descent, then glided slowly and gracefully to a stop on the grassy infield.

Hazel could talk of nothing else on the drive home but the wonders of the Wright biplane and one particular pilot's skill. I found it annoying to keep listening to her prattle.

"Really, Hazel, these farm boys don't understand the extraordinary machines they're flying. You know this whole aviation meet is just an exhibition of the Wright brothers' patent and how successful and popular it is," I said.

"And training some very good pilots how to do just that," she said.

"Like Billy Hitchcock?"

"Like Billy Hitchcock." She turned to face me. "Why won't you admit how great his flight was today?"

I ignored her. The "Man-bird" would have his wings clipped soon enough. His luck wouldn't last.

The sun had set before we left the Speedway, and the night sky was full of drifting clouds. I thought I heard thunder behind us in the west. That didn't bode well for tomorrow's schedule.

I was right. Morning thunderstorms threatened cancellation of Tuesday's events, but a crowd of five thousand people showed up at the Speedway despite the weather. The Wright brothers decided to continue with the meet. Well, they'd been paid to perform, but I wasn't going to fly my aeroplane with such high winds and rainstorms. None of the other amateur pilots would either, and we left the field to the Wright team.

Orville Wright, in his distinctive black-domed hat, was everywhere, fussing over his chickens. Hazel watched him conferring with his pilots.

"He's certainly worried about them, isn't he?" she said.

"He's worried about his planes. What if the wind tosses them all?"

"Oh, don't say that, Eston. His team won't risk their lives or his planes."

She hates it when I laugh at her, but I couldn't resist snickering.

"No pilot has a lick of sense. He wouldn't be a pilot if he did. Or a race car driver as well. It's a fraternity of fools!"

To underline my words, the Wright biplanes, one by one, began a succession of low, careful turns around the course. I was pleased; even the "Man-bird" aimed no higher than 100 feet off the ground, but in the last program of the day, he battled the wind to reach 2,083 feet before safely landing. Hazel never took her eyes off the plane.

After the event, the spectators got a chance to see a Wright biplane more closely. One was rolled out in front of the main grandstand, and the crowd ran from their seats to inspect it.

"Why it looks like a giant kite!" someone said. "It seems awfully fragile up close."

As if she'd never seen an aeroplane before, Hazel lifted her skirts and ran to join them milling around the plane. Suddenly someone spotted Billy Hitchcock near the aerodrome and shouted for him to come closer. The crowd cheered as he slowly approached, and I got a good look at the idol of the day. Still wearing his tie and jacket and that ridiculous cap turned backward, he was quite tall and rather thin, with freckles sprinkled across prominent cheekbones.

Hazel had moved past me to stand almost at his shoulder, and I saw him smile at this pretty girl when he turned toward her. I could see he was thinking she was another conquest.

"What is it like to fly so high?" she asked him, almost simpering.

"The only difference is the temperature. It gets colder and colder as you ascend. I'm sure we'll reach an altitude someday where the aviator will have to wear special clothes to protect him from the cold."

I put my hand on her elbow to steer her away from the crowd of gawkers, and I felt her arm stiffen.

A reporter from the *Indianapolis News*, notebook in hand, pushed past her.

"Say, Billy, how long have you been flying?"

We were walking back to my car but I heard his answer.

"I enrolled at Mr. Wright's school two months ago…"

Damn! Maybe he was half-bird, half-man. All of us had been flying at least six months or more. I could tell from Hazel's flickering smile she had heard him, too.

Word had gotten out about the exploits of the Wright pilots, and the crowds were getting bigger. Wednesday morning there were 19,000 spectators clogging the wooden suspension footbridge into the Speedway infield. The breeze was very strong, fluttering all the little American flags that lined the course. I heard Hitchcock sneer that many of the amateur pilots wouldn't even attempt to fly in such a severe wind. Of course, he was the first to take off and he flew in a figure-eight formation a few times while he circled the course. His showboating was irritating. "Look at me! Look at me!" he seemed to taunt.

I flew next, up about a hundred feet, finishing four laps before I landed safely right in front of the grandstand. I had hoped to dip a wing for Hazel before my runners hit the grass, but the wind was buffeting the plane too much to try it.

Heavy rain and powerful winds soaked my assistants as they pulled my plane back to the aerodrome with all the others. Travis Fletcher was another amateur pilot, ready to thumb his nose at the Wright team. He got to a decent altitude when a gust of wind tossed his aeroplane to the ground and broke his rudder. He scrambled out safely but stood, cursing the damage, while rain pelted his face.

On Thursday, black clouds massed in the west and high winds again decreased the crowds. There were only three days left in the meet. So far it had been a sweep for the Wright biplanes. All of their pilots had made successful ascents by themselves or with a partner in the other seat. Hitchcock's exploits were on everyone's lips, especially both Orville's and Wilbur's. He was clearly their star performer. Seated at an Aero Club table with Carl Fisher, Orville bragged constantly about what a natural pilot Billy Hitchcock was, how even he and Wilbur gasped at his daring. Obviously he was promoting the Wright "School for Skylarks" which had produced such a wonder. Just the name made me laugh.

"I'm going up again today," I said to Hazel. She'd been a brick about coming to the Speedway with me every day, even the rainy, windy ones.

"I don't think any of the others are going to attempt it." She waved to some of the other amateur pilots sitting around the club house. "Travis is still sulking about his rudder."

"I don't know why he entered his precious plane," I said. "These pilots for hire are showing us up badly."

It annoyed me that she didn't seem to share my resentment. I remembered her glowing face when she met Hitchcock yesterday.

"Wouldn't you love to get paid for flying a plane, Eston?"

"I fly without charging for the privilege. The Wright brothers had the genius to create the flying machine, but they're shrewd businessmen as well. I've heard Carl Fisher paid $95,000 insuring their patent, to get them to come here. Hazel ..."

She had stopped listening. The announcer was reporting that William Hitchcock would open the program as planned with a twenty-minute flight.

"He's flying the very same plane my brother flew to circle the Statue of Liberty in New York Harbor," I heard Wright tell the group at his table.

They were all suitably impressed—a solemn nod, pursed lips, a whispered "oh, my!" The pompous fools!

I could feel rage tighten my throat, quicken my pulse. I was sick to death of William Hitchcock and his exploits. I pushed my chair back.

"Hazel, I'm going to the aerodrome. I want to get my plane ready for some trial flights—maybe try to break that altitude record if the wind doesn't worsen."

Two other Wright pilots made successful ascents after Hitchcock's performance, and I managed to get my Farman in the air for a flight at least as long as theirs, a little over twenty minutes. But the wind was an intimidating factor. It seemed to be relentless. The Speedway director suggested we all take a short break to see if the wind might die down a little. The Wright brothers came in the aerodrome to confer with their team, and Wilbur drew Hitchcock aside for what seemed to be a confidential talk. One of my aviator friends had snagged a meteorologist from somewhere. This chap unrolled a map full of cryptic arrows and wavy lines. "I would say Friday's weather won't improve. The winds might even be a bit stronger."

In other words, a literal washout for our team. Some of them shook their heads slightly. All of them were tight-lipped. If the majority weren't already planning to crate up their planes, the next event would have settled the matter.

The Wright team pushed out a biplane, and Hitchcock turned his cap around and followed it. He climbed on to the seat, flew effortlessly to the south and proceeded to put on the most dazzling exhibition of the week. At about a thousand feet in the air, he stood the plane nose down and began a series of death-defying spirals, breaking the record for a complete revolution in 6.4 seconds. Everyone in the stands and all of us in the aerodrome stood breathless. When he came down as easily as he had risen, every pilot joined the awed spectators in a sustained cheer. Both Orville and Wilbur met him on the grass and shook his hand. He turned to acknowledge the crowd with a grin and a small wave. Everyone in the Aero Club was on their feet. I could see Hazel's pale pink dress, and I decided to stay in the aerodrome. I wasn't ready to hear her rhapsodize with the others about Man-bird's feat.

I signaled my mechanics to start my plane. Hitchcock's skills didn't intimidate me. I felt charged. I was going to try for the longest flight time. I knew the record was forty-four minutes, and I knew I could break it.

This time the wind was almost an ally. I could feel it moving beneath my wings, pushing the biplane higher. I turned east, then banked north following the course of the infield. The plane was so responsive it felt alive under my hands. What a glorious thing it is to fly! This time, as I flew south, I tipped my wing toward the grandstand, toward the Aero Club, toward Hazel.

I made another lap around the course, then set the levers to bring me down. I wasn't surprised to hear the announcement: "Pilot: Eston Carter; flight time: a record fifty-two minutes, five seconds." I bounded out of the seat and acknowledged the "thumbs-up" salute from my assistants.

Hazel and my friends applauded as I came into the club.

"You held up the side for us, old man," one of my pilot pals murmured in my ear as I headed for Hazel's table.

This time, her eyes were on me. The dazzling smile was for me.

"I was so proud of you, Eston. That wasn't luck, dearest. That was skill and daring against that awful wind."

By that time the sun was going down rapidly. It was so dark most of the spectators were streaming toward the exit; some stopping at the concession stand for a five-cent soft drink. Suddenly Hitchcock, wearing a heavy green sweater, climbed into one of the Wright biplanes. The sweater meant he was going for the altitude record. He aimed his plane like a bullet for the sky, climbing constantly until we could hardly see him.

When he finally skimmed gracefully down to the grass, those of us still at the meet heard the announcement. His altitude of 3,876 feet was short of his record, but he had stayed in the air for 54 minutes and 20 seconds! Almost casually, he had broken my record.

Hazel and I had a silent ride home. She was acutely aware of my feelings and smart enough not to say anything. I was deep in thought, working out the mechanics of how to bring down that high-flying bird.

It wasn't hard to break into the aerodrome that night. As an aviator entrant and the owner of a plane inside, I just nodded to the security guard at the door and let myself in. It was shadowy inside the cavernous building. I went directly to my biplane and looked through my assistants' shelves for a set of screwdrivers. Tools in hand, I walked to the six Wright biplanes lined up facing the doors. Methodically I loosened a single bolt on the chassis of each one, a different bolt each time. I couldn't know who Wright would pick to fly his biplanes tomorrow, which of these planes would race around a course hundreds of feet above the brick paving that the race cars followed. But luck is part of winning and tonight I would start the roulette wheel spinning. I was pretty sure that weatherman had been right when he read all those squiggly lines on his map. Tomorrow would be stormy again. Some of Friday's pilots would worry about their luck against high winds and rain. Orville or Wilbur might be concerned about their precious biplanes, about what a crash could do to the future of aviation. But I knew one man who didn't seem to care about danger. Hitchcock would fly tomorrow in the teeth of a hurricane. And I would bring the bastard down.

The winds on Friday were so strong all flights were postponed until 4:47 p.m. Many of the people in the record number of spectators left before the all the events were done.

"They're saying the winds are over thirty-five miles an hour," I told Hazel. "That could tip an aeroplane over while it's still on the ground. Today I think I'm just going to enjoy the show. If there is one."

"I can't imagine anyone trying to control a plane with winds that strong," she said.

She had hardly finished saying that when Hitchcock, cap backward, ascended for a fifteen-minute flight. The crowd seemed disappointed. They were hoping for more aerial acrobatics. Only the aviators present were impressed. They knew how difficult it was to just get aloft in such a wind. I knew my man. I knew he'd be the first to fly on such a day. It was almost 7:00 p.m. when Hitchcock swung into the seat of his biplane for his second flight. Immediately after takeoff he began climbing.

"What's he doing?" Hazel asked.

"He's trying to set a new altitude record," I said. "He's crazy. In this wind, he's lucky to get aloft."

Hitchcock was soon a little dot in the air, sailing in a broad circle. He could be seen several miles from Speedway, where people had gathered to watch. Speedway's city engineer measured his altitude at 4,938 feet before he began his descent. He had broken his own altitude record.

Was it worth it?

His plane vanished from sight. Both Orville and Wilbur stopped gazing at an empty sky and ran for their cars to look for him.

"He might have been injured when it came down. Do you want to help look for him?" I asked Hazel.

She nodded mutely.

I grabbed her hand, and we ran to the garage where I kept the Fiat. About a dozen reporters and the ambulance crew were cranking their cars and heading in different directions. Suddenly there was a shout.

"He's been spotted, a field east of the track!"

I knew that field. I drove ahead of the pack to a wheat field I'd spotted flying over the farmlands next to the County Poor Farm. It was the only place I could think of where you could land a plane. As we drove along Crawfordsville Pike, I kept watching for smoke or, God help me, a fire. The anger and jealousy that had energized me for the past twenty-four hours was gone. I felt sick with fear and guilt. Had I killed him, that stupid young fool, someone who knew more about the joy of flying and mastering an aeroplane than anyone I'd ever known? Then I saw the path plowed open by a bigger machine than a tractor.

The plane was intact. Billy Hitchcock was leaning against it, smoking a cigarette, squinting like a cowboy against the sun setting in the west.

"Are you all right?" Hazel asked him.

"What happened? Did something come loose on the plane?"

"Something come loose?" He stared at me for a long second. "Why would you think that? Nah, I always tighten all the bolts before I fly. Mr. Wright drummed that into me for sure."

He flipped his cigarette. "When I started to descend I discovered that my motor was missing out, so I shut it off and headed for the Speedway. Closer to the ground, the wind was really tossing the plane, and I knew I couldn't make it to the course. So I picked out a spot in a nearby farm and glided down the rest of the way."

"You were lucky."

"Yeah, I was, wasn't I? No damage to me or the plane. Every pilot needs luck on his side, don't you think?"

"Well, of course..." I started to say.

"And skill. Superior skill. Think you could pull it off, Mr. Carter?" His eyes were locked on my face.

A car sputtered noisily to a stop behind us. Hitchcock shifted his gaze and grinned. "Hi, boss!" Orville Wright crossed the distance between them in two strides and wrapped his arms around his lost chick.

When the winds increased in intensity the next day, the Wrights cancelled the final day of the exhibition and began disassembling their planes. The exhibition team had another air show the following week in Canada. Hitchcock and the Wright Brothers would dazzle another audience waiting to see a miracle happen.

I'd experienced that miracle for myself. I could fly through the air too. I could race my Fiat over the brick track at the Speedway next year. And Hazel—beautiful, desirable Hazel— was still mine.

Sunday was a bright, clear day, wonderful after the week of rain. When I suggested to Hazel I take her up again in the Farman that afternoon, she smiled with delight. At the Speedway, I parked the car and we walked through the grassy fields where the hot air balloons once were launched. No one was in the grandstands. They were empty and echoing. On our right, the aerodrome loomed over the brick paving for the race cars and the graded oval, within the track, of the aeroplane's course. Inside, there were only four planes shrouded in tarpaulins. I knew which one was mine and began to pull off the cover. Hazel and the security man came over to help.

She had just uncovered the two leather seats when she called back to me, "Eston, you've left your cap on the seat."

I walked up to the front of the biplane to inspect her find and froze. It wasn't my cap, but I knew its owner. He always wore it backward when he was flying. Christ, what had Hitchcock been doing in my plane?

Hazel's eyes widened and her smile disappeared. "What? What's wrong, Eston?"

The First Indy 500
And the Winner Was...or Was It?

by *Phil Dunlap*

The first Indianapolis 500-mile race in 1911 was mired in controversy from the moment a driver pulled into Victory Lane. Ray Harroun, driving the bright yellow #11 Marmon Wasp, was credited with the win. But did he actually win? Some aren't so sure.

The timing and scoring table was a cobbled-together affair with 100 (some say as many as 200) people using a new timing system that had yet to prove itself, at the center of which was the Warner Harograph that scored every passing car (together with handwritten numbers), using twelve reporting points around the track. It was an engineering marvel, although not foolproof.

Near the halfway mark, a car lost control, sending it careening into the scoring table (which sat alongside the track without benefit of a protective barricade), and scattering the scorers. During that time, the cars of Ralph Mulford and David Bruce-Brown passed the timing stand, but Harroun's car wasn't recorded as having passed. It was later determined that he may have been in the pits.

When the final lap flag (green back then) was shown to Mulford, Bruce-Brown and Harroun (in that order), Mulford thought he was in the lead. Bruce-Brown's car didn't finish due to mechanical failure. Mulford's team signaled for him to take the precautionary three extra laps in case of controversy. But Harroun, thinking he was the winner, pulled into Victory Lane without taking extra laps. When Mulford came around and found Harroun in the winner's circle, his team filed a complaint.

Through the night and into the next day, officials engaged in debate, figuring and refiguring, issuing "official" results three times (each one slightly different). In the end, Ray Harroun was declared the winner. The race became history, only slightly tarnished by the controversy that remains to this day.

Driven to Kill

by Phil Dunlap

Phil Dunlap is the author of two historical western/police procedural novels, combining mystery and the Old West. His first novel, The Death of the Desert Belle, *2004, was followed by* Call of the Gun, *2005.* Fatal Revenge, *October, 2007, and* Blood on the Rimrock, *February, 2008, continue the U.S. Marshall Piedmont Kelly series. Phil has been published in magazines and newspapers for over twenty years.*

Engines rev throughout the pit area. The ground shakes with the vibrations of powerful, sleek, open-wheel race cars, their drivers impatient to take to the track. The early morning draws a number of spectators to the stands, others gather along the fence separating them from the pits, jockeying for a spot to catch a glimpse of a favorite driver. It's the opening day of practice for the Indy 500, the kick-off to a month of excitement, and the atmosphere is electric.

Drivers sit tapping fingers on tiny steering wheels, anxious for the action to begin, when suddenly, several track officials run past the line of cars, signaling pit crews to shut down their engines. Race teams and fans alike are greeted by the unexpected silence. Several of the chief mechanics sprint down pit row to the front of the line to find out what is going on.

The driver of the first car in line, K.B. Carson, is not in his car as required by track rules. Being first in line, the team is expected to be ready when the track opening is announced. It is prestigious to be first on the track on opening day. One of the track officials tells Carson's chief mechanic, Eddy Williams, to run back to the garage area to find the errant driver or lose their place in line.

As crews grow restless, Williams comes hurrying back from Gasoline Alley, waving his arms and yelling for help. Police and safety crew respond immediately. Following the mechanic back to Carson's garage, they find the driver lying in a pool of blood, clad only in his underwear, with a nasty wound in his right temple. Paramedics are summoned, although most consider the effort futile. When Carson is transported to the infield hospital, the verdict is quick in coming. There is nothing anyone can do for K.B. Carson. He is DOA.

The news that there's been a dreadful accident to the popular driver blows through the pits and the stands like a spring thunderstorm. The media scramble for answers, as do the other teams and owners. For a young, up-and-coming racer to die from such a common accident as falling on a slick floor is unthinkable. Few are prepared for the verdict several hours later from the county coroner: death from blunt force trauma to the head. The police, who know more than what is being released to the public, begin working on a murder theory.

Speedway police cordon off Carson's garage with yellow crime scene tape and begin their investigation by questioning every one of Carson's team. The Marion County Crime Lab scours the garage area, gathering evidence for their forensic investigation.

Because of the suspicious nature of the death and the potential for it to become a high-profile case, Speedway police officials sought more experienced help. The case was assigned to Indianapolis Metropolitan Police homicide detective, John McGruder, a twenty-year veteran with an enviable track record for solving unusual crimes. This case qualified. Why anyone would want to kill a young race car driver was anybody's guess, and McGruder knew he had only three weeks to unravel this one before teams scattered to numerous locations to prepare for the next race. And now another race—a race to catch a murderer—had the green flag.

While the corner of the garage where Carson suited up for racing was fairly small, the entire compound became part of the overall investigation. With people milling around outside garages, anyone could have wandered into Carson's garage and gone unnoticed, making the number of potential suspects limitless. All it took was a pit pass, and a person could roam throughout the garages with few limitations. McGruder gave the responsibility of interviewing other teams or visitors to the garage area to his partner, Detective Maggie Cooper, while he checked with the forensics team.

"What do you have for me?" McGruder asked as he blew into the crime lab.

"We got zip. No murder weapon. Yet. We went through the trash all up and down the garage area. Got nothing. Fingerprints on everything in the garage—from mechanics to pit crew, owners, unidentified individuals and Carson, himself. That narrows it down to about thirty-five, give or take a dozen. This one's going to be tough, John," said Harold Ornitz, the lead lab tech.

"Coroner says this was no accident. Nothing to indicate he hit his head on anything as he went down. Says someone struck him with a blunt object as he turned away from his attacker. Was anything taken?" McGruder said.

"Nope, nothing to indicate a robbery. We found an expensive watch in his locker, his wallet along with five-hundred in cash, and numerous other items. I'll get you a complete inventory later. Oh, and there was a revealing picture of a stunning babe. I made you a copy."

"I'll take it with me. Maybe we'll run into each other," McGruder said.

"A single guy like you, McGruder, I figured you'd want it."

"Have you tested the clothing in the locker for bloodstains?" McGruder stuffed the photocopy in his jacket pocket.

"Yeah. Nothing. He was killed as we found him, in his shorts and a tee shirt. He wasn't moved."

"The coroner release anything yet on stomach contents?"

"His report says mostly junk food, party stuff: potato chips, onion dip, cheese, ham, bread and coffee."

"What did the coroner say about the time of death?"

"From all indications he died around eleven in the morning."

"I'll get started tracking his whereabouts in the early morning. By the way, how many people know we're considering this a murder?"

"Quite a few. Those who found him, paramedics, doctors, and certain onlookers might be speculating about now. And, I expect the press soon will be making guesses. They have a knack for gathering information."

"Well, let's try to keep it as quiet as we can, at least until we find the murder weapon," McGruder said as he left the lab. "If people think it was an accident, they'll be more willing to talk."

McGruder pulled into the Indianapolis Motor Speedway garage area a half hour later. At Carson's garage, the yards of yellow tape had been removed. He found three mechanics bending over the car he assumed Carson would have driven. They were adjusting the seat configuration. Another was hand-lettering a new name above the word *Driver*. A second car was sitting alongside the one being worked on, with the engine cowling removed.

"You guys don't wait long to make a substitution, do you?" McGruder said, displaying his badge.

A man looked up from tightening a bolt and said, "We have exactly two weeks to get a car up to speed, a new driver comfortable in it, qualified, and our fuel and tire testing completed. What do you think?" His shirt said *Eddy Williams*.

McGruder understood the jam they were in, but he wasn't keen on people wandering through his crime scene like it was McDonald's, even though the CSIs *had* released it.

"Tell me about these cars, Mister Williams. I don't know much about them."

"Not much to tell. They're all about the same now. All the chassis are made either by Dallara or Panoz. The engines all come from Honda and are sealed at the factory. We can't even open them up if we got a problem. We just bolt them on, hook up the accessories, and send them off to do battle. Each has a unique serial number," Williams said.

"What if one goes sour?"

"We send it back and get another one."

"Are they all equal in power and speed?"

"Supposed to be, but with anything mechanical, each one has its little quirks," said Williams. "Some are better than others."

"What happens if you question an engine's performance?"

"We call the Honda rep and let him handle it."

"Any of you guys see Carson yesterday morning before he died?"

"For a minute, maybe. Most were here by seven. Lots to do. Had to get these engines swapped out. Why?"

"Who all was in the garage then?" asked McGruder.

"I already told all this to the other cops."

"Tell it again."

"Okay. We all were, except Carson, who's a late riser. He came strolling in around ten-thirty, just as the rest of us were leaving the garage to roll the car in line. And of course, Carson's bimbo, Angelina Sanders, had yet to arrive to give us all 'moral' support."

"Would she normally have been in the garage area that early?"

"Not that early, but hell, man, at other times she was Carson's shadow."

"Where can I find her?"

"Probably at the motel, getting her beauty sleep."

"When you last saw Carson, how was he dressed?"

"Getting out of his jeans, as I recall."

McGruder turned and wandered outside where he'd been told he could find the team's owner, Jim Blake. He found Blake two garages down in an apparent disagreement with driver Scotty Black's car owner, David Thurston.

As McGruder approached, they ceased their conversation and moved apart, obviously sensitive to anyone overhearing them. Blake was a nice-looking man of about forty. Slim, well dressed, and exuding the confidence one would expect of a race team owner. Thurston looked more the hands-on type, not afraid of getting grease under his fingernails.

"Excuse me, Mister Blake. I need to talk to you." said McGruder, showing his badge. Thurston turned away to let them talk and disappeared into his own garage.

"Make it quick, will you?"

"What can you tell me about Carson? Do you know who might want to harm him? Anyone with a grudge?"

"K.B. was one of the best-liked drivers out here. Why do you ask? Folks say he slipped and hit his head while getting ready. An accident that could happen easily—slick floors, oil spills, water." Blake looked at McGruder as if he were too stupid to realize the obvious. "Is your presence an implication it was something else? Why are the police involved?"

"Were you there when they found him?" said McGruder.

"No. By the time I got there, he was on his way to the hospital."

"Who told you he'd slipped and fallen?"

100

"One of the crew. Are we through here? I gotta run." Blake moved briskly to his own garage and disappeared into the hubbub of activity.

McGruder drove to the motel where he'd found out Angelina was staying. The Brickyard Crossing Golf Resort and Inn was located just to the east of the track on Sixteenth Street, and many visitors, owners and teams made staying there a ritual during May.

After getting her room number from the front desk, he took the elevator to the second floor. He knocked on her door, waited, then tried again. He thought he heard some rustling from inside the room, then a click as the lock was released. A pair of sultry blue eyes peered out at him.

"What do you want? I'm trying to sleep."

"Miss Sanders?"

"Yeah."

"I'm Detective John McGruder. I need to speak to you about Mister Carson's death. May I come in?"

Clearly rattled at being confronted by a policeman, Angelina nervously backed away from the door, clutching at her flimsy robe. McGruder recognized her immediately from the photocopy in his pocket.

"I'll get dressed and be right back. Have a seat, Detective." She disappeared into the bedroom and closed the door.

While he waited, he glanced around the suite's living room. Various articles of clothing were strewn about, ashtrays overflowed, and empty beer cans occupied tabletops.

Several minutes later, Angelina returned to the room, freshly coiffed and smelling of something expensive. She wore not one piece of jewelry. Her eyes were red, either from lack of sleep or crying.

"Now, what can I do for you, Detective?"

"Did Carson stay with you the night before he died?"

"Of course. Why wouldn't he?" She suddenly got misty-eyed.

"What time did he leave for the track?"

"Same time as always. Ten, ten-thirty."

"What was your routine that morning?"

"I always get up and make him coffee, then I go back to bed."

"Did the two of you party the evening before?"

"Yeah. I had some of the crew and a couple of drivers and car owners over for drinks and stuff. Why?"

"What time did the party break up?"

"I don't know. The sun was up. That's all I remember."

"I'd like a list of those who were at your party."

"Okay," she said, rattling off names as he wrote them down.

"Looks like you maybe had a party last night, too. Am I right?"

"I, uh, why do you ask?"

"Are you good friends with Jim Blake?"

She nervously wrung her hands. "I, uh, have known Jim for awhile."

"Was he at your party the night before Carson died?"

"I think I remember him dropping by. I forgot to mention him."

"What do you know about the cause of Carson's death?"

"I don't know anything. I was told he slipped and hit his head. Why do you ask?"

"One never knows what will be important during an investigation," the detective said. "Oh, one more thing. Was Carson upset about anything when he left you yesterday morning?"

"He was always tense before a race. Driver's nerves. Happens a lot."

"Do you know of any recent arguments he'd had with anyone?"

"None that I'm aware of." She looked at the floor with a slight frown.

"Had he been drinking the night before?"

"Never. He only drank soft drinks or coffee."

McGruder left. By the time he returned to Carson's garage, the crew was getting ready to push a car out for a practice run. Eddy Williams was adjusting something in the cockpit.

"Mister Williams, I notice you got Carson's car changed over pretty fast. New driver name and all."

"It's not Carson's car. This is our second team car. Cockpit's different."

"Why's that?" said McGruder.

"The driver, Shooter Strong, is about twenty pounds heavier and a couple inches taller. Couldn't use the same set-up. Each seat is custom-made for the driver."

"Was this Strong fella set to drive before Carson died?"

"Ask Blake. I just get 'em ready and keep 'em running. You'll have to excuse me, I have a lot to do."

Just then a young driver came into the garage. His nametag read "Shooter." McGruder cornered him before he could join the crew gathered around his car.

"Excuse me, Mister Strong, a moment of your time, please."

"Sure. Who are you?"

"Detective McGruder. I'm investigating K.B. Carson's death."

"I thought he fell and hit his head," said Strong, with a puzzled expression. "How come the cops are interested?"

"It's a high-profile death, and we have to make sure we're covering all the bases. No weapon has been found yet that proves murder, however."

"Then how do you know it wasn't an accident?"

"When you've been doing this as long as I have, you get a feel for these things."

"Damn. I can't believe anyone would kill K.B. How can I help?"

"What can you tell me about Carson's relationship with the owner, Jim Blake?"

"Not much. I'm new with this team. I was originally set to drive for Thurston, but Blake made him a deal. So here I am."

"I'm a race fan. So I'm familiar with your stats. You've done all right for yourself," said McGruder.

"Not too bad. I can improve, however. This set-up looks better than what I've had before. Better chance at winning, or at least placing near the front. The money's all about where you finish, you know?"

"Did you get along with Carson?"

"I get along with everybody. He and Scotty Black had a pretty good rivalry going, though."

"Could it have been over Angelina Sanders?"

"Don't think so. Scotty's taste ran more to the mature type with lots of money." Strong smiled and shrugged.

McGruder wandered over to David Thurston's garage stalls. His driver, Scotty Black, had just returned from taking several practice laps.

"Mister Thurston, I'd like to talk to you about K.B. Carson's death."

David Thurston nodded and led the way outside.

"Too noisy in there. Now, what can I tell you?" said Thurston.

"For one thing, how did you feel about Shooter Strong moving over to Blake's team?"

"Mixed emotions, I suppose. His record last year wasn't spectacular. He's a good driver, but I was in need of some quick money, and Blake offered me a deal to buy Strong's contract. I jumped at it. Win-win. Besides, Carson hadn't been doing well, either."

"Do you have any idea who'd want Carson dead?"

"None at all. Are you suggesting it wasn't an accident?"

"We're looking into alternate possibilities. I understand Scotty and Carson didn't get along."

"Nothing serious. Drivers have rivalries going all the time. Friendly competition, that's all," said Thurston.

"I'd like to talk to Scotty," said McGruder.

"I'll send him out," said Thurston. He turned and disappeared inside. Seconds later, Scotty Black stepped out the door and walked up to McGruder.

"Mister Thurston said you wanted to talk to me."

"I understand you and Carson had an ongoing grudge. That right?"

"Nothing like that. We both drive hard and like to win," said Scotty. "That's all there was to it. I'll admit he *was* running better than me this year."

"No competition over women?"

"Naww. He's got himself a squeeze, although he didn't actually have her all to himself, if you know what I mean."

"Oh. Who else was in the loop?"

"Blake, for one."

"Did Carson know that?"

"I'm not certain. If he didn't, he sure had his head in the sand."

"Anyone else?"

"Not that I know of, but then, we *are* talking about Angelina Sanders." Scotty gave a knowing nod and went back inside.

It was clear to McGruder that Angelina played a bigger part than just a girlfriend. He went back to her motel for a second interview. As he neared the entrance, his cell phone rang.

"We found the murder weapon. A chrome-plated socket wrench. A big one. It was hiding in plain sight: a mechanic's toolbox. Found traces of blood and a hair where the socket attaches," said Ornitz.

"How come you didn't spot it before?"

"It wasn't there when we were doing tests for blood residue. We covered that place from top to bottom. It had to have been put there *after* we left the scene."

"Whose tool box was it in?"

"The chief mechanic, Williams. Funny thing though, he had another just like it."

"Did you look to see if anyone had a missing wrench?"

"Normally these guys scratch their initials in the handles of their tools. Sharing tools is apparently a no-no. This one had no initials, but Williams' other one did. What do you make of that?"

"I'll let you know." McGruder hung up just before knocking on Angelina's door.

She greeted him with a seductive smile and swung open the door to let him in.

"I'd hoped I'd see you again, Detective. Would you like a drink?" She closed the door and slipped the chain in place, her former sadness replaced by inviting coyness.

"No, thanks. It's a little early in the day for me." He couldn't fail to notice what a striking young lady she was. A "modelesque" figure and a million-dollar face. No wonder she has a string of men a mile long.

"Suit yourself. What can I do for you?" Her come-hither smile and honey-dripped voice was an instant mantrap, and he had been around long enough to know how to keep from getting snared. In self-defense, he chose a single chair across from where she'd eased onto the plush couch, crossing her shapely legs.

"I'm sure that by now you've figured out that we're regarding Carson's death as something other than an accident. Do you have any idea who'd want to kill him?"

"Good heavens, no. How would I? Are you certain?"

"I understand you have a particular fondness for the racing circuit."

"So? I guess you could say I have lots of friends in the business. I like adventure, the excitement of men putting their lives on the line in fast cars."

"Was one of the men you've dated Scotty Black?"

"No. He's a sweetheart, but he's not my type. When I met K.B., wow, he was hot."

"Was he hot the night of the party?"

"If you mean angry, no, although he was having his problems, I suppose. *Every* driver goes through down times." She shrugged her shoulders and curled her lips as if he should already understand those things.

McGruder got very little else out of Angelina Sanders. When he got back to the crime lab he rechecked his notes. Ornitz was finishing some paperwork.

"Harold, I need something to build a case on. These guys are buddy-buddy one day and in a deadly dual on the track the next. And Angelina Sanders. Boy, if she had the flu everybody at the track would catch it."

"Got around, huh?" Ornitz mumbled. He looked up from his work. "So what can I help you with?"

"Let's start with the murder weapon. No fingerprints?"

"Wiped clean."

"How about Williams' wrench?"

"Yep. His fingerprints were on all his tools. Everyone has his own set of tools, and they lock them up at night. Each mechanic's fingerprints were on all their own tools, just as you'd expect."

"So where did the murder weapon come from?"

"It appears to have been part of a complete set of tools that was owned by the Blake team for replacements if a tool were to break or get lost. No initials on any of them, however. That set *was* missing a socket wrench like the one used to kill Carson."

"Were fingerprints found on any of those tools?" asked McGruder.

"Several, yes, but different mechanics had used various pieces."

"So anyone could have gotten into that toolbox?"

"That's how it looks to me."

"Tell me about everything you found in the locker."

"Blue jeans, a T-shirt with his number on the back over a picture of his race car, a light jacket, sneakers, driving shoes, gloves, a notepad with what appears to be driving schematics, a receipt from Morgan Jewelers, a Tom Clancy paperback with a bookmark about half-way through, a Sharpie marker, a small jar full of change and two driving uniforms. One of them was in a plastic bag like it hadn't been worn for a while, or was fresh from the cleaners. No blood on any of the clothes in the locker."

McGruder looked over items from Carson's locker that were spread out on a table, scratching his head and frowning.

"Did you find anything unusual about either of the cars?"

"Looking for what?"

"I don't know. I'm curious about anything that might have been done to the engines," McGruder said. "Try to match their serial numbers with the cars. Let me know if you find anything. If Carson's engine was swapped with Strong's, there might have been bad blood. Oh, did you find any traces of blood on any of the other team members' uniforms?"

"Nada."

McGruder left the building and climbed into his unmarked Chevy Impala. He sat flipping through his notes and chewing on his lip. He started the car and headed for the Indianapolis Motor Speedway. When he pulled into the 16th Street entrance, he drove around to the parking lot for garage owners and team members. His badge was his parking permit.

He caught up with Blake as he was about to enter his garage. "Blake, I need another word," McGruder said, motioning him to a shady spot near the entrance.

"Again? Can't you see I'm busy?"

"I get the impression that you and Angelina Sanders were 'close.' Would that be a fair characterization?"

"Where'd you hear that?"

"Is it true?"

Blake began shuffling his feet and staring at the ground. "Maybe."

"I'll take that as a yes. How did Carson feel about it when he found out?"

"We had a few words. Nothing serious. He knew what Angelina was like when he started their relationship. It was a fling. A nothing. She liked young drivers, that's all."

"And your relationship, was that also 'nothing'?"

"Not to me. But I indulged her dalliances."

"How long have you been involved?"

"On and off, about four years," Blake sighed and looked away. "That's not for publication, please."

"Jealousy sounds like a motive to want someone dead."

"Murder? Are you implying I killed Carson?"

"No, but evidence points to someone on the team being guilty. You certainly had a motive," said McGruder.

"Nonsense. I would never kill my own driver over a woman. I have too much at stake to risk losing everything."

"I take it you're not married?"

"Divorced."

"She catch you playing around?"

"No. It was the other way around, Detective."

The interview over, McGruder approached his car. The cell phone rang. The read-out said it was the crime lab.

"What do you have for me?" said McGruder as he flipped open the phone.

"Our warrants to search every team members' locker turned up nothing."

"How about homes?"

"Only two of them live here. They volunteered to let us look. Again, nothing. The rest are from all over the country."

"Then they all have motel rooms somewhere. See if Maggie can find a judge that will issue warrants for their rooms. Be sure to check out Angelina Sanders, Jim Blake, David Thurston and Scotty Black. I'm uncertain of their whereabouts at the time of the murder."

Ornitz sighed at the prospect of so much legwork thrown his way. He hung up with a groan. McGruder returned to leafing through his notebook. Too many motives, he thought.

The next day McGruder spent much of the morning poring over paperwork: entrance forms and fees, car registrations, engine numbers, garage fees, requests and payments made for fuel and tires, and security. As he leafed through copies of checks made to the Indy Racing League, he found them signed, not by James Blake, but by Janice Devereau Blake. He set out to find this new player. It didn't take long. Mrs. Blake's home address, as listed on the garage application, was Cincinnati, and she was listed in the phone book. A maid answered and said Mrs. Blake was in Indy for the month of May. McGruder got a phone number for the hotel she was staying in downtown. The desk clerk dialed her room.

"Mrs. Blake, my name is McGruder. I'm with the Indianapolis Metropolitan Police Department. We're investigating the murder of one of your husband's race drivers, K.B. Carson."

"Ex-husband, Detective."

"Yes, sorry. I seem to recall Mister Blake saying you were divorced. The reason for the call is that I'm wondering why all the checks to the Indianapolis Motor Speedway, as well as for tires, gas, payroll and such, were signed by you?"

"I assume you noticed my signature includes my maiden name, Devereau, as in The Devereau Industrial Bank. When my father died, he left his only child a *very* wealthy woman."

"I thought the name was familiar, but in my line of work, guessing is dangerous."

"I'm sure it is. Now what can I do for you?" she said.

"I'm curious why you'd be paying your ex's racing expenses after a divorce."

"Easy, I own the team. Jim works for me. He's a *very* good manager, just a lousy husband."

"Hmm. Would you mind telling me why you got a divorce in the first place, then?"

"I didn't. He did. You see I'd known for years he liked to play around, but I couldn't prove it. At the time, he didn't know I had my *own* romantic interests. Someone told Jim about my fling, and he filed for divorce, that's all. I have a thing for young drivers; he has a thing for bimbos."

He hung up after thanking the ex-Mrs. Blake for her candor.

Harold Ornitz called to give McGruder a heads-up on some new evidence. "You were right to have us look for blood on shoes. We found Carson's blood on the soles of one of his chief mechanic's left shoes. We're still checking on other people."

"Anything on the uppers?"

"No."

"Keep looking." McGruder hung up and flipped to the page with the list of suspects, and put a check mark by Eddy Williams. He sat and tapped his pen on his desktop. A cup of coffee sat untouched off to the side. His partner, Maggie Cooper, walked up to his cubicle.

"Where've you been?" he asked.

"Chasing down anyone who might have been near the Blake garage that morning. That and finding a judge willing to do your bidding."

"You don't look like you're brimming over with good news."

"Nope. I just got back from serving the search warrants with the lab guys."

"Find anything promising?"

Detective Cooper sat across from him and leaned forward.

"Not at first glance. Waiting for some tests. But I don't think we're ready to point fingers, yet. So, where do we go from here?"

"If I get the call from Harold I'm hoping for, you and I are going racing."

That call came minutes later. Harold Ornitz had found a pair of shoes with a tiny speck of blood residue between an eyelet and the shoelace.

McGruder and Cooper walked into the Blake garage. Most of the crew was busily engaged in some activity or another around both cars. He noticed that the cockpit of Carson's car had another name painted on. It came as somewhat of a surprise: Scotty Black.

Scotty was sitting on a stool, leaning against the back wall. Jim Blake was near the door in a heated argument with David Thurston. McGruder, Cooper and two uniformed officers approached the two battling owners.

"Sorry to interrupt your love fest, gentlemen, but we're here on official business." McGruder carried a brown paper sack. "What're you two nearing fisticuffs over?"

"This jackass hired away my *other* driver. Claims he didn't. Yeah, I admit I needed money, but I had no intention of losing Scotty as well as Strong. But Blake here made him a deal, and he walked out on me."

"Didn't he already have a contract with you, Thurston?"

"Not exactly. The money from the Strong deal was my leverage to broker a better deal with Scotty. He had yet to sign on the dotted line. But I know he would have if Blake hadn't gone behind my back. I might as well fold my tent and leave, losing all my up-front fees in the process."

"I doubt that Blake had anything to do with it. I suspect it was his wife, the former Mrs. Blake. She's the one with the money, anyway. Didn't you notice who had signed the check for Shooter Strong?"

Thurston looked stricken. Apparently he *hadn't* put it together.

"Blake got a divorce from his wife because of her cheating." McGruder looked over at Scotty whose attention he had gained. "Someone ratted her out to her husband. My guess is that Scotty was the co-respondent, and that you were the one who told Blake. Am I close?"

Thurston looked at the floor, his face still red with anger. "Yeah."

"Janice Devereau Blake didn't strike me as the kind to let a past indiscretion go unpunished. I'll bet she made the deal for Scotty to jump teams in order to get back at you for ruining her marriage. That about right, Scotty?"

Scotty nodded. "Yeah, she and I were doing just fine until Thurston walked in on us one night. He gave Blake the leverage he needed to get out of his marriage..."

"And get a nice settlement to enter into another marriage, right?"

"Uh, yeah, that's right," stuttered Scotty. "How'd you know?"

"I know because I can add two and two. And in this case, it adds up to three, which is one too many. That's our killer."

"Don't you need some sort of evidence, Detective?" said Thurston, his face still flushed.

McGruder reached into the sack and pulled out a pair of black leather shoes, and held them up.

"That's what I'm holding in my hand, Mister Thurston. Do either of you recognize these?"

"Yeah. They're mine. So what?" said Blake.

"This is the evidence Mr. Thurston was talking about. These shoes have a sprinkling of blood droplets deep in the eyelets, on the top of one shoe. You polished them after killing Carson, but blood doesn't erase easily. That puts you at the scene when Carson was bludgeoned to death. By you, Mr. Blake."

"Why would I do a thing like that? You're crazy."

Detective Cooper spoke up just then. "McGruder, I heard Harold say he also found blood on the soles of Williams' shoes. Isn't that just as damning for him?"

"Nope. The blood on Williams' soles proves he was telling the truth. He found Carson dead. He obviously stepped in some blood. But it was already there, and Carson was already dead. The *killer* had to have splattered blood on the tops of his shoes."

"But why would Blake kill his own driver?" said Cooper.

"Because he was about to lose his girlfriend to Carson, who had asked her to marry him. She had accepted. She was likely wearing the engagement ring the night before he was killed. The jeweler's receipt was still in his locker. When Blake found out, he was probably furious, but he didn't want to make a scene in front of all the crew, so he waited until morning, after the crew had pushed the car out to put it in line, and Carson had just come in, rushing to get dressed to drive."

"I'd indulged her playing around with every young stud she could find, but she had never before agreed to marry any of them. She was mine. She'll never belong to some hack race car driver," Blake blurted out.

"During the argument that ensued, when you likely told him to leave her alone or lose his ride, he told you to get lost since he knew who held the purse strings, anyway. He was rubbing your nose in it. That's when you grabbed a socket wrench out of the unlocked team toolbox and hit him. You're under arrest, Blake, for the murder of K.B. Carson."

The two officers stepped forward and cuffed the man who once had it all, but wanted more. Blake hung his head in defeat as he was led away.

"What's the most powerful motive for murder, sex or money?" McGruder asked, and then answered his own question. "In your case, Blake, it appears to have been both."

Indianapolis Motor Speedway Hall of Fame Museum

by Sheila Boneham

No visit to the Crossroads of America would be complete without a stop at the Indianapolis Motor Speedway Hall of Fame Museum, located on the grounds of the Indianapolis Motor Speedway. Established in 1956, the museum features approximately 30,000 square feet of display space, with the main display area under a canopy of glass to provide natural light. Bus tours of the historic 2.5-mile oval track depart from just outside the museum.

The museum exhibits approximately 75 vehicles, including the Marmon "Wasp," winner of the first Indianapolis 500 in 1911 with Ray Harroun at the wheel, and more than 30 other Indianapolis 500-winning cars. The collection also includes one of only three 1935 Duesenberg Model JN four-door convertible passenger cars ever built. Equipment used for timing and scoring the Indianapolis 500 from the first race until now is displayed and explained, and the 48-seat Tony Hulman Theater features 20 minutes of historic footage and Indianapolis 500 highlights.

To join the approximately 250,000 people who visit the museum annually, or to learn more, log on to the museum's web site:
www.indianapolismotorspeedway.com/museum.

Tracks

by Sheila Boneham

Sheila Boneham writes from her home in Fort Wayne, Indiana, where she lives with her two dogs, Jay and Lily, and her husband, Roger. She is an award-winning author of many books and articles about dogs and cats, and is working on a mystery series starring Tracks characters Janet McPhail and Jay.

It all started when Alberta Shofelter asked me to shoot her dog. She offered triple my usual fee plus expenses and said that Jay could come along, so of course I agreed. Then the whole project whirled out of my control, and I found myself headed for an overnight ordeal in a Speedway motel.

Don't get me wrong—the motel was fine. More than fine. Alberta has plenty of money and knows how to use it, and the Belton Inn was the nicest motel I've stayed in since my first honeymoon. Not that I've had or wanted a second, although the way things are going with Tom, I'm terrified that he'll catch me in a weak moment and I'll end up swilling champagne and wondering what hit me. Alberta also treated us to an outstanding steak at a little place I'd never heard of in Carmel, an up-and-coming little burgh just north of Indy. CARmel—only newcomers or the nouveau pretentious put the accent on the second syllable.

No, the accommodations were fine. It was Alberta herself who made the trip from Fort Wayne an ordeal, gossiping nonstop during the two-hour drive to Indianapolis. I couldn't decide whether to strangle her with a leash or run her down with her SUV when she made a pit stop somewhere around Muncie, so she lived to blather on while I chewed my cuticles raw and Jay snored in the back seat.

By nine o'clock Alberta was in her room, and I was tucked into bed with Jay, and more or less off the hook until morning. Unless she called me. Again.

But maybe I should clarify why Alberta wanted me to shoot her dog. I'm Janet MacPhail, and I photograph pets, among other things. And Indy, spoiled rotten and petted silly, isn't your run-of-the-backyard pet Welsh Terrier. He was at the top of his game in the show ring and in need of a new photo portfolio. Or rather, Alberta, his campaign manager and doting

"Mommy," needed a new batch of photos as she prepared an all out marketing assault in the big, slick show-dog magazines. Wanted to hit 'em hard before Westminster. I was, it seemed, photographer of choice, which was great news for my bank book. For my sanity? Mmmm, not so good.

Alberta wanted the shoot to be special, and she wanted the perfect location, so we had brainstormed a bit. Maybe the Lakeside Park Rose Garden? But when I drove down Lake Avenue to check the place out, there was scaffolding all over the park's giant pergola. Not all that picturesque.

We bounced ideas around for a while, and then one of us, I can't remember who (and hate to admit that it may have been me), said "The museum at the track!" meaning, of course, the Indianapolis 500 Hall of Fame Museum. Which made perfect sense because Indy's official moniker is Champion Welsho Start Your Engines. All of Alberta's dogs are named for the 500—Welsho Checkered Flag, Welsho Pace Car, and so on. Now, I can sit and watch dogs all day, but I'd be bored stiff watching a bunch of cars run around in circles. Not Alberta, though. No sirree. As she'd reminded me two hundred times since noon, she went to her first 500 in 1960 and hadn't missed a race in forty-six years.

I was just falling off the edge into la-la land, my arm wrapped around Jay's warm body, when the phone jangled me back from the brink. *If this is another question about which lens I'm going to use, I'll shove my tripod...* I let the rest of the thought go as I put the receiver to my ear. "We can talk about this tomorrow."

"Uh, sure," said a voice much more masculine than Alberta's.

"Oh, Tom." Jay groaned, rolled toward me, and planted a big wet kiss on my cheek. I nudged him off so I could talk, a pang of guilt nestling into my gut. "Sorry I didn't call. I must have drifted off." I gave Tom an abridged rendition of my day, leaving out Alberta's gossip and her detailed instructions on how to conduct a photo shoot. "Indy's a cute little booger, though. How's Leo?"

Tom was cat sitting for me. His idea. Leo would have been fine at home, but he's so adaptable and social that Tom insisted on a sleepover. Besides, he helped save my life not long ago. Leo, not Tom. So we hold him in high regard.

At the sound of Leo's name, Jay's lids lifted and he gazed at me, the soft look in his brown eyes enough to break your heart. I ran my fingers lightly through the silvery hair behind his ears.

"Leo is cuddled up on the couch next to Drake. Jay enjoying the trip?"

I rolled Jay away from me, wrapped an arm around him, and wove my fingers into the thick hair of his chest. "Oh, I think so."

"Lucky dog." I smiled. One of the things I like most about Tom is that he understands my love affair with Jay. He feels much the same about his own dog, Drake. "Tell him I hold him responsible for your well-being. And try to stay out of trouble."

I'd met Tom three months earlier, back in May, when I got tangled in a web of murders involving members of our dog-training community. I wasn't keen to get into a situation like that again. Had I known that history was threatening to repeat itself, I probably wouldn't have gotten any sleep.

As it was, though, I conked out as soon as I hung up the phone and bounced out of bed at 5:30 a.m., pulled on some jeans, a T-shirt, and a pair of low rubber boots for the dew-laden grass. My involvement in the murders I mentioned had shown me how useful a good tracking dog can be, and I'd gotten serious about training Jay to follow human scent trails, something best done before the humid heat of Indiana summer days. I took Jay out for a quick pee, then grabbed his breakfast kibble, already stashed in a plastic container, plus my orange flags. I ignored the you're-not-taking-me-with-you look on Jay's face as I shut the door.

I had scoped out a field just east of the motel the night before. Most people would call it an eyesore, filled as it was with weeds and grass grown to mid-calf height. For my purposes, it was perfect. I laid out a 540-yard track with four turns, left and right. I put the container with Jay's breakfast at the end of the track. Finding it would be his reward. I wanted to

age the track at least thirty minutes before we ran it, so I figured I'd hang out in the room for a little while and catch the
news. But when I approached my door, I found Indy sniffing
at the threshold while Alberta pressed her ear against the metal,
testing it with a steady pattern of rap-rap-rap, listen-listen, rap-
rap-rap.

"Hi ya!"

Alberta jumped, and Indy wriggled and snorted around
my ankles. I bent to pet him.

"Oh, Janet! I thought we could go over the plan before
breakfast."

*And at breakfast, and on the way to the museum, and at the
museum,* I thought, but I buttoned my lip. She was paying me
pretty good money, after all.

"Okay, Alberta, we can do that in a few minutes." I opened
the door to my room, put a leash on my dog, and grabbed his
harness and long line. "But I want to run a track with Jay, and
I've already laid it. Will that work?"

She started to protest that we should get ready, but I pointed
out that since the museum didn't open until nine, we had three
hours, and Jay would run this track in less than five minutes.
Besides, I was halfway back to the start of my track, and Alberta
was too busy trying to keep up to argue further. She's maybe
four-eleven if she pulls herself up straight, and not in the best
possible shape. The little baby cigars she smokes don't help.

"Why don't you watch from here and catch your breath?"
I smiled at her. She panted and gasped at me, nodding and
pressing her palm against her heaving bosom. Indy bounced
in happy circles at her feet, then gave up on that and started
dancing around Jay, darting under his belly and between his
legs until his retractable leash was twined and tangled with
Jay's short leather one. By the time I separated the dogs and
put Jay's tracking harness and long line on him, the track was
half-an-hour old. At least we weren't bored while we waited.

Jay beat my estimate and ran the track in four minutes. He
sat beside the food container, his way of indicating that he'd
found something. He wriggled and bounced while I removed
the lid, and he sucked up a cup of kibble in the time it took me
to arrange his forty-foot line into a tidy coil. The air was heavy

with August humidity and the temperature climbed with the morning sun, so we crated the dogs in our motel rooms and headed for breakfast.

Twenty minutes later, I shoved a fork full of cinnamon French toast into my mouth and listened as Alberta went over the pictures she wanted. Again. Then, to my surprise, she said, "Jay's good."

"Yeah, he's a good boy."

"No, I mean tracking. I was impressed."

I smiled at her. Flattery concerning my dog is always welcome.

"No, really! If I were lost, I'd want you and Jay looking for me. You should join a SAR team."

High praise indeed, but search and rescue isn't something you do as a hobby. It's a lifestyle commitment, and I didn't think it was one I could make. "Tracking is just a hobby for us, but thanks. He is pretty good."

A half hour later we pulled into the museum parking lot. A pot-bellied little man with a fringe of straight gray hair encircling a shiny scalp rushed out to meet us as we approached the building's entrance. He took in the two dogs, the camera bag and the tripod and said, "You must be Ms. Shofelter? I'm Nelson Parker. Call me Nelson." The name tag pinned above the Ralph Lauren pony on his shirt confirmed that and identified him as assistant museum manager to boot.

Nelson stood just out of handshaking range and kept an eye on Indy and Jay. He looked like he was ready to turn tail if either of them made a move toward him. Intrigued, the two dogs leaned against their leashes to poke their noses as close to the nervous little man as possible.

As we moved onto the main floor of the museum, Nelson's cell phone played a tinny rendition of "Lil' Deuce Coupe" and he excused himself. I put my bag and tripod down, and Alberta and I looked at the seventy-some cars that surrounded us. Dust motes danced in the light from the glass canopy above our heads, and a faint potpourri of fuel, rubber and wax crawled into my nose. A handful of early birds wandered through the museum.

Most of the cars on display have raced flesh and dreams around this track at America's crossroads and elsewhere in the world, and about half of them are Indy 500 winners. Some Indy pace cars and vintage models of special note round out the collection. Among the visitors was one feral-looking character, gaunt and reptilian. Years of working with dogs have honed my sense of body language, and my instincts told me the guy was jumpy. I watched him for a minute or two, but he could hardly pocket a car, so I turned back to the task at hand.

Alberta couldn't decide which would suit Indy better, Ray Harroun's yellow Marmon "Wasp," winner of the first Indianapolis 500 in 1911, or one of A.J. Foyt's four winning cars. I was about to suggest that I just shoot him in whatever cars we could and sort out the best shots later, when Nelson's phone conversation turned both our heads.

"But I have Alberta Shofelter here for a photo shoot."

Pause.

"How long?"

Pause. Sigh.

"Okay, stall if you can." He pocketed the phone and turned back to us.

"I'm sorry. Um, we have a sort of, um, problem."

Jay, Indy and Alberta all cocked their heads, two to the right, one to the left, and listened. I wished I had my camera out.

"There's been a scheduling mix up. We have a field trip of third graders coming in."

"In August?"

"Summer school group." Little sparkles of sweat danced across Nelson's wide forehead. "I'm so sorry."

"Not a problem. You can just keep them back from whatever car we're using at the moment." Alberta is rich, famous in certain circles, and accustomed to being obeyed. "We'll be fine. Won't we, Janet?" The tiny black curls across the top of her face bounced as she nodded her head at me. She looked back at Nelson. "When will they be here?"

"They're outside. But they're going for a bus ride around the track, so you have maybe half an hour."

Alberta had brought a suitcase full of mats, rugs and assorted fabrics to protect automobile finishes from Indy's smoothly "dremeled" nails. She busied herself selecting the perfect piece to complement each car. Indy, it turned out, was quite the ham, and in the next twenty minutes we got some great shots of him in, on and in front of various cars. My favorite prop wasn't a race car at all but the 1935 four-door convertible Duesenberg JN passenger car. It's one of three ever built, and it was one snazzy ride in its day.

We were just wrapping up a series with Indy and the '57 Corvette when the museum filled with the patter of sneakers and high-pitched young voices oohing and aahing and settling on, "Look! Dogs!"

I knew I wouldn't be able to take photos and keep an eye on the kids swarming Jay, and it was too hot to leave him in a closed car, so I suggested a half-hour break. The kids would have had enough of the museum by then anyway. I stashed my camera in my bag, hoisted the bag to my shoulder, tucked my folded tripod under my arm, and headed out with my dog.

The man in gray stood round-shouldered against the wall just inside the front door, hands shoved deep in his pants pockets as he watched the kids and flicked the tip of his tongue in and out between narrow lips. Our eyes met for an instant before he looked away. My own body reacted with no conscious direction from my brain, arcing my path away from the man, and I heard a low rumble rise from my dog's throat. I was not surprised.

Ten minutes later, Alberta bustled out with Indy tucked tight against her. She did not look happy. "This is impossible. Let's go. We'll have a cup of coffee and come back and finish later when those kids are gone."

I couldn't convince her to wait it out at the Speedway, so we loaded the dogs and set off in search of coffee. Not just any coffee, mind you. Alberta had to have Panera's "Dark and Vibrant," along with one of their ooey-gooey double-chocolate calorie bombs. My hopes of getting home by early afternoon raced away.

When we pulled back into the museum parking lot ninety minutes later, the school bus was still there. That was startling enough. The flashing lights of the three Speedway police cruisers parked in front of the door were absolutely hair-raising.

Nelson paced back and forth outside the entrance, wringing his hands and swiping a sodden hanky across his slick forehead. When he saw us, he scurried over and addressed Alberta.

"I don't think they'll let you back in. Not now, anyway. Oh, it's just terrible. Terrible." Beads of perspiration flew into the air as he shook his head.

"What's happened?" I couldn't think of anything third-graders could do to attract three police cars.

"One of the children has disappeared."

Alberta clapped her hands to her mouth.

"Disappeared?"

Nelson shifted his round-eyed stare to me. "When they loaded the kids to leave, they did a head count, and a little boy is missing. We've looked everywhere."

I thought about the layout beyond the entrance and couldn't imagine anyone hiding in the wide-open display area, unless the kid had crawled under a car. The two gift shops might offer possibilities, I supposed, for a small child to hide, although it seemed unlikely. "Could he have gotten into one of the offices in back?" I scanned the clusters of people gathered in front of the museum, looking for the shifty-eyed loner who gave me the willies earlier. He was nowhere to be seen.

Nelson shook his head. "I don't see how. No one's here, really. I mean staff. Everyone's out for vacations or other things, and the offices are locked unless someone's working." He appeared to be trying to wring one of his hands right off. "Except now, of course. The police wanted them all opened so they could search."

A giant in brown slacks and a blue shirt with wet crescents under his armpits joined us. He was at least a foot taller than my 5'4" and somewhere between slim and fat. He ignored me and Alberta in favor of Nelson. "We've called for a K9 from Indianapolis."

Never one to be ignored, Alberta shoved her hand in front of his tie tack and introduced herself, adding, "And this is Janet MacPhail, and Jay."

"Garza. John Garza. Detective, Speedway PD."

I had no idea if it meant anything, but I told him about the odd character I'd seen lurking in the museum earlier, and how my dog and I both got bad vibes from the guy. He pulled a radio from his belt and passed the description along to the other officers, then gave Jay an appraising look. "She's a pretty dog." Jay gets that a lot, probably because he *is* pretty. "Border Collie?"

"Australian Shepherd. Male."

Our dog talk was interrupted when a red Cavalier whipped up to the curb, and a tear-streaked young woman leaped out almost before she had fully stopped. She was built like a runner, long and lean enough to look good in her turquoise spandex shorts and coral tank as she sprinted to the nearest cop. Her brown hair hung in a wild tangle to her shoulders, and she didn't seem to know what to do with her hands. The mother. The officer pointed toward Garza, who met her halfway. One of the teachers moved to her side and wrapped an arm around her shoulder. Grief and guilt and fear buzzed around the little group like hungry bees, and I had to look away.

Three quarters of an hour later, I sat on the warm concrete in front of the museum with one hand on Jay's panting side, the other holding Alberta's Tweetie Pie umbrella for some shade. I hadn't seen Alberta for a while and was just wondering where she'd gotten to when I heard Detective Garza shouting into his cell phone.

"How long?" Garza scowled into the distance. "Dammit!" He punched the air with his phone. "Then I need more people. We have to find this kid."

He listened for a moment, grunted something while gesturing for one of the uniformed cops, and shoved the phone back into its holster. "The K9 is working a scene in Madison County. Can't get here for at least another couple of hours. We need to search this whole place." He waved his arms as he spoke. "Track, bleachers, the works."

I struggled to my feet, one of which seemed to have disappeared. Hard surfaces have gotten harder since I turned fifty. I winced as I got my feet under me and forced myself to ignore the needles scampering up and down my flesh as I tottered toward the detective, stomping a little more life back into my foot with each step.

"Excuse me."

He looked down at me like I was a gnat. Small, annoying and irrelevant. "What?"

"I heard what you said about the K9 being delayed. Maybe I can help."

Garza lifted one eyebrow in a "yeah, sure" look, but I pushed on, gesturing toward Jay.

"My dog tracks. If you have something with the child's scent, he could track him."

"Ma'am, I'm sure she's a nice doggy." Jay cocked his head, and Garza let out a long tired breath. "Look, I appreciate the offer, but we have a sick child out there. We can't afford to waste time with an untrained team."

Alberta bustled up with the same suggestion I'd just made. "Janet, why don't you see if Jay can track the little boy?" She looked at Detective Garza and went on. "Jay is a wonderful tracker."

"Yes, ma'am. As I was explaining to Ms., uh," he glanced at his notebook, "MacPhail, I appreciate your concern, but we need a trained search team, not somebody's pet. So we'll just go on with the search as is." He started to turn away, dialing his cell phone again.

"Excuse me, Detective Garza." He looked at me. "Did you say the little boy is sick?"

"Diabetes. Mom says he's overdue now for a blood sugar test and will need insulin soon." He walked away, phone to his ear.

"Damn fool!" Alberta looked apoplectic. "Come on!" She took me by the elbow and steered me toward the child's mother, who stood with Nelson Parker and one of the teachers. The teacher tried to run interference when she saw us approaching, but Alberta pushed past her and introduced the two of us. Then, pointing at Jay, she announced, "And this is Jay, and he's going to find your son!"

I groaned inside. I hate to make promises we may not be able to keep, and I really hate it when other people make them for us.

"Billy." The young woman whispered the name and choked on a sob, then gathered herself and, turning her dark eyes toward mine, held her hand out. "Julie Wentworth. Can you really find my little boy?"

My heart climbed into my throat, but I tried not to let my doubts show. "I don't know. But my dog is a pretty good tracker, and we can try."

"We have to find him soon." Her face was chalky, her eyes wide. "If he doesn't get his insulin he could have a seizure." She sobbed. "He could die."

"I need something that smells like Billy."

She frowned, then brightened. "The car! I have something in the car!" She sprinted for the red Cavalier, and I got Alberta's keys and took Jay to the Lincoln to get his harness and line. On my way, I invoked every deity I could think of and placed a special request with St. Roch, patron of hunting dogs. We needed to find this quarry.

Our only real hope was that Billy had walked away from the museum on his own two feet. If someone had carried him away, it was doubtful that Jay could track him, even though all human beings shed tons of scent-loaded skin cells and other gunk all the time. *I didn't share my doubts, though, or the King Kong of worries that loomed in my mind—that someone had loaded the child into a car and driven off.* I'd have felt better if the creepy character I'd seen earlier was still lurking within sight.

I cast Jay in front of the museum doors in hopes that he would pick Billy's scent out from all the others. He swept his nose back and forth over the concrete, pausing here and there to clack his tongue against the roof of his mouth as he tasted the scent. He moved toward the museum doors twice, which of course made perfect sense, but I called him back and encouraged him to try again.

After four or five minutes of that, I once again showed him the little boy's shoe that Julie Wentworth had brought from the car. It was well worn and grubby, and saturated with Billy's scent. Jay sniffed with interest, looked at me, and whined as if to say, "Yes, that's the kid I'm searching for."

"You have to try to find him, Bubby." I stroked the dog's copper cheek, and holding the back of his harness with one hand, led him off the curb and onto the track. "Go track!"

Jay began again to work his nose along the ground, moving away from the building in widening arcs. Then without warning, he took off, nose skimming the hard, hot surface and tail nub wagging like mad. He had the scent. I let the nylon line glide through my hand to the knot I had tied twenty feet from the slide bolt, giving my dog plenty of room, so I wouldn't overrun him if he stopped.

As it happened, my immediate problem would be keeping up. Now that Jay had the scent trail, he ran, nose about nine inches above the ground, shoulders bearing into the harness with what felt like twice his fifty-four pounds. I scrambled to keep up, letting another ten feet of my forty-foot line play out between my fingers, then grasping the thirty-foot marker knot with both hands.

I have never liked running. My memories of gym classes are dominated by the agony of stabbing pain under my ribs from gasping my way through JFK's presidential fitness six-hundred-yard torture test on the cinder track behind Kekionga Junior High. But there I was, trying to keep up with my four-legged speedster on the Indianapolis Motor Speedway. Just when I thought I'd blow a gasket, or whatever the cardiovascular equivalent might be, Jay reached the stands and slowed to a trot. I gasped and panted as I watched him search for the scent. Julie Wentworth and Alberta jogged up behind us, Alberta wheezing and panting enough for both of them, and I called to them to stay back at least ten yards.

My breath was still coming in gasps and my heart threatened to beat its way out of my chest when Jay spun once around, sniffed, wriggled his nub, and moved up to the next row of seats. And then the next. And the next.

We worked our way up the risers until we were at the top of the stands, and then Jay set out between the top bench and the one below it, his nose to the concrete. The knots in my line swung and threatened to catch in the bleachers, so I did something I almost never do when tracking. I stopped my dog.

"Down!" I figured that if he just lay down, Jay was less likely to lose the track he was on. In any case, he kept running. "Jay! Down!" He slowed and, with obvious reluctance, sank to the ground and whined. I caught up, leaned across his body, and unhooked the nylon line from the harness. "Okay. Go track!"

Jay took off again at a slow run. I glanced at Alberta, pacing in front of the stands below us, and heard Julie come up behind me.

"You let him go?"

"He's faster in these bleachers without me." As if to confirm that, Jay bounded over the bench to his right and raced along the concrete in front of the uppermost row of seats. We followed on the path we were on.

Jay stopped. He was about thirty feet ahead of me and a row of seats higher, and all I could see was his rear end. Then he lifted his head and looked back over his shoulder at me. One bark, and his head went down again. He'd found something. I let myself breathe.

"Billy!" Julie's voice was raw with fear. Unable to pass me in the narrow space, she shoved me forward, pointing through the space beneath the bench. A blood-red flash was just visible beside Jay's snowy leg. As I came closer, I saw brown hair and an arm. A little boy, and he was down. Julie screamed her son's name again. My breath caught somewhere deep in my chest, and my heart stood still again.

And then Jay was whining and wriggling, and I knew.

The red morphed into a T-shirt. A lock of brown hair, lighter than his mother's, lifted and fell in the hot south wind. Billy slowly rose to his feet, smiling and petting my beautiful Jay. "Hi, Mom. Isn't this a great dog?"

Two hours later I called Tom to tell him we were on our way home. The AC in Alberta's Navigator felt like heaven as we left the Hamilton County congestion north of Indianapolis and shot northeastward on I-69. Jay was stretched out and dozing on the back seat. I had just told Tom how scared I was that the man in gray had kidnapped Billy. Or worse.

"He ran away?"

"Yeah. I guess they had a big fight that morning, and he said he was going to find a new mom who would let him have a dog. I thought for a minute he was going to adopt me."

Tom chuckled. "Maybe you *should* do search and rescue." As Tom knew, this wasn't Jay's first find. A few months earlier my mom, whose mind isn't what it used to be, wandered away, and Jay found her. "So you think his mom is going to cave in to his demands?"

"She was a bit incoherent, but I wouldn't be surprised. The little booger played up the idea that a dog saved him so much, no one seemed to remember that he kidnapped himself."

"And I bet you told her that dogs can be trained to signal when a person's blood sugar is low."

No wonder Tom scares me. He knows me way too well.

Indy's Indy-Car shots were a huge hit. I won't take credit, but the little guy raced to another string of big wins after *Dogs in Review* published his Marmon Wasp portrait. Jay was nominated for a hero award, and his picture was in several newspapers.

A special delivery package arrived in early October, addressed to "Janet and Jay MacPhail." In it was a frame with race cars circling the glass, and a card in childish scrawl that said simply, "Thank you. Your friends Billy + J.J." Another note from Billy's mom said they'd contacted the Australian Shepherd Rescue and Placement Helpline after they met Jay, and the framed photo showed Billy in front of the Motor Speedway gate, an enormous grin on his face. Next to him, with a matching grin, sat a blue merle Aussie named after my best friend and me. That was the best shot of all.

Billy Arnold, Hard Luck Champ

by Phil Dunlap

A short dramatic career is the best way to describe hard-driving Billy Arnold, the 1930 Indianapolis 500 winner. Though he had been driving at several Midwest tracks since the mid-1920s, his first start at Indianapolis netted him a seventh-place finish.

He captured the pole for the 1930 race and was guaranteed a place in the record books after leading all but two laps to win the Indianapolis 500. He won two more races that year, giving him the AAA National Championship title. He was the first driver to win the 500 at a pace of over 100 mph without relief. Billy Arnold seemed to be unstoppable. That is until informed that, while he was driving the race, someone had stolen his personal car which had been parked outside the track.

He was quoted as saying, "I'd like to find whoever took it. I'd give him title to the darn thing."

During the 1931 race, he was again leading strongly with just 39 laps left, when a broken axle sent him and his riding mechanic over the fence coming out of the northwest turn. Tragedy had struck. Both he and his mechanic sustained serious injuries. The rear wheel of his car broke off and became airborne, crossing Georgetown Road and striking twelve-year-old Wilbur Brink who was in his yard. The impact killed him.

Arnold was leading the 1932 race when he crashed, again sustaining serious injuries to himself and his riding mechanic, Spider Matlock. After the race, Arnold's wife reportedly gave him an ultimatum: quit racing or face divorce. He never raced again.

Arnold appeared as himself in a cameo role in the 1932 movie *The Crowd Roars*, starring James Cagney and featuring other notable race drivers. It was partly filmed at the Indianapolis Motor Speedway.

Driven to Death

by Tamera Huber

Tamera Huber writes short stories, screenplays and poetry. She has completed her first mystery novel, and three of her short stories appear in the mystery anthologies, Derby Rotten Scoundrels *and* Low Down and Derby. *Huber is also an award-winning professional freelance journalist. Photography is her other creative outlet. She resides in the Louisville, Kentucky area.*

As I turned away from the television, a crisp breeze parted the curtains and raised the hairs on my arms. The smell of charred beef wafted from my neighbor's backyard. Part of me wanted to go outside and enjoy the cool night, but I couldn't look away from the circus on my television screen.

CNA and *MNX*, the major cable news networks, arrived early on the scene. No surprise there. *What passed for news these days?* Little more than endless celebrity sightings, rumors and innuendos galore, and scandal watches. Over and over and over.

The crawl at the bottom of the screen read: *INDY 500 HOPEFUL'S MANAGER DEAD.* They had me at Indy. After all, I lived in Carmel, a nice Indianapolis exurb only ten minutes from the home of the dead man, Martino 'Marty' Cavaletti. Despite the unusually cool weather beckoning me outside, the tube commanded my rapt attention. I flipped from channel to channel, embracing the sights and sounds. One by one, each network cut into their normal mind-numbing regurgitation of pseudo news to report the actual news.

Let the musings begin, I thought. One station announced that an unidentified witness had seen a man with wavy black hair fleeing Cavaletti's million-dollar digs in Noblesville. Another station reported that Cavaletti had been bludgeoned to death. A third reporter informed viewers that the Indy driver had committed suicide. Statements such as "We cannot confirm any of this information" didn't stop the talking heads (journalists in name only) from spouting hearsay and speculation.

Did the police find a suicide note? Did Cavaletti's ex-wife turn to murder? Or did he surprise a burglar? Who had a grudge against Indy driver Jeff Patrick's charismatic manager?

The thought of microwave popcorn beckoned me away for a moment. I popped a mini-bag saturated with butter, clicked open a diet cola, and settled in, propping my feet on the ottoman and snuggling into the afghan Elise had made for me.

My little sister had always been sickly—a bad heart. Ten years her senior, I had taken care of Elise after our parents died. That is until she met Jeff, the strong, handsome and attentive race car driver. For two years they lived in wedded bliss; I thought she couldn't be in better hands. They shared everything, and with his celebrity and connections, Jeff even managed to get a million-dollar life insurance policy on Elise, despite her frail nature.

The harsh ring from the phone interrupted my thoughts. No one spoke for a few seconds. Then, "Susanne?"

The call came sooner than I'd expected. "Hey, Jeff. What's up?" I knew perfectly well what Jeffrey Patrick wanted. I pressed mute on the remote control.

"Did you hear? The news?" he asked.

I grunted in the affirmative. "It's awful. Isn't it?"

"You have to tell them. I was with you."

"What? Why? You think the police will ask?"

"They've already called. They want me to come into headquarters."

"You *were* best friends. I'm sure they just want to know who might have wanted him dead. You have nothing to hide. Do you?"

"Of course not," he said, but I heard the fear, not sadness, in his voice.

"I haven't been this scared since Elise died," he said with iciness traveling over the phone line.

Elise. Soon, I would celebrate her life rather than mourn her death.

"But you're my only alibi," he went on.

Questions swirled through my head. I picked one. "Are they sure he was murdered? Or was it suicide?"

"Someone shot him."

"When?" I asked.

"My contact at the sheriff's office said Marty died sometime between six and seven this evening. While I was waiting for you at Cool Creek Park."

Elise's favorite place. Her life ended too soon, two weeks and two days ago, three days shy of her twenty-first birthday. I thought it was an appropriate place, and I was sure Jeff would come, if for no other reason, out of curiosity.

"I was at the park. Where were you?" he asked, sounding like my father when the teenaged me snuck in late after a date with Steve Miller, now a respectable civil servant.

"What? I was waiting for you at five-thirty, as you asked," I said.

"*Six*-thirty. I said to meet at six-thirty."

"I called your cell phone at six and then again at six-thirty and some other guy answered, each time, saying wrong number."

"I lost my phone this morning. You have to tell them. I was there from six to seven, waiting for you." I could hear the tightness in his voice.

"But how could I possibly know you were actually there?"

"It's me, Susanne. You have to tell the police that we met at the park."

"You want me to *lie*?"

"It's not a lie. Not really. I was there and we were supposed to meet." His voice was thicker than I had ever heard it.

"I don't know, Jeff."

"Don't do this for me. Think of Elise. She wouldn't want me to go to jail for something I didn't do. She was—an angel."

"At least she is now." I felt the blood rise into my cheeks.

"What about it, Susanne? After all, we're family."

I pulled in a quick breath and tasted salt as I sucked the popcorn kernel stuck between my teeth. "I guess I could. We were *supposed* to meet. You can count on me to make this right."

"You're the greatest. I'll take you to Ruth's Chris Steak House after the 500. My treat."

Your treat, I repeated in my head, and then hung up.

Around two in the morning, the background flickers of the newscast lulled my lids to sleep. When I opened my eyes, the Sunday morning sun sat low in the sky. I stumbled to the kitchen and breathed in the raspberry teabag before dropping it into hot water. The combination of the tea's strong scent and the doorbell brought me closer to awake. The peephole illuminated a police badge. Still in my robe, I opened the door and ushered the two detectives into the foyer.

They didn't stay long. I had plenty of time to get ready.

My walk-in closet was divided into two sections—my clothes and accessories on the left and Elise's things, from the penthouse apartment she and Jeff shared, on the right. I brushed my fingers across her clothes and stopped at a bright sundress, the sundress that had hidden Marty's revolver, long forgotten in a box of Elise's rumpled clothes he had mailed to me last week.

I pulled the dress, Elise's favorite, to my face and breathed in her still-present scent. Next I chose the sling backs, floppy hat and Wayfarers she had worn to our last outing. As I stuffed a tote bag with sunscreen, bottled water and a digital camera with a long lens, I found myself humming a tune I couldn't place.

My image in the full-length mirror brought back more memories. Cascading strawberry curls, small breasts, curvy calves. Although older, we had nearly always passed for twins. I slipped on the outfit. "I'm ready," I said, turning away from the mirror.

The twenty-five mile drive to the Indianapolis Motor Speedway didn't take as long as I'd thought. While I waited in line at the main gate on West 16th, I fished the press credentials out of my bag. One thousand dollars for the media pass let me go pretty much anywhere, and the camera provided great cover. *Worth every penny.* I staked out a position sitting on a retaining wall close enough to view Jeff Patrick's pit area through my eighty-millimeter lens.

I killed time alternately watching a quarter of a million spectators and keeping an eye on the finish line. Many hours and buckets of sweat later, Jeff's car passed under the black-and-white checkered flag, signaling his second Indianapolis 500 victory.

The fans rose, but I stood for a very different reason, as did Detectives Connelly and Miller, about ten yards from me. I followed, snapping pictures as they approached Jeff's crew.

Jeff pulled the winning Indy car into the pit, climbed out and threw his arms around his team. They poured him a glass of milk. As he drank it dry, applause and shouts erupted from the stands. The media, including me, pushed forward, sticking microphones and cameras in the winner's face.

I noticed that the detectives watched the media circus at a polite distance, allowing it to go forward until the trophy presentation. Jeff, on the Jumbotron, kissed the "Baby Borg," the smaller version of the Borg-Warner sponsor trophy. Then he solemnly dedicated the win to the memory of Marty Cavaletti and his recently deceased wife and asked for a moment of silence.

As the crowd bowed in unison, the officers moved in, each grabbing the crook of one of Jeff's arms. I was close enough to watch them slap on the handcuffs and to hear Jeff's rights read to him. Then the detectives marched him to an unmarked car, passing within two feet of me. Detective Miller nodded in my direction as he pushed Jeff into the back seat, ignoring the stunned crowd left wanting for an explanation.

When none came and the car containing their hero drove away at much less than Indy speed, the fans filtered slowly out of the gates, murmuring to one another as they left. Then cell phones sounded and clarity dawned, one fan at a time, in what I knew was news from home. A collective gasp erupted from the spectators as they learned the news—Jeff Patrick had been arrested for the murder of Marty Cavaletti.

Although it took two hours to travel twenty-five miles, I don't recall driving home. After I arrived, I sank into the sofa and clicked on the television. The flickering blue light reflected in the photos of my sister that lined the living room wall.

I retrieved a worn memory box from the bookshelf and sat it at my side. I stroked the silk embroidered top and opened it gingerly, then picked up the dried rose, one of a dozen Elise had sent on my birthday three years ago. The fragile flower crumpled in my hand, and the smell, although long gone, came back to me.

The answering machine tape nestled against a ribbon from Elise's wedding bouquet in the box's corner. I placed the cassette in the player. Elise's voice, angry and sharp, boomed from the speaker as my tears splashed onto the player.

"Hey Suz. I finally got a signal." A guttural sound escaped Elise's throat. "You know the millions that Jeff supposedly had socked away to open that art gallery for me? Gone! He and Marty lost all of it on a land deal. I picked up an extension in the hotel and heard it all, Marty and Jeff arguing about what to do. They borrowed money from a loan shark. To get square with that guy, they sabotaged the Indy frontrunner's car in the lead-up to the race. I've had it! Jeff's a player. He gets what he can, whenever he can. This vacation was our last chance. But when he comes back, I'm telling him off. I wish you were here, Sis. I know you're out of range, but when you get back, I'll be waiting in your house, eating your food, and not washing your towels. See ya."

And that was it. The last time I heard her voice. When Elise and Jeff had decided to go to Fiji, I had decided to go on my own adventure. I'd always wanted to go to the Amazon. A guide led me through the dwindling rain forests of South America. No cell phone, no contact with the outside world for two whole weeks.

When I'd had a hot bath at the hotel, I checked my messages. I listened to Elise's rant and tried to call her, but the signal was gone. Then Jeff called and left the message that changed my life. I stared at the cassette player, unsure whether I wanted to hear his message one last time.

Click.

"Susanne. It's Jeff. I-I don't know how to say this to you of all people. I know how close you and Elise had been." *Had been?* I remembered thinking, but he continued. "You know about her heart. I don't know how else to say it, but she's dead. She died in my arms. With her last breath, she asked me to cremate her and spread her ashes across the South Pacific. Right away. My lovely Elise."

By the time I arrived in Fiji, Jeff was long gone and Elise had been reduced to ashes, floating on the choppy sea. The doctor who had signed the death certificate looked like he could have been bought for the price of a bottle of rum, and the police chief didn't care if an American died. "One less tourist to worry about," he said.

Back in the States, I called the only person I could think of—Steve Miller, now a police detective. He informed me that without a body there was little he could do. But he remembered my beautiful kid sister and told me he'd do anything to help. Anything, including stealing Jeff's cell phone earlier in the day.

I had kept everything that Jeff had sent me from Elise's closet, even Jeff's hairbrush with his wavy black locks.

When I arrived at Marty's place, his shocked and horrified expression (mostly at the gun, Jeff's gun, which I held) did nothing to dissuade me. I told him to confess and I'd think about sparing his life.

"Poison," he said. From his father's drugstore.

Jeff had slipped it into her drink, even before she had confronted him about the sabotage. The insurance money would pay off the loan shark. Marty begged, he pleaded on his knees. I told him the big lie—that he could live if he called the police and told them about the sabotage—but not about Elise. Then he would tell the cops that he was afraid Jeff would shift the blame to him or get nervous and decide to kill him.

He asked why I didn't want him to confess about Elise. "Just make the call!" He did. And when he had hung up, I squeezed the trigger. Twice. As he lay dying on the Italian marble, he asked forgiveness. Instead, I crushed Jeff's hair into his fist and held it closed for over a minute until he died. Then I called 911 from a public phone to report a man with wavy black hair running from Marty's house.

When the detectives, including my old pal Steve, questioned me about Jeff's alibi, I told the truth—well, mostly. Jeff and I had planned to meet, but he never arrived. I called Jeff's cell phone sometime between six-thirty and seven. He seemed anxious, nervous and a little scared. He said something, I recalled to the police, like "What have I done?" Of course, I told the officers I had no idea what he had just done.

I stared into Elise's deep green eyes, the last photo I'd taken of her a month before she died. Eyes that had been drained of life, drop by drop.

As I walked out the patio door, the greenness that I had ignored for the past month sprang to life. I breathed in the aroma of early honeysuckles and the fragrant air of spring passing the baton to summer. My heart that had ached for so long seemed somehow lighter.

I sipped iced tea and relished the revenge that lingered in my mouth. Combined with the raspberry flavor, it created a taste sweeter than I had ever known. A taste I shared with Elise.

Indianapolis 500 Trivia

by Wanda Lou Willis

- The 500 was first called the "International 500-Mile Sweepstakes Race." The name changed to "Liberty Sweepstakes" for one year in 1919. The original title continued until 1980 when it changed to either "International Sweepstakes Race, Distance 500 Miles" or the "International 500-Mile Sweepstakes Race." Beginning in 1981, it was officially named "Indianapolis 500-Mile Race." Unofficially it's known as "The 500," "Indianapolis 500," or "Indy 500."

- The 1916 race was limited to 300 miles, with a field of only twenty-one cars. The track closed for the next two years owing to the World War I.

- Auto racing suffered through the Great Depression. The 1933 purse was reduced, which resulted in a short-lived drivers' strike.

- World War II brought another closing to the track in 1941, and the track deteriorated. Four years later, Eddie Rickenbacker sold it to Tony Hulman for $750,000.

- At a cost of $1.4 million, the double-decked Paddock Grandstand was erected in 1961 on the main straightaway.

- The Speedway Motel opened in 1963. The Speedway Hall of Fame and Museum followed thirteen years later.

- From 1909 until after World War II, the Indiana National Guard patrolled the grounds. By 1948, the Speedway had its own Safety Patrol. The original uniforms of navy blue wool were replaced in the early 1970s by short-sleeved yellow shirts and baseball caps.

- The original track surface of crushed rock and tar was

replaced in the fall of 1909 with 3.2 million street-paving bricks. Later, patches of asphalt were applied to the rougher portions of the turns. By the 1939 race, only about 650 yards of the main straightaway still had the original bricks. The track has been resurfaced several times with a fresh batch of bricks inlaid at the start/finish line.

Pole Day at the Track

by Sherita Saffer Campbell

Sherita Saffer Campbell is a great-grandmother, freelance mystery writer and poet, who has been published in Alfred Hitchcock's Mystery Magazine, Fate Magazine, Branches, Sagewoman, Humpback Barn Festival, *and* Country Feedback. *She facilitates a poetry workshop with Jeff Pearson, a Just Journaling writing group, and a fiction critique group with Linda Johnson at Danner's Bookstore in Muncie, Indiana where she lives. She is co-director of the Humpback Artists and Poetry Festival with Jeff Pearson.*

Jessie Bland pulled into the parking lot beside the big ugly prison building and leaned her head back against the seat. *Three more weeks until the term is over. Three weeks until John is released. Providing, of course, he doesn't get into any trouble. St. Jude, if you exist...or is it St. Dismiss?*

She let out a deep sigh and got out of the car, opened the trunk, put purse, metal objects, everything but her car keys in the lock box she kept there.

Oh God, St. Jude, I forgot. Watch after him when he gets out.

Then she put her poetry books, papers she had graded and lesson plans into her book cart, slammed the trunk shut and walked up the sidewalk, pushing the cart to the prison entrance.

"Hi, Jessie. When do you think you'll be ready to start testing?" asked Peggy, her teaching partner and best friend.

"I don't know. I guess next week, so I can grade before the term is out."

"Still worried about your student?"

"I worry about all of them, but him..."

"I know, he's special. We all have one."

"I think he could make it back on the outside if he doesn't do something stupid."

"If he doesn't do something stupid,' is the mantra we all say when they get out of here. It's what we all hope won't happen. You need a break. How about coming to work with me at the American Business Women's Association's booth at the 500 race?"

"I don't like races."

"You won't see one. You'll be selling souvenirs."

"I could be reading."

"It's for women's scholarships. And you don't have to go race day. We can go Pole Day."

"Pole Day? Interesting. I keep hearing about it from one of my students."

"*The* student?"

"*The* student. I'm busy that day."

"You don't know what day. You need a life."

They went through the prison search and walked to the classroom section of the prison.

Once inside the classroom, Jessie set the papers on her desk and looked over her class. Orange uniforms made them look like novice Buddhist monks. They had prison tattoos in vivid shades of green, red and black that crept out of their necks and wrists like vines crawling all over their bodies. This body art placed them in the tangled justice web of the court system. She had no illusions they were bad boys. Some, however, had begun to realize it and were desperately trying to do penance. Some men, like John, were going to get a release. Others were trying to write poems to convince the younger generation not to walk the path they walked. She knew her St. Jude prayer-student wanted revenge. She shivered.

She began to pass out papers. John walked into the room, winked at her, and then sat down.

"You did well on this essay," she said. "How you were framed was well-written. I wonder about the redemption. A little too thick."

John just nodded and smiled as he placed his books on his desk.

"Thank you," was all he said.

She wondered what was going on in that mind. What thoughts were rolling around the synapses like pinballs rolling around the pinball machine he had told her he liked to play when he was "outside?" She went to the front of the room and began to write three suggestions for poems on the board. She turned to face the class. He smiled at her. The class looked first at her, then at him. *God, even they know how worried I am about him. No secrets in prison. Even for the instructors. They knew he was one of her favorites. But... she looked them over... they all know I would stand up for each of them. She knew they understood she believed in each one of them, even the lifers.* Always honest with them, she had fought to get them into the prison college program. To keep them studying and working, she would have moved heaven and earth.

John Cavenal was a special case. She had always believed in his innocence and had helped him with the Law Library assignments that enabled him to obtain his soon-to-be release.

"I have only two more transition classes, then I'm gone," John told her.

"Where will you go?" *Did her voice falter just a wee bit? Was it overly curious?*

"Home... Indy. If it goes well, I'll get out in time for the 500. Maybe get to go to Pole Day."

"What is Pole Day? You write about it, Peggy talks about it."

"When the fastest driver and car gets the Pole position for the race. The front place. That can give him an advantage."

"Or her."

"I forgot again. Her."

"Things have changed a great deal since you've been here."

He smiled and nodded. *He didn't think he would like all the changes on the outside. Maybe that's why some guys came back. They couldn't stand change. Well, by God, he'd get used to change. He was never coming back.*

"Is it that important, I mean, for you to be there?"

"Yes, until I went in this last time, I never missed Pole Day." *He didn't want to tell her how important it was this year.*

"Your stories and poems suggest the interest in Pole Day is more than just racing."

"It's not exactly just an interest. It's something too important. Pole Day. I don't know how to write about it. I like the party and the excitement. OK. I bet on who would win the prized position. I didn't care except if I won. This year it's just something I have to do."

She looked at him, giving him her teacher look. *It was more her reading-his-mind look.*

"What do you have to do on Pole Day?"

"Just go and sit back."

"No. What else do you have to do? Don't lie to me. I've been your English instructor for four years. Your writing tells me why you're here."

"Then you know why I like Pole Day."

"I know of one reason you don't like Pole Day." The men in the class were barely breathing. No one was moving, scratching his arm, or even fiddling with a pencil. They were waiting.

John looked at her for a long time. *Damn. Did he write that, too? She had this sweet, baby-wise face. Her soft voice gave them ideas for their themes when she taught. He was always a sucker for women. Damn again. But ole baby-face had a mind like a steel trap. It would never let him forget his promises to her or the threats he might have tried to conceal in his fiction writing.*

"OK. Maybe…just maybe, I can prove my innocence. Even though you're not allowed to talk to me about it."

"You wrote about it. I'm giving you writing advice. Don't con me, mister. You will never be a better con artist than a schoolteacher. Of my generation, anyway. We've seen it all."

"OK. If, and I say if, I nose around and find out anything about who might have done the deed that got me in here, I intend to tell my probation officer. Who knows? Oh, by the way, she knows that I'll be going to the track and working at the 500 on Pole Day, and every other weekend, including race day, if they need me."

"No booze. Probation."

"I know. I just want to be there. The sun shining on me. Be free, drink pop, smoke when and where I want. Walk. Roam. The track on Pole Day is one big party. I can afford it. It's just $10.00 to get in that day. I'm going to work for a guy that has a concession stand. They give free passes when you work. I won't have to pay, but no play. They give away all kinds of free merchandise. I'll be free," he said.

"Make sure you stay that way," she said as she handed out more papers. "By the way, you can't smoke when and where anymore. And if it doesn't quit raining, you don't have to worry about missing the sun." *What else could she say? All she had left was a teacher's prayer for his…what? Safety? Staying out of trouble? Finding the guys whom he thought had framed him?*

"Write three poems," was all she said.

She sat down and watched them as they wrote. *I want to be clairvoyant, just for a few days, God, St. Jude. Whoever listens to these things.*

She picked up a theme she'd been saving and began to read as she waited for them to finish their poems.

The Prison Experience, or How I Lost My Innocence
By John Cavenal

My decline into prison started in this bar when I sat down beside this man about my size whose face looked as if it had been used for dartboard tournaments. Some of the chiseled marks were still pink and fresh. The man just stared ahead. I thought maybe his brain was also pox-marked.

He bought me a drink because he said his old man told him to be kind to strangers. We drank a lot before we left The Sleazy Bar. I swear to God, that was the name of the bar.

We got in a car and I almost passed out in the back seat, but all at once some black-headed woman with a mean and evil look in her eye got in the car beside me. My drink-buying buddy said it was his mom. I did pass out then. I'd come to and she was patting me down.

Someone started singing. They asked me to sing along. I just kept passing out and coming to, over and over. Once someone put a beer in my hand and said drink. It was the foulest-tasting stuff I ever tasted. Guess what? It had something in it and I really went to la-la land this time.

Then I heard police sirens. Cops pulled me out of the car. They searched me. They found a gun. They showed it to me. Waved it in my face. I hate guns. I was terri-fied.

They found some jewelry in my pocket. Stolen, they said, in a robbery. Then they read me my rights.

Jeez, Louise, if I ever stole jewelry I would have more sense than to put it in my own pocket. Still, I was drunk. For a long time, I thought maybe I did it.

Jessie laid the paper on the desk. She picked up the next page.

My lawyer didn't even try to defend me. How could he? I didn't know what had happened that night. They wanted to know where I had stashed the jewels. "What jewels?" I asked them.

I found out later that the money and jewels had belonged to someone at the track. Out-of-towners come to the race for a good time, all the time. They stash their jewels in their rooms at hotels or wear it to the track with them to show off in those fancy suites. Then they wonder why they get robbed.

It took me seven years of sleepless nights in prison, trying to reconstruct what happened that last Pole Day I had been free.

That was the first theme he had written for her junior class.

"You have 45 minutes to finish the poems." She looked at all their faces, then picked up the next theme. She knew it by heart, but she was searching for something, some way to understand Pole Day.

I Investigate
by John Cavenal

For a long time I couldn't remember why I was drunk. I'd won a bet about something on Pole Day. I still can't remember what.

When I first arrived in jail, I really thought I'd done the robbery. The excitement of winning something, and the booze had made me overcome my fear of guns. Then I talked this over with my cellmate. He recognized the man with the scars on his face. He said it was someone called Baby Boy Wayne and his Ma.

"They pull that scheme all the time. I remember readin' about the robbery in the paper."

My cellmate told me to check the files on the microfiche. Then he told me the most important thing I ever heard. He told me to get my GED, use the library and apply for college classes.

Now, because of that cellmate and my teacher, Mrs. Jessie Brand, I'm getting out soon. I want to remember a good Pole Day. The rush, the excitement, the cars.

The sound of those cars. I haven't heard them for so long. God, I love those sounds: people laughing, music from everywhere, the live bands, speakers, boom boxes. The couples dancing, women wearing shorts and halter tops. God. The wild clothes. The smell of hot dogs, pizza. Beer everywhere. A whole damn festival of fun. I want that again. When I get out.

She looked up. John was watching her. He knew she was getting his papers ready for him to take with him when he left. Was he trying to remember what he had written in two years of themes in advanced composition class?

John was the last to leave class, and he placed his poem on top of the stack. He winked as he strutted out.

She waited until the door closed, then turned to the stack to read his poems. He only wrote two.

Revenge
They told me
Revenge is a dish best served cold
I wonder, Will ten years be enough
To make me cold?

The Reaper
The reaper walks the streets of the city.
Glides through prison walls
Lives on thoughts of hatred
Follows to the gallows
Or speeds out the walls that hold me here
Meets me on the race track
Stalks with me under bleachers
Rides in cars that collide
Becomes the enforcer on Pole Day.

Oh, my God, he is going to do it. How am I going to get to Pole Day? Then she remembered. What was it Peg had asked her just this morning? About good old Pole Day? She turned down the offer. But hey, people could always use help on race day or, she smiled a grim reaper smile, on Pole Day.

She gathered up her books slowly and tried to think like John. He was up to something. *What, and how could she stop it?* She was going to Pole Day.

It was still raining when he went back to his place, just like this morning. It had been three weeks of rainy days. When the day arrived for his release he wanted the sun to be shining.

Manny the Trader came up to him, looked around as he continued mopping the floor. Manny ran a big outfit inside the joint and outside. He traded information, fenced illegal merchandise and protection. His specialty was enforcing his own rules. Sometimes he rented out this expertise.

"I hear you're gettin' out in a few weeks."

"Yeah, I am."

"And lookin' for Big Mama and her baby boy."

"You know anything?"

"They just pulled a job. Friend of mine fences the stuff."

"You don't say?"

"Still got it, under the counter, so to speak."

"That a fact?"

"Yep. For a small fee, I can put you in touch with the information you need. Maybe a lot more than you need." He raised his eyebrows and turned from looking at John as he mopped. He concentrated on his mopping as two guards walked by. John became absorbed in mopping in the opposite direction. Manny was the complete prison link to the outside. No one knew how.

"What kind of fee?" *Dear God, I hope it's not what I think. I can do no more... Manny had been here a long time. Still....*

"I don't have library privileges. I want a college degree."

"OK." *This was beginning to sound promising. Maybe something he could handle, except he knew from the prison grapevine that Manny could add up the proceeds from a job or scam faster than a computer. But he couldn't read a stop sign.*

"I see."

"I need you to research my case. You gettin' out and all, maybe you could find me a way to get me into the college program. Fact is, John, I don't know nothin'."

"That a fact?"

"Yeah. My daughter's in the smart kids' class."

"Gifted program?"

"That's it. She comes to see me and I don't know how to talk to her."

John nodded. He'd been there.

"I figure if I get into the college program, we can talk on the same level."

He smiled and nodded his head. This long speech had been an effort.

"She graduates high school in six years. I want to be out for that and have a degree, so I can get a straight job and pay for her college and be..."

"I know. A role model or good dad." *Manny had a daughter, something to file away for another trade someday.*

"Yeah. What's a role model?"

"Someone you look up to. First you need to get more library privileges. Study for your GED." He paused unsure of how to go on. His life could hang in the balance if he wasn't real careful with the wording.

"What?"

"The GED, library time and some good trading may get you into the college program. You can't do nothin' wrong, ever."

"And?"

"You've got to study. I can help with that. Tutors and teachers can help."

"So?"

"Having done that, getting out with your record in that amount of time is hard. Might not be possible."

"I was afraid of that. But I heard you would tell me the truth."

"Now if you get into the library, you can study the law books and maybe find some kind of something to get a new trial or an appeal. How long before you can get into the GED program?"

"About six more months, they said. Can you help me? I'm a lifer. Longterm lifer. If you get my drift."

"GED is time off."

"Right now I just want to talk to her."

He looked at Manny long and hard for a while. *Dear God, what was he getting into? Maybe he would need the enforcer guys. Manny was The Enforcer Guy. Jeez...*

"Manny, I think we can deal." *His part might be a piece of cake. Could ole Manny come through for him?*

For the next few days, John and Manny mopped the floor as close together as they dared.

"Listen to me. Big Mama and Baby Boy hang out at Pole Day, every year," Manny said.

"That a fact?"

"Did you know they always get a suite?"

John looked surprised. He stopped mopping.

"Mop."

John mopped. "How do you know that?"

"Got ways, man. I got lots of ways." *God, did he have ways.*

The last day before John got out, they were in the exercise yard, and the sun was just hanging there behind a rain cloud, peeking out when no one was looking. John was leaning against the fence. Manny walked by.

"My friend has the merchandise ready."

John barely nodded.

"When you get off the bus in Indy, have a cup of coffee in the bus stop waiting room. You'll get the claim check for the pawn shop then. You've done me good so far. I got limited library now. I'm on the GED list. Just keep it coming. You have to lead me step by step. Like pulling a good bank job."

"OK." *I have no idea what a bad bank job is.* "How do I send this information to you?"

"Man at the coffeehouse will help you a bit there." Manny walked away.

It started raining before they went inside. John hoped it would stop, but it was still raining the next day when he walked out of prison a free man.

Thursday he caught the bus into Indianapolis and began the trip from one rainy, cold place to another. Home of the Speedway track where the same cold rain was still pouring. He knew because the bus driver took it on himself to become the weather forecaster for the passengers.

It was 6:30 a.m. on Pole Day, and Peggy, Jessie and the other volunteers working the souvenir booths were unloading their Coke coolers, chairs and sleepy bodies into the souvenir booth.

"You guys have to tell me what to do. I don't have a clue." *I'm only here to keep John from doing someone in.*

"We won't be doing much, not in this rain, I can tell you that." Peggy handed her another Coke cooler to put in the small storage room in the portable souvenir trailer.

"We've got enough food here to take care of all the silly people who come to Pole Day in this rain."

"Whenever you women get tired of unloading your junk, we could use help in here putting out the sweatshirts." This voice from Bess, the organizer of the expedition, reverberated from inside the booth.

Jessie went inside and began taking sweatshirts out of the box. It was while she was folding them that she saw this guy hurry by in a sweat suit, hood pulled down over his eyes, hands in his pockets, carrying a Coke cooler. He looked very cold. *Because he'd spent the long cold winters inside a warm building!*

"Buy some gloves, mister? You look very cold." Her voice dripped with honey.

John put his head down and just kept walking. She recognized that walk and just smiled like a man from the tax office. *Got to follow him.*

"I'm freezing. No customers. Can we walk around to get warm? I need coffee."

"OK. Let's go."

They walked and walked. Keeping John in sight, Jessie looked around in amazement.

"I had no idea the place was so big." There were booths like the one she and Peg just left. Food booths, souvenir booths, most with volunteers for non-profit organizations that used the money for philanthropic projects like scholarships, food, clothing and shelters for the needy. This city was in a pavilion that surrounded the track under bleachers, in front of bleachers and scattered beneath the suites.

"Coffee," she and Peggy said at the same time. She was sipping the coffee when she saw the elevators. "Look," she elbowed Peggy. "Those must take you to the rich folks' seats in the suites."

"Guarded, too, from us common folks."

Out of the corner of her eye, Jessie saw John walking toward the elevators. He stopped, turned and went into the restroom.

"Peggy, I'm going to stand in the freebie line. Free DVD's of past races." She started toward the line, watching the restroom all the time.

"You've never seen a race, why do you want a DVD of one?"

"Background, to learn." She kept her eyes on the restroom.

"Now that you mention it, why did you all of a sudden beg to volunteer?"

"You needed help here."

"You sounded desperate."

"I live in Indiana, time I learned about the 500." To change the subject, she asked, "Those the suites?" She was looking up, when out of the corner of her eye she saw someone emerge from the restroom. Not John, it was a man in a service outfit. One of the catering service volunteers.

"Those suites look like prison cells."

"Oh, honey," the woman in back of her said. "They are so luxurious, we stayed in one last year. The company paid."

She watched the service worker take a tray off the food cart that was rolling by. Did they have to check in or something? Then he walked over to the elevator. Up he went.

The line to get the free DVD's went slowly. She watched the upstairs folks as they talked to each other while leaning against the buildings, laughing and drinking out of long-stemmed glasses. She hoped they were plastic. Everyone in the whole place was having a party while waiting for the rain to stop and the race to begin. She saw the food service worker walk down the runway outside the suites, carrying a tray.

It was John. She would recognize that strut anywhere. He went to the first suite and knocked on the door and was admitted. She watched in horror. *Was he really working for someone? Was she witnessing his revenge? Whatever it was?*

"Hey, wake up, the man is handing you your DVD. You know, the one you wanted so badly."

"Thanks." She took the flat box, still watching the suite.

"You seem fascinated by those things up there."

"I can't get over how much they look like prison cells."

"Maybe you need a vacation."

Just then John came out of the suite, shut the door and began walking down the walkway to the elevator. Slow and easy like he did in prison when he strutted down the hall between classes.

So she was paranoid. He was working here, just delivering food to rich people. Like he said, enjoying the day. She sighed, sipping the last of her coffee. She and Peggy started strolling to the next line. People were talking and looking at things in giveaway lines and on tables.

"Excuse me, ma'am," said a young man carrying a uniform, as he cut between her and Peg.

"There's a restroom right there," she said as she pointed to the restroom John had used.

"You can't change company uniforms in the public restroom. We have to use a special one," he said.

"Oh," she said. Just then, she saw John entering the same men's restroom. The man behind her sprinted past it. She slowed her walk, dropped her empty cup into the trash can and watched the door as Peggy talked on about the Scottish Highlander band that came marching into the pavilion.

She nodded. She was listening to the bagpipes, watching the band with one eye, the restroom door with the other. *I'm going to get a headache.* Just then John came out the door in the same blue hooded sweatshirt, minus the Coke cooler, wearing the gloves.

He walked right past her, winked and moved into a faster strut. It started to rain again.

"Come on, Peg. They'll be wanting us back, I bet, to close up."

She took off at a fast dog trot, weaving in between the people watching the band. *What had John done?*

"What is the hurry?"

Peggy was trying to keep up with her. *Did John know she was behind him?*

John was scurrying as fast as his little strut would allow him. He walked faster, slipping in and out of open booths, mingling with other race fans hurrying to get away from the rain.

Jessie speeded up, looking around for John's darting form. *Did he rob someone? Did he find whoever had set him up and kill them?*

"Jessie what is with you—one minute the freebie line, the next a marathon run?"

"See, they're closing up now."

"Yeah. I bet we're in trouble."

Jessie kept John in sight all the way to the booth. He wove between clumps of people like he was a needle pulling thread. He slid around bicycles and golf carts like he was on a skateboard.

Jessie was breathing hard. *Why was he in a hurry? What had he done?*

"They've closed up the booth," Peggy said.

"There they are, waiting for us."

"Hurry up. We're taking the money to the bank," Beth said.

Jessie was grabbing stuff to hand to Peggy when she saw him. He was going down the lane to the exit.

She held her breath until he was out of the lane. She could see him slowing down. Then he disappeared from sight.

Sirens started screeching from all over the racetrack.

"My God, what is that?" Peggy said as she handed her a cooler.

A security guard standing by said, "There's been a murder or a robbery or worse. Terrorists maybe." Then he put his whistle in his mouth and blew hard.

Gates started closing. All the track parking areas and walkways were flooded with police. They began to search people.

A track security car drove by. "There's been a robbery," the driver said.

I knew it!

Another security guard walked by.

"Where was the robbery?" asked Jessie

"Our friends just went to turn in the money," explained Peggy.

"Naw. They're all right. It had somethin' to do with the suites. There's always somethin' with the suites."

An announcement came over the loudspeaker. "You can open the gates now."

A security shuttle came by.

"Hi. Did they catch someone?" asked Jessie, thinking of the suites.

"You'll never believe it. We caught these jewel thieves, Big Mama and Baby Boy Wayne in a suite with the loot from last week's jewel robbery.

"What suite were they in?"

"The one over where they pass out the free gifts. Band plays there a lot."

Jessie smiled, picked up her Coke cooler and chair, smiled again and said, "Isn't it a wonderful, beautiful day?" The rain pounded down in her face. "Oh, who won the pole place thing?" Peggy just shook her head. They began walking to the car.

It Almost Made History

by Phil Dunlap

The date: May 31, 1967. The place: the Indianapolis Motor Speedway. The driver of the number 40 STP Turbine racer: former Indy 500 winner, Rufus Parnell "Parnelli" Jones. By all accounts, this car was poised to turn the racing world on its ear.

In 1963 Parnelli won the big one, the Indianapolis 500. In 1965, he placed second and then failed to finish the 1966 race due to mechanical problems. He'd won the USAC stockcar championship in 1964. He'd also won the Pikes Peak Climb twice. That said plenty about this accomplished driver. What else was there to say? He decided to retire from racing.

But when opportunity knocked on the door of this consummate racer, he answered. In 1967 he was asked by the Granatelli brothers, Andy, Vince and Joe, to drive their radical new turbine-powered design in the Indy race. The USAC rulebook allowed such a design, but no one had tried it before. And there was much excitement surrounding the car that "whooshed" around the track like it was on rails. What a departure it was from the earsplitting roar of gasoline-powered, reciprocating engines.

The 1967 Memorial Day 500 was rained out after only nineteen laps, forcing a restart the next day, after the weather broke. Parnelli and the turbine were on a tear, leading 171 laps, and it looked like nothing could beat the rocket on rubber. Nothing that is, except the failure of a $6.00 bearing three laps short of the finish line. Parnelli coasted to a disappointing sixth place finish.

Joe Leonard, Art Pollard, and Graham Hill each drove turbine cars in the 1968 race and each experienced similar misfortunes. It marked the end of a grand experiment. In 1969 USAC changed the air inlet rules, effectively excluding turbine engines from the 500.

Death of a Best Friend

by P.J. Robertson

P.J. Robertson lives in South Central Indiana with her husband and four dogs. She spends her time playing with the dogs, searching for antiques, reading, and trying to find time to work on her writing. Her short stories have appeared in Derby Rotten Scoundrels *"The Long Shot", and* Low Down and Derby *"Orinoco", both published by Silver Dagger Mysteries.*

"Sorry I couldn't provide a murder or two to spice things up during *this* race," I said straight-faced, referring to the murder of a jockey Jake and I had witnessed during my first Kentucky Derby earlier in the month. My companion, Jake Carter, an investigator for the Major Crimes Unit in Louisville, had led the team that solved that crime.

He looked at me seriously for a moment before a grin appeared, revealing dimples in each tanned cheek and laugh lines crinkling the corner of each eye. He winked. "Can't say I don't show a lady a good time when she comes to my town." Then his face sobered. "Truthfully, C.J., I'm glad we missed any fatalities today, intentional or accidental. The race was exciting enough as it was. Thank you for bringing me." He hefted the bags weighed down with our water bottles, dish, blanket and other dog supplies.

We'd waited for some of the masses to disperse from the Indianapolis Motor Speedway before we'd left the handicapped seating area. Crowds were difficult for my assistance dog, Oliver, and I to negotiate. As we left the racetrack behind, he stayed close by my side, and my hand cradled the handle of his harness to steady myself. My balance was unpredictable and the dog served to steady me. He was also trained to brace himself so I could use him to help regain my feet if I fell. Happy to be moving after hours spent crouched beside me, his stub of a tail moved to a tune only he could hear as we crossed busy streets where police directed race-goers pulling from parking areas and side streets onto the crowded thoroughfares. We headed for a grassy area where he could relieve himself.

The sounds of revelry and traffic paled in comparison to the roar of Indy cars and fans that had caused our ears to ring during the race itself. Foot traffic thinned as we started down

156

30th Street, past the legions of cars, trucks and motor homes waiting to blend into the traffic on the main streets. Nearly every yard sported a sign offering parking, for a price. Some signs were professionally lettered, most were simply brushstrokes on wood or cardboard. Some were ancient, and I wondered how many decades these same signs had been pulled from the garages and put into place; how many race goers had the signs seen pass over the years?

Early that morning, we'd parked our car in Jake's old friend's driveway and walked the several blocks to the track. Now we were reversing our way toward Tom Gage's house, salivating at the thought of the barbecue we'd been promised. Tom had been on duty all day—all area police officers were on duty when the Indy 500 was taking place, even homicide detectives, but he'd hoped to be home in time to join his family and friends for their annual cookout. For the first year, Jake and I would be joining them.

I picked my way carefully along the cement, watching my feet rather than where we were heading, as the sidewalks were cracked and lifted from the soil freezing and thawing over the years, plus a few tree roots tunneling underneath. So I was surprised when Jake pointed out the flashing light bars on the police cars filling the street ahead, the evidence van, and the obligatory cluster of people blocking our way.

We slowed and watched the activity that seemed to center on a beat-up Honda parked beside a swaybacked garage. Paint that had once been white or gray or some other nondescript neutral tone barely covered the aluminum siding cloaking the home and attached garage; I could see bare metal in places. Vivid yellow dandelions scattered sunlight along the gravel drive. Rust and gray duct tape were the predominant colors of the old Honda, although traces of faded red showed here and there. The driver's side door hung open, and even from here we could hear the buzz of flies swarming around the still form within.

Beside the car, a dark-haired man in a wrinkled suit and a loosened tie stood issuing orders to a small group of uniformed police officers. "Isn't that Tom?" I whispered.

"Uh-uh, looks like the cookout will have to wait. Wonder what's up?"

We approached the yellow crime scene tape and stood quietly, waiting for Tom to notice us. Eventually he did. A man and woman accompanied by a hairy black Bouvier des Flandres were hard to ignore.

Tom walked over to us. "Well, Jake, how are your barbecue skills? I called Heather and told her to start the grill. You'll have to take my place. I've no idea how long I'll be here—some old man's dead. A head wound—probably moved to the car after he died—not much blood. We're trying to get some search dogs over here to backtrack the man, if they can after all the cars and people who've wandered through this yard today. Unfortunately, the only ones in the area are out tracking a toddler who walked away from the family's picnic, so it may be a while."

Jake glanced at me, and I took the look for approval, so I volunteered, "Tom, Oliver can track, and I've taught him to backtrack, just as a game. I can't guarantee anything, but we're willing to try, if you're okay with it."

Tom hesitated, and Jake spoke up. "I've heard about Oliver's tracking ability, both from my sister and the sheriff down where C.J. lives. Seems to me it's worth a try."

Raising the yellow tape, Tom motioned us through. "See what you can do. Might save us some time. And thanks," he added belatedly. He didn't look optimistic.

I rummaged through the bag Jake carried for me and brought out a handful of soft treats and a long fabric leash. "Tom, can Jake put our bags somewhere out of the way?"

Tom threw Jake a set of keys. "Put 'em in the back of my car."

While Jake took our bags to the car, I clipped the long line to Oliver's harness and stuffed the short lead in my pocket. "Come on, Ollie. Let's track."

The dog's dark eyes sparkled and his body quivered as he waited for me to tell him what to do next. He loved to play games, and to him, tracking was a game. I didn't know how he'd handle the scent of blood, but it wouldn't be the first dead body he'd sniffed. And face it, gross as it seems, dogs tend to be drawn to dead animals—any dead animal, including homo sapiens.

We followed Tom to the open door of the Honda. "Who found him?"

Tom nodded at the black SUV parked next to the red car, "Some guy came to get his vehicle after the race and noticed the man in the next one over had blood on his clothes. After we questioned him, we let him go home; he wasn't feeling any too good as it was—day in the hot sun, a few beers, and finding a dead body. Good thing he called us—hate to think what the body would have been like after a few more hours in this heat."

I'd rather not think in those terms. Sometimes I did research into crimes for people, and I'd found more than my share of bodies, but I'd not become as inured to it as these police officers who worked with death on a daily basis.

"May I have something from the man for the dog to sniff?"

Tom handed me a pair of thin latex gloves and motioned toward the body. "Take your pick; the techs are done until the body's moved. We're waiting on the coroner before we can do that."

I brought Oliver close to the body of an elderly African American male. He probably wasn't very big to begin with, but now he looked like an elf napping behind the wheel, a gnome with muscular arms and a cotton tonsure encircling his head. The rank metallic odor of blood reached out and threatened to gag me. Swallowing, I pointed to the man's hand dangling over the seat's edge, and urged, "Sniff, Ollie. Sniff the man."

The dog turned dark eyes to me, puzzled. His moist nostrils quivered at the strong scent of blood. He looked from me to the man, and then gently sniffed the man's hand.

"Good boy! Backtrack, come on, where did he come from?" I released the handle on his harness and held tightly to the long lead.

Ollie moved away a few feet, his nose near the ground. Then he trotted back to the car and sat looking from the slumped body to my face. "Good boy, there he is! Now search back." I motioned away from the car, in no specific direction.

This time, the dog stretched his neck until his black nose reached the man's chest. He inhaled, sneezed, and started away from the car, moving behind it and then along the passenger side, his nose searching the air and ground. He moved in the direction of the fence dividing the back yard from the front, then cut in front of the car and walked directly to a peeling white door set into the side of the garage. After sniffing at the threshold, Ollie tossed his head and gave an impatient bark. I stepped forward and tried the knob, but the door was locked.

"Can someone unlock the door?" I called over my shoulder.

"Let me check with the owner. He's told us to look around all we want." Tom walked off toward the front door of the ranch house. In a moment he returned with a key, unlocked the door for us, and stepped back. He was looking more interested and less pessimistic than before.

Oliver bounded inside and I followed, feeling along the doorframe for a light switch. A click and then a feeble glow from a single bulb hanging from the ceiling cast shadows everywhere. The garage smelled dank, even in the heat. An older sedan took up most of the room, while an old workbench ran the width of the building, guiding us toward a door at the top of a single step. Looking ahead, I nearly stumbled over my dog, stopped at a rolled rug wedged under the bench. Tom, Jake and a patrolman moved into the space and I motioned toward the rug. "Worth checking out?" They nodded affirmatively.

Ollie pawed at the rug until I pulled him away and reminded him "Back," then he headed toward the step into the house, nose down. After a quick knock on the door, I twisted the knob and pushed. Ollie stepped slowly into the small dining area and past a chrome dining set, its chair seats patched with duct tape. He picked up confidence, trotting into a crowded living room. An old man sat slumped in a wide-armed chair from the 1950s, its nubby beige upholstery worn and stained, polka-dotted with cigarette burns. The man's ropey arms were crossed, shielding his sunken chest. Faded blue eyes, red and watery, followed the dog's movements. The man's tapered fingers wore nicotine stains built up over a period of decades. His thin white hair lay lankly across his forehead, yellowed by years of cigarette smoke. Shoulders sagged under the thin white T-shirt. An empty ashtray sat on the end table beside a pair of silver-rimmed bifocals. An open beer can rested on one wide arm of the chair; a wooden cane with a rubber tip leaned against the other, partially obscuring the small oxygen canister topped by tubing.

Perpendicular to the chair, a matching sofa sat against the wall, facing a television set topped with a radio and numerous pictures. A blonde wood table with metal-tipped legs sat in front of the sofa, a rocking chair filled with pillows pulled to one side. Behind the rocker, a basket overflowed with dog balls and chew toys. A plush dog bed was pushed against the wall.

Barely glancing at the man, Oliver moved decisively across the room and stopped near the table. He sniffed the floor, and I commanded "leave it," as he started to lick the bare floorboards. His nose traveled to the nearest corner of the table, sharp and triangular, and then he sat.

"Tom, is that far enough, or do you need him to track further?"

"No, it's enough, I think."

Praising Oliver, I called him to me, offering a palmful of treats, and looked at the old man. Glancing at the kitchen doorway, I saw Tom and Jake staring at the table with its sharp corners, and at the spotless floorboards the dog had wanted to lick.

The old man leaned forward, his elbows resting on his knees, and began to speak, more to the dog than to any of us. "I killed them, my two best friends in all the world. I killed 'em both, sure as I'm sitt'n' here." He raised a shaking hand to dash tears from his eyes.

Tom held up his hand in an attempt to stop the man's words and began to recite the Miranda warning. Then, he called out to one of the uniformed officers and conferred with him briefly before turning back to us, a small notebook in his hand. He jotted a few notes.

"Mr. Selenski, is there a place we can talk privately? My men need to seal off this room while we wait for a search warrant. Maybe the bedroom?" At the old man's nod, Tom crossed the floor and helped him from the chair. Jake, Oliver and I followed the pair down a hallway. At the end, the old man turned right and sank down near the head of the double bed centered on the long outside wall. A double dresser, blonde and shiny like the coffee table, sat opposite. Matching bedside tables cluttered with more pictures, mostly framed snapshots, and small crystal lamps, flanked the bed. A chrome-and-vinyl chair, matching those in the kitchen, sat beside the dresser. Tom sank onto it while Jake, Ollie, and I remained in the doorway. Pulling out a small tape recorder, Tom placed it on the dresser, gave the date, time and name of those present. "Mr. Selenski, is it okay with you if I tape our talk?"

The old man shrugged. He opened a drawer on the nearest table, pulled out an unopened package of Camels and an ancient metal lighter. His hand shook so, it took several tries for him to get a grip on the silvery foil and tear open the pack. Once he had a cigarette in his mouth, he flicked the wheel on the lighter, but no flame appeared. Finally Tom stepped forward with a lit match and held it to the cigarette's tip. Mr. Selenski drew in the smoke from the cigarette as though it would be his last, then coughed a long wet cough. "I'm not supposed to smoke. Lung cancer, you know. Guess it don't matter much now."

"Why don't you tell us about killing your friends? Why did you kill Charles Avery?" Tom began.

The man sat and smoked and said nothing. Tears leaked from his eyes, ran down his wrinkled face, and dripped off his chin. "I killed him. Just put me in jail, it don't matter no more."

And that's all he would say. Tom tried to convince the old man to explain, but he sat there, hugging himself with his arms and smoking one cigarette after another as a torrent of tears washed his face.

Ollie whined and pulled away from me, so I let him go to the old man, then walked into the bedroom and asked permission to sit on the end of the bed, looking only to Mr. Selenski for permission. I could hear Jake and Tom murmuring behind me, but I focused on the elderly man who claimed to have killed his two best friends. Ollie sat on his haunches, putting first one, then two paws on the old man's leg. Mr. Selenski reached out to the dog, rubbing his ears and stroking his head, but stayed mute. Finally he stretched to the ashtray on the nightstand and stubbed out his last cigarette.

It was obvious there was a lot more to the story. I gave him a few seconds of silence, and then, before Tom could object, I asked, "How did it all start? Help us understand."

After a bit, he wiped his face on his shirt sleeve and looked over the pictures on his nightstand. Finally he selected three and laid them on the bed beside him. Picking up one, he handed it to me. "This is Tiny. She was about all I had left after my wife died—be ten years ago in November. We'd moved up from Kentucky and bought this house when I got on at the auto factory, but neither of us had kin around here, except our daughter and now her family.

A curly-haired toy poodle looked out at me from the photo. "She's a cutie," I said as I handed the picture back to him. "I'll bet she was a lot of company."

"Yes, she was. She and Charlie were about all that kept me alive. My daughter was having troubles of her own: her man sick, helping out with her grandkids, and missing her mother. I mean, she tried, but... Charlie worked at the auto plant too, and we'd become friends, way back. We fished a lot after we retired, went where we could take Tiny with us. Hung out at the bar down the street—they let me bring Tiny in if it wasn't crowded—and it never was." He smiled at the memory.

"When Tiny died 'bout a year ago, I thought maybe I wouldn't get another dog at my age. But my granddaughter, she volunteers at the shelter. She seemed to think I needed another buddy. When this little girl came in and no one claimed her, she put my name down for her." He handed me a second picture, one of a matted and filthy little dog. It was impossible to know what breed or breeds constituted her makeup, but dark eyes smiled from the mats, a black button nose hovered above the pink tongue that was busy licking the old man's hand as he held her. I could see the light reflecting off tears on his cheeks as he carried her from the shelter that day, frozen in time by his granddaughter's camera. "We didn't know what she was or where she came from, but the vet at the shelter thought she'd had puppies at least once before, and she had an infection in her female parts so maybe someone dumped her instead of paying to make her well. She was 'spaded' before she came to me, and she didn't have no problems after that. We named her Princess. My granddaughter said she'd take Princess if anything happened to me, so I thought it would be okay."

I murmured my encouragement as I handed back the second picture. It might be a long story, but we'd understand more, hearing it all. I just hoped Tom and Jake had the patience to let the old man tell the story his way. The floor creaked as Jake shifted his feet, but no one spoke.

Fresh tears fell as he handed over the third and last picture. In it, a freshly groomed Bichon wearing a jaunty pink bow smiled out from the old man's lap, her dark button eyes looking at the camera. "Here's Princess last week, after my daughter got her groomed for me. The groomer says she's a "bee shon." I never heard of 'em, but they're on them dog shows on television all the time, she says."

"She's beautiful. I noticed the dog bed and the toys in the living room and wondered where your dog was." I handed the picture back. "Where is she?"

The old man clasped the picture to his chest. His wheezing sounded bad, but he coughed for a long moment and then went on. I couldn't imagine this old fellow lasting a week in prison.

"Day 'fore yesterday, I let Princess out in the back yard to do her business. I go out with her—too many animals have disappeared from our neighborhood. Nobody knows for sure what happens to them, but they never git seen again so we have our suspicions. But the phone rang, and I was expecting a call from my doctor, so I hurried inside, fast as I was able, and grabbed it. Nobody was there, but when I got back outside, Princess was gone! I was pretty sure she couldn't have gotten under the fence, but I searched and called her name." The tears continued to fall. Ollie whined and licked the old man's creased cheek.

"I searched until dark. I hadn't been back in the house ten minutes when I got a call. A man said he had my dog and if I did what he said, I'd get her back. And if'n I didn't, he'd throw her in with his pit bulls and send back what was left in a box."

A gasp escaped me. I knew only too well how I'd feel if Oliver were missing and threatened, as he'd been not that many months ago. I dashed tears from my own eyes.

A uniformed officer leaned into the bedroom and handed Tom a sheet of paper without any words being exchanged. I became aware of the sounds of people moving about and speaking in low voices in other parts of the house.

"What did the man want?" Tom was leaving it up to me to get the story.

"I make a little extra money lett'n' people park in my yard during the races. Charlie and me, we usually go to the races together. Sometimes I bet a little on one of the drivers. The man told me to take all the money I took in from the parking and put it in a grocery sack and send it with Charlie. He'd be taking bets in one of the tents that sold souvenirs, he said. He described the tent and its location well enough I thought Charlie could find it, so I did what he said. He told me to stay home and wait for Princess."

"Did he use Charlie's name?" Tom interjected softly.

"No, he said the old geezer who was at my place all the time. I knew who he meant."

"So what went wrong?" I asked.

"I sent the money with Charlie and told him who to bet with and what driver to tell 'em. But Charlie, he came back early, when the car he'd bet on was real far ahead, and wanted me to listen to the race on the radio. He told me he'd put my money on that one too—had some inside information, he said. When he told me that, I knew he'd same as killed Princess and so I killed him. That's all there is to it."

"How much money did you send with Charlie, Mr. Selenski?" Tom asked.

"All of it. Dunno how much there was, but I have a double lot...." He shrugged. Lots of cars park here. It was a goodly amount."

"Do you usually bet it all?" Tom questioned.

"Nope, I usually just bet a little, save most for dog food and vet bills and such, but this year I sent it all, like he said."

"Didn't Charlie find it odd that you sent so much? Why didn't you tell him why you were doing it?" Now that the old man was talking, Tom took over the questioning.

"Cause the man on the phone told me not to. Said not to tell anyone or Princess would pay. Everyone knew Charlie never could keep a secret." The old man shook his head sadly. "If Charlie wondered, he didn't say so."

"Okay, so tell us how you killed him."

"Don't matter. Both Charlie and Princess are dead and it's my fault, and I don't care what you do to me."

By this time, Tom was standing and pacing the width of the room, from the door to the wall, past the foot of the bed. He was impatient but trying to get the full story. He stopped and tried another tack. "What did you do after you killed Charlie?"

"I took the betting slip he'd given me and I tried to go to the track. I thought if I could give the winning slip to the man, maybe he'd bring Princess back. I couldn't walk so far, so I took my car. The police wouldn't let me get to the parking area 'cause I didn't have a ticket. I did get close enough to notice that a lot of the vendors were tearing down their booths, so I figured it was too late. I came on home and hoped the man would call me to find out why I never sent the money." He stopped to croon to Oliver and pulled him tight against his chest. Ollie squirmed, but didn't pull away.

"Why didn't you go to the man's house, if you knew who he was?" I interjected.

The old man's face flushed. "I would've if I thought it would do any good. He's a bad man, ma'am. He'd just laugh at me, and it wouldn't help Princess none if I angered him. He raises pit bulls and teaches 'em to fight, I hear. There's a place near here where they fight them, or at least that's what I hear from the neighbors."

"Why did you put Charlie's body in his car?" Tom asked, changing the subject.

"I couldn't just leave him in the middle of my front room. Couldn't call the police in case the man came about Princess, and I thought no one would notice Charlie 'til later out there. I knew I had to move him before his body stiffened up like you see on TV, so I rolled the rug around him and managed to pull him out through the garage. Like to never got him into his car. Thought it'd kill me doing it, but knew Charlie would understand. I put all his stuff out there too." He lowered his face into the fur on Ollie's neck and began to sob. "Now it's too late. I've killed Princess too, and Charlie died for nothing."

The metal bedsprings made a squeaky sound as I rose and moved closer to the old man. Bending slightly and placing my hand on his arm, I gently asked, "Mr. Selenski, did you intend to kill Charlie for what he'd done?"

He shook his head, still nestled against my dog's fur. "No, ma'am, but I was so mad, I stood and shook my cane at him. He didn't realize what he'd done. He jumped back and slipped on that danged old rug of mine and hit his head on the corner of the coffee table. I couldn't believe he was dead, but he just lay there, and he wasn't breathing no more. He wouldn't get up..." He looked down at Ollie, a confused look on his face.

"Tom, I'd like your permission to call his daughter to come get him. Unless the autopsy shows something inconsistent with his story, I assume the prosecutor won't charge him. He did move the body—I realize it's a crime. But if he's charged, I'll help him hire the best attorney we can find. I don't think anyone is going to convict a dying old man for what was a tragic accident."

Tom nodded. "We don't have to take him anywhere right now. Long as we know where to find him, it will be okay. And thanks, C.J., for getting the whole story out of him. If there's anything I can do for you..."

I grinned at Jake, standing beside Tom. "There is. If I can find out who Mr. Selenski thinks stole his dog, I'd like to visit him. And I could use an escort."

Mr. Selenski didn't know the address, but he thought he could find where the man lived. I called his daughter, and while we waited for her to arrive, we all piled into Tom's unmarked car and drove to a house a few blocks from where we'd been all afternoon and into the evening.

Toys littered the yard, and other than a huge metal building nestled behind the one-car garage, this house looked little different from its neighbors. Oliver and I walked to the front door; the metal storm door was missing its screen and hanging from one hinge. We waited until Jake and Tom positioned themselves to one side, shielded from the doorway by some overgrown yews, before knocking at the door.

Muffled barks and deep growls erupted from the back yard, but I couldn't hear anyone approach the door. Just as I was ready to knock again, the door was yanked open and a burly dark-haired man in his thirties appeared there. His T-shirt bore an advertisement for a popular brand of beer and was pulled tight over a protruding stomach. If a man could look nine months pregnant, he did.

"Yeah?"

I plastered a big smile on my face and held out my hand. Surprisingly, he shook it before stepping back and reaching for the door, prepared to close it in my face.

"What do you want?"

"I've heard that you're a dog breeder and I wanted to introduce myself." I gestured to Ollie who stood quietly by my side. "Since I use an assistance dog, I often speak to breeders about donating a puppy to be raised as a guide or assistance dog. Do you think you'd be interested? What do you breed?"

A smirk appeared. "Oh, I don't think you'd want my pups. They aren't what you'd call friendly to people." He glanced down at Ollie. "That's a nice-looking dog. Bet he could hold his own in a fight. What breed is he?"

The thoughts of this man getting his hands on any of my breed or any other made my insides crawl, but I pushed these thoughts aside and looked down at my group-placing American Kennel Club Champion Bouvier des Flandres dog, sending him a silent apology. "Him? He's a mutt. Got him at a shelter. They thought there might be some schnauzer in him, maybe some sheepdog."

A high-pitched yelp came from another part of the house. A girl, perhaps kindergarten age, came running into the hall, a dirty white dog clutched tightly in her arms. Bruises ringed the girl's wrists and dotted her thin legs, exposed by her shorts and dirty tee. The dog was struggling to break free, but the child grasped her too tightly. I recognized the pink bow from the picture I'd been shown earlier, although now it was limp and drooped over one dark eye.

The dog scratched at the girl's chest. In desperation, she reached down and nipped the arm encircling her. As the dog slipped from her grasp, I bent forward and called, "Princess, Come!" She propelled herself into my outstretched arms and I quickly passed her to Jake who'd materialized behind me. A glance showed Jake hurrying toward Tom's car, where the old man struggled to pull himself from the back seat.

The girl began to scream and kick at the man's leg. "Daddy, you said I could keep her. She's mine!"

I wanted to smack her, but instead I took a deep breath and held the man's eye. "If any more animals go missing in this neighborhood, not only will the police be looking into it, the Department of Agriculture will be holding unannounced visits to your kennel." He pushed the child away from him, hard. She ricocheted off the wall before landing on her bottom, where she shrieked for her mother. He started forward, fists clenched, but found Oliver in front of me, teeth bared.

"Not to mention," I added, as Tom stepped up beside me, "the Internal Revenue Service will be interested in the money from dogfights and illegal betting that you almost certainly haven't paid taxes on." I smiled. "And there's always the Child Protective Service to harass you even further. I suggest you try to clean up your act, and soon."

Tom had one hand on his gun as we backed away from the doorway. We'd gone only a few feet when the wooden door banged shut, bouncing open again from the force. A woman's thin face, edged by straggly dishwater blonde hair, peered out and then quickly closed the door. We heard the lock engage as we headed to Tom's car.

We'd take a grateful Henry Selenski and his dog to meet his daughter, and then Tom could drop us by our car; he had paperwork to do and phone calls to make. Child Protective Services would be interested in what we'd witnessed, and if the Vice Squad hadn't been aware of the man's involvement in local dog fighting, they soon would be. And as I'd threatened, there was always the IRS.

I was starved. No barbecue for us, but maybe Jake and I could cadge some leftovers from Tom's wife before we headed back to Persimmon Creek. Tomorrow was another day, and we could relax before Jake headed back to Louisville.

Indianapolis 500 in Hollywood

by Andrea Smith

Hollywood is just as fascinated with the Indianapolis 500-Mile Race as Hoosiers. The race has been the subject of nine films and referenced countless times on television in commercials and other media. The first film to feature the race was *Racing Hearts*, released in 1922. While this silent film does not actually have the Indianapolis Speedway in it, the movie did feature some of its star drivers, including Jimmy Murphy and Ralph DePalma.

Speedway was made in 1929 and was filmed in part at the Indianapolis Speedway. It was the story of a cocky race car driver who falls in love with the daughter of an airplane manufacturer.

But perhaps the most memorable film was *Winning*, which starred Paul Newman and Joanne Woodward. The film is about a rising star on the race circuit who dreams of winning the big one—the Indianapolis 500. But to get there he runs the risk of losing his wife to his rival. Bobby Unser and Tony Hulman played themselves in the movie, and reviewers wrote that the racing sequences leading to the Indianapolis 500 were superbly staged.

Murder in the Snake Pit

by D.B. Reddick

D.B. Reddick is a policy analyst with a national insurance trade association and is busy at work on a cozy mystery featuring Candi and Mandy. He lives in Camby, Indiana.

"...And then there was that time in '81, when this guy was murdered in the snake pit."

Phil from Greenwood had been droning on for ten minutes about his memories of the Indy 500 when he dropped that bomb. Unfortunately, I was overdue for a commercial break. Believe it or not, we do sell airtime on my all-night radio talk show.

"Hang on, Phil. I've got to sell some stuff. But when we come back, I want to hear more."

My producer, Zach Berman, punched up the commercials from our second-floor control room, while I waited impatiently in the studio next door. It's no bigger than a phone booth and is used for news breaks during the day. Management doesn't want us using the main studio on the first floor that faces onto Monument Circle. They're afraid too many drunks will rap on the window at night if we do our show from there. I've worked in bigger studios in my career, but I have to say the computer equipment at WZMN-AM, News Talk Radio 790, is state-of-the-art.

Right now, though, none of that mattered. I was more interested in finding out if I'd heard Phil correctly. A murder in the snake pit? The pit used to have an "anything goes" reputation in its heyday, but murder? That seemed a little far-fetched. Maybe Phil was just spinning an urban yarn.

"Okay, folks, we're back," I said when the last commercial ended. "It's twenty after the hour. I'm Charley O'Brien. Before the break, Phil from Greenwood was telling us about a murder in the snake pit back in '81. Who was murdered?"

"Freddie Olds."

"Did you know him?"

"Nope."

"Anything more you want to say?"

"Don't know much more, Charley. Freddie's story didn't surface until a few days after the race. His family must have reported him missing. Anyway, the cops learned he'd been in the snake pit with some friends on race day, but nobody saw him leave. It was like he disappeared into thin air. The local TV stations had a field day. They showed nightly video clips of Boy Scout troops helping the cops look for Freddie in every nook and cranny. When the cops didn't find him after a week, the media lost interest and that was that."

"Sounds more like Freddie just disappeared."

"But word on the street has always been that he was murdered. The cops couldn't prove it, though. No body and no crime scene to speak of after a party like that. A sheriff's deputy I once knew told me the cops couldn't find any credible eyewitnesses. Nobody saw anything."

"Thanks for telling us that story, Phil."

Eight months ago, I moved back to Indy to start this all-night talk show after being away nearly thirty years. I grew up in the shadow of the Indianapolis Motor Speedway, and talk of a murder in the snake pit made me real curious. I wondered if any other listeners knew about Freddie Olds. I asked them and didn't have to wait long for an answer. Wayne McLean's name popped up on my computer.

"What's on your mind this morning, Wayne?"

"I knew Freddie Olds."

"You did? Tell us about him. Were you buddies?"

"Sort of. He used to date my sister, Margie. He treated her pretty good. For Valentine's Day, he even bought her some earrings that looked like fishing lures."

"The message on my computer screen says you're from the Westside. You probably went to the race every year, right? Remember seeing Freddie there in '81?"

"Yeah, we were all there. Me and my pals. Knockin' back a few out of the bed of my pal's pickup. Freddie and his pals were sittin' on a blue-striped couch next to us, eyeing the babes and having a few beers themselves."

"How'd that couch end up in the pit?"

"Bobby Matthews had it in his big red van. He was one of Freddie's pals."

"So when did Freddie disappear?"

"I don't know."

"What do you mean?"

"Didn't see the end of the race. I passed out with fifty laps to go. Must have been the heat and the cold beer. You gotta watch that when you have pale skin. My pals picked me up and tossed me in the back of their pickup. Didn't come to for three or four hours."

"Hmm. Did any of your friends see what happened to Freddie?"

"Nope. They were too busy talking to everybody who walked by and asked about me. 'Is he dead?' folks would say. 'He looks dead.' Pretty soon, my pals started telling everyone that I died from heat stroke. They were even gonna charge folks a quarter for a peek. How funny is that?"

"Pretty funny. Too bad about the heat stroke. I was hoping you'd help us solve the Freddie Olds mystery."

"Afraid I can't do that."

It was 1:35 a.m. Time for another two-minute commercial break. The Freddie Olds story was beginning to pique my interest. Even though Wayne hadn't been much help, at least he'd confirmed that Freddie was at the track in '81 with some guy named Bobby Matthews. That was a start, I guess.

When we went live again, Raymond from Indianapolis was holding on Line One.

"How can I help you this morning?"

"I just heard you talking to that guy, Wayne. Heard him telling you about Freddie Olds and all, so I thought I'd call, too."

"Great. What can you add to the story?"

"He was an okay dude. Freddie, that is. We used to work together. We were welders. Freddie was a guy who'd give you the T-shirt off his back. But he couldn't hold his liquor. When he got drunk, he'd do crazy things."

"What kind of crazy things?"

"He once told me how he got arrested for drag racing down Madison Avenue. Turns out the other car was an unmarked police cruiser. Stuff like that."

"Were you with him at the track in '81?"

"Naw, we never hung out much. I was married back then, and didn't drink neither. That day, I drove my old lady to a family reunion. Besides, I've never really liked Indy cars. I prefer NASCAR."

"What about Freddie's friend, Bobby Matthews? Know anything about him?"

"Never met the guy, but Freddie once told me that Bobby was a bad-ass dude. Apparently did time at Pendleton. Beat up a bartender real bad."

"Did Freddie disappear or was he murdered?"

"If I was a bettin' man, I'd say he was murdered."

Another vote for murder. This story definitely was getting better. It was beginning to sound like Freddie got crossways with somebody. All I needed now was to hear from someone who was there that day and saw what happened. Maybe this mystery might get solved after all.

"Hiiiiiiiiii, Charleeeeeee."

"Is this Candi from Indianapolis?"

Zach had typed her name across my computer screen.

"Yeah," she breathed heavily into the phone.

"Whoa, Candi. Turn down your radio. I'm getting too much feedback."

As Candi dropped her phone to fix the radio, I thought I heard someone in the background.

"Hi, Charley, it's me, Mandy. Did anyone ever tell you that you have a sexy voice? And I bet you're a real hunk, too."

I hated to shatter Mandy's fantasy, so I took the more chivalrous path and kept quiet, hoping Candi would come back on the line soon.

"I'm back, Charley."

"What's happening with you two lovely ladies this morning?"

"You're such a real sweet talker, Charley. No wonder Mandy's sitting here cooling her forehead with a beer bottle. We just left Pete's Hideaway Lounge on Lynhurst and flipped on the car radio. Heard you talking about poor Freddie Olds, so we decided to call."

"Did you know Freddie?"

"Hell, yes. Every girl on the Westside knew Freddie. He was a little bitty guy, but nobody seemed to notice, if you get my drift. And he was one damn fine kisser. He used to get me all fired up. What about you, Mandy?"

Great. Turns out Freddie was some kind of a love machine. I really wasn't interested in knowing that. I just wanted to find out if anybody saw him get murdered.

"Ladies, can I get you to focus on other parts of Freddie's personality?"

"Other parts. That's funny. Mandy, did you hear what Charley said? About Freddie's other parts."

I was beginning to think Candi and Mandy were a lost cause, when Candi piped up.

"We were there that day. We saw what happened to Freddie."

As Candi dropped that revelation, I heard Zach rap on the large picture window that separates the control room from my studio. I hadn't been watching the clock. Time for the Fox News feed at the top of the hour. Damn. I was afraid I'd lose Candi and Mandy if I put them on hold. Then I got an idea.

"Does Mandy own a cell phone?"

"Sure," Candi replied. "Why?"

"Cause I want to do a three way."

"Charleeeee!"

"Nothing like that. Have her call in like you did. Zach will patch her into our conversation so we can all talk at once. How's that?"

"Mandy, find your cell and call Charley."

Good. That should keep them busy during the ninety-second news break and the two minutes of commercials. I ran next door and told Zach to tape Candi and Mandy. I had a hunch that once they got talking, they might say something worthwhile about Freddie. I also took Maria Rodriguez's business card from my wallet and handed it to Zach. "Call and have her listen to the show." Maria is a homicide detective with the Indianapolis Metropolitan Police Department and an occasional dining companion.

I rushed back to my studio. In the interim, Mandy had found her phone, dialed our number and was hooked up with Candi and me.

"Okay, folks, we're back," I said. "Let's pick up where we left off. Ladies, tell me more about Freddie Olds being at the track in '81."

"He was pretty drunk," Mandy began. "He started passing out free beer to any girl who'd show him her assets."

"Where were you two?"

"Standing next to him, drinking a few free beers," Candi said. "Then Bobby Matthews gets mad. Says Freddie is giving away too much beer and there won't be enough left for them."

"What happened next?"

"Freddie starts mouthing back. Says he paid for part of the beer keg and he wants to look at some more assets."

"Then what?"

"Bobby jumps up off the couch and pushes Freddie to the ground. Then Freddie gets up and tries to wrestle with Bobby. They grab and clutch at each other and fall backward over the beer keg and the tub of ice it's sitting in."

"Yeah, then the whatchamacallit falls off the keg and beer starts spilling all over the ground."

"The whatchamacallit?"

"What's the name of that thing, Mandy?"

"You mean the doohickey?"

"Yeah, maybe that's what it's called."

"Ladies, can one of you please describe the whatchamacallit or doohickey?"

"It's that hard metal thing on top of the beer keg."

"The beer tap?"

"That's it."

"So the beer tap somehow comes loose."

"Yeah, beer is spilling all over the place," Mandy said. "Bobby picks up the doohickey and whacks Freddie over the head with it. Freddie falls down. Then Bobby walks over and fixes the keg like nothing happened."

"Yeah, everybody is pointing and laughing at poor Freddie," Candi said. "Bobby pours a beer on his head, but Freddie doesn't move. Bobby reaches down and pokes Freddie, but then Bobby jumps up and whispers something to his pals. Next thing you know, they hoist the couch in the van. Then they scoop up Freddie and throw him on top of the couch and take off."

"Did anybody do anything?"

"Wayne McLean's friends wandered over and picked up the beer keg and bucket of ice and threw it in their truck," Mandy said.

"What did you two do?"

"I can't remember exactly. Mandy, didn't we walk over and have a beer with Wayne's friends?"

"Yeah, and then we headed for the exit. The race was nearly over and we wanted to beat the crowd."

"Why didn't you call the police and tell them what happened to Freddie?"

"That he got whacked on the head by one of his pals?"

"You didn't think it was more serious than that?"

"What are you trying to say, Charley?" Candi said defensively. "That we aren't good citizens or whatever?"

"Nothing like that, I just thought that when you heard later how Freddie was reported missing, you might have called the cops and told them what you knew."

"We never listen to the news, Charley," Mandy said. "It's too depressing. Besides, why would we want to cross Bobby? He's a bad-ass. We once heard how he reached across a bar one night and cracked open a bartender's skull with an empty beer bottle 'cause the guy wouldn't serve him last call."

I looked up at the clock. It was 2:18 a.m. I'd been on the phone with Candi and Mandy for almost a half-hour. I was mentally drained. And with all that effort, I still didn't know if Freddie Olds had been murdered or if he simply had disappeared with a big lump on his head.

I thanked Candi and Mandy for their time, reminded Mandy that it was against station policy to date my listeners, and asked them to stay on the line so Zach could get their last names and home numbers. I figured that if anything came of our conversation, Maria would want to talk to them.

As I waited for the latest commercials to end, I rubbed my eyes before peering down at my computer. Was I reading Zach's message correctly? Bobby Matthews was holding on Line One.

"What's going on this morning, Bobby?" I said nonchalantly.

"You that Charley guy? Just got home from work. Wayne says he done called you a ways back. Says you a right nice feller. I shoulds call you and tell you about Freddie Olds myself."

"That's right. Was he a friend of yours?"

"You talkin' of Wayne?"

"Sure," I replied. I really didn't care how well Bobby knew Wayne McLean. I just wanted him to stay on the line and talk to me. "How long have you known him?"

"Probably thirty years. I used to date his sister, Margie, for a time. Me and Wayne are roomies now on account of how his old lady done throwed him out last month and I had an empty couch."

That was more than I really wanted to know. I took a deep breath and pressed on.

"Interesting, Bobby, but let me ask you. Were you at the track in '81? That's the year Bobby Unser won his third Indy 500 race."

"I remember that race. Them Unser boys were damn fine racers."

"Let me ask you another question. What kind of vehicle did you drive back then?"

"Big red van. Had large curly yellow waves on each side. Sure did. Why you askin'?"

"Just wondering. I had a yellow Corvair myself. Remember them? The engine was in the rear. A really dorky-looking car, but it was all I could afford. I was a DJ back then. I didn't make much money. But my Corvair got decent gas mileage. Wish I had her today with gas prices as high as they are."

"That's for damn sure. Hey, Charley, I gotta go."

Damn, I shouldn't have spent so much time trying to ease Bobby into a conversation about Freddie Olds. Now I'll probably never find out what he knew about Freddie's disappearance.

We went to another commercial break and took a few other calls before I noticed Bobby's name on my computer screen again.

"Is that you, Bobby? What happened?"

"I had to shake the worm and gets a beer. Workin' sure makes a feller thirsty."

178

"Let's pick up where we left off. You were telling us about your big red van. It must have been a real chick magnet. Bet you had a mattress in the back in case you got lucky with the ladies."

"Huh, I had a couch. Used it for love engagements, and then I'd pull it out at the drive-in."

"By the way, what color was it?"

"It had blue stripes."

"Wow, my neighbor's looking for a couch with blue stripes. Still got it?"

"Been thirty years, man. It's long gone."

"What did you do with it?"

"Why you askin'?"

"Just trying to make late-night conversation."

"Dumped it on my daddy's farm."

"Now, did I ask if you knew Freddie Olds?"

"You sure ask lots of questions. Me, Freddie and my pal, Pete Gibson, was tight."

"Somebody told me that you and Freddie were at the track in '81 and Freddie disappeared before the race was over."

"It were that shit, Wayne, weren't it? That big mouth. Mouths off when he's drunk. Can I say 'shit' on the radio?"

"Sorry, Bobby, you can't. The FCC is very anal when it comes to words like that. They love to fine us, but we have a 10-second taped delay system, so my producer caught it and bleeped you."

"You're taping me? I don't like that. I'm hanging up."

"No, no, Bobby. Don't do that. Calm down. We throw the tape away after every show."

I didn't hear anything on the other end of the line, but it didn't sound like Bobby had hung up. What's he doing now?

"Friggin' phone fell on the floor. What was we talkin' about? Right, that shit, Wayne."

"Wayne told me that he passed out during the race. His buddies threw him in the back of their pickup. Everybody thought he was dead. But Wayne said it was just heat stroke. Right, like I believe that."

"I remembers now. That silly little shit. Can't hold his liquor."

"What's that noise in the background?"

"A siren, dude."

Maria to the rescue? I decided to go ahead and ask the sixty-four-thousand-dollar question.

"Why did you whack Freddie over the head with a beer tap?"

"What?"

"And why did you leave the beer keg behind?"

"Man, you knows too much. I'm gonna kill that Wayne."

Bobby slammed down the phone. I didn't care. The sirens sounded even closer than before. I hoped Maria and her colleagues arrested him. I'd call her when my show ended at five and find out for sure. And I can already imagine our conversation.

"Why do you keep trying to solve every murder that happens in Indianapolis?" she'd ask. "I thought we'd straightened that out after the last murder. Remember? You agreed. I'm the crime fighter; you're the all-night talk show host."

"Yeah, right," I'd reply. "Let's go grab some breakfast."

The Gray Ghost

by Wanda Lou Willis

Ralph DePalma (1/23/1884 – 3/31/1956)

In motor racing circles, Italian-American race car driver DePalma is considered a true pioneer of the sport. He retired from racing with an astonishing record of 2,557 wins out of 2,889 races. In 1991 he was inducted into the International Motorsports Hall of Fame. His uncle, Pete DePaolo, won in 1925, the first race to average over 100 miles per hour.

DePalma's career began with racing motorcycles. In 1909 he switched to auto racing when the American Automobile Association established the national driving championship. He was immediately successful, winning the first Milwaukee Mile Championship Car Race in 1911.

His first race at the Indianapolis Speedway was in 1911, finishing in sixth place. His only win at the Speedway was in 1915 after having led 132 laps.

He's remembered more for the dramatic manner in which he lost the 1912 race than his 1915 win. Taking and holding the lead in the third lap, suddenly on the 199th lap and half way through the fourth turn, his car malfunctioned. He and his mechanic, Rupert Jeffkins, pushed his car, which would later be known as the "Gray Ghost," across the finish line to take twelfth place.

DePalma had a small role in a 1920 Hollywood film, *High Speed*, and was in the 1924 *Racing for Life*. He went on to establish a company in Detroit for the manufacture of race cars and engines for both automobiles and aircraft.

DePalma died in 1956 and is buried in Holy Cross Cemetery, Culver City, California.

Pre-Race Jiggers

by Wanda Lou Willis

Wanda Lou Willis is a folklore historian who specializes in Hoosier folktales and historic research. A popular presenter at schools, universities, libraries and historical societies, she has also been a guest on local TV stations as well as local, national and Canadian radio. In 2006 Wanda appeared in the docudrama, Central State, Asylum for the Insane. *She is the author of two books,* Haunted Hoosier Trails *and* More Haunted Hoosier Trails. *She is currently working on a third book.*

May dawned as it always does in Indiana—capriciously as a beautiful woman teasing promising pleasures and excitement that stirs the imagination, and yet, just like a budding romance, the weather would change, the days becoming gray and rain soaked.

That is how it started this year, and yet there was a sense of festivity and excitement. When the roar of the engines filled the air, the vagaries of May's weather did not dampen the spirit of the Indianapolis 500-mile race fans.

Before the day of the race, there are many events planned, and this year there would be even more in celebration of the fiftieth anniversary of the 500 Festival. There would be the Mini Marathon, the 500 Festival Parade, cocktail parties to cook outs, the gala Snakepit Ball and many thrilling pre-race track events.

I attended a late afternoon cocktail party at historic Tuckaway, once the home of George and Nellie Meier, an internationally renowned palmist of the early twentieth century. The Meiers loved parties and during their day hosted many. They would have been pleased to know that the current owner was continuing this tradition.

The day started with a bright sunlit sky as clear as a newborn's conscience. The guests, with drinks in hand, ventured outside to take advantage of the late-afternoon gentle spring breeze and sun. Suddenly a large dense dark cloud settled ominously in front of the sun, and the gentle breeze turned into a chilling wind. Without further warning, an intense spring storm erupted. Guests scurried back into the house as the wind-lashed rain beat down, accompanied by thunder and lightning. Within the house, the party continued with much laughter. Our host was kept busy mixing the Speedcity cocktails he had created especially for this occasion.

No one seemed to notice that the shades of night had fallen as the storm continued to rage. The rain pounded the windows and drummed on the roof. It was a night perfect for a fright. A flash of lightning seared across the dark sky. The lights began to flicker. Suddenly the house was plunged into darkness. Someone gasped, and then, dead silence.

The host asked everyone to be calm as he quickly struck a match; his face eerily lit from below sent a shiver up my spine as he began lighting candles. He next bent to the task of lighting the fireplace logs. Soon the house throughout was aglow. A swirling curtain of rain wrapped around the house, while within, the rooms glowed in the candle and firelight. As the wind buffeted the walls, the house sighed and creaked. The day you see, the night you hear.

A nervous voice asked, "Are you sure you didn't have someone pull the plug on purpose just to give us a fright?" Our host assured us that he would not dream of it, even though there was a legend that the house was haunted. Someone gave a nervous laugh. To ease the tension the host offered everyone another round of his special cocktail. At that point, the laughter and conversations resumed.

The room was not as dark as it would have been without the candles and the fireplace, but it was spooky. The flickering light created a multitude of strange, quivering shadows dancing their eerie pas de deux on the walls. Writhing fingers of flames pirouetted upward as shards of embers fell from the logs.

No one seemed to want to leave, especially while the storm continued. We all settled into the cozy convivial atmosphere, enjoying hors d'oeuvres and delicious Speedcity cocktails. The conversations centered on the 500-Mile race and the past winners — familiar and colorful names such as Ray Harroun who won the first race in 1911 in his Marmon Wasp; the 1919 winner, Howdy Wilcox; three-time winner Wilbur Shaw; A. J. Foyt and the Unser family. I enjoyed discussing my favorite race and the near win of the Gray Ghost in 1915. Ralph DePalma had run a smooth race, leading for nearly 196 laps in his

Mercedes Gray Ghost, when the car cracked a piston. With only two laps remaining, he and his mechanic pushed the car across the finish line to take twelfth place.

Suddenly a blood-chilling scream echoed through the house as one of the guest's wives ran down the stairs in near hysteria. "The house is haunted. I saw two ghosts. I am telling you I saw two ghosts."

Her husband caught her just as she started to fall. Sitting her in a chair, he began patting her hand, trying to calm her.

"I know what I saw. They were there and then they just disappeared into thin air. Ghosts! That is what they were. Ghosts!"

She had gone upstairs to the bathroom and then decided to walk onto the summer porch which overlooked the back gardens. With a loud crack, a blue-white bolt of lightning illuminated the sky and porch. With a frightened gasp, she noticed a couple standing a few feet from her. Introducing herself, she apologized for the intrusion and hoped she hadn't frightened them. After commenting on the sudden ferocity of the lightning, she waited for their comments. Once again, a thunderbolt of lightning lit up the sky and the porch. Startled, the woman discovered the couple was no longer on the porch. They couldn't have left without passing her.

The rest of us edged ourselves away from the scene. I could hear whispered comments that what she had seen were hallucinations brought on by one too many Speedcity cocktails. Though the rain was still pouring down, she insisted that they leave immediately. Her husband thanked the host and apologized for his distraught wife's outburst.

Looking toward the stairs, I smiled. I had been blessed, or cursed depending on your view, with an intuitive ability to know or sense things that others could not. Some would say I was psychic, a sensitive, or clairvoyant.

Though a sense of unease had settled over the guests, after a brief period of nervous whispers and clinking ice, the conversations pertaining to the May events continued. Several of the female guests decided to remind the men that the 500 was not just a "good old boy" activity any more and began discussing female drivers. There was Janet Guthrie, Lyn St. James and especially Danica Patrick who, in 2006, became the first female to run in the lead. Pit problems and nearly running out of fuel slowed her down, though she did finish fourth.

The men drifted into small groups, some discussing the race while others discussed other sports, politics or their businesses. The women began talking about the Snakepit Ball and the gowns they planned to wear.

"Did you notice the stuffed peacock in the corner of the dining room? Isn't that somewhat strange?"

Some of the women turned their attention toward the dining room. A couple stood beside the heavy Spanish dining table near the peacock, smiling. The women nodded and then turned back to their group.

"How strange," one of them commented. "I don't recognize them. Do any of you?"

No one seemed to know who they were, but then there were quite a few people in attendance.

"Did you see what they were wearing? It appeared to be clothing from the 1920s,"another woman remarked.

"Oh, surely not. Besides that, how could you tell? Candlelight is not the brightest you know, and they were standing in a shadowy corner." As an afterthought, she added, "Almost as if they really didn't want to be seen." Glancing back into the dining room, she gave the couple a friendly nod and smile. She was just starting to turn back to the group of women, when out of the corner of her eye, it appeared that the couple was evaporating. She quickly turned toward the dining room: No one was there. Thinking it must have been a trick of the flickering candlelight, she turned back to her circle of friends.

Standing near the fireplace, I watched a couple on the couch in what appeared to be a very deep and personal conversation. A young woman approached them. She stopped and just stood there. Finally, the man looked up. "Yes, may I help you?" She didn't answer or move. "If you don't mind, this is a private conversation." Again, she did not respond.

The man helped his companion from the couch, and as they walked away he commented, "How curious. I wonder who she is." The woman was no longer standing in front of the couch. He looked around the room. She was nowhere among the lively crowd. "That's strange. I wonder where she went."

The host overheard and asked, "Who?"

"There was this woman who approached us by the fireplace and just stood there looking at us. I asked if there was something she wanted, and she never answered nor moved, and now I don't see her."

"Perhaps she went into another room or even upstairs," the host suggested.

"Perhaps. But it was strange."

At this time one of the women spoke up, "My friends and I saw two people standing in the corner by the peacock. Then a few seconds later, out of the corner of my eye, I saw them seem to 'evaporate.'" She could tell no one believed her. "Nonetheless, I'm almost sure that's what I saw. I hadn't seen them before and haven't since. Just like his woman, they seemed to vanish."

Once again, I smiled to myself. It is amazing how people often refuse to accept what they see with their own eyes, especially if it's something that their mind will not allow them to believe exists.

The storm stopped, and the lights came back on. The guests had seemed to be having a good time; however, they also appeared to be anxious to leave the house. They shook hands, thanked the host and hurried out the door. I was the last to leave. I assured our host that it had indeed been an interesting evening.

As the door shut behind me and I stepped off the porch, I looked out into the yard. Shreds of mist drifted between the trees and swirled sensuously along the ground. The only element missing from this scene were real ghosts.

Turning back, I saw George and Nellie Meier watching me, illuminated by the porch light. Standing beside them was their niece, who had sold the house to the present owner just a few years before she had died. George winked, Nellie smiled, as I raised my hand in a farewell.

There was no mystery here, only the ghosts of the past being a part of the present, having a little fun and enjoying the cocktail party.

Speedcity Cocktail

½ ounce orange liqueur
1 ounce Bombay Sapphire Gin
Juice of ½ lime
½ ounce white cranberry juice

Pour all ingredients into mixing glass with ice.
Shake and strain into martini glasses.
Garnish as desired.

Adjust ingredients to taste.
It is recommended—no substitution for Bombay Sapphire Gin.

Indianapolis 500 Superstitions

by Wanda Lou Willis

Superstitions abound in auto racing. Green was considered unlucky. This can be traced back to 1920 when Gaston Chevrolet, the youngest of the three brothers, won the 1920 Indy 500 driving a green Monroe-Frontenac. This was his last stroke of luck. On November 25, 1920, driving the same car, he was killed racing on a board track in Beverly Hills, California.

This seemed at one time to be an American superstition. The British Lotus was green since that was Britain's world championship color. Nonetheless, there have been other green cars at the Indy 500, such as Jimmy Jackson's bright emerald green, dubbed the Green Hornet, and the Gatorade green car.

There are several superstitions in the racing realm. Another car superstition is getting in and out of the car from the left, which dates to front-engine cars, when some drivers claimed it was bad luck to cross the tailpipe. Or having your picture taken before a race is unlucky. It could be the last one taken. Also, numbers that would be legible when read upside down should never be used. Some drivers wear the same "lucky" underwear every race (laundered, of course) or eat the same pre-race meal. And then there's the one about making sure their shoelaces aren't twisted.

Many race drivers have at least one superstition. Especially if they've won a race, it would stand to reason they'd want to do the same things they did that day to insure another win.

One of Those Days

by Debi Watson

Debi Watson is a native of Indiana. She recently retired as a family nurse practitioner where she worked in a variety of settings: Hospital, street clinics, and a jail. She currently works as a contributing editor to Shore Magazine.

Shari, the receptionist, recognized Gillian had been shopping again at the Fashion Mall. She wore a perfectly tailored Donna Karen suit and tasteful Jimmy Choo heels. Diamonds dangled from her ears, hugged her neck, cuffed her wrist and decorated her fingers. Although flawless in her appearance, she reeked of K-Mart. "Mrs. Koehler, good to see you again. May I offer my condolence on your recent loss?" Shari held the learned empathic expression of the perfect host. Gillian waved her hand in the air as if to erase the proffered words of the model-thin receptionist. Shari arched an eyebrow in surprise at Gillian's dismissal.

"It's vital to my karma, Mary," explained Gillian, while digging for her cell phone in her Louis Vuitton bag.

"Shari," she interrupted, "Mrs. Koehler, my name is Shari."

"Well, Kerry, either I cut my hair today or kill my husband."

"It's Shari, madam." Standing now, she met Gillian at eye level.

Hints of Gillian's New Jersey accent rose and mixed with her newly acquired Southern lilt. "Cherry, surely you understand I'm having one of those days when something has to change? I know André will work me in." Gillian continued without a breath. "My husband gave me a new tiara and he insists I wear it during the Indianapolis 500 Gala tonight. Thoughtful as that might be, the tiara won't look good unless I cut my hair."

Shari, who read social cues for a living, peered into Gillian's demanding steel-blue eyes and said, "Mrs. Koehler, André only has you scheduled for a wash and style today. I'm sure you're aware this is our busiest day of the year with the gala this evening."

Gillian glowered at the receptionist as if she hadn't spoken. Shari pushed her designer eyeglasses up on her nose, watching anger color Gillian's cheeks while still fishing in her handbag for the cell phone.

Gone now was any pretense of a Southern lilt, "No one, including my dear husband Jules, appreciates how traumatic it will be for me to cut my hair. Over the last year I've suffered too many bad hair days growing all the layers out. Not to speak of all the weeks I've spent hunting for the precise dress and shoes to complement my hair color and style."

Gillian raised her phone in triumph and took a calming breath. A cape of calm seemed to settle on her shoulders as she exhaled. In her most Southern drawl she continued, "Unfortunately, killing my husband isn't an option today, so the hair must go."

Acquiescing, Shari got up and strolled the salon floor to discuss the schedule change with André. Phone in hand, Gillian called out, "I'll just let the chauffeur know he can take Jules for a ride while I'm getting my hair done. Oh...and tell Mark he can do my manicure since André is sure to make me wait."

Surprise then annoyance wafted across the receptionist's face at the request. Conditioning taking over, she forced a smile, turned and asked, "Would you care for something to drink, Mrs. Koehler?"

Mark watched as Gillian sashayed toward him, working the room as if she were a politician running for re-election. He stilled his tapping toe as Gillian stopped to accept condolences, hugs and air kisses from other customers before she made her way back to his work station. She leaned forward, blew an air kiss, and gave him a shoulder hug. "Mark, I've missed you. These last eight weeks while you were out with your broken shoulder have been totally horrible for me. Estelle doesn't know Champagne Pink from Fire Engine Red, let alone how to carry on a conversation, she's so...so average, oh, very ordinary. I've missed your flare for news."

"Gillian, I was so sorry to hear about Jules," he began, but Gillian cut him off.

"Mark, darling, you must fix my ladies," she said, wiggling her fingers as if playing a piano.

His eyes were immediately drawn to the huge diamond on her left hand. He pulled his eyes from her huge rock and scrutinized Gillian's hands. They were covered with a multitude of cuts, bruises and torn nails. He gently submerged them in a healing bath of eucalyptus and lemon oil. "I don't know if I can repair the 'ladies' in time for the gala tonight. The only thing we can do is cut them off."

"Isn't that a little drastic?"

"They'll grow back. Honey, this is beyond criminal; you've been performing manual labor. Jules threaten to cut off your clothing allowance?" Without waiting for an answer, he nodded toward her hand, "Is that ring three or four carats?"

Gillian lifted her hand, admiring the diamond and crooned, "You know my Jules; he gave me this little bauble as an incentive to ensure I carry out his plans explicitly for the insurance company's float entered in the 500 Festival Parade. Jules'll be hell to live with if he loses again. He's placed second so often they're calling him 'Second Hand Rose.' I had my marching orders this year that we were winning come hell or high water. He is adamant, after last year's loss to Eli Lilly; his float will finally take the grand prize this year."

Mark gave her a quizzical look, shook his head and then squeezed cuticle softener onto her nails. "He must want to win if he's got you performing common labor."

Gillian laughed, threw back her shoulders, and mimicked her husband Jules shooting his cuffs. Then in Jules' slow baritone drawl she said, "If you ever meet a good loser, you've just met a loser." Continuing to mock her husband holding court as he often did, her voice boomed now. "Gillian, you know that the Indy 500 Parade is the crème de la crème of parades, one of the top three in the good ole U.S. of A. They rank New York's Thanksgiving Day Parade first, the Rose Bowl number two, and then us. I'm telling you, the 500 Festival Parade outclasses Macy's." Gillian mimed smoking a stogie and swirling a glass of eighteen-year-old port, continuing in Jules "Foghorn Leghorn" southern drawl, "I know everyone oohs and ahs over those big cartoon character air balloons. However, those ugly contraptions only require hot air. It takes architectural brains and a sea of flowers to finesse a float that can compete in the

Rose or Indy Parade, not just hot air." Her shoulders dropped back to her natural posture. "I know I shouldn't make fun, Jules's my gem. I couldn't live without him."

"Seems odd not to see the handsome old devil in the paper at this time of year, decked out in an Armani suit and bragging how he hired the best Disney designers to create the Diamond Insurance Company's float extraordinaire, assuring everyone who will listen, he's going to take the grand prize." Mark wiped the chipped polish off her short nails. "I didn't realize Jules had recouped from his heart attack."

She waved a hand dismissively, silencing him. "Jules just wasn't up to an interview this year." We hired that big company out of Arizona to build the float. You know, the ones who build their own chassis and frame. The process usually has me crossing my eyes, but this year they made it so easy, just like paint by the numbers. They put the chicken wire on, spray-painted different colors to match the color of the flowers. Then you just follow the painted grid and apply all the dried flowers, seeds and structures. The fresh flowers can't be added until a day or two before the parade."

Mark, puzzled by Gillian's shifting mood, continued to file her nails and listen to her babble.

"When you're adding 500,000 water-filled plastic vials holding roses and orchids, it takes a legion of volunteers' hands to twist and push those vials into the chicken wire. You know Jules was never one to waste or squander a resource. So even though he didn't do 'manual labor,' he wasn't above making sure his wife helped out. I finally got all the glue off my hands this morning." Mark clipped a jagged nail and Gillian yelped, "Careful, that hurts."

"I know Jules writes off the expense, says it promotes corporate and civic pride. I understand, but he never fails to constantly remind me that the insurance business is what pays for all of my necessities in life. But $100,000 to indulge his ego, even to me, seems extravagant."

Mark stopped in mid-stroke of buffing Gillian's nails, eyes wide, and mouthed, "$100,000?"

Gillian leaned toward him and in a low conspiratorial voice said, "More like $300,000." Leaning back into the chair, she continued in an exasperated tone. "That doesn't include the entry fee, the hours recruiting and managing volunteers. Jules expects me to manage all those details; he doesn't care what else I have on my plate. Do you know the florist told me the amount of flowers we used on the float this year is more than he goes through in five years?" Wistfully Gillian continued, "Oh hell, I was willing to do anything just for him to win this last time."

Gillian turned at the touch of André's lips on her cheeks. He hugged her and whispered, "I'm so sorry I couldn't attend Jules' memorial service."

Mark watched as tears welled in Gillian's eyes. André turned to walk away then looked back at Mark and said, "I'll be ready for Mrs. Koehler in ten minutes. Do you need more time?" Mark shook his head no and watched while tears spilled over and slid down Gillian's cheeks.

A look of puzzlement crossed Mark's face. As he began to paint her nails, he asked quietly, "I thought you said Jules was with you?"

"He is," Gillian said, showing off her diamonds. She waited a beat then continued. "Jules died several months back, right after his heart attack. It was all the liquor, food and cigars. The man never exercised a day in his life. Hell, he was seventy; I couldn't believe he lasted as long as he did." Gillian's eyes widened now, remembering the scene. "What finally did him in, though, was when he found me in bed with the Parade Marshal. He yanked me out of bed to throw me out on my ass. I held onto his leg, pleading. I reminded him he told me to do whatever it took so his damn float could win." Gillian's hands balled into little fists. "He just kept screaming and dragging me naked to the door, all the time calling me stupid and ungrateful. He even had the nerve to call me a whore." She paused, eyes wide and feral. "All of a sudden, he started sputtering and coughing. He turned purple, grabbed his chest, and then he just collapsed. By the time I got the Marshal out of the room and called 911, he was dead when the ambulance arrived."

Mark realized his fingertips and toes were numb with disbelief as he listened to Gillian's revelation. He tried to compose his features into a neutral expression, but without much luck.

"Oh, Mark, don't look so aghast. At first I was angry at Jules for the way he treated me. He never understood just how much I loved and needed him." A slow grin rose like a sunrise on her face as she continued. "He was always preaching to me waste not, want not. Then I remembered how much Jules enjoyed new technology. Well, I took him at his word. I had him cremated and took his remains to a company that made them into diamonds. It's extremely cutting-edge technology. They extracted the carbon from the cremains by heat and pressure to make man-made diamonds. Then they cut and faceted the synthetic stones. I couldn't think of a better tribute to my dear late Jules, now that I'm CEO of Diamond Insurance."

Stunned speechless, Mark watched as the chauffeur walked in and handed Gillian a velvet-covered box. She opened the box and turned it around so Mark could see inside. A tiara covered in diamonds lay in the center of the velvet drape. Surrounding the headband were hairpins adorned with small diamonds. "I've always called Jules my gem, and now he'll always be close. Jules even inspired me for next year's parade entry theme." A look of pure joy crossed her face as she blurted out, "A brilliant mind will race you into a brilliant future."

Mark opened and then closed his mouth. He covered his lips with his hand. Standing on wobbling legs he said. "Gillian, let me see if André is ready for you and Jules." Leaving Gillian petting her tiara as if she were rubbing Jules' cheek, he walked across the salon in search of André.

Where They Are Now
by Wanda Lou Willis and Tony Perona

The Founders

The four founders of the Indianapolis 500 and several others connected with the event are no longer with us. All of them are interred in the historic Crown Hill Cemetery.

Allison, James A.
b. 08/11/1872; d. 08/03/1928

Businessman and Indianapolis Speedway co-founder. In 1915, he founded the Indianapolis Speedway Team Company, which, years after his death, would be purchased by General Motors and lead to the Allison Gas Turbine Division, which made aircraft engines and was sold to Rolls-Royce in the 1990s, and the Allison Transmission Division, which makes transmissions for a variety of vehicles. In 1927, James Allison sold the Indianapolis Speedway track to World War I hero, Eddie Rickenbacker, who then sold it to Anton Hulman, Jr. in 1946.

Fisher, Carl G.
b. 01/12/1874; d. 07/15/1939

Fisher came into the automobile business through the bicycle business, where he developed a flair for promotion. When he was in his late teens, he and his two brothers opened a successful bicycle repair shop in Indianapolis. He turned to the automobile business when the bicycle craze wound down and became one of the founders of the Prest-O-Lite company. In his later years, Fisher turned to developing and became a major developer in Miami Beach.

Newby, Arthur C.
b.12/29/1865; d. 09/11/1933

Newby was one of the founders of the Indianapolis Chain & Stamping Company, which would become Diamond Chain Company. His interest in bicycle racing culminated in his building the quarter-mile pinewood Newby Oval bicycle racing track with seating for 20,000. Newby came from a Quaker family background, and during his lifetime, he made gifts totaling

$100,000 to Earlham College. In his will, he made a joint bequest to Earlham and Indianapolis First Friends. Newby never married and was a very private person.

Wheeler, Frank H.
b.10/24/1863; d. 05/27/1921

Wheeler was an Indianapolis businessman involved in the manufacturing of carburetors, magnetos and brass fittings. He was a founder of the Wheeler-Schebler Carburetor Company, which later became Marvel-Schebler, one of the founding companies of the Borg-Warner Corporation in 1928. Today the Borg-Warner Trophy is awarded to the winning driver of the Indianapolis 500 each year.

The homes of Allison, Fisher and Wheeler are now a part of Marian College campus. Newby's home, which was located on North Meridian Street, no longer exists. Each of the four elementary schools in the town of Speedway, Indiana is named for a founder of the track.

Dust to Dust

by Sheila Sowder

Sheila Sowder had a long career in advertising, priding herself on having never been fired in a field notorious for mass dismissals whenever accounts are lost. She semi-retired a few years ago to work at a church, from which she was fired not just once, but twice. She loves writing neighborhood bar stories because she spent many hours in first-person "research" of the subject when she was much younger.

When a splash of light hit the bar, I looked up from the sink where I'd been rinsing beer mugs. A tall thin man with a stoop was silhouetted against the sunlight of the open door.

"Hey, Mac, how you doing?" I called. The door swung shut, cutting off the sunlight and fresh air before it had a chance to taint the fragrance of booze, smoke and sweat that had been marinating for decades in the murky interior of the bar.

Mac had a special place in my heart. When I'd applied for the bartender job at Speedy Joe's Tavern, the manager had a small smile on his face all during our interview. It was not a smile that said, "I like your style." It was a mean smile that said, "I'm going to get those bastards."

My first day on the job, I figured out who the bastards were. Mac, Nate, Walter, Bill, Charley and Fred. The bar's most loyal customers. Every afternoon about five, sure as death and taxes, these old geezers would plop their butts down at one end of the bar. Except for frequent trips to the john, there they'd sit, rehashing old Indy 500 races until *Fox News at Ten* came on the TV above the bar.

Now, I grew up out near the drag strip in Clermont, so I know plenty of race fans. And with the bar being just a block from the Speedway, I expected to hear some race talk. But these guys knew every driver and every detail of every race since the beginning of time. And they replayed it every evening for hours on end.

On that first afternoon, though, you'd have thought the manager had announced the place was changing into an artsy-fartsy wine bar, the way they glared when he introduced me.

"Gentlemen, this here's Angie. She's taking Sam's place." His smile was pure spite as he grabbed his jacket and left.

I pasted a grin on my face as I scanned the line of old men, each with a mug of the draft beer in front of him. "Hey, fellas, good thing you're all beer drinkers since I almost failed the cocktails class at bartending school."

Six pairs of eyes stared back at me. There wasn't a friendly gleam in any of them. *Okay, then, if that was the way they wanted it.* I gave up and got busy refilling the beer cooler. They went back to arguing about who caused the pile-up on turn three in the 1974 race.

They managed to ignore me all that evening, just shoving their glasses forward for refills of our cheapest beer. This went on for the next few days. Every time I tried to be nice to one of the old codgers, I'd get frozen out. Worse than that, none of them tipped, yet they took up six barstools during prime drinking hours. I guessed that's what got the manager's goat—these slow-drinking, cheap-beer-guzzling old farts taking up the best bar seats and chasing the high-end drinkers away with their boring old race talk.

One day, after I'd been there maybe a week, Bobby Owens, this guy I went to school with, came in and sat at the end of the bar.

"Hey, Angie, how long you been working here?"

I gave Bobby the lowdown on my new career path, and we shot the bull for a while about old times. I could tell by the silence at the other end of the bar that the old geezers were listening, even though none of them looked in our direction.

"So, you got any kids?" Bobby asked.

I dug into my purse and handed him a picture of my three kids. After he looked at it, he passed it down the bar. When it reached Mac, he looked at it for such a long time I got a little nervous.

Finally he handed it back to me and cleared his throat. "Nice looking youngsters."

I was so surprised, I couldn't even think of *thank you.*

"You and your husband must be real proud."

My stomach clenched at the thought of that worthless piece of slime. "Yeah, they're good kids," I said, "but it's just me and them now. Ever since their daddy, may he rot in hell, walked out a few months ago."

He was looking at me like he was seeing me for the first time. Somehow I ended up telling him how I'd never worked before and how, after the asshole left, my brother suggested bartender school. It was only a six-week course, and then they help you find a job. Besides, I could work evenings when my sis was home to watch the kids.

All Mac said was, "That's a big job for a girl to take on by herself." But that night he left a fiver by his glass. The next night they all left me fivers and even managed to growl out hellos and goodbyes aimed in my direction. It didn't take long before we were cutting up like a bunch of school kids. They turned out to be pretty good guys once they got used to a female bartender.

So the afternoon I'm talking about, they were all here as usual when I said, "Hey, any of you know why this bar's called Speedy Joe's?"

And Nate said, "Crymenetly, Angie, don't you know who Speedy Joe Forsythe was?"

I shook my head. They looked at me like I'd just served them Heinekens.

Nate crossed his arms on the bar and leaned forward. "Back in the spring of '56, there was this driver everyone called Speedy Joe, though it seems he got that name because he talked real slow. Anyway, he came up out of the bush leagues down South where he never gave no one reason to think he was anything special." He looked down the row for corroboration. Four heads bobbed up and down while Bill, who is a little deaf, poked Charley next to him to ask what Nate was talking about. "He took a room at a motel that used to be down on the corner. Stopped in here once in a while to shoot the breeze and wet his whistle. Pretty good guy, Speedy Joe."

Mac took over. "Joe was real hot that May, driving a fast car rumored to be backed by Lou DeFranco."

"Who was Lou DeFranco?" I asked.

Mac and Nate looked at each other and shook their heads.

"Lou DeFranco owned the main liquor distributorship in the Midwest back then," Mac said, speaking slowly like I was a halfwit. "He also had his hand in all the gambling and prostitution in the area. It was pretty common knowledge he was part of the Family up in Chicago. In fact, he was in line to become Boss after Sam Giancamo was ousted in the midsixties, but "Teets" Battaglia had him wiped out so he could get the job himself."

"And Speedy Joe was working for Lou DeFranco?"

Charley nodded. "Well, officially he was working for DeFranco's wife's nephew, but it was DeFranco's money, sure enough. In other words, the mob's money. We used to tease Joe about it, said he'd better win or he'd be swimming with the fishes."

"And he'd say the White River was too dirty for fish, and more 'n likely he'd end up under the cee-ment floor of DeFranco's new liquor warehouse down in Southport," Walter chimed in, poking Fred with his elbow.

I was starting to get real suspicious. These guys got a kick out of feeding me a tall tale, then listening to me spread it around like it was the gospel truth. "You're putting me on, aren't you?"

"No, sirree," Mac said. "Every once in a while the mob would try to get into the racing game, more than just controlling the betting action in Vegas and Atlantic City. Happened back in '51, then this time in '56 with Joe driving for them. And let me see," he looked at the boys, "wasn't it '71 when they gave it another shot?"

Five heads nodded again.

"So here's Joe," Mac continued, "with this spiffy car beating all the records during practice. And everyone watching to see what he's going to do at time trials. Never been a rookie on the pole before."

"Did he get the pole?" I asked, still not quite sure they were on the up and up.

Mac gave me a squinty-eyed look because I was trying to rush the story, which I knew from past experience couldn't be done. If anything, he'd just slow down on purpose to be ornery.

"As luck of the draw would have it, Joe didn't get to qualify until late in the day. We were all over there at the track, sitting up right behind his pit crew when he finally got his shot."

He took a sip of his beer, and Nate jumped in. "First lap, he was going like a house afire. Second started out the same. Then, for no reason anyone ever figured out, his car started wobbling. He hit the wall in the second turn, bounced off, and rolled over a couple of times."

"Oh, my God, was he killed?" I asked, picturing the way an Indy car can shed pieces of itself during a crash like a meteor breaking up when it hits the earth's atmosphere.

"Nope, he walked away from it. Pretty banged up but all in one piece. Last we saw him, he was sitting up front in the ambulance, on his way to Methodist Hospital." Mac drained his mug and slid it forward for a refill. "And that night, he disappeared."

My hand just stopped in the process of reaching for his empty mug. "What do you mean, *disappeared*?"

"That's all we know. Hospital wanted to keep him for observation, but sometime during the night, he was gone. Didn't show up at his garage the next day. His chief mechanic checked his motel room. All his things were still there. Only there was blood smeared all over, some on the wall and some in the bathroom. Cops couldn't determine if it was Joe's because no one had a sample of his blood. And this was long before DNA, so they couldn't have been sure anyway."

"So, what are you saying? The mob killed him?" I leaned my elbows on the bar, all bartending forgotten.

"No one knows," Nate said. "Though that's what was generally believed."

"But why? Just because he crashed the car? Shoot, if every driver who ever crashed a car got executed by its owner, the sport would have been wiped out years ago."

Charley leaned forward from the end of the row. "One of his grease monkeys was in here drunk, not long after Joe disappeared. Telling everyone that he'd heard talk there was some money missing. Envelope full of it that the nephew was supposed to deliver to DeFranco's office. Said it was probably payoffs from their poker machines in bars."

"Did he say Joe took it? Was Joe that dumb?"

Mac frowned down the row at Charley. "That guy was probably talking through his ass. Joe might of talked slow, but his brain worked just fine. He knew you don't steal from the mob and get away with it."

Charley held up his hand, palm forward. "All I'm saying is Joe disappeared, there was blood all over his room and some money missing. Ain't brain surgery to figure out what happened. Anyway, the cops never did get any leads, and his body never turned up. Finally they just called it a missing person and dropped the case."

"But how did this bar get his name?"

"I'm getting to that," Mac said. "Gol durn, girl. A man could die of thirst in here." He looked pointedly at his mug still sitting empty on the bar. After I filled it, he took a gulp and set it down. "About a month after Joe disappeared, a package arrived here at the bar, addressed to us guys." He pointed up behind my head. "See that urn up there?"

I turned around and looked up at the shelf that stretched across the back of the bar. It held fancy bottles of booze that, to my knowledge, had never been opened.

"That bottle there, between the kahlua and the triple sec," he said.

"The white one, looks like it's carved out of marble?"

"Yep. That's Speedy Joe. His ashes, anyway."

"No shit!" I said, which got me a frown from Fred, who didn't approve of women cussing.

"Yep. Some lawyer fella down in Texas sent it here. His letter said it just showed up one day with some money to cover his fees and instructions to send it on to us. Once word got around, so many people came in to see the urn, the owner at the time thought it would be good for business to change the bar's name to Speedy Joe's."

"So how'd he die?"

"Don't know."

"Did you tell the cops?"

"Nope."

We all looked at the short fat urn on the shelf for a minute, no one saying anything.

"Fifty fu-frigging years—sorry, Fred," I said.

I couldn't get that story out of my head for the next couple of days. It seemed like there ought to be a better ending. Something to make it feel like it was done. I tried to explain how I felt to the guys, but they just looked at me like I was suggesting they drink their beer at room temperature.

A couple days later, before the guys could decide which year's race they wanted to beat to death for the evening, I brought it up again. "Didn't you ever open it?"

Six pairs of eyes looked at me like I'd just stuck little paper umbrellas in their beer mugs.

"Why'd we want to do that?" Nate asked.

"Well, gee. Curiosity, maybe? I mean, it's just ashes, right? Not like a real dead body." I looked down the row of old-timers and realized if they had an ounce of curiosity between them, they'd find something better to do with their evenings than sit in this bar yammering about the same things over and over. "Hey, I've got a great idea. Let's open it now."

They looked as shocked as if I'd spit in their beer mugs. But like my brother tells me, I've always got to go right off the deep end when I get a bright idea instead of thinking it through. So I got the ladder out of the storeroom and climbed up. Got the urn, carried it back down, and set it on the bar.

As dust from the urn's surface caught in the breeze from the ceiling fan and swirled around my head, I wrinkled my nose, then sneezed. "Ugh, that thing's got to have more dust on the outside than it does inside." I examined the lid. "I think I can pry this open."

I grabbed a church key from under the bar.

"Here, Angie, you can't do that." Mac leaned over the bar to grab the urn.

"Watch me," I moved it out of his reach. I pried the church key under the lid. It didn't budge. "Shit."

"Cusses like a line-haul driver," Fred said. While I was distracted for a second, trying to figure out why a line-haul driver would cuss more than anyone else, Mac managed to grab the urn out of my hands. He passed it down the line to Bill at the end. Then they gave me the evil eye.

"OK, fine," I said, "but it's been fifty years. Fifty goddamn years—sorry, Fred. Hows about we have some kind of memorial or something? After all, the bar *is named* after him."

I could see them kind of warming up to the idea, so I plowed on. "What we need to do is figure out what kind. How about a party?"

That perked the old guys up a little, but then Fred shook his head. "Don't seem right, having a party to celebrate someone dying. Seems sacrilegious to me."

I tell you, I, for one, could live without Fred. Too bad he's not against drinking. The others seemed reluctant to give up the party idea, too, but finally, one by one, Fred shamed them into it. They sat looking kind of depressed while I filled a few beer mugs and gave it some more thought.

Then Bill, who almost never says anything, probably because he can't hear what's going on, cleared his throat. "We could scatter Joe's ashes somewhere. That's what my wife's niece did when her husband died. We had to drive down to Brown County where they had a cabin and stand around getting ate up by mosquitoes while a minister read some Bible verses. Then they sprinkled the ashes around the woods."

"Bill, that's a great idea," I said, although the other guys were looking at each other all squinty-eyed. "And there's only one place to do it." I looked at each guy down the line for dramatic effect. "The track."

They all started talking at once, but finally Mac out-shouted the others. "Now just you hold on a minute, Missy. If you think the track management's going to let us toss ashes around on their property, you got another think coming." The guys chuckled.

I could feel my dander getting up. Everyone in my family could have told them, when I get my dander up, it doesn't do any good to stand in my way. "Then we just won't tell them," I said.

And that's how we happened to be there at midnight a couple of days later, huddled in the shadows outside a small gate not far from the main track entrance. Shivering in the October night. Except Walter. He was our inside man. See, he used to volunteer for security every May and bragged he knew all the exits. He'd visited the Hall of Fame Museum that afternoon and sneaked into the track from there. At the moment, though, my main worry was that he might have fallen asleep waiting for us. Back at the bar, it had taken two pots of coffee to keep the gang awake this far past their bedtime. I almost lost them around eleven until I brought up the subject of our governor and his union-busting mentality. Nothing gets these retirees from Allison's assembly line going like a threat to the UAW!!

I'd put my cell phone on vibrate and slipped it in Walter's pocket before he set out that afternoon. I'd tried to call him before we left the bar but got no response. Nate said he was probably carrying it over his artificial hip, where the feeling still hadn't come back two years after surgery!

After ten minutes of crouching in the chilly night air, the troops were close to mutiny. "Damn fool idea."

"My knees are locking up."

"End up in the hoosegow for trespassing."

I tried to ignore their bitching and prayed that last complaint hadn't already happened to Walter. He's got a real mean wife, and I sure didn't want to be the one to tell her he was in jail.

I wondered how much longer I could hold them there, when we heard footsteps. None of us moved a twitch until we heard Walter whisper. "Hold on a minute 'til I squirt some WD-40 on these hinges."

Then we were inside.

"Shhh!" I said, as they all tried to talk to Walter at once. But no one heard me, so I started poking arms. "I SAID SHHH," I whisper-yelled. After a few "ouches," they quieted down. Walter was making "follow me" motions, so I lined them up single file behind him. The noise made by all those old feet shuffling on the tarmac seemed to echo off the empty buildings. We followed Walter through the space between bleacher sections and up to the edge of the pit area. He hesitated just inside the line where the shadows ended. The track itself was lit almost as bright as day.

"Should have waited for a new moon," Mac whispered in my ear.

I tensed as we looked around for guards, then Walter's shoulders rose as he took a deep breath and moved out into the moonlight. We followed him to the middle of the track and stopped.

"Bill, hand me the bag," I whispered.

Of course, Bill was at the end of the line and didn't hear me, so I poked Mac who poked Nate who poked, well, you get the picture. Finally a plastic Kroger bag was shoved into my hands. I removed the urn and held it out. "OK, fellas, this is it. Who's giving the eulogy?"

Charley stepped forward. "I had some Bible verses written down, but it's too dang dark to read. Guess I'll have to wing it." He bowed his head, and we all followed suit. "Lord, Speedy Joe, that's Joe Forsythe to you, he was a good man deep down. Never hurt no one on purpose far as we know, maybe drank a little too much sometimes, but then who doesn't? And he never started no fights, leastways not that some bastard didn't deserve."

"You can't say 'bastard' in a prayer," Fred said.

"Why not, if that's what he was?" Charley answered. "You think the good Lord don't think some guys are just pure bastards?"

"Stop arguing, damn it," I hissed. "Charley, keep going before we all freeze to death."

We bowed our heads again. "Anyway, Lord," he continued, "we're here to scatter Joe's ashes on the place he loved best. Well, maybe not this particular track, 'cause I remember he once said he loved Talladega the best, but you know what I mean." He looked up as Mac snorted with irritation.

I nudged Charley's arm. "Keep going." Christ, this could take all night. My hands holding the urn were shaking so much with the cold, old Joe must have felt like he was a milkshake.

"So, Lord, we're commemorating the fiftieth anniversary of the life and death of Joe Forsythe. We ask your blessing on him and his family, if he has any." Charley raised his head and nodded toward the urn. "You want to open 'er up, Angie?"

I tried to turn the large cap on the top of the urn, but my hands were too small to get a grip. I handed it over to Nate. Even his big mitts couldn't budge the cap. Fred dug a Leatherman's tool out of his pocket and handed it to Nate, who used one of its little arms to pry the cap loose. He twisted the urn the rest of the way open and held it up. I suddenly realized he was about to toss around corpse dust and took a couple of steps back.

"Here we go," he said as he tipped the urn upside down.

Out dropped a long white envelope but no ashes. We all stared at it. Then the lights went on, and someone yelled, "Put your hands up."

Well, I'm surprised we didn't all pee our pants, what with how scared we were and the old coots' weak bladders. A couple of guys with jackets that said "Security" herded us off the track. They marched us over into a small lit building just out of sight around the turn from where we came in. You'd have thought we were a bunch of hardened criminals, maybe terrorists, the way they kept their guns pointed at us.

Thank goodness the head guy sitting behind a desk recognized Walter. But even then it took a lot of explaining before he was willing to let us go. His guards were biting their lips to keep from smiling, and at one point, the head guy excused himself and went outside for a minute or so.

Finally, after making sure we understood what *could* have happened and probably what *should* have happened, he said, "Well, considering there weren't actually any ashes in the urn, so you didn't damage any track property, I'm going to over-look the breaking and entering and trespassing and let you off with a warning."

We all mumbled our thanks and turned to get out of there, but then I remembered. "Hey, where's the envelope?" The codgers turned back around.

The head guy looked confused, but one of the guards reached in his pocket. "Here it is, Chief, what should I do with it?"

The head guy just looked disgusted and waved toward me. The guard held it out and I grabbed it. We hauled ass out of there faster than those old farts had moved in years.

Back at the bar, I poured little shots of Jack Daniels for everyone, on the house, because the guys were looking a little peaked and shaky. I held up the letter. "It's addressed to you, Mac. Says, 'Mac and the guys'. Want me to open it?"

A shrug went down the line, and no one said not to. I lifted the flap that was no longer glued down and removed a sheet of lined paper and two little packets wrapped in Scotch tape.

I waved the sheet of paper. "Should I read it?"

Mac held out his hand. He silently checked with the group, then fished his reading glasses out of his shirt pocket and began to read out loud.

Dear Mac and the rest of you guys,
I ain't dead. Leastwise, I hope I still ain't by the time you
read this. But if I'd hung around Indy any longer, I'd be
deader 'n a doornail by now. See, a briefcase with a big chunk
of change from one of Mr. DeFranco's businesses come up
missing. Harry Reidenbach, that good-for-nothing nephew
of DeFranco's wife, stole it.

Mac looked up. "Harry Reidenbach. *Harold* Reidenbach.
Ain't that the sorry son-of-a-hyena who's running for Con-
gress right now on the holier-than-thou ticket?"
"Go on, read the rest," I said.

There's this secretary in Mr. DeFranco's office who's sweet
on me. She knew something was up with Harry so she
started listening in on his phone conversations. One week
he was begging his bookie for more time, the next he was
telling him how he'd suddenly come into a lot of dough.
That's when a couple of DeFranco's goons started watching
me. I figured Harry's set me up. This girl's a real smart
cookie, smarter than Harry, and she got her hands on a
note that proves the weaselly little moron did it. Trouble is,
we didn't know who to trust. I knew I was taking a chance
by crashing up that car, but I needed to get away from the
goons long enough to slip away into the night. And one
bonus from that hospital visit was the bag of blood I lifted
from this big old refrigerator in the basement. I put the note
in a safe deposit box in the Indiana National downtown
branch, and me and Miss Smarty-Pants high-tailed it out of
there. By the time you get this, we should be drinking
margaritas down south of the border. I'm not going to tell
you any more because it's best if you don't know where we
are. But here's the key to that safe deposit box in case the
time's ever right to hand it over to the authorities. I'd ap-
preciate it if you all keep mum about this here note. And
that second packet, well, have a beer on me.
Joe Forsythe

Mac handed the letter to Nate who read it and then passed
it on down the line.

"What are you going to do?" I asked, unwrapping the smaller packet and handing him the key.

"I move first thing in the morning we see if that safe deposit box has survived the ownership changes at the bank." Mac looked at the others, who nodded their agreement. "And if it did, maybe we can use that note to wipe the self-righteous smirk off that slimy politician's face."

I unwrapped the other packet. A tight wad of money fell out. I pried it apart and spread it out on the bar. Six one-dollar bills.

"What the hell?" I looked up. The old coots were grinning at me, even Fred.

"Draft beer was seventy-five cents back in 1956," Mac said. "And two bits for the bartender."

Pre-Race Track Traditions

by Wanda Lou Willis

- The Fastest Rookie of the Year Award has been held by three generations of the Andretti family.

- Every year since 1972 the "Last Row Party," a charity event, has been held on the Friday before the race. This event serves as a roast for the three final qualifiers who will be starting on the eleventh and final row.

- On the day of the race, an explosion is set off to signal the opening of the gates.

- As a Memorial Day remembrance since 1919, the Purdue University Marching Band plays "Taps," while military aircraft do a fly-by, often executing the missing man formation.

- Hoosier born, actress/singer Florence Henderson for most years since the mid-1990s has performed the song "God Bless America," which then is followed by "The Star-Spangled Banner," sung by a different guest artist each year.

- In most years since 1972, Jim Nabors has been performing "Back Home Again in Indiana" accompanied by the Purdue Marching Band. Thousands of multicolored balloons are released from the infield as he sings "...the new mown hay..."

- "Gentlemen, start your engines!" was changed when female drivers began competing to "Lady/Ladies and gentlemen, start your engines!"

- Believing it would be safer than the standing-still start, the founder, Carl Fisher, lead the inaugural race field of 40 cars around the track one lap, then released them to the flagman as he pulled into the pits. This is believed to have been the first mass-rolling start for any automobile race anywhere in the world, and now is commonplace.

Killer Traditions

by Jaci Muzamel

The daughter of a Navy photographer, Jaci Muzamel learned at an early age that being around a camera was a way of life and a method to observe people as she moved across the United States. The step to writing came after many people encouraged her to record some of the stories she delights in telling about the amusing events in her life. An avid race fan, she found this story a way to combine her interests.

"I don't care. It doesn't make sense to call it Carb Day if the cars don't have carburetors anymore. I realize it's a tradition, but give me a cute driver and pit crew any day to a stupid tradition," Tammi said for what seemed like the twentieth time.

"They had to adjust the carburetors to make cars run faster and smoother, but even after the introduction of fuel injection in the late 1940s, the original term, carburetion runs, continued to be used," Brian began. "Since the tradition was already in place, they never changed it." He saw that trying to explain was useless. Tammi had walked away before he could finish.

He sat down on the bleachers and wiped his face. The late afternoon sun was brutal, and Brian's shirt was drenched with sweat. Heat rose from the famous Yard of Bricks in a shimmering wave, obliterating the outline of the start/finish platform, making it look as if the flagman was standing on thin air. There was a distinct smell to a race track that Brian loved. Hot metal, burning rubber and super-heated asphalt created an odor that was almost as famous as racing itself. He watched Tammi ease into her photographer mode, focusing her camera on one of the pit crews, and wondered when she had become a fanatic race fan. He loved racing and had always imagined himself in the ultimate dream: racing in the Indianapolis 500.

Over the years, they'd lived near Dover and Texas Motor Speedways, so whenever they had the chance, they'd head to the track. Now she kept up with NASCAR like a fiend and spouted facts like a sportscaster. Most summer Sunday afternoons, she'd be glued to the television, and any interruption would be met with a stony glare and a quick, "Can't you see

211

Jimmie's in the lead?" Her favorites changed yearly, depending on how *cute* the driver was or how good he looked in his uniform.

Brian was thrilled when they moved to Indianapolis. Instead of just NASCAR racing, he'd have a chance to see the Indy 500. It wasn't as good as actually driving in the race, but it would do. After they'd settled in, he'd gone to the Speedway website and purchased a weekend pass for the race. It included pit passes on Carb Day and decent seats for the race.

His thoughts were interrupted when he heard Tammi's excited whispering, "I think that's Helio there now…isn't he a doll? I'm going to try to get closer."

One thing Brian knew for sure, if he dragged Tammi's photo equipment to the track, she'd be occupied chasing pictures, and he'd have a few minutes of peace to watch the cars speed past and imagine himself in the driver's seat.

Tammi's enthusiasm was evident. "I think I just got some great shots; I can't wait to get home and look at them on the computer. We've never gotten this close to the NASCAR guys, and the Indy crews are friendlier. A couple came over and talked to that guy."

Brian glanced over but dismissed the long-haired guy as some sort of track groupie, ever present with their cheap beer and knowledge of racing trivia. "That's one reason I wanted to come for the entire event. I think you'll get to see and do more today then on Race Day. Look around. This area is practically deserted. I'm surprised we've been able to get this close to the cars."

"This is great. There's nothing better than the sound of the engines when they drop the flag, but this is pretty cool, too. I didn't know you could get this close. Hey, isn't that A.J. Foyt? I think so. I know I saw Michael Andretti earlier." She was so excited she bounced. "Do you think any of the other old guys are here?"

No sooner had she said that than the guy standing by the rail hollered, "Hey, Rick, over here." Rick Mears, four-time winner of the Indy 500, flashed his million-dollar smile and waved.

"Wow, how cool is that? Rick Mears," she said and dug her elbow into Brian's side. "Thanks for pointing him out," she said to the guy. "I thought he looked familiar, but I wasn't sure." She tossed Brian one of those *someone*-knows-what-this-is-all-about looks.

With a sip of his beer, the guy turned toward Tammi. "If you hang around long enough, you'll see most of them. I've been coming all my life. I like Carb Day actually better than the race. You can get up close and personal, and the guys are a lot more at ease. They'll stop sometimes and talk if they see you're interested. Man, on Race Day, you won't be able to get within a mile of the pits."

"You sound like you know a lot about racing."

"Well, like I said, I've been coming all my life. I take the whole week off, bring my gear down and camp on a friend's yard. He lives in the tract housing right under turn three, so it's not a long walk. I wouldn't miss the 500 for any reason. I've met most of the crews." He nodded at two crew members hurrying toward a car that had just pulled onto pit row.

Brian looked down and saw the guy had a cooler full of empty Budweiser cans floating in a sea of melting ice. That might explain the beet-red color of his face, although the heat rolling off the track no doubt contributed. Brian shot a glance across the pit area and saw he wasn't the only one watching their new friend. The crew chief for Russ Miller's number 21 car was watching him pretty intently, too. Why? Because he'd yelled at Rick Mears, or because crew members wasted time when they stopped and talked? Most of the teams seemed pretty laid back, but Miller's crew was intensely focused for a non-race day. The crew chief waved his arms and yelled the entire time they gassed the 21 car and got it rolling back out onto the track. The times they'd been setting were hot, and Brian wondered if it was one of the fastest cars in the field.

The guy on the rail looked out at the last remaining cars. "It's about time for me to head out. There won't be many more cars on the track this afternoon. I'll bet you won't see any faster than the speed Miller just set. My name's Tim, by the way. First time here?" He swapped the last dripping can of beer to his left hand and extended his right toward Brian. The icy cold made Brian shiver as he introduced himself and Tammi and said they'd recently moved to the area. He wasn't sure he wanted to talk with this guy, but Tammi started asking questions about the races he'd seen. So much for not liking tradition.

While Tim talked about famous people and the sights he'd seen, Brian looked the guy over. He appeared to be in his mid-thirties, but it was hard to tell. His stringy brown hair looked like it hadn't been washed all week, and he was missing a few teeth. He had on torn shorts and no shirt, but wore a pair of Merrell Wilderness Hiking Boots. No wonder he camped out instead of getting a hotel room. The guy was standing in a $250 pair of boots.

"I know all the teams pretty well," he said, "and I've seen a lot of the drivers come and go. The better ones stick around, mostly 'cause of their skill. But every now and then, you see a driver get pretty far in the standings, and you have to wonder why when you watch them practice. Sometimes I swear it's just luck."

He picked up his cooler, closed the top, and said, "Well, looks like I'm out of beer, and it's getting late. I'm outta here." He paused. "It gets in your blood. I'm sure I'll see you here next year." He laughed and headed toward the tunnel to the parking lots. As he went, he yelled at someone in the garage area.

"Man, what a loser," Brian said as Tammi peered over the fence at the television system the crews use. "Funny how he can afford a cooler full of beer and those hiking boots, but not a decent place to stay. Guess it all depends on your priorities."

"Well, I think he's kinda fun. He sure knows a lot about the track." Tammi raised her camera to her eye and hollered at Tim, who was fast disappearing into the gloom of the tunnel. "Hey, Tim," she yelled out and took several pictures of him as he turned and saluted her.

By the time Brian lost sight of Tim, things *had* quieted down on the track. Crews had packed up most of the equipment and were pushing the cars into the garage area. One driver sat on the concrete barrier talking to his crew chief. Brian gathered up Tammi's equipment, thinking all the while that he made a great pack horse.

Tammi looked around at the emptying pit. "You know, Tim was right. There's nobody left to watch. Are you about ready to head home? I love to look at the memorabilia at the Union Jack Pub. Want to stop there for dinner on our way out?"

"I thought you weren't into tradition and memorabilia?"

With an exaggerated why-me-Lord sigh, Tammi picked up one of her cameras. "Oh, don't be silly. I love to look at all that old stuff. Where on earth did you get the idea I don't like tradition? You've been in an odd mood today. Is it the old, wish-it-were-me-out-there deal?"

Brian didn't feel like talking about his life-long desire to race, so he kept quiet and started to walk away.

As if she'd been nothing but Miss Sweetness and Light all day, Tammi perked up and said, "So, do you want to stop at the Union Jack? I'll buy you a beer. I need to hit the restroom on the way out, though."

"Me, too." Brian was amazed at how quickly her moods changed.

With a last glance at the track, they turned toward the tunnel and walked past the entrance to the garage area. "I'd love to get passes into the garage one day. Do you think we could?" Tammi asked. "That would be terrific. To see what they do to the cars."

Since Brian knew she'd have no idea what they actually *do* to the cars, he just smiled. "Sure. Let's try to get them next year."

They headed toward the restrooms carrying her camera equipment and their hats. When they got to the doors, Brian offered to wait with their belongings so they didn't have to split the load and drag their stuff in with them. There was nothing worse than setting your things on the floor of a men's restroom. Tammi went in and, in a few moments, was back, taking the camera bags from Brian's hands.

"I'll be out in a minute," he said over his shoulder and disappeared through the door.

Within seconds he shot out the door and almost knocked Tammi over. He was flushed and his hands were shaking.

"What on earth's the matter?" she asked, a look of concern on her face.

"Get help," he stammered. "Hurry...RUN!"

"Why? What's wrong?"

"Just go find somebody, Tammi. NOW!"

Tammi dumped the camera bags on the concrete and ran toward the nearby souvenir shop. "Get help right away," she screamed. "In the men's room...there's something wrong in the men's room!" Before the startled gift shop clerks could ask questions, Tammi turned and ran back to Brian. He was trembling all over.

"Brian, for God's sake, what's wrong?" She grabbed his shoulders. With a shake she demanded, "What is in there? BRIAN!"

Before Brian could answer, two security guards appeared, followed by a lady from the shop. One guard held a half eaten sandwich in one hand and a bottle of Coke in the other. They were out of breath and clearly not happy they'd been dragged away from a late lunch.

"What's the problem?" the guard asked, gesturing toward Brian with the sandwich. A slice of half-ripe tomato dropped on the concrete.

Brian didn't answer. He walked to the restroom door and pointed inside. The guards went in. Moments later they were back out. One blocked the entrance, while the other threw his sandwich into the trash and spoke rapidly into his radio.

Brian took Tammi by the arm and tried to steer her away.

She snatched her arm out of his grasp and started toward the men's restroom. "I want to know what happened, and if you won't tell me, I'll find out for myself."

"In the restroom..." he tried to sound calm, "that guy you were talking to in the pit area... he's dead. I'm sure it's him. He's face down, but who else would have boots like that?"

"How do you know he's dead?"

"There's so much blood around his head, I don't see how he *could* be alive."

"Oh, my God," Tammi said. "What are we going to do?"

"Do? We're going to let the cops handle this, and we're going home."

"We can't just leave," she said in a tone Brian knew all too well. "What if the police need to talk to you?"

"Okay, okay," Brain conceded. "Let's just stand over here and see what happens."

Soon the tunnel was alive with activity. Police officers must have been on the grounds. Additional track security arrived along with members of the Speedway's board of directors whom Brian recognized from pictures in the *Indianapolis Star*. If it weren't for the dead man in the men's room, Brian was sure Tammi would have been thrilled to be so close to guys who'd be sitting in the Pagoda on Race Day. She didn't seem to realize who they were, which was probably just as well. Brain had visions of her going over to *chat* with them.

An ambulance arrived, but Brian thought it was probably too late. A coroner's wagon would be more appropriate. He and Tammi were shuffled to one side of the tunnel. Brian was starting to think they could just slide away, when a security officer, two policemen dressed in street clothes but with badges attached to their belts, and the CEO for the track approached them.

"You found the body?" the track security officer asked. Tammi took a deep breath, but before she could say more than "Well, we were…," Brian shot her a warning glance and took over the conversation. He told the group how they had met Tim, talked with him about racing, and that he'd left the pit area a few minutes before.

"Had you noticed anything odd about him?" one of the police officers asked.

"Nothing other than the fact he had obviously been drinking," Brian answered. "He seemed to be steady enough, and his speech wasn't slurred, but his cooler was full of empty beer cans, so he must have been drinking all afternoon. He was pretty loud, but I wouldn't say he was obnoxious, although he did yell at several different crew members. We're not the only ones who noticed. Russ Miller's team was watching him pretty closely, too."

Their conversation was interrupted by a uniformed police officer who approached the group with what looked like a white pill in his hand. "Sergeant Kellham? We found something I think you need to see." The group of officials scuttled off to the side like a bunch of crabs side-stepping on an ocean beach.

Tammi's giggle had a nervous edge to it. "Do you think they realize how silly they look?"

Brian shushed her and strained to hear. He wasn't sure, but he thought he heard one of the board members say, "You can't be serious. That would never work." They had their backs turned and were speaking softly.

After a few more hastily spoken words, a police officer came over to them. Brian saw a couple others head to the pits, and the rest hurried toward the garages. As he approached, the officer said, "You'll have to stay here a while longer. You can sit over there on the grass if you'd like. You might as well make yourselves comfortable, but stay where I can see you, okay? I'm Officer Layton."

"How long will we have to stay?" Tammi asked. "Can you tell us what's going on?"

"No, ma'am. You'll just have to sit tight until Sergeant Kellham comes back. Thanks for understanding."

Brian headed toward the shaded grass. Tammi followed, straining to see what was happening behind her. He took her arm, making sure she didn't stumble.

She didn't pull away this time but huffed at him, "Don't you hate how they say that kind of stuff? He should at least tell us *something* since *you* found the body."

"Well, I guess we'll just have to wait. At least it's cooler here. I thought when we left Texas we'd left the heat behind. Who'd have thought it got so friggin' hot and humid in Indiana? I'll go see if I can find something to drink."

Brian unceremoniously dropped the camera bags on the ground, held Tammi's hand as she plopped on the grass, and walked toward a Coke machine. He hated soft drinks but figured if Tammi had a cool drink in her hands, she'd be more likely to accept that they weren't going anywhere any time soon.

As they opened the sodas, they watched the uniformed personnel remove the body. Tammi stretched to get a better view, but when she actually saw the body on the stretcher, she picked up her camera bag and peered inside. Sometimes it takes a good picture to make you understand reality.

The emergency vehicles pulled away. The police and security guards who were left behind kept to themselves and talked quietly. They had blocked off the tunnel about fifty feet from the restroom, so no one else was close by. It was quiet as dusk began to settle on the Speedway. Occasionally Brian could hear crew members making laughing references to whose turn it was to buy beer as they closed and locked their garages. Even though most were rivals, the crews had known each other for years. It wasn't unusual for crew members to move from one team to another.

Tammi was focused on reorganizing her camera equipment. Brian wondered how much money they had invested in those bags. Maybe saving money to buy new equipment was why she was so agreeable to eating at home almost every night. Not that it really mattered to him. He loved that she had a hobby that kept her so entertained. Honestly, he thought she was good enough to have some of her work published. She just had to get some confidence in herself and try.

Brian was the first to notice Sergeant Kellham and the head of security walking toward them. Kellham pointed to Tammi's camera bag. "Did you by any chance take pictures in the pit area today?"

With a tight grip on the bag, Tammi frowned. "Yes. I got some great shots of the guys, I think. Why?"

"Have you looked at them yet? We'd like to see what you got."

She looked at him with suspicion. "Why?"

He shot a questioning glance at his silent partner, who nodded. "We've looked at the track security cameras. The pit area cameras show nothing out of the ordinary. We could see that you were taking photos and wonder if you might have taken a picture that could be helpful to us."

Brian saw Tammi's concerned look change as a smile broke over her face and she realized what they were asking. They wanted to see *her* pictures.

"I can show you right on the camera screen with the review." She stood up, digging in her bag for the right camera. "Or we could download them to a computer, but that can be tricky. I have my USB cord with me. I don't know a lot about computers, but I'm sure one of your computer geek guys can help me. Or we could take the memory stick out if you have a computer with a slot for one and the software." She shifted back and forth with excitement, talking faster and faster. It was hard to keep up as the words spilled out. "I took a lot of pictures, but I'm not sure I got Tim in any of them. I guess that might not matter though."

He took the camera out of her hand. "Thank you so much ma'am. If you don't mind, we'll let the track's security guys take a look. I think you'd be more comfortable if you just waited here. We'll get your camera back to you as soon as we can." The two turned and walked toward the administrative building.

Brian braced himself for the verbal explosion he was sure was coming and was surprised when Tammi said, "You know, if they find something on one of my pictures that leads them to the killer, they'll have to give me some credit for helping solve this crime."

He felt a flash of irritation at her cavalier attitude. "You do realize that they're looking for something that will help them figure out how a guy you were talking to less than an hour ago died. This isn't one of your silly who-done-it books." He wanted her based in reality but didn't want to scare her. He knew her well enough to know some of her chatter came from being nervous. The straight line of her mouth and the set of her back as she turned away let him know he'd said too much.

They stood in an I'll-never-speak-to-you-again marital silence until they saw the police returning. Brian saw they had Russ Miller's crew chief handcuffed between them. They led him to one of the police cars and pushed his head down as they shoved him into the back seat.

"That's interesting. Wonder what's going on?" Brian asked no one in particular as they watched the car pull away.

Without explanation, Officer Layton returned the camera to Tammi and told them they could go.

Tammi couldn't contain herself. "You mean you're not even going to tell us what happened in there, and why you arrested that guy? Did you use any of my pictures?" She obviously refused to believe their day would end with so much having happened and no one to tell her why. "You can't just leave it like this and tell us to go home. I think you should tell us what happened."

Layton looked at her, opened his mouth to say something, and then started to laugh. "Do you put up with her every day of the week?" he asked Brian, shaking his head. "I can't. I'm sorry. Since the race is Sunday, there'll be a press conference in an hour. Usually it wouldn't happen so fast, but management doesn't want people worried about coming to the track. You can read about it in the paper tomorrow morning."

Brian took a step back. He knew Tammi would not let it go at that. With a determined look on her face she moved closer to Officer Layton. "What? No way. We want to go, too. We were the ones who found the body. And you guys took my camera. My pictures helped, didn't they?"

"Man, you can be tough." Layton looked out at the Pagoda, his brow creasing in thought. He keyed the mike on his radio and stepped away from them. A moment later he smiled at her. "Okay. You can go sit in on the press conference. You can't say anything though. Get your stuff together and come on. I'll take you over and be sure you get in."

They sat in the back of the room and watched as the track CEO and police personnel came in and faced a bank of cameras. Brian was amazed how fast this had all taken place.

The CEO said a few words about security at the track and how the security team should be complimented on their speed in resolving the situation. Brian considered the use of the word "situation" odd since they were, after all, talking about a death. After his short spiel, Sergeant Kellham stepped to the microphone. He cleared his throat and gave a brief description of the events.

Brian became more alert when he heard Kellham say, "A spectator was murdered. His name is being withheld pending notification of relatives. Cause of death will be determined by an autopsy. When we moved the body, we found a white tablet. One of the tech guys noticed that it had a pretty strong smell of naphthalene, commonly associated with the smell of moth balls. It's a very distinct odor and is the smell emitted from the newest additive for fuel efficiency. It's sold in a pill form that is dropped into the gas tank. Our techs were sure they knew what it was."

"A review of the photos taken by security cameras and…other sources…" Brian could feel Tammi stiffen, "showed that the victim was followed into the restroom by Russ Miller's crew chief, Bob Anderson. Following that lead, we went to Miller's garage to question Anderson, and found him there alone. We confronted him with the pictures and he confessed. After searching the area, more pills were found as evidence."

"We don't want to make assumptions since we don't have all the facts, but one theory is that Miller hadn't been doing well, so Anderson was trying to find some way to boost his sagging stats. There's no guarantee that this action would have won him the race. Track officials check the fuel tanks before and after each race. The pill would have melted once they added the fuel, but our forensic techs think it still would have left some residue in the tank. You have to understand what's at stake on this track—millions in prize money and advertising are awarded on Race Day."

He took a few questions from the press, and then brought the news conference to a close.

Brian watched Tammi make her way to Officer Layton. "Did you use my pictures or not?"

"I think they did," he said. "I heard you got a shot of the victim just as he headed into the men's room, and Anderson could be seen beside him. He must have thought the victim saw him throw some pills in the fuel tank, and that was what he'd been yelling about. You said he yelled at Rick Mears and talked to different crew members, but Anderson couldn't have known what was said. He obviously left to find him while his guys pushed the car into the garage."

"The papers are going to have a field day. I hate that the Speedway will have this kind of cloud over it. But what can you do? People will do anything to be on top," Layton said as he walked away.

Their car was the only one in the lot as they crossed the street to leave. Everyone had gone home. "Man, what a day." Brian took the cameras from Tammi and wrapped his arm around her waist, giving her a playful hug. "How about that beer you promised me?"

On Sunday, getting to the track for the actual race wasn't as difficult as people said it would be. Brian had purchased a parking pass when he got the tickets, so they headed to the lot off Crawfordsville Road, then toward the gates. Once inside, they picked up their pre-ordered Marsh Box Lunches, a must according to local race fans. Brian insisted that they stop by one of the concession stands, where they bought a couple of bottles of water, a bag of peanuts and some chips.

As they headed up the steps to their seats, Tammi wondered why they'd gotten so much food before the race even started. "I'm beginning to feel like a pack horse," she gasped as they slid into their seats, juggling the food and her now ever-present camera bag. "Why on earth did we have to buy this stuff now? I'm going to have a hard time taking any decent pictures with all this on my lap. You never know…one of my pictures could be…the one…again. Not that I got any credit for it though. That still kind of torques me. You'd think they would have said who the 'other sources' were."

"Oh, well. I'll tell you what, I'm not getting out of this seat until the race is over," Brian said.

With precision timing, they heard the first notes of "Back Home Again in Indiana," and the red, white, and blue balloons started their annual ascension. The man beside Brian leaned over and said conspiratorially, "Be glad you got everything you think you'll need. We always bring a cooler with us. You won't want to get up once the race starts. You could miss something."

Brian laughed and settled into his seat to watch the "Greatest Spectacle in Racing" with a whole new perspective.

Indianapolis 500 Pace Car History

by Wanda Lou Willis

YEAR/CAR/DRIVER

2007	Chevrolet Corvette Z06	Patrick Dempsey
2006	Chevrolet Corvette Z06	Lance Armstrong
2005	Chevrolet Corvette	Gen. Colin Powell
2004	Chevrolet Corvette C5	Morgan Freeman
2003	Chevrolet SSR	Herb Fishel
2002	2003 Chevrolet Corvette	Jim Caviezel
2001	Oldsmobile Bravada	Elaine Irwin-Mellencamp
2000	Oldsmobile Aurora	Anthony Edwards
1999	Chevrolet Monte Carlo	Jay Leno
1998	Chevrolet Corvette	Parnelli Jones
1997	Oldsmobile Aurora	Johnny Rutherford
1996	Dodge Viper GTS	Robert A. Lutz
1995	Chevrolet Corvette	Jim Perkins
1994	Ford Mustang Cobra	Parnelli Jones
1993	Chevrolet Camaro Z-28	Jim Perkins
1992	Cadillac Allante	Bobby Unser
1991	Dodge Viper RT/10	Carroll Shelby
1990	Chevrolet Beretta	Jim Perkins
1989	20th Anniver. Pontiac Trans Am	Bobby Unser
1988	Oldsmobile Cutlass Supreme	Gen. Chuck Yaeger
1987	Chrysler LeBaron	Carroll Shelby
1986	Chevrolet Corvette	Gen. Chuck Yeager
1985	Oldsmobile Calais	James Garner
1984	Pontiac Fiero	John Callies
1983	Buick Riviera Convertible	Duke Nalon
1982	Chevrolet Camaro Z28	Jim Rathmann
1981	Buick Regal V-6	Duke Nalon
1980	Pontiac Turbo-Trans Am	Johnnie Parsons
1979	Ford Mustang	Jackie Stewart
1978	Chevrolet Corvette	Jim Rathmann
1977	Oldsmobile Delta 88	James Garner
1976	Buick Turbocharged V-6	Marty Robbins
1975	Buick Century Custom "Free Spirit"	James Garner
1974	Hurst/Olds Cutlass	Jim Rathmann
1973	Cadillac Eldorado	Jim Rathmann
1972	Hurst/Olds Cutlass	Jim Rathmann
1971	Dodge Challenger	Eldon Palmer
1970	Oldsmobile 4-4-2	Rodger Ward
1969	Chevrolet Camaro SS0	Jim Rathmann

YEAR/CAR/DRIVER

Year	Car	Driver
1968	Ford Torino GT	William Clay Ford, Sr.
1967	Chevrolet Camaro	Mauri Rose
1966	Mercury Comet Cyclone GT	Benson Ford
1965	Plymouth Sports Fury	George W. Mason
1964	Ford Mustang	Benson Ford
1963	Chrysler "300"	Sam Hanks
1962	Studebaker	Sam Hanks
1961	Ford Thunderbird	Sam Hanks
1960	Oldsmobile Ninety-Eight	Sam Hanks
1959	Buick Electra 225	Sam Hanks
1958	Pontiac Bonneville	Sam Hanks
1957	Mercury Turnpike Cruiser	F. C. Reith
1956	DeSoto Fireflite Pacesetter	L. I. Woolson
1955	Chevrolet Bel Air	T. H. Keating
1954	Dodge Royal 500	William C. Newburg
1953	Ford Cresline Sunliner	William Clay Ford, Sr.
1952	Studebaker Commander	P. O. Peterson
1951	Chrysler New Yorker V-8	Dave Wallace
1950	Mercury	Benson Ford
1949	Oldsmobile 88 "Rocket"	Wilbur Shaw
1948	Chevrolet Stylemaster Six-Series	Wilbur Shaw
1947	Nash Ambassador	George W. Mason
1946	Lincoln Continental V12	Henry Ford II
1941	Chrysler-Newport (Phaeton)	A. B. Couture
1940	Studebaker Champion	Harry Hartz
1939	Buick Roadmaster Series 80	Charles Chayne
1938	Hudson "112"	Stuart Baits
1937	LaSalle Series 50	Ralph DePalma
1936	Packard One-Twenty	Tommy Milton
1935	Ford Model 48	Harry Mack
1934	LaSalle Model 350	"Big Boy" Radar
1933	Chrysler Imperial (Phaeton)	Byron Foy
1932	Lincoln Model KB	Edsel Ford
1931	Cadillac 370 Twelve	"Big Boy" Radar
1930	Cord L-29	Wade Morton
1929	Studebaker Series F-10 President	George Hunt
1928	Marmon "8" (Model 78)	Joe Dawson
1927	LaSalle V-8 Series 303	"Big Boy" Radar
1926	Chrysler Imperial E-80	Carl G. Fisher
1925	Rickenbacker Eight	Eddie Rickenbaker
1924	Cole V-8 Series 890	Lew Pettijohn
1923	Duesenberg Model A	Fred S. Duesenberg
1922	National Sextet	Barney Oldfield

1921	Harry C. Stutz Series 6	Harry C. Stutz
1920	Marmon Model 34	Barney Oldfield
1919	Packard 335	Col. J. G. Vincent
1916	Premier Model 6-56	Frank E. Smith
1915	Packard Model 5-48	Carl G. Fisher
1914	Stoddard-Dayton	Carl G. Fisher
1913	Stoddard-Dayton	Carl G. Fisher
1912	Stutz	Carl G. Fisher
1911	Stoddard-Dayton Model 11-A	Carl G. Fisher

The Volunteers

by Tamara Phillips

Tamara Phillips moved to the Midwest in 1985 after growing up and living in Alaska for thirty years. Most of her previous writing has been work-related. She has worked for the federal government, owned an antique shop, and been a fundraiser for public television and radio. She is currently employed as an insurance adjuster. She has a degree in journalism, three daughters and three grandsons.

"You'd think it would be pretty dangerous walking around with thousands of dollars in a beat-up little beer cooler," Trish said to her friend, Sylvia.

Sylvia pressed her lips together hard enough that little dimples shot into each side of her mouth as she considered Trish's comment. "I'll bet no one thinks about someone stealing one of these, though. Everyone is carrying a cooler, and besides, the people working these booths don't stand out at all from the rest of the people here. It's not like they're wearing uniforms or anything. I'm sure it's safe. Don't worry so much, let's just enjoy ourselves."

"Just the same, it could be dangerous, and a person should watch out," Trish countered.

Sylvia shrugged. She had already taken one trip to the deposit area and back, escorting the person carrying the cooler. "I agreed to do it for the experience," she'd said in Trish's direction. "I'll tell you all about it later so you'll know what to do if you have to go."

Trish nodded, but secretly thought the whole thing sounded risky, and began folding T-shirts into stacks and sorting them into the proper sizes. *I don't think it's a good idea for people to call unnecessary attention to themselves when they are carrying a large amount of money. It had occurred to me last year that hauling money around in a beer cooler is not very secure.*

Trish and Sylvia had gone through school together, inseparable from first grade through graduation at Grayley High School in Harrisville, about twenty miles southeast of Fairmount, Indiana (the hometown of James Dean). Harrisville is one of those small towns where everyone knows everyone else and their business. The two were town terrors, and there wasn't a prank pulled in over fifteen years that they didn't either do or instigate.

They'd started out in grade school with the usual joke phone calls, but quickly found out when their whole group of friends was involved, the next call was to their parents. Soon after, it was just the two of them. One of their favorites was the simple "out of order" signs they put on all the men's restroom doors at the regional basketball tournament. Trish and Sylvia grew to enjoy the planning and execution of their practical jokes, and it did keep them occupied while the years moved slowly toward graduation.

They couldn't wait to grow up and leave for someplace more exciting. Trish's Aunt Fay was known to say frequently, "If you girls don't settle down some, the farthest you're likely to get from Harrisville is the state prison in Pendleton."

As fate would have it, they had both ended up back in Harrisville permanently, each alone and trying to settle into semi-retirement. Both sets of parents were now gone, but good old doomsayer Aunt Fay was alive and well and still regarded everything they did with suspicion, which amused both of them to no end.

Last year had been Trish and Sylvia's first visit to the Indianapolis 500. A mutual friend had asked them at the last minute if they could help out at one of the many concession stands that surround the track. They'd agreed and enjoyed themselves so much that they offered to volunteer again this year. They ended up scheduled to work the first shift on Race Day itself, volunteers, as usual, being in short supply.

Trish had looked forward to working at the Indianapolis 500 all winter. She and Sylvia spent hours discussing and researching the race track. Their planning provided an enjoyable diversion during an otherwise boring Indiana winter. By spring they were rattling off the names of drivers and sponsors of cars like they'd been avid fans their whole lives.

Trish crawled out of bed at 2:00 the morning of the big race. Her eyes, squinty with sleep, looked out the kitchen window at her 1998 Honda. It sat packed and ready to go in the half shadow from her front porch light. Within minutes she was dressed and driving slowly through the dim streets to Sylvia's house.

Just as she pulled up, the front door opened and Sylvia came out carrying a large cooler and dragging a folded-up lawn chair.

Trish got out to help and stood by the just-opened trunk.

"Here, don't forget to put this on your rear view mirror," Sylvia said.

The handicapped parking tag was from Sylvia's knee surgery the previous fall. Even though the knee was back to normal, the tag was still current and would allow them to park within a block of the concession stand they were working at. Trish felt a little guilty about using it, but the thought of trudging through the dark for several blocks from the regular parking area for volunteers, toting their chairs and coolers, pushed that feeling right out of her mind.

She helped her friend arrange the cooler and chair in the trunk alongside her own and waited while Sylvia ran back inside to grab two umbrellas, "just in case." With every eventuality covered, they climbed in the car, buckled up and headed out of town, anticipating a busy and exciting day.

The two-hour drive to Indianapolis was uneventful until they turned off I-465 at Speedway. There they drove through miles of the temporary tent city that surrounds the track every year. The fast food trailers and concessions were dark for the night. Empty cans and assorted wrappers littered the streets. Every available driveway and field was filled with campers and tents. In the distance they could hear the yell of a lone reveler, still going from the night before.

"There's Gate 10," said Sylvia, as they approached an area that looked better lit. "Just drive through like you know where you're going."

"Get our volunteer passes out just in case," Trish said. "I hope they don't try and divert us to another parking lot since we know the handicapped one is so convenient."

It was dark as they pulled up to the lighted area. An orange-vested security guard stepped into the light, the flashlight in his hand angled politely toward the ground.

"Good morning," Trish said with a smile, "ready for the big day?"

"Sure am," he responded.

Trish waived the passes out the open window, "We're volunteering today and we already know where we're supposed to park."

He nodded, swung his light toward the track, and turned to the cars coming in behind them.

"Perfect," breathed Sylvia.

They drove a short distance and pulled into the second row of handicapped parking. They could see the souvenir stand about 500 feet to the right where they would be meeting the other volunteers.

The concession was actually close enough to the car for them to come back for the umbrellas and lightweight jackets if they needed them, so they just took out the two coolers and folding chairs and started walking toward the stand.

They had been sitting on the large pink cooler only a couple minutes when the other volunteers started arriving. They had already stopped for the keys and a small cooler just like Trish's small one. This cooler, which was blue, was the one used to transport money from the booth to the central location for deposit.

The booth opened at 5:00 a.m. and was busy from the start. Some of the more popular caps were sold out after two hours. When their replacements showed up just before race time, Trish and Sylvia were both relieved. The timing was great for them to eat a quick bite and have the rest of the day to enjoy the race.

They each grabbed one of their coolers and the folding chairs and headed around the track to see if they could find a picnic table. They finally found an empty one in a shady spot just barely under the bleachers. Sylvia put out lunch, and Trish took the binoculars out of her tote bag and began looking around at the crowd.

She focused in on a concession in one of the small freestanding trailers. It was something like the one they had been working in that morning. To Trish's appraising eye, it had a far better location and seemed to be even busier than they had been.

"It's true when they say location is everything," Trish commented as she watched the customers pushing to pay for their T-shirts and caps.

Sylvia took a bite of her sandwich and wiped her mouth with a napkin.

She gestured to her left. "The place where the money is deposited is two or three blocks up there. It's tucked in under the bleachers alongside the maintenance and storage rooms. The way it was explained to me, the concession workers from this area put the money in their coolers, deposit their money, and then take the deposit slip back to their booths. That way they don't end up with a lot of money in the booth. You know, Shirley, the one I went with this morning guessed they would take in over $20,000 today. A booth in a high traffic area like that one could take in twice that much." She pointed her sandwich toward the booth Trish was looking at.

"Here, take a look. I'll bet it won't be too long before they take a deposit back." Trish passed the binoculars to Sylvia.

Sylvia took a quick look. "Possibly. Do you want to finish up eating and head down that way? I know you want to see how it's done."

"Sounds good to me. I'll carry the binoculars and our lawn chairs, if you'll carry the coolers."

"Good, it will keep me sort of balanced."

As they went past the back of the 24-foot trailer they had been watching, they again joined the surging crowd of race fans and partiers. They had gone about a block when Sylvia swung the smaller cooler forward, pointing to an area up ahead.

"See where those two ladies with the small blue-and-white cooler are turning? The deposit area is right back there," Sylvia said.

"Very sneaky."

They walked along past more concessions and over to where the food stands were doing a brisk business. Customers were lined up for half a block at each one. The beer stand had three lines, and the end of the closest one almost reached where they were standing.

All of a sudden, all heads turned toward the track as a roar went up from the fans in the stands and the sound of engines blasted at the same time. The race had begun!

"Look, Trish," Sylvia said, pointing. "Two people from the trailer we were just watching are coming this way, with one lady carrying a small cooler."

They turned and watched as the two approached them. They were about ten feet away when a young guy on a skateboard weaved through the crowd behind them and hit Trish in the side, hard. Both feet flew straight out in front of her and higher than her head. The binoculars swung out to the side and up, still tethered to her neck by their black strap. She landed with her arms and legs all askew. There was a chorus of gasps all around them, and as the lawn chairs clattered to the ground, Sylvia began screaming.

"Oh, my God, Trish, are you all right?" She grabbed the lady closest to her and screeched, "Help her, help her!"

The crowd around them seemed to stop simultaneously in their tracks. Sylvia had a death grip on the lady and was sobbing and yelling.

A young man smelling of beer reached down to help Trish up. She carefully moved one leg and then the other until both feet were under her, and then pulled herself up straight. She squeezed the forearm of the man who helped her and looked around as if dazed.

Sylvia patted the lady she had all but attacked in her hysteria. She kept saying, "I'm so sorry, I was just scared."

Trish moved her shoulders back and forth to make sure everything was still working and stepped toward Sylvia.

"For heavens sake, Sylvie, pull yourself together," she hissed into her mussed hair, "and pick up your stuff."

"Thank you, young man," Trish said, turning to her inebriated rescuer, who stood behind her shuffling uneasily from foot to foot.

"Are you sure you're okay?" he asked. "Should we call the paramedics? They've got wagons all over."

"No, I don't want to ride in one of those golf cart things. I've been enough of a spectacle, and I think I'm all right." Trish brushed at her clothes and straightened the waistband on her pants.

The onlookers smirked and moved away. The rest of the crowd pretended nothing had happened.

Trish picked up the chairs and put them under her arm. Sylvia tucked the small cooler inside the larger one. She put her free arm through Trish's. "Hang on to me," she said. "I think we should head home. This is enough excitement for one day."

They hobbled toward handicapped parking.

This time they didn't bother opening the trunk. They just tossed everything in the back seat and got in. Trish took her place behind the wheel.

She started the Honda and expertly backed out. She headed toward the exit. Not many people were leaving since the race was still going. As they left the racetrack, she made a right hand turn and headed north away from Speedway. At the next major crossroad, they drove west until they were able to pull onto the freeway.

Trish concentrated on her driving until traffic thinned out to almost normal. As they merged onto I-69 North, she took a quick look at Sylvia sitting smugly in the passenger seat.

She couldn't help but smile.

Sylvia grinned back and said, "I swear, Trish, you are such a show-off. I have never seen such a fall. You must have been at least four feet off the ground. I don't know how you landed like that, either."

Trish chuckled, "Body recall...and you, you acted absolutely demented. You're lucky they didn't decide to just haul you away. And that poor woman...I thought you were going to pull her arm off!"

"Nah, just enough of a tug to loosen her grip on that cooler so I could switch them," Sylvia said.

"And Trish, our timing...it was perfect," she continued excitedly. "We popped that small cooler full of money into the larger one and just left."

"You're right, Sylvie, we're not just older, we're better!"

"Shall we count it now?"

"No, you know I love surprises; let's wait until we get home. Maybe we'll take Aunt Fay out to celebrate just to hear her carry on about what hellions we were."

"You mean *are*, don't you, Trish? Actually, we never stopped; we just got good enough not to get caught!"

"Well, Sylvie, I think we have just touched the tip of the iceberg as far as the races in Indianapolis go. Maybe we should consider the Brickyard next time..."

Sylvia settled into her seat. "I do love the racetrack."

Trish made her usual careful two-handed turn onto their exit, "...and they always need volunteers."

Post-Race Track Traditions
by Wanda Lou Willis

- After winning the 1936 race, Louis Meyer asked for a glass of buttermilk. His mother had suggested he drink his favorite drink after the race to revive his energy. Anton "Tony" Hulman in 1956 made the drink a permanent part of the Victory Lane celebration. No longer buttermilk, but Grade A milk is served to the winner in a replica of a 1936 glass milk bottle. Besides the bottle, the American Dairy Association also presents a cash award to the winner and his chief mechanic.

- The winner's face, name, average speed and date of his victory are added to the Borg-Warner Trophy, which was introduced in 1936. Since 1988, a smaller replica of this trophy has been presented to the winner. Prior to that they received a replica mounted on a wood plaque.

- Almost every year since 1936, the winner has received the pace car or a replica. George Robson was to receive an oil painting and a trip to Italy in lieu of a pace car. Before he received them he was killed in another competition. The 1991 Dodge Viper pace car was still a prototype with only two in existence. Instead Rick Mears was awarded a Dodge Stealth. The Stealth had been chosen as the original pace car. The UAW protested this selection since the car was an import built by Mitsubishi in Japan. They were instead used at the track as festival cars.

- Jim Rathmann received the first Winner's Wreath consisting of exotic-looking, dark-yellow-and-brown flowers. The following year A. J. Foyt received a garland of white and red carnations, the type normally associated with horse racing. Today the wreath features 33 ivory-colored orchids, plus 33 miniature checkered flags intertwined with red, white and blue ribbons.

Photo Finish

by Diana Catt

Diana Catt has three children, a husband, two dogs, two cats and a Ph.D in Microbiology. She is currently an instructor and postdoctoral research fellow at the IU School of Dentistry in Indianapolis. She is also the owner/operator of a private lab for the analysis of mold in the environment. Diana enjoys writing, reading, racquetball, birding and hiking.

Maggie Wheeler drove along 16th Street toward the track entrance used by employees of the Indianapolis Motor Speedway Museum and felt a tingle of anticipation. There was not a cloud in the sky, and the radio announcer promised that today was "finally, race fans, the day you've been waiting for," a rain-free practice day. Throngs of people were already descending upon the track, carrying coolers, jackets, radios and stadium seats.

The front door to the museum, usually deserted an hour before opening, was hidden by a sea of red jackets, the uniform of the regular museum staff. Maggie was a "yellow shirt," the description for, and uniform of, the temps hired for the month of May. An ambulance with its back doors open was parked in front of the museum on the circular drive, flanked front and rear by police cars.

"What's going on?" Maggie asked the assistant director, Mrs. Thompson, who turned toward her as Maggie approached the group. "Is someone hurt?"

"You'd better go on in, Ms. Wheeler. The detective wants to speak with you."

"Detective?"

The buzz of the crowd stopped and heads turned toward her. Lou Hawkins, museum security, stepped forward and opened the door, giving Maggie a nod and a questioning look.

"She's here," Mrs. Thompson called through the doorway to the man standing at the information desk. "This is Maggie Wheeler."

Maggie crossed the lobby and eyed the man at the desk. He was old, maybe thirty even, but really cute.

"Please have a seat, Ms. Wheeler. I'm Detective Morgan with Speedway P.D."

"Hi," she said. "I'm Maggie. What's going on?"

"Do you know J.D. Butler?"

"J.D.? Yeah. He's a guy who works across the street. Comes in here a lot to talk. Why are you asking about J.D.? Is he okay?"

"I was informed that Mr. Butler was your boyfriend."

"J.D. my boyfriend? No way. We only met last week. Why?"

"When did you last see Mr. Butler?"

"Well, we had lunch yesterday outside by the fountain. But it was chilly. I ate fast and, well, that was about it."

"Do you have a key to the museum, Ms. Wheeler?"

"Lord, no. Temps don't get keys. What's this all about? Has something happened to J.D.?"

That's when Detective Morgan told her what had happened.

J.D. Butler, the biggest flirt Maggie had ever met, knocked the Borg-Warner Trophy off its pedestal in the Indianapolis Motor Speedway Museum and got himself murdered in the process. At least, that's what Maggie thought the detective said. The words stunned her, and she had trouble making any sense out of it all. Did he really say J.D. had been shot?

"Oh, my God," she said. "Are you sure? He was just here yesterday. I can't believe this."

The detective nodded.

"But why would he even be here in the museum?"

"I was hoping you might be able to answer that."

"Me? I barely knew the guy." She paused, overwhelmed by the sudden intrusion of death. J.D. was too young to die. She couldn't quite come to grips with the idea. He had been so alive yesterday, and now he was dead. Dead. Shot right here in the museum. During the middle of the night. Was he a thief?

"Was he stealing something?" Maggie asked.

"Why do you ask that?"

"Well, he was in the museum after hours," Maggie said. She almost added "duh," but thought better of it. "What was he after?"

"The museum will be inventoried."

"This is so weird," Maggie said. "I never dreamed J.D. was a thief."

The detective cocked his head and looked closely at her. "You seem to be the only one around here who knew the victim, Ms. Wheeler. Did he ever say anything about the Ferretti necklace?"

Maggie paused to think a minute. She and J.D. had never discussed jewelry. She said no.

"Where were you last night, Ms. Wheeler? Around nine p.m.?"

"At home. Just call my mom. I went there for supper right after work and stayed until the news came on at ten. Then I drove to my girlfriend Sheena's apartment in Plainfield. Took about twenty minutes."

"Thanks. Write down the names, addresses and phone numbers for you, your mom and girlfriend, and we'll check it out. That's all the questions for now. I may need to reach you later on if something else occurs to me."

Maggie was relieved and disappointed at the same time. "Sure. I guess we won't be opening today, huh?"

"The gift shop can open. We'll try to wrap up the crime scene and get the museum open ASAP. Town Hall hates to see anything dampen the 'Greatest Spectacle in Racing.'"

Maggie headed across the lobby toward the gift shop. The news of J.D.'s death hung like a black cloud over her spirits. On impulse, she changed direction and headed into the women's room, where she pulled out her cell phone and called Sheena. She needed her best friend's perspective right now.

Sheena had never met J.D., but she was still shocked by the news.

"Oh, man, that's awful," Sheena said. "Plus it sounds like you're a suspect."

"Me? I don't think so. I'm just the only one here who knew J.D."

"My point exactly."

"J.D. was nice to me."

"Well, don't get all melancholy over him. He was obviously up to no good."

"Still, it's sad though."

"Yeah. But, tell me more about the detective," Sheena said.

"Cute. Old. A little stuffy maybe."

"Married?"

Maggie giggled. "I don't know. The subject didn't come up."

"Gotta notice these things, girl."

"Well, too late now."

"Uh-uh. Just sneak into old Mrs. T's office again and Google him."

"You're nuts," Maggie said with a laugh. "But thanks for being there. I feel better now. Catch you later."

Maggie pocketed the phone and headed for the gift shop. She literally bumped into Lou Hawkins, who was standing just outside the restroom door.

"Oops, sorry, Lou." He was on the frail side, but she didn't seem to have hurt him.

"Better watch your step, Ms. Maggie," Lou said. "You don't want to end up knocking over the displays and hitting your head like your boyfriend in there." He nodded toward the main museum display area, which the police had taped off.

"You know he's not my boyfriend, and besides, he didn't hit his head. He was shot."

"Must be losing my touch," Lou said. "I can usually spot trouble a mile away. That young man didn't seem too bad. Otherwise, I'd have never sent him in your direction."

"What?"

"When he was in here last week asking about you and whether you were single. I said you were and suggested he talk to you. That's all."

"That's enough."

"My apologies. What did the police ask you?"

"Oh, how well I knew J.D., where I was last night, that sort of thing."

"Did they say what the boy was up to?"

"They asked about some jewelry. Maybe J.D. was trying to steal something."

"Jewelry? Let's see. We have some winners' rings on display, some commemorative watches and some historic diamond-studded European stick pins. Any of those?"

"No. This had a name. Sounded like one of those expensive cars. Ferrari maybe? Ferrari necklace?"

"Well, I'll be. You mean Ferretti. Do the police think the Ferretti necklace was here in the museum?"

"What the heck is the Ferretti necklace, and why would J.D. get killed over it?"

Mrs. Thompson interrupted. "Ms. Wheeler, please stop gossiping and get to work. All this police activity will attract curiosity seekers, meaning extra business for the gift shop. We have a lot to do to get ready. Come along now, young lady."

"Meet me for lunch?" Maggie whispered to Lou. She enjoyed lunches with him. He was a walking history book.

Lou nodded, and Maggie scurried into the gift shop. Mrs. Thompson sure called it right; the morning was her busiest since taking this job. Rumors were flying all day about the murder and the Ferretti necklace connection. Maggie learned that the necklace had been lost in the pit area during last year's running of the 500, and a huge reward was still being offered. The young Ferretti heiress who had carelessly worn the family antique had been blasé about the whole incident, citing a faulty clasp as the culprit, but her grandmother had been livid. Grandmother's phone calls had prompted searches of everyone leaving the pit area, and she had also put up the reward.

Maggie overheard Mrs. Thompson confiding to a fascinated group of customers that a piece of the necklace had been found at the murder scene, and it appeared that it had been hidden all year in that big face-covered trophy. But if the assistant director had any idea who put the necklace there or how J.D. found out about it, she was keeping it to herself. Maggie looked forward to lunch and her chance to talk it over with Lou. He had been around the museum forever, knew practically everyone, and would surely have a theory.

Maggie heard one rumor floating around, that the famous Borg-Warner Trophy had been damaged during the murder. The first version had the trophy as the murder weapon, but Maggie knew J.D. had been shot, and anyway, how could you bean someone over the head with a five-foot, one-hundred-fifty-pound object? They'd be looking for the Hulk if that were true.

Another version had all the faces on one side of the trophy getting knocked off and the 24-karat-gold head portrait of Tony Hulman, the late Speedway owner and president, still missing. Postcards featuring the trophy quickly became a popular purchase item. Mrs. Thompson was driving the clerks crazy trying out different ways to display them.

Maggie was restocking Danica Patrick T-shirts when she remembered something J.D. had said at lunch yesterday. The cute detective had asked her to relay anything she remembered, so she went to locate Mrs. Thompson for permission to take a break. Detective Morgan was with Mrs. Thompson in her office, examining the computer.

"Yes, Ms. Wheeler?" Mrs. Thompson said. It sounded to Maggie as if her last name had taken on a new meaning, sort of on par with a dead skunk.

"Um, excuse me, Mrs. Thompson. But I remembered something that I thought the detective might want to know."

He looked up from the computer terminal and smiled at her. "Would you excuse us, Mrs. Thompson?" he said.

He couldn't have seen the glare Mrs. Thompson sent her way. Did the assistant museum director have the hots for the cute detective?

"Do you know much about computers, Maggie?"

He called her Maggie. Her heart flipped.

"Yeah, I guess. Why?"

"I'm printing out a list of the names of everyone who has used this terminal recently to send e-mails or use the Internet."

Maggie felt her heart sink. She and J.D. had used the computer yesterday after lunch while Mrs. Thompson was still on her break. Would they be on that list?

"That's sort of what I wanted to tell you," Maggie said. "I mean, I remembered someone J.D. mentioned at lunch, then he wanted to, you know, send the guy an e-mail. So I sort of, well, let him in here." She stared at the carpet.

"What was the name?"

She looked up. "Huh?"

"The name of the guy J.D. told you about?"

"Oh. J.D. just called him Crash. He works for the Penske team pit crew. Changes tires or something? Anyway, J.D. was impressed. Said the guy had it made and wanted to hire him."

"And the computer?"

"Well, he needed to let the guy know he was going to take the job offer, didn't he? They may not have phones in the pit area, but they can get e-mails."

"So you let J.D. use Mrs. Thompson's computer?"

"Yes. Does she know?"

He shrugged. "She might figure it out. But thanks for coming clean with me."

She felt a surge of hope. Mrs. T. might be mad at her, but at least he wasn't.

"We also know that you and J.D. were responsible for the screen image that startled Mrs. Thompson when she came back from lunch."

Maggie laughed. "Oh, J.D. did that. You should've heard her. She went freaking ballistic. You'd think she hadn't seen any naked men before. But J.D. didn't really mean any harm, detective, just a little joke. Too bad he didn't stick around to hear her reaction."

"Oh, he stuck around, all right," the detective said. "We've watched the surveillance tapes. J.D. used that distraction to hide himself in the old Cadillac on display on the museum floor."

Maggie's mouth fell open, but she couldn't think of a thing to say.

"How old are you, Maggie?"

"Eighteen," she said, avoiding eye contact with the detective. When he didn't say anything, she looked up to meet his stern gaze. "Well, okay, I'm only seventeen, but I'll be eighteen soon."

"Why aren't you in school? Drop out?"

"No, of course not. I graduated early, last December. I should be in college, I guess. But I just don't know what I want to do."

"There are phones in the pit area, Maggie."

"But J.D. said…"

"I think J.D. was using you to gain access to the museum."

"Using me? Now wait just a minute. He didn't need me to get into the museum. He always paid admission like everybody else."

"The way I see it," Detective Morgan said, "he needed to scout out the place. He couldn't very well come here every day without a reason, or someone might get suspicious. So you became his reason."

Maggie was stunned. "I thought he liked me," she said. "I was feeling bad for him, being dead and all. You really think he was using me?"

"Looks that way. We think someone, probably this Crash person, hired J.D. to retrieve the necklace from where it was hidden last year." The detective smiled. "One of the Penske drivers won last year, and the pit crew had a photo op with the driver holding the Borg-Warner Trophy. It would have been a good opportunity for this guy Crash to hide the necklace in the base of the trophy. There's a felt pad on the bottom which is loose on one corner. He probably slipped it in through there. I'll bet anything Crash thought the trophy was going to leave the racetrack with the driver or the car owner. I'd love to have seen his face when he learned the driver only gets a replica, and the big one comes right back here to the museum."

"I wouldn't have known that either," Maggie said. "So why wait a whole year to try a break-in?"

"Don't know. Maybe they travel so much, this was the first chance he had to get back to Indy. Anyway, now that we have someone to look for, we can ask him. Thank you, Maggie."

"But why kill J.D.?"

"Don't know that yet, either," the detective said. "If you think of anything else, please call me." He handed Maggie his business card. She was thrilled. No one had ever given her their business card.

"Oh, I will, Detective Morgan. You can count on me."

Maggie left the office and spotted Lou Hawkins standing in the museum lobby. She glanced at her watch. Lunchtime. She went behind the cashier's counter, retrieved her purse, and ran into the lobby.

"Let's go," she said, "before Thompson fires me."

They walked out of the front entrance and headed for the nearest food tent.

"Want to eat out on the lawn?" Lou asked.

Maggie agreed. Once settled in the sun, she filled Lou in on her discussion with Detective Morgan.

"There's a lot of people nicknamed Crash around here," Lou said. "I could probably come up with ten without even trying."

"Bet they don't all work for the Penske team," Maggie said. "That should narrow it down a lot."

"It still seems far-fetched to me," Lou said. "There's always such a crowd around the winner's circle. Someone would have noticed a person messing with the bottom of the trophy."

"Hmm," Maggie replied with her mouth full. "I'd like to look through some pictures taken at the winner's circle. I bet there's a lot of extra ones that don't get displayed."

Lou finished his sandwich and looked at Maggie. "You're a pretty smart cookie," he said. "There are boxes and boxes of photos somewhere upstairs, but I doubt we could find them."

"Can we look?"

"No time now," he said. "Tell you what. If I get a chance, I'll scout around for them."

Maggie caught glimpses of cute Detective Morgan through-out the afternoon, and she tried hard to think of something else to tell him. She pulled out his business card and entered his number in her cell phone on rapid dial, just in case something occurred to her. The police finished with the crime scene around three that afternoon, and the museum was allowed to reopen. It immediately filled with tourists snapping pictures of the murder site.

Maggie's day was just about over when Mrs. Thompson freaked out because the postcards were running low. Maggie volunteered to go upstairs to the storage area and bring down another case. She was thrilled to see Detective Morgan still on-site. He even gave her a little nod when she walked through the museum toward the stairway.

Maggie never located the postcards. While looking around the crowded storage room, she noticed a stack of boxes labeled "2006 – 500 photos." She pulled down a box from the top, opened it, and peered inside. It was stuffed with large manila envelopes. Some of the labels read: "2006 start;" "Laps 1-50;" "Laps 51-100;" "Wreck-lap 48-turn one." She flipped through them until she came to one labeled "Winner's Circle." She was standing in front of the boxes holding the envelope when the door to the stairway opened, and Lou appeared.

"Thompson left for the day and said you were up here. Did you find the postcards?"

"No, but I found something more interesting." She pointed to the stack of boxes.

"Those the pictures you were wanting?"

"Maybe. Let's take a look."

Lou nodded, ambled over, and looked at the label on the envelope.

"Probably should've let it be, Ms. Maggie," he said. "Leave this for the cops."

She grinned at him. "I'm trying to impress Detective Morgan."

Lou just shook his head.

Maggie poured the contents of the envelope out onto a table. There were eight smaller envelopes. She picked one at random, read the photographer's name on the front, and removed the pictures. "Wow, just look at these," she said.

Maggie recognized Sam Hornish, Jr. wearing the winner's wreath and drinking from the victory bottle of milk. She spotted the Borg-Warner Trophy beside the car. Lou was right. There were lots of people around Mr. Hornish and his car. It would be hard to do anything secretive. All twenty prints were pretty much the same.

The next envelope contained smaller prints of the same scenes taken from a different angle. She pointed this out to Lou.

"There are lots of photographers around the track all month," he said. "Some are pros hired especially for this event, and most of the pictures are theirs. Then there's the private photographers who hope to get one of their prints chosen to be used on a postcard or put on our website or in the museum. Their prints are stored here, too."

"You mean they might make money doing this?"

"Sure. I had a shot get used as a postcard a few years back."

"No way," Maggie said. "I didn't know you were a photographer." She picked up another envelope and read the name on the face. "Hey, here's some of yours."

Maggie slid out the photos and looked them over—a series of pictures taken after the crowds had dispersed. These photos were of the crew, the driver, the owner, the car and, of course, the Borg-Warner Trophy, front and center. She scrutinized the shots and noticed that it took several men to lift the trophy into position by the driver. In one picture, she could actually detect the hand of one of the pit crew on the bottom of the trophy.

Maggie realized she was holding something that would get Detective Morgan's attention. Without saying anything to Lou, she pulled her phone out of her pocket and pressed the speed dial number for the detective.

"Don't call anyone," Lou said. His voice had a stern edge to it that Maggie had not heard before. "And hand over those prints."

Maggie looked up.

"I mean," he said somewhat softer, "don't bother trying to get a signal up here. It won't work."

Maggie looked at her phone. The call was going through. An alarm went off in her head. She carefully placed the phone in her pocket without disconnecting.

"Tell me about these pictures, Lou."

"I told you. You should have let it be. But what's done is done."

"You have a photographic record of someone hiding the necklace. Why didn't you claim the reward?"

Lou sighed and began picking up the photographs and re-placing them in the envelope.

"I didn't realize what I had until last week when I was looking through my negatives at home," he said. "They want to use one of my pictures for an ad, and I needed to find the negative."

"What, you were just waiting for someone to come and get the necklace?"

"It takes a strong man to move that trophy. I couldn't do it. And the necklace might have already been removed. I couldn't tell."

Maggie couldn't quite believe where this was heading. "My God, Lou. Why did you have to kill J.D.?"

"I knew you were a smart cookie," he said. "I'm sorry you figured it out, Ms. Maggie, but J.D. wouldn't let me have the necklace. I could tell from the pictures that Crash was the one who hid it, and I was reasonably sure he wouldn't try to re-cover it himself. He might be recognized around here, you see.

I figured he would hire someone. So I've been watching. I figured it would happen this month, when everyone's back in Indy. I'd just watch and wait and take my time. When J.D. first came in, I suspected he was the one Crash had hired. I've been watching him scout out the place for a week. That distraction yesterday with Mrs. Thompson's computer didn't fool me one bit. I made sure he wasn't discovered in the Caddie, and then I hid out, too. Of course, it was a lot easier for me to remain behind undetected."

"And J.D. had to die because he could identify you," Maggie said, her heart pounding in her throat. "What about me?"

"I wish you hadn't been so curious about this, Ms. Maggie. I like you, I really do. I would have removed these prints, but I didn't dream anyone would think of looking through them so closely. Now I'm afraid you've become inconsolable since the death of your boyfriend. You grabbed my gun, vowed to join your young lover in death, and pulled the trigger."

Maggie nodded. "That's pretty good. But J.D. wasn't my boyfriend."

"Publicly, no. Secretly, yes. I was your only confidante. I'll be convincing."

She had no doubt of that. He certainly had her fooled all this time. What if Detective Morgan wasn't listening? She needed to get downstairs, maybe someone was still on the premises.

"I'm sure you will. This is probably not the best spot, though."

"You're right again. We'll go downstairs and have the tragic event take place at the site of J.D.'s demise. Much more poetic." He glanced at his watch. "I'm sure everyone's cleared out by now. Let me have those pictures, and put the rest back in the box."

Maggie's hands were shaking as she straightened up the files. Lou wasn't holding a gun, but she was sure he had one. She hoped Detective Morgan had heard the confession over the cell phone.

"By the way," she said, "where's the necklace now? I heard it was in pieces."

"Never mind about that. I've got it stowed away. And put that box back up there where it was," Lou said. "I don't want anything to confuse the police investigation."

"Okay," Maggie said. "But, you know Detective Morgan's going to figure this out and bust you." She prayed it would happen sooner than later.

"Your innocence and trust are charming, my dear. Now let's go."

Maggie led the way down the stairs. When she turned the first landing, her cell phone rang. She nearly fainted. The line was supposed to be open, and the police were supposed to be listening and waiting at the bottom of the stairs. What could she do now?

"Don't answer it," Lou said.

"No," she screamed and lunged at Lou. She knocked him off balance. He fell back against the wall, and Maggie took off. She rounded the doorway at the bottom of the stairs and ran directly into the waiting arms of Detective Morgan.

"I got him," a man called from the stairwell.

Maggie looked up into the handsome face.

"Are you okay?" he asked.

"What are you doing here?" she blurted out. "I mean, yes, I'm okay, but how'd you know?"

He released her and explained. "Well, your friend, Hawkins, has been at the top of my suspect list ever since I found out he volunteered to do the security check on this section of the museum yesterday. J.D. couldn't have hidden out in that car without someone on the inside covering for him. And thanks to your tip, we found Crash. He readily admitted hiding the necklace and hiring J.D. to retrieve it, but he had a solid alibi for the time of the murder. Then I saw Hawkins follow you upstairs."

"Why didn't you do something?"

"I was standing on the landing, just out of sight the whole time," he said. "And my partner went up the back stairway, had you covered from behind. You were never in any real danger. Good job getting him to open up like that."

The praise did the trick. Her good humor returned.

"I tried to phone you."

"I was standing on the stairway," he said. "Had my phone turned off. Ever think of going into police work? We're always looking for bright young people like you."

Her heart did a flip. *The Police Academy? Wait till Sheena hears about this.*

Founding of the Town of Speedway

by Tony Perona

The town of Speedway was founded in 1926, fifteen years after the first running of the Indianapolis 500 in 1911. Although called the "Indianapolis Motor Speedway," all 539 acres of the track actually lie within the town limits.

Today the town of Speedway is completely surrounded by Indianapolis, but it maintains a fierce independence. The town has its own police force, fire department, town hall, public library and school system. The school's team name, the Speedway Sparkplugs, even reflects the racing heritage.

Although having three races is good for the Speedway economy, it also brings a lot of visitors. Not all residents enthusiastically embrace the traffic, the trash and the transitory migration that now occurs three times a year along with the excitement of having the greatest drivers and the greatest cars in motorsports racing.

The Land Grab

by Tony Perona

Tony Perona is a former General Motors advertising/public relations manager, who in 1991 became the first man at GM to take the company-sponsored leave of absence to care for his children. He didn't go back. Today he is a freelance writer and author of the Nick Bertetto mystery series. This is his first story to feature new characters, Charlotte and Francine, and their list of sixty things they want to do after turning sixty. Tony grew up in Speedway, Indiana, and is a 1974 graduate of Speedway High School.

The glazed-over look in Charlotte's eyes put Francine on alert. Whenever she saw it, she knew her friend was about to say something that hadn't been fully processed by her brain. Sometimes Charlotte said whatever the other person wanted to hear; other times she said whatever popped into her mind. So Francine was braced to head off trouble when Charlotte told the policeman, "Someone killed my uncle, and I know who did it."

Francine sighed. It had been a rough afternoon for Charlotte, but this was an unexpected development. The two women had suspected the worst when they used Charlotte's key to let themselves into her Uncle Harold's house just after lunchtime. Charlotte hadn't heard from the 82-year-old widower in two days, despite having left numerous messages. They'd found him in bed, unmoving. Being a retired nurse, Francine had immediately checked for a pulse but found none. She'd called 911, and then comforted Charlotte while they waited for the Speedway Police to arrive. She'd sat by her friend's side during questioning.

But this latest twist had exasperated Francine. "You don't know that he was murdered, Charlotte. I think it was just natural causes. There wasn't anything about him that made it look otherwise. And he'd been taking heart medications. They were sitting on his nightstand."

Charlotte shifted away from Francine on the couch. "I bet the paramedics found something. Or the deputy coroner. They've been in the bedroom awhile."

Francine got up and looked out the living room window. The paramedics had arrived within a few minutes of her call. Their ambulance was parked in the driveway, the deputy coroner's car now alongside. Two police cars had also responded. They were parked in front of the house. One had contained a rookie officer, Brett O'Neal, and his field training officer, Lt. Joe Helphenstine, who'd both come in. The other policeman had remained outside. Francine could see him questioning Harold's neighbor, Lloyd Monroe.

O'Neal, who'd interviewed them, came over and stood next to Charlotte. "What makes you think he might have been murdered, Mrs. Reinhardt? Did he have enemies?"

"I'm just saying that he was very healthy, even though he was taking medicines. He power-walked two miles three times a week. He could dance for hours at a time."

Francine had seen Harold "power-walk." It might have seemed fast to Charlotte, who'd had to slow down when her hip replacement surgery hadn't gone so well. But to Francine, watching Harold power-walk was like watching someone run through Jell-O—the motions looked fast, but he didn't cover much ground. And while he might have been a dancer, she guessed he didn't jitterbug anymore.

O'Neal looked at his notes. "Earlier you said you and Mrs. McNamara last saw him two weeks ago during the 500. Did he give you the impression he was worried about his life?"

"He was too busy parking cars on his lawn," Francine offered. "We hardly talked to him at all."

Charlotte sniffed. "He didn't have much time to visit with us that day. Being directly across from the track makes his parking pretty attractive. Did I tell you he makes almost $700 on Race Day? Because of my hip surgery, he was very nice this year about letting me park for free."

O'Neal tucked his notebook under his arm and joined Francine by the window. He peered past the rutted front lawn and Georgetown Road to the first-turn bleachers. "You can't get much closer than this. You been a race fan long?"

"Didn't give a hoot about it until I met that Brazilian driver Helio Castroneves at the Marsh grocery on Crawfordsville Road three years ago." Charlotte leaned heavily against the armrest and stood up. She made her way across the room until she was standing next to O'Neal. She had to look up to make eye contact since he was a good nine inches taller. "He was such a nice young man. And good looking, too. You're not so bad yourself, you know?"

Francine wasn't so sure about Charlotte's assessment. The policeman's hair was shaved to his scalp, and he had an ultra-lean, muscular build that gave him a hard edge. But when he smiled, which he did at Charlotte's remark, his hazel eyes sparkled. It made him less intimidating maybe, but not handsome.

O'Neal thanked her and appeared embarrassed by the compliment. "I prefer the Brickyard myself. Tony Stewart's my favorite. He's a fighter."

"I'm not surprised you like fighters," Charlotte said. "You kind of look like one with those long strong arms. I bet you've got six-pack abs, too. I bet you know how to take a punch." She playfully jabbed at his stomach.

O'Neal was grinning as Lt. Helphenstine came out from the bedroom. Francine placed him in his late 40s. Although he was quite a few pounds overweight and had a receding hairline, he had very few lines in his face. O'Neal dropped his smile.

The lieutenant motioned Charlotte and Francine to the brown leather couch. "Ladies, please have a seat."

Francine tried to help Charlotte, but she gently pulled her arm away. "I'm okay, Francine." She looked at the officers. "All my friends seem to think I'm an invalid. I hobble a bit, but I've still got spunk."

She has that in spades, Francine thought, settling into the couch beside her.

"The deputy coroner is trying to get hold of your uncle's doctor," Helphenstine told Charlotte. "If she's successful, and the doctor signs the death certificate, she says she can release the body to you this afternoon."

"But what about the autopsy?" Charlotte exclaimed. "Aren't you going to find out how he died?"

Helphenstine stared at her with a puzzled look. He glanced at O'Neal.

"Mrs. Reinhardt believes her uncle may have been murdered," O'Neal said.

Francine thought she saw a look of bemusement pass between the two officers.

Helphenstine turned a sympathetic smile to Charlotte. He squatted down so he could be at her eye level. "I'm very sorry about your uncle's death. I'll ask the deputy coroner to explain her findings to you as soon as she's finished. Let me go see if she's done." He disappeared into the bedroom.

The paramedics came out and nodded at O'Neal as he let them out the front door. Then he squatted in front of Charlotte as Helphenstine had done. "I'm just curious, Mrs. Reinhardt. How do you think he was murdered? And who do you think did it?"

Charlotte had a gleam in her eye. She leaned in close. "As for how it was done, poison. He threw up before he died. You noticed that, didn't you? In the bathroom? There's a poison that gives a victim a heart attack, but it makes them sick first. I read lots of mysteries."

"Oleander, isn't it? I read a lot of mysteries, too. But what would be the motive? And who would do it?"

Before she could answer, Helphenstine reappeared with the deputy coroner. The slightly built woman, who Francine guessed to be in her twenties, wore bright red lipstick that made her pasty complexion seem even paler.

"Mrs. Reinhardt, I'm Susan Clement," she said, shaking Charlotte's hand. "I'm so sorry about your uncle. I've examined him, and everything would seem to indicate he died of natural causes. I've called his physician. Based on his age and the type of medications he's been taking, his physician has agreed to sign the death certificate."

"No! He couldn't have just died! Don't you have to do an autopsy?"

"I understand this isn't easy. But despite what you see on television, when the deceased is elderly and has a pre-existing medical condition, and there are no signs of foul play, an autopsy is not required."

Francine knew that was especially true in a big city like Indianapolis, where they had to be budget-conscious. Autopsies are expensive.

"But what if he were poisoned?" Charlotte's voice peaked when she said it. Francine was afraid her friend might become hysterical.

Clement's voice remained calm. "Is there a reason to believe someone wanted him dead?"

"Yes." Charlotte set her jaw. "My uncle refused time and again to sell this land. It's prime property, sitting across the street from the Speedway. Lots of people wanted to buy it. I bet the owners of the track would pay a pretty penny to get it."

Francine saw the surprised look on the coroner's face. She herself was surprised. While it was reasonable to believe that a prominent family might want the property, since they also owned a lot of the surrounding land, the idea that they would kill for it wasn't. If anyone could offer the right price, it would be them.

Clement took a deep breath. "Now Mrs. Reinhardt. It's my understanding that housing values have declined in this area over the last few years. Ever since the Motor Speedway started hosting three races a year, it's a major hassle for the people who live here. Very few want to put up with the congestion."

Charlotte looked puzzled. "Well, Harold said that Lloyd Monroe who lives next door has been trying to buy him out for years. Why would he want the land otherwise?"

"I grew up in Speedway, and I know Lloyd Monroe," Clement said. "He owns a bunch of other properties. Maybe he sees it as a long-term investment. It's possible that someday the Motor Speedway may decide that they want this land. Probably not soon, since they own a large chunk of property across 16th Street that hasn't been fully developed. I think they'd use that land before they'd buy any over here."

"So, it's not valuable?"

The coroner shrugged. "Not now, it isn't."

Charlotte looked to Officer O'Neal for help.

"I live in Speedway, too," he said. "Land values have been declining." He ran a finger across his prominent jawline. "Although, now that I think of it, the Redevelopment Commission does have a plan to straighten up the intersection where 16th Street, Main, Crawfordsville and Georgetown Road come together. If they did that, they would have to shift Georgetown

Road to the west, and that would change whatever property remained on this side from residential to commercial. That would make it more valuable."

Francine knew the intersection well. It was a pain to negotiate. Everyone knew it needed work, especially since the businesses that operated on the Crawfordsville Road side had become seedy. The worst was the strip club at the corner.

O'Neal's suggestion made Charlotte perk up. "Then if they decided to go through with it, the land value could appreciate at any time."

Francine noticed that Helphenstine had moved closer to the group at the mention of the Redevelopment Commission. Now he shook his head.

"My brother Jerry's a commissioner. It's pretty far down on the Commission's wish list. They're divided on whether to do it or not. Half want it. Half don't. They're letting my brother sway the issue since he represents the folks who live around here. And they don't want it."

"Why not?"

"To relocate Georgetown, they'll have to tear down all the houses on this side. Then a whole new set of houses west of the track will bear the brunt of the traffic and depreciate in value."

Charlotte shook her finger at Lt. Helphenstine. "I'm still suspicious of Lloyd. The minute Francine and I arrived, he rushed over to see why we were here. I told him Harold wasn't answering the phone. That's when he said he hadn't seen Harold in a couple of days. Wouldn't you think he'd have called or something?"

O'Neal sighed. "What people should do, and what they actually do, are two different things. I haven't been a policeman all that long, and I've seen it a hundred times. And just because he wants to buy the land doesn't mean he would kill your uncle for it."

Charlotte's face went glum. Francine felt a little sorry for her, but her accusation did seem off base.

Clement put her hand on Charlotte's shoulder. "If you have that much concern, I can do a tox screen on your uncle. It'll allow us to rule out some poisons, but it will take several weeks to get the results back."

"I'd like that."

Clement stood up. "Let me get it underway, and then I'll be gone. Have you selected a funeral home?"

Charlotte nodded. "Conkle's, on 16th Street."

"I'll give them a call," Helphenstine said. "And I'll let headquarters know what's going on." He left the house.

Charlotte started to get up from the couch. O'Neal took her by the arm and helped her up. Charlotte winked at him. "Thank you, handsome." She clung to the officer's bicep to steady herself.

Francine almost rolled her eyes. She knew once Charlotte was on her feet she was fine.

After groping the officer's muscles, Charlotte let go and moved toward the hall. "Can I get something out of Harold's office to show you?"

O'Neal raised his eyebrows. "Let me come with you. What is it?"

"I'll show you."

Francine caught up with O'Neal as they followed along behind Charlotte. She whispered, "We've been worried about Charlotte for some time. Between her hip replacement and the chemo she's taking for breast cancer, she's gotten testy. We're not sure what she'll do or say anymore."

"Who is 'we'?"

"Our bridge club. Eight of us."

"Why does she want her uncle to have been murdered?"

Francine felt her cheeks redden. "Well, when we all turned sixty, we made lists of the sixty things we wanted to do before we died. One of Charlotte's was to solve a mystery."

As Francine and O'Neal trailed into Harold's office, Charlotte turned around to see them talking. Francine closed her mouth immediately.

O'Neal spoke up. "What are you looking for, Mrs. Reinhardt?"

Charlotte didn't answer but turned back to a bulletin board near Harold's desk. Only a few notes were tacked to it. Charlotte scratched her head, and the blond wig shifted to one side. Francine made a mental note to fix it later.

"I know it was up there." Charlotte pointed to the bulletin board. "He showed it to me just the other day."

Lt. Helphenstine entered the office. Everyone glanced at him.

O'Neal turned back to Charlotte. "What's missing?"

"A photo. For the past few weeks, Harold's been staying up late at night, photographing the comings and goings at that strip club on Crawfordsville Road. He had a platform built in the tree out back so he could easily see the back exit. This one photo had someone standing in the doorway, pawing a stripper."

Lt. Helphenstine cocked his head. "Were there other photographs?"

"He had a bunch of them in his desk drawer, except for the one that used to be on the bulletin board."

"I'd like to take a look at them," Helphenstine said.

Charlotte switched on the desk lamp. She opened the drawer and pulled out thick stacks of photos, handing them to the lieutenant.

Helphenstine sat at the desk and began to separate them into piles. Francine estimated there were at least two hundred photographs. Toward the end, he pulled a couple of photos close to his face and studied them.

"Was there anyone in the picture your uncle could identify?" he asked Charlotte.

"He didn't say, but he was excited about it. Those two photographs you have were taken at the same time, I think, but you can't see the guy's face."

"Did he have any distinguishing features?"

"Honestly, I don't remember what he looked like. I wasn't paying attention." She reached for the photos but Helphenstine didn't let go of them. She squinted at the images. "If it's the same guy in those photos, you can see he has a bald spot on the back of his head. The security light's reflecting off it."

"I think you're right. I'll just take these two along with me, give them a little more thought," he said, pocketing them.

O'Neal frowned and started to say something, but just then the woman from the coroner's office called out for Lt. Helphenstine. Everyone followed him out of the office. Susan Clement was in the living room.

"I'm finished," she said. "I'll send you the results of the tox screen as soon as I have them."

There was a knock at the door. Charlotte opened it, and the men from Conkle's Funeral Home came in to retrieve Uncle Harold's body. Clement left after them. Before the officers left, Lt. Helphenstine gave Francine and Charlotte each a business card and told them to call if they had questions.

Charlotte went into the bathroom and got a tissue to wipe her eyes. "He saw something in those photos. He just doesn't want us to know what it was."

Francine rested a hand on her friend's shoulder. "I wouldn't put a lot of stock in that, Charlotte. The coroner is probably right about natural causes. They see a lot of cases like this."

Charlotte broke into tears. Francine put her arm around her friend and guided her into the kitchen. Charlotte sat in a padded chair at a small table.

"How about if I make you a hot toddy, Charlotte? It'll calm your nerves."

"But it's June!"

"Oh, you're right. Maybe I'll just spike some lemonade."

About an hour later, Charlotte looked a whole lot better. *Rest and a couple of my hard lemonades work wonders*, Francine thought. The two women drove over to make the funeral arrangements, and Charlotte had another good cry, but Francine thought her friend seemed resolved about the death. She hoped that Charlotte would get off the kick that Uncle Harold had been murdered.

"It's suppertime," Francine announced after they were finished. "Why don't we stop at MCL Cafeteria and get something to eat before we head back to Brownsburg?" Francine and Charlotte loved to stop at MCL, and the Speedway shopping center had the closest location to their homes, about fifteen minutes away.

Charlotte's eyes glazed over. "Let's go to the library, instead. I want to look up information on the Redevelopment Commission."

"Charlotte..."

"Uncle Harold wouldn't just die of natural causes without being sick first. I want to check out some things."

Francine groaned. "Okay, but first we have to get food."

After a stop at MCL, the two drove to the library on 25th Street. There they read the previous year's minutes from the Redevelopment Commission.

"Look at this map," Charlotte said. "If they were to align Georgetown Road with Main Street, Uncle Harold's property would still be fully intact and redesignated as commercial property."

Francine traced a finger along the route. "It would go right through the middle of the strip club, so that building would have to come down."

"That would make a lot of people happy."

"It looks like a bunch of residential properties would have to go, too, but some of these lots are already vacant."

"I wonder how many of the properties Lloyd owns? I bet we can find that online somehow. Let's ask the librarian."

With a little help, Charlotte searched a property tax database and found the answer. "Lloyd Monroe owns them all," she told Francine triumphantly. "All except Uncle Harold's."

Francine had been examining newspaper clippings. She held one up. "Here's a shot of the Redevelopment Commission. Look at this guy here, the one turning around. He's got a bald spot on the back of his head. Do you think it could be the same guy Uncle Harold caught at the strip club?"

Charlotte bit her lower lip. "It's hard to tell, but it could be. Does it say who he is?"

"No, it just identifies the group as the Redevelopment Commission."

Charlotte took the clipping from Francine and went to the copy machine. When she returned, Francine looked at her watch. "It's almost eight! The library's going to close soon. Let's put this file back and go home."

"Francine, I appreciate you being with me today, but I want you to drop me back at Harold's house. I've decided to stay there tonight."

"And sleep in your clothes?"

"I'll just sleep in the buff. I do that sometimes."

"Charlotte! You cannot sleep naked in the bed where someone just died."

"Of course not. I'll put on one of Harold's robes and sleep on the couch."

Francine frowned at her.

Charlotte put her hands on her hips. "You read all the time about the homes of recently deceased people being robbed because no one's staying there. That could happen here. And don't worry. I'll put on every light in the house."

Charlotte wouldn't be dissuaded, so Francine was forced to return to Brownsburg without her. *This is so unlike her*, Francine thought as she drove away. She picked up Lt. Helphenstine's business card and dialed the number on her cell phone. Officer O'Neal answered.

"My friend has decided to stay at the house alone tonight," Francine said after identifying herself. "I'm worried, and I wondered if you could maybe look in on her."

"My shift ended earlier, and I'm just clearing up a few things," he said, "but I'll leave word for someone else. Thanks for calling and letting us know."

"Will you please let Lt. Helphenstine know as well?"

"I'll make sure he gets the message."

Francine felt a little better, but she couldn't help recalling the far-away look in Charlotte's eyes. I hope she doesn't get herself in trouble, Francine thought.

Charlotte watched her friend drive away yakking on the cell phone. "Francine, you'll get yourself in trouble doing that," she said. As she turned and headed back into her uncle's house, Lloyd Monroe came over. Charlotte despised seeing him twice in one day. He had a narrow flat face and black hair with long thick sideburns, and she thought he would have looked exactly like a ferret if his hair were a different color.

"We're not selling the property, Lloyd."

"You're not? Don't you need to check with his other relatives?"

"No, he left me the property in his will." Charlotte felt the words roll off her tongue.

They sounded true, even to her.

"Oh."

"Is there anything else?"

"Umm. I'll be happy to look after the place until you get back tomorrow."

"Thank you, but I've decided to stay the night."

"Really? I thought you'd be headed back home."

"It's just that there's so much to do. I've got to go through his computer files. He put a bunch of photos on his computer, and the police want me to see if I can find a specific one."

Lloyd's mouth dropped open, but he quickly closed it. "I didn't think Harold had a computer. He couldn't even program a VCR."

"Oh, he liked to let on that he couldn't do that stuff, but he could. He kept a laptop hidden away. Like I said, I've got to look through it."

"I won't keep you. Listen, if you need anything, don't hesitate to call."

Charlotte watched Lloyd Monroe scurry back to his house. *Now why do I do things like that?* she thought after she closed the door.

Charlotte waited all evening for Lloyd to make his move, but nothing happened. Four hours of anticipation, only to be let down. She'd even put Francine's number on speed dial, just in case. Now she lay on the couch, willing herself to sleep. She sat up and looked at the clock: 2:05. Her body was tired, but her brain kept reviewing the day. If the photos had nothing to do with her uncle's death, why had the policeman taken them? She was still sure Lloyd Monroe was involved, too. He'd looked suspicious when she implied a copy of the missing photo remained on Harold's nonexistent computer.

Charlotte struggled off the couch. She retied Harold's robe and put on his slippers, but they were so big she had to rubber-band them to her feet.

She went into Harold's office. Everything was just as she'd left it. She sat in his chair and went through the photos again but didn't see anything suspicious. If there were something, she told herself, it would be in either the missing photo or the two taken by Lt. Helphenstine. She'd ask to get those back in the morning.

Charlotte looked out the window, trying to see Lloyd's house. A tree and tall shrubbery blocked her view. Charlotte partially turned away when something caught her attention. Though it was night, the street lights never let it get too dark, and she could see the tree in the back yard from which Harold had taken his photos. He had built a platform about eight feet off the ground. *High enough*, Charlotte thought, *to see into Lloyd's house.*

She went into the kitchen. Harold kept a flashlight and binoculars by the door, and she snagged those as she left. She hobbled into the grass. Dew had already settled on the lawn, and she could feel the wetness on her toes. *The slippers must be getting soaked*, she thought. For a moment, she considered putting on her shoes, but it was either comfort or momentum, and she decided on momentum. Then she giggled. *I bet Miss Marple would have done the same thing.*

Charlotte aimed the flashlight into the tree. Because she was only five feet tall and not in the best of health, the platform looked very far away. But she had it in her mind that she was going to get up there.

I'll take it one step at a time, she assured herself. The homemade ladder looked sturdy enough. She slipped the flashlight into a pocket, put the binoculars around her neck, and placed a foot on the first step. She pulled herself up with effort. She managed the second step, and then the third. But at the fourth rung, her feet began to hurt. *Should have put on the shoes*, she thought. But Charlotte was nothing if not determined, and five minutes later, she pulled herself, exhausted, stomach-first onto the platform.

Once her heart stopped pounding, she sat up and looked around. The platform was about five feet by five feet, made of thick plywood. There was no railing of any sort, and it made Charlotte wary. She gingerly scooted to the back where she could lean against the tree trunk and face Lloyd's house. Unfortunately, she could only see the back yard. She thought maybe there was a light on in one of the rooms, but it was just a guess.

Charlotte shined her flashlight into the back yard. Lloyd had a patio off the back porch where Charlotte could make out pots of tall plants with white flowers.

That looks very much like oleander, she thought. *I need to tell Francine about this tomorrow.*

With not much else to look at in Lloyd's back yard, she checked out the view in other directions. She didn't need the flashlight to see the strip club on Crawfordsville Road, which was well lit and had a security light, but she did use the binoculars. Still, nothing was happening there. She rested her head against the tree.

It wasn't comfortable, but Charlotte felt drained. Soon she dozed off, only to be startled awake by the sound of someone climbing the ladder. Her first thought was to move, but she was stiff from climbing.

Lloyd Monroe pulled himself onto the platform. He was wearing a black T-shirt and jeans and seemed to blend in with the night. "What are you doing up here, Charlotte?" he asked.

"I wanted to see what Uncle Harold could see. What are you doing here?"

Lloyd looked around. His glances were quick and furtive. "The same. Have you seen what you wanted?"

"Oh, yes. I've seen your back yard with its pots of oleander. And the back side of the strip club, which Harold photographed."

"I'm going to need your help, Charlotte. You see, I can't let anyone else get a copy of that photo. I want you to tell me where Harold's computer is."

She shook her head. "You killed him, Lloyd. Somehow you gave him oleander. The police might not think so, but I do. Why'd you do it?"

"You think this is some Agatha Christie mystery where the killer spills his guts at the end?"

Charlotte was trying hard to keep her cool, but inside she was trembling. "Yes. And I'm playing the role of Miss Marple, so let's have it."

"Trust me, I'm going to let you have it. But first I want the computer."

"You won't get away with this, Lloyd. It's public record that you own every home on the block except this one. If you kill me to get the property, someone else will figure it out. You'll be a prime suspect. What I don't understand is why you want a property that isn't worth anything."

"It'll be worth plenty if they align Main Street and Georgetown Road."

"But it's not going to happen."

"Only because the person standing in the way is Commissioner Jerry Helphenstine. And Harold's telephoto lens caught him at the strip club. So this is my chance to get the property and make it valuable at the same time. I had to stop Harold before he exposed Helphenstine. Now I'll buy the property, then blackmail Helphenstine into pushing for realignment. Or expose him and let public opinion do it for me. Either way, I make a bundle."

Lloyd didn't have much room on the platform. To move anywhere, he would have to cross over Charlotte's legs, and that's what she was watching for. Her goal was to kick a foot out from under him and send him falling off the platform.

He took a step toward her. "Where's the computer, Charlotte?"

She heard a rustling in the yard.

Lloyd's head jerked up. "Who's there?"

Silence.

"I know someone's out there."

Lt. Helphenstine stepped out of the bushes in the back of the property. He had a gun in his hand.

Thank goodness, thought Charlotte.

"Please go right ahead and kill her, Lloyd," Helphenstine said. "I'm tired of cleaning up my brother's messes. If he weren't sharing his bribes with me, I'd turn him in myself. But you can take care of this problem. You kill her, and I'll take away the evidence along with your photo and the computer. You can buy this property, but you won't be able to accuse my brother of anything. In time, maybe they'll vote to realign Main Street, and then you'll get your money. But you'll have to wait."

Lloyd snorted. "I won't be your stooge. If I can't turn a profit right away, it's not worth it. She won't sell me the property anyway."

"Don't turn around, Joe," said a tight, controlled voice. Charlotte recognized Officer O'Neal at the corner of the house. "Just drop the gun," he said.

Lt. Helphenstine didn't turn around, but he didn't drop the gun, either.

"What are you doing here, Brett?"

"I got suspicious when you took the photos without a search warrant and then kept finding excuses not to let me see them. There've been rumors that your brother was 'in' with the strip club, and that he was paying you to keep his record clean. So when Mrs. McNamara asked me to pass the message onto you about Mrs. Reinhardt being here alone, I made sure you saw it. If you were involved, you'd take the opportunity to do something. And you did. Now drop the gun."

"I'm your training officer, Brett. Don't do this. Accusing me without proof won't look good on your record." The gun remained in Helphenstine's hand.

"Don't be stupid, Joe. There's no way out. I've had my radio channel on. The car is taping everything, and I've already sent for backup."

Helphenstine dropped the gun by his feet.

"Now get in a kneeling position with your hands behind your back," O'Neal said.

"No." The lieutenant remained standing.

"We'll just wait for backup to get here."

Charlotte felt a long tense silence take hold.

Helphenstine nudged the gun a little ways off to the left with his foot. "How's that? You can take the gun away from me now."

"We'll wait."

Charlotte could hardly breathe. She looked at Lloyd. His face was getting redder by the minute. He looked bad. "Lloyd?"

Lloyd held his chest and gasped.

"Officer O'Neal, I think he's having a heart attack," she said.

Lloyd Monroe fell off the platform.

Charlotte was never quite sure of the sequence of events after that. She knew she screamed. She heard shuffling feet in the grass. Fists hitting, and men grunting. Something heavy hitting the tree. Sirens in the distance. The sound of handcuffs snapping shut. Someone climbing the ladder.

O'Neal stuck his head above the platform. "Are you all right, Mrs. Reinhardt?"

"Yes, but what about Lloyd?"

"Mrs. McNamara is giving him CPR."

"I'm so glad you're okay, Charlotte," Francine called. Her voice sounded labored.

"What are you doing here, Francine?"

"I couldn't sleep, so I drove out here and found Officer O'Neal in the driveway. He let me stay but made me get back in my car until it was over."

The sirens got louder, and two medics arrived to take over.

O'Neal helped Charlotte down from the platform and into the kitchen where she could sit comfortably. An on-duty officer took statements from everyone. Francine prepared hard lemonades for her and Charlotte. O'Neal declined.

"So I was wrong and I was right at the same time," Charlotte said, taking a sip.

"Lloyd Monroe killed my uncle, but not for the reason I thought."

"That's right. He wanted the land, but more than that, he killed your uncle to get control over Jerry Helphenstine. He hoped to get the land afterward, but it was just a hope."

"Then I really didn't solve the mystery."

O'Neal's eyebrows lifted, and he smiled at her. "Almost. Now I want you to promise me you won't try anything like this again. If Mrs. McNamara hadn't called to let me know what was going on, it might have ended badly."

Charlotte didn't say anything.

The officer's voice was tight. "Promise?"

Charlotte felt her eyes go out of focus. She wondered if it was Francine's concoction. "I promise," she said.

But from the way Officer O'Neal and Francine looked at each other, she got the impression neither of them believed her.